BY ERICH MARIA REMARQUE

# A TIME TO LOVE
# AND A TIME
# TO DIE

# A TIME TO LOVE
# AND A TIME
# TO DIE

*A Novel*

*Erich Maria Remarque*

*Translated from the German by Denver Lindley*

RANDOM HOUSE TRADE PAPERBACKS

NEW YORK

2014 Random House Trade Paperback Edition

Published in the United States by Random House Trade Paperbacks, an imprint of Random House, a division of Random House LLC., a Penguin Random House Company, New York.

RANDOM HOUSE and the HOUSE colophon are trademarks of Random House LLC.

This translation was originally published by Harcourt Brace Jovanovich, Inc., in 1954.

ISBN 978-0-449-91250-8
eBook ISBN 978-0-8129-8560-3

Printed in the United States of America on acid-free paper

www.atrandom.com

Book design by Christopher M. Zucker

*To P. G.*

# A TIME TO LOVE
# AND A TIME
# TO DIE

# Chapter One

DEATH SMELLED DIFFERENT in Russia than in Africa. In
Africa, under heavy English fire, the corpses between the lines
had often lain unburied for a long time, too; but the sun had
worked fast. At night the smell had come over with the wind,
sweet, stifling and heavy—gas had filled the dead and they had
risen like ghosts in the light of the alien stars as though they
were fighting one last battle, silent, hopeless, and each for himself alone—but by the next day they had already begun to shrink,
to nestle against the earth with infinite weariness as if trying to
crawl into it—and if later they could be brought back some were
light and dried out and the ones that were found weeks after
were hardly more than skeletons that rattled loosely in uniforms
suddenly far too big for them. It was a dry death, in sand, sun
and wind. In Russia it was a greasy, stinking death.

It had been raining for days. The snow was melting. A month
earlier it had been three yards deeper. The ruined village, which
at first had seemed to be nothing but charred roofs, had silently,

night by night, risen higher out of the sinking snow. Window frames had crept into sight; a few nights later the archways of doors; then stairways that led down into the dirty whiteness. The snow melted and melted, and with the melting came the dead.

They were old dead. The village had been fought over several times—in November, in December, in January, and now in April. It had been taken and lost and taken again. The snowstorms had come and covered the corpses, sometimes within hours, so deep that the medical corpsmen often could not find them—until finally almost every day had thrown a new layer of white over the devastation, like a nurse stretching a sheet over a bloody, filthy bed.

First came the January dead. They lay highest and came out at the beginning of April, shortly after the snow began to slip. Their bodies were frozen stiff and their faces were gray wax.

They were buried like boards. On a little hill behind the village where the snow was not so deep it had been shoveled away and graves were hacked out of the frozen earth. It was heavy work. Only the Germans were buried. The Russians were thrown into an open paddock. They began to stink when the weather turned mild. When it got too bad snow was shoveled over them. It was not necessary to bury them; no one expected that the village would be held for any length of time. The regiment was in retreat. The advancing Russians could bury their dead themselves.

Beside the December dead were found the weapons that had belonged to the January dead. Rifles and hand grenades had sunk deeper than the bodies; sometimes steel helmets too. It was easier with these corpses to cut away the identification marks inside the uniforms; the melting show had already softened the cloth. Water stood in their open mouths as though they had drowned. In some cases a limb or two had thawed out. When they were carried off, the bodies were still stiff, but an arm and a hand would dangle and sway as though the corpse were waving, hideously indifferent and almost obscene. With all of them, when they lay in the sun, the eyes thawed first. They lost their glassy brilliance and the pupils turned to jelly. The ice in them melted and ran slowly out of the eyes—as if they were weeping.

Suddenly it froze again for several days. A crust formed on the snow and turned to ice. The snow stopped sinking. But then the sluggish, sultry wind began to blow anew.

At first only a gray fleck appeared in the withering white. An hour later it was a clenched hand stretching upward.

"There's another," Sauer said.

"Where?" Immermann asked.

"Over there in front of the church. Shall we dig him out?"

"What's the use? The wind will dig him out by itself. The snow back there is still a yard or two deep, at least. This damn village is lower than anything else around here. Or do you just want to get your boots full of ice water?"

"Hell no. Any idea what's to eat today?"

"Cabbage. Cabbage with pork and potatoes. Pork nonexistent."

"Cabbage of course! For the third time this week!"

Sauer unbuttoned his trousers and began to urinate. "A year ago I still pissed in great arcs," he explained morosely. "In good military fashion, the way it's supposed to be done. I felt fine. Advance each day so-and-so many kilometers. Thought I'd soon be home again. Now I piss like a civilian, half-heartedly and without pleasure."

Immerman stuck his hand under his uniform and scratched himself comfortably. "I wouldn't care how I pissed—if I were a civilian again."

"Me either. But it looks like we'd go on being soldiers forever."

"Sure. Heroes to the grave. Only the S.S. still piss in great arcs."

Sauer buttoned up his trousers. "They can do it too. We do the dirty work and those beauties get all the honors. We fight for two or three weeks for some damn town and on the last day up come the S.S. and march into it triumphantly ahead of us. Just look at the way they're looked after! Always the thickest coats, the best boots, and the biggest chunks of meat!"

Immermann grinned. "Now even the S.S. aren't taking towns any more. They're going back. Just like us."

"Not like us. We don't burn and shoot what we can't carry off with us."

Immerman stopped scratching himself. "What's got into you today?" he asked in surprise. "You're talking like a human being. Take care Steinbrenner doesn't hear you or you'll soon find yourself in one of those disciplinary companies. Look—the snow over there has settled! Now you can see a piece of the fellow's arm."

Sauer looked over. "If it goes on melting like this by tomorrow he'll be hanging on a cross. He's in the right place. Right over the cemetery."

"Is that a cemetery there?"

"Of course. Didn't you know? We were here once before. During our last counterattack. Around the end of October. Weren't you with us then?"

"No."

"Where were you? Hospital?"

"Disciplinary company."

Sauer whistled through his teeth. "Disciplinary company! I'll be damned! For what?"

Immermann looked at him. "Former Communist," he said.

"What? And they let you out? How did it happen?"

"A fellow has to have luck. I'm a good mechanic. Apparently they are more useful now here than there."

"Maybe. But as a Communist! And here in Russia! They're

always sent somewhere else." Sauer suddenly looked at Immermann with suspicion.

Immermann grinned derisively. "Take it easy," he said. "I haven't turned spy. And I won't report what you said about the S.S. That's what you meant, wasn't it?"

"I? Not a bit of it. Never thought of such a thing!" Sauer reached for his mess kit. "There's the field kitchen! Quick— otherwise we'll only get dishwater."

The hand grew and grew. It was not as if the snow were melting but as if the hand were slowly stretching up out of the earth—like a pale threat or a paralyzed gesture for help.

The company commander halted abruptly. "What's that over there?"

"Some Panje or other, sir."

Rahe looked more intently. He could recognize a piece of the faded cloth on the sleeve. "That's no Russian," he said.

Sergeant Muecke wriggled his toes in his boots. He could not bear the company commander. To be sure, he stood before him with irreproachable rigidity—discipline transcended personal feelings—but privately, to express his contempt, he kept wriggling his toes in his boots. Stupid ass, he thought. Numbskull!

"Get him out," Rahe said.

"Yes, sir."

"Get a couple of men to work at once. That sort of thing's not a pleasant sight!"

Babe in arms, Muecke thought. Twaddler! Not a pleasant sight! As though that was the first dead man we've seen!

"That's a German soldier," Rahe said.

"Yes, sir. For the last four days we've found nothing but Russians."

"Have them get him out. Then we'll see what he is." Rahe walked across to his quarters. Conceited ass, Muecke thought. Has an oven, a warm house, and the Ritterkreuz. I haven't even the Iron Cross first class and I've done just as much to earn it as he has with his whole hardware store. "Sauer!" he shouted. "Immermann! Come here! Bring shovels along! Who else is there? Graeber! Hirschland! Berning! Steinbrenner, take charge of the detail! That hand over there! Dig it out and bury it if it's a German! I bet it isn't."

Steinbrenner sauntered over. "You're betting?" he asked. He had a high, boyish voice which he vainly tried to keep low. "How much?"

Muecke was disconcerted for a moment. "Three rubels," he said then. "Three occupation rubels."

"Five. I don't bet less than five."

"All right, five then. But pay up."

Steinbrenner laughed. His teeth glistened in the pale sunlight. He was nineteen years old, blond, with the face of a Gothic angel. "Pay up of course. What else, Muecke?"

Muecke did not like Steinbrenner either; but he was afraid of him and therefore cautious. Steinbrenner came from the S.S. He possessed the golden insigne of the Hitler Youth. Now he belonged to the company, but everyone knew he was an informer and a Gestapo spy.

"All right, all right." Muecke pulled out of his pocket a cherrywood cigarette case that had a flower design burnt into its lid. "Cigarette?"

"Sure."

"The Fuehrer doesn't smoke, Steinbrenner," Immermann said casually.

"Shut your trap."

"Shut yours, you bastard."

Steinbrenner lifted his long eyelashes in a sidewise glance. "You seem to be feeling pretty good. Forgotten all sorts of things, haven't you?"

Immermann laughed. "I don't easily forget anything. And I know just what you mean, Max. But don't you forget what it was I said: The Fuehrer doesn't smoke. That was all. Here are four witnesses. And the Fuehrer doesn't smoke. Everyone knows that."

"Stop jawing!" Muecke said. "Get on with the digging. Orders from the company commander."

"All right, move!" Steinbrenner lighted the cigarette Muecke had given him.

"Since when is smoking permitted on duty?" Immermann asked.

"We're not on duty," Muecke explained irritably. "Now cut the talk and get going! Hirschland, you too!"

Hirschland came up. Steinbrenner grinned. "First-rate work for you, Isaac! Digging out corpses. Good for your Jewish blood. Strengthens the bones and the spirit. Take that shovel over there."

"I'm three-quarters Aryan," Hirschland said.

Steinbrenner blew smoke from the cigarette into his face. "That's what you say! As far as I'm concerned you're one-quarter Jew—and through the generosity of the Fuehrer you're allowed to fight side by side with true German men. So, dig out this Russian swine. He stinks too much for the Lieutenant's delicate nose."

"This is no Russian," Graeber said. He had dragged a few boards up to the dead man and by himself begun to cut away the snow from around the arm and breast. The wet uniform was now clearly visible.

"Not a Russian?" Steinbrenner came over, quick and sure-footed as a dancer on the teetering boards, and squatted down beside Graeber. "It's a fact. That's a German uniform." He turned around. "Muecke! It's not a Russian! I've won!"

Muecke walked over heavily. He stared at the hole into which water was slowly trickling from the sides. "I can't understand it," he declared disgustedly. "For almost a week now we've found nothing but Russians. He must be one of the December lot that sank deeper."

"He might just as well be from October," Graeber said. "Our regiment came through here then."

"Nonsense. There can't be any more of them left."

"There could be. We fought a night engagement here. The Russians retreated and we had to go on at once."

"That's true," Sauer announced.

"Nonsense. Our replacements must have found all the dead and buried them."

"That's not so certain. By the end of October it had started to snow very hard. And at that time we were still advancing fast."

"That's the second time you've said that." Steinbrenner looked at Graeber.

"I'll be glad to let you hear it again if you like. At that time we were counterattacking and we advanced more than a hundred kilometers."

"And now we're retreating, eh?"

"Now we're here again."

"That means that we're in retreat, doesn't it?"

Immermann nudged Graeber warningly. "Are we perhaps going forward?" Graeber asked.

"We're shortening our lines," Immermann said, staring derisively into Steinbrenner's face. "For a year now. Strategic necessity. Everyone knows that."

"There's a ring on his hand," Hirschland said suddenly. He

had gone on digging and had exposed the dead man's other hand. Muecke bent down. "A ring," he said. "And a gold one too. A wedding ring."

All of them looked at it. "Watch yourself," Immermann whispered to Graeber. "That swine will do you out of your furlough. He'll report you as an alarmist. He's just waiting for the chance."

"He's simply showing off. You're the one who'd better watch out. He's got it in for you more than for me."

"I don't care. I won't get any furlough."

"Those are the insignia of our regiment," Hirschland said. He had gone on digging with his hands.

"So then it's dead certain that it's not a Russian, eh?" Steinbrenner turned and grinned at Muecke.

"No, it's not a Russian," Muecke replied angrily.

"Five rubels! Too bad we didn't bet ten. Cough it up!"

"I haven't got it on me."

"Where then? In the Reichsbank? Come on, cough it up!"

Muecke glared fiercely at Steinbrenner. Then he produced his wallet and handed over the money. "Everything's gone wrong today, damn it!"

Steinbrenner pocketed the money. Graeber bent over again to help Hirschland dig. "I believe it's Reicke," he said.

"What?"

"This is Lieutenant Reicke. There are his bars. And here, on his right hand, the last joint of the index finger is missing."

"Nonsense. Reicke was wounded and sent home. We heard that later."

"It is Reicke."

"Clean off his face."

Graeber and Hirschland went on digging. "Careful," Muecke shouted. "Don't poke him in the head."

"He won't feel it now," Immermann said.

"Shut your trap. Here lies a fallen German officer, you Communist!"

The face emerged from the snow. It was wet and made a strange impression with the hollows of the eyes still filled with snow: as though a sculptor had left a mask unfinished and blind. A gold tooth gleamed between the blue lips.

"I can't identify him," Muecke said.

"It must be him. We didn't lose any other officer here that time."

"Wipe out his eyes."

Graeber hesitated an instant. Then he cautiously wiped the snow away with his glove. "It's him," he said.

Muecke became excited. He took command himself. Since an officer was in question a higher rank seemed necessary. "Lift him! Hirschland and Sauer take the legs, Steinbrenner and Berning the arms. Graeber, take care of his head! Come on, all together—one, two, pull!"

The body moved. "Once more. One, two, lift!"

The body moved again. From under it out of the snow came a hollow sigh as the air rushed in.

"Sergeant! The foot's come off!" Hirschland shouted.

It was the boot. It had come half off. The flesh of the foot had rotted in the melting snow and was giving way. "Let go! Let him down!" Muecke shouted. It was too late. The body jerked loose and Hirschland held the boot in his hand.

"Is the foot inside?" Immermann asked.

"Put the boot down and go on shoveling," Muecke shouted to Hirschland. "How was anyone to know he was already so soft? And you, Immermann, shut up! Show some respect for the dead!"

Immermann looked at Muecke in amazement, but he kept quiet.

A few minutes later they had finished shoveling the snow

away from around the body. In the wet uniform they found a wallet with papers. The handwriting had run but was still legible. Graeber had been right: it was Lieutenant Reicke, who had been a platoon leader in the company during the fall.

"We must report this at once," Muecke said. "Stay here, I'll be right back."

He went over to the house where the company commander lived. It was the only one that was still in some degree habitable; before the Revolution it had probably belonged to the village priest. Rahe was sitting in the big living room. Muecke stared spitefully at the broad Russian oven in which a fire was burning. On the oven bench Rahe's sheepdog was lying asleep. Muecke made his report and Rahe went out with him.

He looked down for a while at Reicke. "Shut his eyes," he said then.

"That can't be done, sir," Graeber answered. "The lids are too tender. They would tear."

Rahe looked over at the shell-torn church. "Take him over and put him in there for the time being. Have we a coffin?"

"The coffins were left behind," Muecke reported. "We had a few for special occasions. The Russians have them now. I hope they'll have use for them!"

Steinbrenner laughed. Rahe did not laugh. "Can we make one?"

"It would take too long, sir," Graeber said. "The body's very soft already. Besides, it's not likely there are any suitable boards in the town."

Rahe nodded. "Lay him on a strip of canvas. We'll bury him in that. Hack out a grave and make a cross."

Graeber, Sauer, Immermann, and Berning carried the sagging body over to the church. Hirschland followed uncertainly with the boot with a piece of foot still in it.

"Sergeant Muecke!" Rahe said.

"Yes, sir!"

"Four captured guerrillas are being sent here today. They are to be shot early tomorrow morning. Our company has received orders to do it. Ask your section for volunteers. If you don't get them the master sergeant will select names."

"Yes, sir."

"Heaven knows why it has to be us. Oh well, in all this confusion—"

"I volunteer," Steinbrenner said.

"Good." Rahe's face was expressionless. He stumped back over the pathway shoveled in the snow. Back to his oven, Muecke thought. The dishclout! What does shooting a few guerrillas amount to? As though they hadn't picked off hundreds of our comrades!

"If the Russians come in time they can dig the grave for Reicke too," Steinbrenner said. "Then there won't be any work for us. Get it all done at once. What do you say, Muecke?"

"It's all right with me!" Muecke's stomach was bitter. That schoolmaster, he thought. Thin, overgrown, a long lathe with horn-rimmed glasses. Lieutenant from the time of the first war. Never promoted in this one. Brave all right, who wasn't? But not a leader by nature. "What do you think of Rahe?" he asked Steinbrenner.

Steinbrenner looked at him uncomprehendingly. "He's our company commander, isn't he?"

"Certainly, but what else?"

"Else? What do you mean?"

"Nothing," Muecke replied crossly.

"Deep enough?" asked the oldest Russian.

He was a man of about seventy with a dirty white beard and very blue eyes, and he spoke broken German.

"Shut up, Bolshevik. Speak only when you're spoken to," Steinbrenner replied. He was in fine spirits. His eyes followed the woman who was one of the guerrillas. She was young and strong.

"Deeper," Graeber said. He, together with Steinbrenner and Sauer, was supervising the prisoners.

"For us?" the Russian asked.

Steinbrenner sprang down quickly, lightly, and hit him hard in the face with the flat of his hand. "I told you, grandfather, to hold your tongue. What do you think this is? A country fair?"

He smiled. There was no malice in his face. It was simply filled with the satisfaction of a child pulling the wings off a fly.

"No, this grave is not for you," Graeber said.

The Russian did not move. He stood still and looked at Steinbrenner. Steinbrenner glanced back. His face suddenly changed. It became tense and watchful. He thought the Russian was going to attack him and he was waiting for the first move. It would have made no difference to anyone if he had shot him then and there; the man had been condemned to death anyway and no one would question very closely whether or not it had been a case of self-defense. But for Steinbrenner it was not the same. Graeber could not tell whether it was a kind of sport for him to provoke the Russian so far that he would forget himself for a moment, or whether he still possessed a remnant of that strange pedantry which seeks through some subterfuge always to appear legal when committing murder. Both existed. And both at the same time. Graeber had seen it often enough.

The Russian did not move. Blood ran out of his nose into his beard. Graeber considered for a moment what he would do in the same situation—whether he would throw himself on the other and risk instant death for the satisfaction of returning the blow, or accept anything in order to gain the few more hours, the one night of life. He did not know.

The Russian bent slowly and lifted the pick. Steinbrenner took a step backward. He was ready to shoot. But the Russian did not straighten up again. He resumed his hacking at the bottom of the hole. Steinbrenner grinned. "Lie down there," he said.

The Russian put the pick aside and laid himself in the trench. He lay there quietly. A few pieces of snow fell on him as Steinbrenner stepped over the grave. "Is it long enough?" he asked Graeber.

"Yes. Reicke wasn't tall."

The Russian was looking upward. His eyes were wide open. The blue of the sky seemed to be reflected in them. The white hairs of the beard around his mouth stirred with his breath. Steinbrenner let him lie there for a while. Then he said, "Out!"

The Russian climbed out. Wet earth clung to his coat. "So," Steinbrenner said, and glanced at the woman. "Now we'll go and dig your own graves. They don't need to be so deep. It makes no difference if the foxes eat you next summer."

It was early morning. A pale red band lay along the horizon. The snow crackled; it had frozen again during the night. The open graves were very black. "Damn it," Sauer said. "The things they load on us. Why do we have to do this? Why not the S.D.? After all, they're specialists in shooting people. Why us? This is the third time. We're supposed to be respectable soldiers."

Graeber held his rifle loosely in his hand. The steel was very cold. He put on his glove. "The S.D. keep busy farther back."

"Right. They don't come this near the front. Wasn't Steinbrenner with the S.D. earlier?"

"I think he was in a concentration camp. Block warden or something like that."

The others came up. Steinbrenner was the only one fully awake and rested. His skin had the rosy glow of a child's. "Listen," he said. "There's that cow in the bunch. Leave her for me."

"How do you mean for you?" asked Sauer. "There's not enough time for you to get her pregnant. You ought to have tried sooner."

"That's just what he did," Immermann said.

"Who told you that?" Steinbrenner asked. "The International?"

"And she wouldn't let him near her."

Steinbrenner turned around angrily. "You're mighty sly, aren't you? If I had wanted to have the red cow I'd have had her."

"Maybe not."

"Oh, cut the jawing." Sauer bit off a chew of tobacco. "If he means he wants to shoot her all by himself he's welcome as far as I'm concerned. I won't fight him for that."

"Nor I," Graeber declared.

The others said nothing. It grew lighter. Hirschland looked at his watch. "Aren't things going fast enough for you, Isaac?" Steinbrenner asked. "Be thankful you've been picked out for this. It's just the thing to cure your Jewish tearfulness. Shooting—" he spat, "much too good for this gang! Ammunition wasted for that! They should be hanged. Like everywhere else."

"Where?" Sauer looked around. "You see any trees? Or shall we build a gallows? And with what?"

"There they are," Graeber said.


Muecke appeared with the four Russians. Two soldiers marched in front of them and two behind. The old Russian came first, after him the woman and then the two younger men. The four arranged themselves, without being told to, in a row in front of the graves. The woman glanced down before she turned around. She was wearing a red woolen skirt.

Lieutenant Mueller of the first platoon came out of the company commander's house. He was Rahe's representative at the execution. It was laughable, but formalities were still for the most part strictly carried out. Everyone knew that the four Russians might be guerrillas and then again might not; they had been formally tried and condemned without ever having any real chance. What had there been to find out? They had been charged with possessing weapons. Now they were being shot with due formality and in the presence of an officer. As if it mattered to them one way or the other.

Lieutenant Mueller was twenty-one years old and had been assigned to the company six weeks before. He examined the condemned and then read the sentence.

"The cow's for me," Steinbrenner whispered.

Graeber looked at the woman. She stood calmly in her red skirt in front of the grave. She was strong and young and healthy and made to bear children. She did not understand what Mueller was reading, but she knew it was her death sentence. She knew that in a few minutes the life that pulsed strong and healthy through her veins would cease forever—but she stood there calmly as if it were nothing and she were only a little chilly in the cold morning air.

Graeber saw that Muecke was officiously whispering to Mueller. Mueller glanced up. "Can't that be done afterward?"

"It's better this way, sir. Simpler."

"All right, arrange it as you like."

Muecke stepped forward. "Tell that one over there to take off his shoes," he said to the old Russian who understood German, and pointed at one of the younger prisoners.

The old man told the other. He spoke in a low, almost sing-song tone. The other man, a gangling fellow, at first did not understand. "Come on," Muecke growled. "Shoes! Take off your shoes!"

The old man repeated what he had said before. The younger one understood and, like someone who had neglected his duty, hastened to take off his shoes as quickly as possible. He wobbled, standing on one foot while he drew the shoe off the other. Why is he rushing so? Graeber thought. So that he can die a minute sooner? The man took his shoes in one hand and offered them obsequiously to Muecke. They were good shoes. Muecke snorted an order and pointed to one side. The man placed the shoes there and then stepped back into line. He stood in dirty foot bandages on the snow. His yellow toes protruded from the wrappings and he kept curling them in embarrassment.

Muecke inspected the others. He found that the woman had a pair of thick fur gloves and ordered her to lay them beside the shoes. The red skirt held his attention for a moment. It was un-torn and of good material. Steinbrenner grinned surreptitiously, but Muecke did not tell the woman to take it off. Either he was afraid that Rahe might be watching the execution from his win-dow or he did not know what could be done with the skirt. He stepped back.

The woman said something very rapidly in Russian. "Ask her what more she wants," Lieutenant Mueller said. He was pale. This was his first execution.

Muecke questioned the old Russian.

"She doesn't want anything. She is just cursing you."

"What?" shouted Mueller who had not understood any of it.

"She is cursing you," the Russian said louder. "She is cursing you and all Germans who stand on Russian soil! She is cursing your children! She hopes that her children will some day shoot down your children just as you are now shooting her down."

"What impertinence!" Muecke was staring at the woman.

"She has two children," said the old man. "And I have three sons."

"That's enough, Muecke!" Mueller shouted nervously. "We're not chaplains. Attention!"

The group of soldiers came to attention. Graeber took hold of his rifle. He had taken off his glove again. The cold steel seemed to suck at his thumb and index finger. Beside him stood Hirschland. He was yellow but he stood firm. Graeber decided to aim at the Russian farthest to the left. In the beginning, when he had been commanded to take part in executions, he had shot into the air, but that was past. Doing it was no favor to those who were to be shot. Others had had the same idea and there had been times when almost everyone had intentionally missed the mark. The shooting had to be repeated and so the prisoners were executed twice. Once, to be sure, a woman had thrown herself on her knees after not being hit and had thanked them with tears for the minute or two of life she had gained. He didn't like to think about that woman. Anyhow, that sort of thing did not happen any more.

"Take aim!"

Over his sight Graeber saw the old Russian with the beard and blue eyes. The gun sight cut his face in two. Graeber lowered it. The last time he had shot away someone's lower jaw. The breast was safer. He saw that the barrel of Hirschland's rifle was raised and that he intended to shoot over their heads. "Muecke's watching you. Aim lower. Sidewise!" he murmured. Hirschland lowered the barrel. "Fire!" came the command.

The Russian seemed to rise and come toward Graeber. He swelled out like a man seen in a convex mirror in some fun house at a country fair. He swelled out and then fell backward.

The old man had been hurled half in and half out of the grave. His feet protruded from it. The two other men had sunk down where they stood. The other one without shoes had thrown up his hands at the last minute to protect his face. One hand hung like a rag from the tendons. None of the Russians had had their hands tied or their eyes bandaged. It had been forgotten.

The woman had fallen forward. She was not dead. She had propped herself on her hands and was staring with lifted face at the group of soldiers. Steinbrenner wore a satisfied expression. No one else had aimed at her. She had been shot in the stomach. Steinbrenner was a good marksman.

The old Russian struck at something from the grave; then he was still. Only the woman still lay propped up there. She stared out of her broad face at the soldiers and hissed. The old Russian was dead and now no one could translate what she was saying. She lay there with her arms braced like a great bright frog that could go no farther and she hissed without turning her eyes aside for an instant.

She seemed hardly to notice as Muecke approached disgustedly from the side. She hissed and hissed and only at the last moment did she see the revolver. She thrust her head to one side and bit Muecke in the hand. Muecke cursed and with a downward blow of his left hand knocked her lower jaw loose. As the teeth let go he shot her in the nape of the neck.

"Damned bad marksmanship!" Mueller growled. "Don't you know how to aim?"

"It was Hirschland, sir," Steinbrenner reported.

"It was not Hirschland," Graeber said.

"Quiet!" Muecke shouted. "Wait till you're asked!"

He glanced over at Mueller. Mueller was very pale and stood without moving. Muecke bent over the other Russians. He put his revolver behind the ear of one of the younger men and fired. The head jerked and lay still. Muecke put his revolver back and looked at his hand. He took out a handkerchief and wrapped it.

"Have some iodine put on it," Mueller said. "Where's the infirmary?"

"In the third house on the right, sir."

"Go there at once."

Muecke went. Mueller looked across at the dead. The woman lay sunk over forward on the wet ground. "Put them in and cover them up," he said. He was suddenly very angry without knowing why.

# Chapter Two

THAT NIGHT the rumbling on the horizon got heavier. The sky was red and the flickering of the artillery fire was more distinct. Ten days earlier the regiment had been withdrawn from the front and was now in reserve. But the Russians were coming closer. The front shifted from day to day. There was no longer any exact line. The Russians were attacking. They had been attacking for months. And for months the regiment had been going back.

Graeber awoke. He listened to the rumbling and tried to go to sleep again. He could not. After a while he put on his boots and went outside.

The night was clear and not cold. From behind the woods on the right came the sound of explosions. Parachute flares hung like transparent jellyfish in the air and showered down their light. Further toward the rear searchlights were probing for airplanes.

Graeber stopped and looked up. The sky was moonless but full of stars. He did not see them; he only saw that it was a good night for fliers.

"Nice weather for men on leave," someone beside him said.

It was Immermann. He was on sentry duty. Although the regiment was in reserve, guerrillas had filtered in everywhere and sentries were posted at night.

"You're early," Immermann said. "You still have half an hour before the change. Turn in and get some sleep. I'll wake you."

"I'm not tired."

"Furlough fever, eh?" Immermann looked questioningly at Graeber. "What luck! Furlough!"

"I haven't got it yet. They could still cancel all leaves at the last moment. That's happened to me three times before."

"It could be. How long have you been due?"

"Nine months. Something always interfered. Last time it was a flesh wound that wasn't good enough for a trip home."

"Tough—but at least you're eligible. I'm not. Unreliable. A hero's lot, and nothing else. Cannon fodder and fertilizer for the thousand-year Reich."

Graeber glanced around.

Immermann laughed. "The German glance. Don't worry, everyone's snoring. Steinbrenner too."

"I wasn't thinking of that," Graeber replied angrily. He had been thinking of it.

"So much the worse." Immermann laughed again. "It's got so far into our bones we don't even notice it any more. It's comic that in our heroic age the informers spring up like mushrooms in the rain! It makes one stop and think, doesn't it?"

Graeber hesitated a moment. "If you know that so well you ought to look out for Steinbrenner," he said finally.

"I don't give a damn for Steinbrenner. He can do me less harm than he can do you. Simply because I don't care. For somebody like me that's a sign of honesty. Too much tail-wagging would make the big boys suspicious. An old rule for former party members, to keep from being suspected. Don't you agree?"

Graeber blew on his hands. "Cold," he said.

He did not want to get into a political discussion. It was better not to get involved in anything. He wanted to have his furlough, that was all, and he didn't want to endanger it. Immermann was right; distrust was the commonest quality in the Third Reich. One wasn't really safe anywhere. And when you aren't safe you'd better keep your mouth shut.

"When were you home last?" Immermann asked.

"Two years ago."

"That's a damn long time. You'll be amazed when you get back."

Graeber made no reply.

"Amazed," Immermann repeated, "at all the changes."

"What changes can there be?"

"You'll see."

Graeber felt for a moment a sharp fear like a stab in the stomach. He was familiar with that; it came now and then suddenly and without reason, and was not surprising in a world in which for so long nothing had been sure.

"How do you know that?" he asked. "You haven't been on furlough."

"No. But I know. In the disciplinary company you hear more than you do here."

Graeber stood up. Why had he come out? He did not want to talk. He had wanted to be alone. If he were only away! It was almost an obsession. He wanted to be alone, alone for a couple of weeks, alone in order to think, that was all. There was so much he wanted to think about. Not here—but back there, at home, alone, away from the war.

"Time for sentry change," he said. "I'll get my stuff and wake Sauer."

The rumbling went on through the night. The rumbling and the flickering on the horizon. Graeber stared across. The Russians—in the fall of 1941 the Fuehrer had announced they were done for, and it had looked that way. In the fall of 1942 he had announced it again, and it had still looked that way. But then had come the inexplicable time in front of Moscow and Stalingrad. Suddenly there were no further advances. It was like witchcraft. And all at once the Russians had had artillery again. The rumbling on the horizon had begun, it had drowned out the Fuehrer's speeches, it had never ceased, and then it had driven the German divisions before it, the road back. They had not understood, but suddenly rumors were abroad that whole army corps had been cut off and had surrendered and soon everyone knew that the victories had transformed themselves into flight. Flight as it had been in Africa, when Cairo had already seemed so close.

Graeber stamped his way around the village. The moonless light distorted all perspectives. The snow caught it and threw it back diffusedly. Houses seemed farther away and woods nearer than they actually were. There was a smell of strangeness and of danger.

The summer of 1940 in France. The stroll to Paris. The howling of the Stukas over a disconcerted land. Roads jammed with refugees and with a disintegrating army. High June, fields, woods, a march through an unravaged landscape. And then the city, with its silvery light, its streets, its cafés, opening itself without a shot fired. Had he thought then? Had he been disturbed? No. Everything had seemed right. Germany, set upon by war-hungry enemies, had defended itself, that was all.

And later, in Africa, during the enormous daily advances, in the desert nights full of stars and the clatter of tanks, had he thought then? No—not even during the retreat. It had been Africa, a foreign land, the Mediterranean lay between, then France and only after that came Germany. What was there to think about in that, even if it were lost? One couldn't win everywhere.

But then Russia had come. Russia and the defeats and the flight. And this time no sea lay between; the retreat went straight toward Germany. And it was not just a few corps that had been defeated, as in Africa—the whole German army had gone back. All at once he had begun to think. He and many others. That was easy and cheap. As long as they had been victorious everything had seemed to be in order, and whatever was not in order had been overlooked or excused because of the great goal. What goal? Had there not always been two sides to it? And had not one of them been from the start dark and inhuman? Why hadn't he thought about that sooner? But hadn't he really done so? Hadn't he often enough felt doubt and disgust and driven them away again and again?

He heard Sauer cough and walked around a couple of ruined cottages to meet him. Sauer pointed toward the north. A mighty, billowing fire thrust upward from the horizon. There was a sound of explosions, and sheaves of flame arose.

"Is that the Russians? There already?" Graeber asked.

Sauer shook his head. "No. Those are our engineers. They're blowing up that place over there."

"That means we're retreating farther."

"What else?"

They remained silent and listened. "I haven't seen an undamaged house in a long time," Sauer said after a while.

Graeber pointed over to the house where Rahe lived. "That one is still in pretty good shape."

"You call that good shape? With the machine-gun holes and the burned roof and the wrecked barn?" Sauer exhaled noisily. "An undamaged street is something I haven't seen in an eternity."

"Nor I."

"You'll soon see them. At home."

"Yes, thank God."

Sauer looked over at the conflagration. "Sometimes when you see how we are destroying Russia you could get scared. What do you think they would do to us if they got across our border? Have you ever thought about that?"

"No."

"I have. I have a farm in East Prussia. I still remember how we had to flee in 1914 when the Russians came. I was ten years old then."

"It's still a long way to the border."

"That depends. It can go damn fast. Do you remember how fast we advanced in the beginning?"

"No. I was in Africa then."

Sauer glanced again toward the north. A fiery wall was rising there and then came a series of heavy explosions. "You see what we're doing there?" he said. "Now just imagine the Russians doing the same thing in our country—what would be left?"

"No more than here."

"That's what I mean! If we keep on going back it will happen."

"They're not at the border yet. You heard the lecture we had to go to day before yesterday. According to that we're shortening our lines in order to bring our new secret weapons into a favorable position for attack."

"Oh, nonsense! Who believes that sort of stuff? Then why did we advance in the first place? I'll tell you something: when we get to the border we must make peace, there's nothing else to do."

"Why?"

"But man, what sort of question is that? So they won't do the same thing to us that we've been doing to them. Don't you understand that?"

"Yes. But what happens if they refuse to make peace?"

"Who?"

"The Russians."

Sauer stared at Graeber. "They can't refuse! We offer to, and they have to accept. Peace is peace! The war will stop and we'll be saved."

"They'll have to make peace only if we surrender unconditionally. Then they will occupy all of Germany and you'll have lost your farm just the same. That's what you mean, or isn't it?"

Sauer was disconcerted for a moment. "Of course that's what I mean," he declared then. "But it is not at all the same thing. They wouldn't be allowed to destroy anything more if we surrender." He squinted his eyes and suddenly became a sly farmer. "Then our country will be undamaged and theirs will be smashed. Sometime or other they'll have to get out of Germany again and so in spite of everything we'll still practically win the war."

Graeber made no reply. Why am I talking again? he thought. I didn't want to get involved. Talking does no good. In these years what hadn't been talked over and picked to pieces? Every belief. Talking was dangerous and pointless. And the other thing, which had crept up noiselessly and slowly, was much too big and too vague and too sinister for talk. One talked about the service, about the food and about the cold. Not about the other thing. Not about that and not about the dead.

He returned along the road through the village. Planks and boards had been thrown across the streets to make it possible to cross the melted snow. The planks shifted as he walked over them and it was easy to slip off; there was no longer anything firm underneath.

He went past the church. It was little and bullet-scarred and Lieutenant Reicke was lying inside it. The door stood open. The evening before two more dead soldiers had been found, and Rahe had ordered that all three be given a military burial next morning. One of the soldiers, a lance corporal, could not be identified. His face had been eaten away and he had no identification marks. His stomach, too, had been torn open and the liver was missing. Foxes, very likely, or rats. How they had got at him was a puzzle.

Graeber went into the church. It smelled of saltpeter, decay, and the dead. He threw the beam of his flashlight into the corners. In one of them stood two broken images. A couple of torn potato sacks beside them showed that under the Soviets the room had been used to store vegetables. Nearby a rusty bicycle without chain or tires stood in the snow that had drifted in. In the middle of the room lay the dead on strips of canvas. They lay there severe and aloof and alone, and nothing mattered to them any more.

Graeber closed the door and went on around the village; shadows hovered about the ruins and even the feeble light seemed traitorous. He climbed the rise on which the graves had been dug. The one for Reicke had been widened so that the two dead soldiers could be buried with him. He heard the low sound of water trickling into the hole. The earth that had been shoveled out shimmered dully. A cross with the names on it leaned there. Anyone who wanted to could, for a couple of days, find out from it who lay there. Not for longer—the village would soon be a battlefield again.

From the rise Graeber looked out across the land. It was barren and dreary and treacherous; the light magnified and obscured, and nothing was familiar. Everything was foreign and penetrated by the chill loneliness of the unknown. There was nothing that one could rely on; nothing that offered warmth. Everything was as endless as the land. Without boundaries and alien. Alien outside and in. Graeber shivered. That was it. That was what had become of him.

A clump of earth freed itself from the pile and he heard it fall with a thud into the hole. In this hard-frozen earth had the worms survived? Perhaps—if they had burrowed deep enough. But could they live yards deep? And what did they find there to live on? From tomorrow on they would have plenty if they were still there.

They had found enough in recent years, he thought. Everywhere we have gone they have been able to feed on superabundance. For the worms of Europe, Asia and Africa we have been the Golden Age. We have turned over to them armies of corpses. Not only soldiers' flesh—women's flesh, too, and children's flesh and the soft bomb-torn flesh of the aged. Plenty of all. In the sagas of the worms we will be for generations the kindly gods of superfluity.

He turned away. The dead—there had been too many. At first the others; principally the others—but then death had encroached more and more upon their own ranks. The regiments had constantly to be re-formed; of the comrades who had been there at the beginning more and more had disappeared, and now they were just a handful. Of the friends he had had there was only one left—Fresenburg, commander of the fourth company. The others were dead or transferred or in the hospital or in Germany unfit for service, if they had been lucky. All that had once looked different. And it had been called by a different name, too.

He heard Sauer's step and saw him climbing toward him. "Has anything happened?" he asked.

"Nothing. I thought for a moment I heard something. But it was only the rats in the paddock where the dead Russians are."

Sauer glanced at the mound under which the guerrillas had been buried. "They at least got a grave."

"Yes. They had to dig it themselves, though."

Sauer spat. "You can really understand the poor beasts. After all, it's their land we're ruining."

Graeber looked at him. By night one had different thoughts than by day, but Sauer was an old soldier and not excessively emotional. "How did you hit on that?" he asked. "Because we're retreating?"

"Of course. Just imagine their doing the same thing to us some day!"

Graeber was silent for a while. I'm no better than he is, he thought. I too kept pushing the idea away as long as I could. "It's funny how you begin to understand others when you get your own ass in a sling," he said then. "As long as everything's fine you just don't think about it."

"Of course not. Everyone knows that."

"Yes. But it's not much of a testimonial, is it?"

"Testimonial? Who cares about a testimonial when his own neck's at stake?" Sauer looked at Graeber with a mixture of amazement and irritation. "The things you educated fellows keep thinking up! We two didn't start the war and we're not responsible for it. We're only doing our duty. And orders are orders. Aren't they?"

"Yes," Graeber replied wearily.

# Chapter Three

THE SALVO WAS quickly smothered in the gray wool of the huge sky. The crows perched on the walls and did not fly up. They simply replied with scattered cries that seemed louder than the shots. They were accustomed to more than that.

The three canvases lay half sunk in the melting snow. The one around the faceless man had been tied shut. Reicke lay in the middle. The torn boot with the remnant of foot in it had been laid in its proper place. But while he was being carried across from the church it had been pushed to one side and now hung down. No one wanted to put it back in place again. It only looked all at once as if Reicke were trying to dig his way deeper into the earth.

They shoveled in the wet clods. When the grave was filled there was still a pile of earth left over. Muecke looked at Mueller. "Shall we stamp it down?"

"What?"

"Stamp it down, sir. The grave. Then we can get the rest of the dirt in and put a few stones on top. Because of the foxes and wolves."

"They won't come here. The grave is deep enough. And besides—" Mueller thought the foxes and the wolves had enough to eat in the open without digging up graves. "Nonsense," he said. "What made you think of that?"

"It has happened."

Muecke stared at Mueller blankly. Another of these bone-headed fools, he thought. Always the wrong people get to be officers and the right ones get killed. Like Reicke.

Mueller shook his head. "Make a mound of the rest," he directed. "That is suitable. And put the cross at the head."

Mueller ordered the company to form up and march off. He shouted his commands louder than was necessary. He always had the feeling the older men did not take him seriously. They didn't, either.

Sauer, Immermann, and Graeber shoveled the rest of the earth into a mound. "The cross won't stand up for long," Sauer said. "The ground is too soft."

"Of course not."

"Not for three days."

"Are you related to Reicke?" Immermann asked.

"Shut up! He was all right. What do you know about it? You didn't meet him in your disciplinary company."

Immermann laughed. "That's all you have kept in your mind, isn't it? Disciplinary company—you ignorant bumpkin!" He was suddenly furious. "There were better people than you there."

"Shall we set up the cross?" Graeber asked. Immermann turned around. "Ah, our furlough boy. He's in a hurry."

"I suppose you wouldn't be in a hurry, eh?" Sauer asked.

"I'll get no furlough. You know that very well, you dung beetle."

"Sure. Because you wouldn't come back."

"Perhaps I would come back."

Sauer spat.

Immermann laughed contemptuously. "Perhaps I'd even volunteer to come back."

"Yes, perhaps. With you nobody can tell what's up. You have lots of stories to tell. Who knows what secrets you have?"

Sauer picked up the cross. The post had been sharpened to a point. He set it in place and hit it a few times with the broad side of his shovel. It sank in deep.

"There, you see?" he said to Graeber. "It won't stand up even three days."

"Three days are long enough," Immermann replied. "I'll give you a piece of advice, Sauer. In three days the snow in the cemetery will have sunk so far that you can get at the gravestones. Fetch a stone cross from there and set it up here. Then your servile soul will be at rest."

"A Russian cross?"

"Why not? God is international. Or isn't even He any more?"

Sauer turned away. "You're a wit, aren't you? A genuine international wit!"

"I've become one. Become, Sauer. Earlier I was different. And the suggestion about the cross came from you. You made it yourself yesterday."

"Yesterday! We thought Reicke was a Russian then, you distorter of words!"

Graeber picked up the shovel. "I'm leaving," he declared. "We're all through here, aren't we?"

"Yes, furlough boy," Immermann replied. "Yes, you model of prudence! We're all through here."

Graeber made no reply. Outbreaks like this were nothing new. He walked down the hill.

———

The section was quartered in a cellar, lighted by a hole in the roof. Under the hole four men were squatting and playing skat on a board. A couple of others were asleep in the corners. Sauer was writing a letter. The cellar was large and must have belonged to one of the party bigwigs; it was partially waterproof.

Steinbrenner came in. "Have you heard the latest news bulletins?"

"The radio's on the blink."

"Why? It's supposed to be kept in order."

"You fix it, baby," Immermann said. "The man who used to keep it in order has been lacking a head for the last two weeks."

"What's the matter with it?"

"We have no batteries for the set," Berning said.

"No batteries?"

"No." Immermann grinned at Steinbrenner. "But perhaps it will work if you stick the wires up your nose—you've always had a head full of electricity. Just try it."

Steinbrenner smoothed back his hair. "There are some people who won't hold their tongues until they get properly burned."

"Don't talk so mysteriously, Max," Immermann replied calmly. "You've already reported me several times. Everyone knows that. You're a sharp fellow. And it suits you nicely. Unhappily I'm an excellent mechanic and a good machine-gunner. Right now that sort of skill is more needed here than yours is. That's why you've had so little luck. How old are you really?"

"Shut your trap."

"About twenty, eh? Or just nineteen? In that time you've managed to put a fine life behind you. Five, six years of chasing Jews and betrayers of the people. My compliments! When I was twenty I chased nothing but girls."

"One can see that!"

"Yes," Immermann replied. "One can see that."

Muecke appeared in the doorway. "What's going on here?"

No one answered. Muecke annoyed them all.

"I asked what was going on here!"

"Nothing, sir," said Berning, who was nearest him. "We were just having a conversation."

Muecke looked at Steinbrenner. "Has something happened?"

"The latest news reports have come through." Steinbrenner straightened up and looked around. No one was interested. Only Graeber was listening. The card players went on playing stolidly. Sauer did not lift his head from his writing paper. The sleepers snored on.

"Attention!" Muecke shouted. "Are you all deaf? The latest news reports! Look alive! This is official!"

"Yes, sir," Immermann replied.

Muecke cast a glance at him. Immermann's face was alert and betrayed nothing. The card players spread their cards face down on the board. They did not push the hands together. That way they saved a second by being ready to go on playing at once. Sauer half straightened up from his letter.

Steinbrenner threw back his shoulders. "Important news! Announced in the 'Hour of the Nation.' Serious strikes in America. The steel industry is completely tied up. Most of the munitions works are at a standstill. Sabotage in the airplane industry. Demonstrations everywhere for immediate peace. The administration is shaky. Its overthrow is expected."

He paused. No one said anything. The sleepers had waked up and were scratching themselves. Through the hole in the roof melting snow dripped into a pail below. Muecke breathed noisily.

"Our U-boats have blockaded the entire American coast. Two huge troop transports and three freighters carrying war materials were sunk yesterday; that makes 34,000 tons this week alone. England is starving amidst her ruins. Shipping lanes have been broken up everywhere by our wolf packs. New secret weapons have been perfected. We now have bombers that can fly to America and back without landing. Our Atlantic coast is a giant fortress. If the enemy attempts an invasion we will chase them into the ocean just as we did before, in 1940. *Heil Hitler!*"

"*Heil Hitler,*" about half the section responded indifferently.

The skat players took up their cards again. A lump of snow fell with a splash into the pail. "I wish we were quartered in a decent dugout," growled Schneider, a vigorous man with a short red beard.

"Party Member Steinbrenner," Immermann asked, "have you brought us any reports about Russia?"

"Why?"

"Because we're here. Some of us are interested in the subject. Our comrade Graeber, for instance. The furlough boy."

Steinbrenner hesitated. He did not trust Immermann. But his Party loyalty triumphed. "The shortening of the front has been almost completed," he announced. "The Russians are exhausted by their gigantic losses. New enlarged positions for the counterattack have been prepared. The strategic disposition of our reserves has been achieved. Our counteroffensive with the new weapons will be irresistible."

He half lifted his hand, then let it fall. He didn't say *Heil Hitler* again. Russia and Hitler no longer went together very well. It was hard to say anything inspiring on the subject; everyone saw for himself exactly what was happening. All at once Steinbrenner was like a frantic student making a final desperate effort to retrieve an examination. "That of course isn't all by a long shot," he said. "The most important news is strictly secret. At this time it cannot be announced to the nation. But this much

is absolutely certain: we will annihilate the enemy this year."
Somewhat lamely he turned about and made his way off to the
next quarters.

Muecke followed him. "Look at that brown-noser," one of
sleepers said, and immediately fell back and started snoring
again.

The skat players began to play. "Annihilate," Schneider said.
"We annihilate them twice each year." He looked at his hand. "I
bid twenty."

"The Russians are born traitors," Immermann announced. "In
the Finnish war they purposely gave the appearance of being
much weaker than they were. That was a low Bolshevik trick."

Sauer lifted his head. "Can't you ever leave us in peace? You
know all about the Communists, don't you?"

"Of course. They were once our allies. Besides, that crack
about the trick in Finland comes personally from our Reichsmarshal Goering. Any objections?"

"Children, just cut out the wrangling, will you?" someone
said from beside the wall. "What's the matter with all of you
today?"

They quieted down. Only the cards went on slapping against
the board and the water dripped. Graeber squatted in his place.
He knew what was the matter. It was always like this after executions and burials.


In the late afternoon crowds of wounded came through. Some of
them were sent on immediately. They came with their bloody
bandages out of the gray-white plain and moved on toward the
pale horizon on the other side. It seemed as if they would never
find a hospital and would somewhere sink into the endless gray-
white. Most of them were silent. All were hungry.

For the remainder, who could not walk any farther and for whom there were no more ambulance cars, an emergency hospital was established in the church. The shell-torn ceiling was screened over and a dead-weary doctor and two assistants came in and began to operate. The door stood open as long as it was not dark and stretchers were carried in and out. The white light over the operating table hung like a bright tent in the golden dusk of the room. In one corner leaned what was left of the two images. Mary held her arms outstretched; she had no hands, and Christ had lost a leg; it looked as if they had crucified an amputee. The wounded did not often cry. The doctor still had anesthetics. Water boiled in kettles and nickel basins. Amputated limbs gradually filled a zinc bathtub that had come from the house of the company commander. From somewhere a dog had appeared. He stayed close to the door and every time they drove him away he came back.

"Where could he have come from?" Graeber asked. He was standing with Fresenburg near the house in which in the Tsar's time the priest had lived.

Fresenburg looked at the shaggy creature that trembled and held its head stretched far out. "From the woods, probably."

"What could he find in the woods? There's nothing there for him to eat."

"There is. Plenty. And not just in the woods. Everywhere."

They walked closer. The dog turned its head watchfully, ready to flee. The two men stood still.

The dog was tall and thin with a reddish-gray coat and a long narrow head. "That's no village cur," Fresenburg said. "That's a good dog."

He made a low clucking sound. The animal lifted its ears. Fresenburg clucked again and spoke to him.

"Do you think he's waiting here for food?" Graeber asked.

Fresenburg shook his head. "There's plenty to eat out there.

He hasn't come here for that. Here is light and something that resembles a house. And here there are human beings. I think he's looking for company."

A stretcher was carried out. On it lay someone who had died on the operating table. The dog leaped back a couple of yards. He leaped without effort as though propelled by a spring. Then he stood still and looked at Fresenburg. The latter spoke to him and took a slow step in his direction. Instantly the dog sprang back warily but then stopped and, barely perceptibly, wagged his tail a few times.

"He's afraid," Graeber said.

"Yes, naturally. But he's a good dog."

"And a man-eater."

Fresenburg turned around. "We're all that."

"Why?"

"We are. And we think, just like that dog, that we are still good. And just like him we are looking for a bit of warmth and light and friendship."

Fresenburg smiled with one side of his face. The other was almost immobile because of a broad scar. It looked as though it were dead, and Graeber always found it strange to watch the smile that died at the barrier in his face. It did not seem to be an accident.

"We're not different from other men. It's the war, that's all."

Fresenburg shook his head and with his walking stick tapped the snow from his puttees. "No, Ernst. We have lost our standards. For ten years we have been isolated—isolated in a hideous inhuman and ridiculous arrogance that cries to heaven. We have been proclaimed Herrenvolk whom the others have to serve as slaves." He laughed bitterly. "Herrenvolk—to obey every charlatan, every command—what has that to do with Herrenvolk? This is the answer here. And as usual it hits the innocent harder than the guilty."

Graeber stared at him. Fresenburg was the only human being out here that he trusted completely. They came from the same city and had known each other for a long time. "If you know all that," he said then, "why are you here?"

"Why am I here? Instead of sitting in a concentration camp? Or being shot for refusing to serve?"

"That's not what I mean. Weren't you too old to be drafted in 1939? Then why did you volunteer?"

"I was too old then. Things have changed since. Now they take older classes than mine. But that's not the point. And it is no excuse. Being here solves nothing. One simply argued oneself into it! Not to leave the fatherland in the lurch in time of war, no matter what the cause was or who was at fault or who had started it. It was a pretext. Exactly the same as the earlier pretext that one would go along in order to prevent something worse. That too was an excuse. For oneself. Nothing more!" He struck hard at the snow with his stick. The dog leaped away noiselessly behind the church. "We have tempted God, Ernst. Can you understand that?"

"No," Graeber replied. He did not want to understand it.

Fresenburg was silent for a time. "You can't understand it," he said then more calmly. "You are too young. You have hardly known anything except that hysterical monkey dance and the war. But I was in an earlier war. And I knew the time between." He smiled again; half his face smiled; the other half stayed rigid. The smile surged against it like a tired wave but could not cross it. "I wish I were an opera singer," he said. "A tenor with an empty head and a convincing voice. Or old. Or a child. No, not a child. Not for what's coming. The war is lost. You know that at least, don't you?"

"No."

"Any responsible general would have given it up long ago.

We're fighting here for nothing." He repeated, "For nothing. Not even for endurable terms of surrender." He lifted one hand toward the darkening horizon. "With us no one will negotiate any more. We have behaved like Attila and Genghis Khan. We have broken every agreement, every human law. We have—"

"That was the S.S.," Graeber said despairingly. He had met Fresenburg because he wanted to get away from Immermann, Sauer, and Steinbrenner; he had wanted to talk to him about the peaceful old city on the river; about the linden-bordered roads and about old times. But now it was even worse than before. Everything seemed jinxed these days. From the others he had not expected any help. But he had from Fresenburg, whom he had not seen for a long time in the confusion of the retreat—and it was just from him that he heard now what he had so long been unwilling to admit, what he had intended to think about only after he was home, and what he was more afraid of than anything.

"The S.S.," Fresenburg replied contemptuously. "The Gestapo, the liars and chiselers, the fanatics, the murderers and the insane—only for them are we still fighting. So that they can stay in power for a year longer. For that and for nothing else. The war was lost long ago."

It had become darker. The doors of the church were being closed so that no light could escape. At the windows dark figures could be seen hanging blackout cloths. The entrances to the cellars and dugouts were being protected too. Fresenburg looked at them. "Moles, that's what we've become. In our damned souls too. We've certainly made glorious progress."

Graeber pulled an open package of cigarettes out of his coat pocket and offered them to him. Fresenburg waved them aside. "Smoke them yourself. Or take them with you. I have enough."

Graeber shook his head. "Take one—"

Fresenburg smiled briefly, and took a cigarette. "When do you leave?"

"I don't know. The papers haven't come through yet." Graeber drew the smoke deep into his lungs and exhaled it. It was good to have cigarettes. Sometimes even better than friends. Cigarettes did not confuse one. They were silent and good.

"I don't know," he repeated. "For some time now I haven't known anything at all any more. Earlier everything was clear and now everything is confused. I'd like to go to sleep and wake up in another age. But things aren't made that easy. I have begun to think damned late. I'm not proud of it."

Fresenburg rubbed the scar in his face with the back of his hand. "Don't let it bother you. During the last ten years they've drummed our ears so full of propaganda that it was hard to hear anything else. Especially anything that doesn't have a shrill voice. Doubt and conscience. Did you know Pohlmann?"

"He was my teacher in history and religion."

"When you get home call him up. Perhaps he's still alive. Give him my regards."

"Why shouldn't he be alive? After all, he's not a soldier."

"No."

"Then he's sure to be alive. He can't be more than sixty-five."

"Give him my regards."

"Yes."

"I must go now. Take care of yourself. We probably won't see each other again."

"Not till I get back. That's not long. Only three weeks."

"Yes, of course. Well, take care of yourself."

"You too."

Fresenburg stamped off through the snow to his company quartered in the ruins of the next village. Graeber stared after him till he disappeared in the dusk. Then he went back. In front of the church he saw the dark shadow of the dog. The door opened and a very narrow beam of light shone out for an instant. Canvas had been hung in front of the entrance. The brief light seemed warm, and it would have been almost like home if one had not known why it was there. He approached the dog. The animal sprang away and Graeber saw the damaged images standing in the snow outside the church. Beside them lay the broken bicycle. They had been carried out; every scrap of space inside was needed.

He walked on toward the cellar where his section was quartered. A pale sunset hung behind the ruins. Near one side of the church lay the dead. In the melting snow three more old ones from October had been found. They were soft and looked as though they were already half earth. Beside them lay the others who had died only that afternoon in the church. They were still pale and hostile and strange and not yet resigned.

# Chapter Four

THEY WOKE UP. The cellar was shaking. Their ears rang. Debris was falling everywhere. The anti-aircraft battery behind the village was firing madly. "Out of here!" shouted one of the recruits.

"Quiet! Don't strike a light."

"Out, out of this rat trap!"

"Idiot! Where to? Be quiet! Damn it, are you all still recruits?"

A dull crash shook the cellar. Something broke and fell in the darkness. There was a crackling and shattering sound of stones, plaster, and wood. Pale lightnings whipped through the opening in the cellar.

"Some have got buried back there!"

"Quiet! That was just part of the wall."

"Out! Before they bury us here!"

Figures could be seen in front of the dim cellar entrance. "Imbeciles!" someone swore. "Stay down here! You're safe from bomb fragments here."

The others paid no attention. They did not trust the unreinforced cellar. They were right; just as were those that stayed. It was a matter of luck; one could just as well be crushed as killed by fragments.

They waited. Their stomachs were hollow and they breathed cautiously. They were waiting for the next hit. It must come close. But it did not. Instead they heard several explosions that followed one another in quick succession and were much farther away.

"Damnation!" someone shouted. "Where are our pursuit planes?"

"Over England."

"Shut up!" Muecke shouted.

"Over Stalingrad!" Immermann said.

"Shut up!"

The sound of motors came through in the pauses in the flak. "There they are!" Steinbrenner cried. "Those are ours!"

Everyone listened. Machine-gun fire trickled through the howling outside. Then came three explosions one after the other. They were hits close behind the village. Pale light skimmed through the cellar and in the same instant nightmarish white and red and green rushed in, the earth rose and burst in a storm of thunder and lightning and darkness. As it ebbed away there were screams from outside and the grating sound of walls crashing together in the cellar. Graeber pawed his way out from under the plaster. The church, he thought, and felt as empty as though only his skin was left and everything else had been squeezed out of him. The entrance to the cellar was still there; it was grayly visible as his blinded eyes began to see again. He moved. He had not been injured.

"Damn it!" Sauer said beside him. "That was close. I think the whole cellar behind us has been blown in."

They crawled over. The noise outside began again. In the midst of it one could hear Muecke shouting commands. A flying stone had hit him in the forehead. Blood was running over his face, black in the flickering light. "Come on! Everyone! Dig them out! Who's missing?"

No one replied. The question was too silly. Graeber and Sauer were clearing debris and stones away. It was slow work. Iron supports and big chunks of stone got in their way. They could barely see. There were only the pale sky and the glare of the explosions.

Graeber pushed the mortar aside and crept along the collapsed wall of the cellar. His face was close to the rubble and his hands kept feeling about. He listened intently, attempting to hear a cry or groan in the uproar, and at the same time he was groping through the ruins for human limbs. It was better this way than to dig at random. Time was vital when rubble fell.

Suddenly he found a hand that moved. "Here's someone!" he shouted. He dug away, searching for the head. He could not find it and pulled at the hand. "Where are you? Say something! Say where you are!" he shouted.

"Here," the buried man whispered in a pause in the firing, almost beside his ear. "Don't pull. I'm caught fast."

The hand moved again. Graeber tore the mortar to one side. He found the face. He felt the man's mouth. "Over here!" he shouted. "Help me here!"

There was only room in the corner for a couple of men to dig. Graeber heard Steinbrenner's voice. "Move over! Keep his face clear! We'll have to get at him from this side!"

Graeber squeezed himself aside. The others were working quickly in the darkness. "Who is it?" Sauer asked.

"I don't know. Who are you?"

The buried man said something. Graeber could not understand him. The others were working at his side. They pushed and pulled at the rubble. "Is he still alive?" Steinbrenner asked.

Graeber ran his hand over the face. It did not move. "I don't know," he said. "A couple of minutes ago he was still alive."

The noise began again. Graeber bent over the face in the rubble. "We'll have you out right away!" he shouted. "Do you understand me?"

He thought he felt something like a breath on his cheek but he was not sure. Above him Steinbrenner, Sauer, and Schneider were panting.

"He doesn't answer any more."

"We can't go on." Sauer struck his spade in front of him on something that rang. "There are iron girders here and the stones are too big. We need light and tools."

"No light," Muecke shouted. "Anyone who strikes a light will be shot."

They knew themselves it would be suicide to strike a light during the raid. "Idiotic ass!" Schneider growled.

"We can't get anywhere. We must wait till we can see."

"Yes."

Graeber crouched against the wall. He was staring up at the heavens from which the din poured down like a torrent into the cellar. He could recognize nothing. He only heard death, invisible and raging. It was nothing unusual. He had waited often before like this—and it had been worse.

Cautiously he ran his hand over the unknown face. It was now free of dust and dirt. He felt the lips. Then he felt the teeth. The open mouth closed. He felt the feeble bite on his fingers. The bite became stronger, then relaxed. "He's still alive," Graeber said.

"Tell him two men have gone out to find tools."

Graeber brushed his fingers once more over the lips. They no longer moved. He searched for the hand in the rubble and held it tight. The hand too had ceased to respond. Graeber held it tight; that was all he could do. He sat thus and waited until the attack was over.

They brought tools and dug out the buried man. It was Lammers. He had been a tall, stringy fellow with eyeglasses. These, too, they found. They were lying a yard beyond him on the floor, and were unbroken. But Lammers was dead.

Graeber went on sentry duty with Schneider. The air was turbid and smelled of explosives. One side of the church had been blown in. The same thing had happened to the company commander's house. Graeber wondered whether Rahe was dead. Then he saw him standing, thin and tall, in the half-darkness behind the house; he was superintending the cleaning-up operations at the church. Some of the wounded had been buried. The rest lay outside. They lay on blankets and on strips of canvas on the ground. Their eyes were directed upward. Not for help. They were afraid of the heavens.

Graeber walked past the fresh bomb craters. They stank and looked as black in the snow as if they were bottomless. Fog was already collecting in them. There was a small one near the hill on which the graves had been dug.

"We can use that one for a grave," Schneider said. "We have enough dead for it."

Graeber shook his head. "Where are you going to get the earth to fill it up with?"

"We can pry away from the sides."

"That won't help. The grave will still be deeper than the ground around it. It's simpler to dig a new one."

Schneider scratched his red beard. "Do graves always have to be higher than the ground around them?"

"Probably not. We're just used to it."

They walked on together. Graeber saw that the cross was missing from Reicke's grave. The explosions had hurled it somewhere into the night. Schneider paused and listened. "There goes your furlough," he said.

They both listened. The front had suddenly come alive. Parachute flares and rockets hung on the horizon. The artillery fire was heavier and more regular. The banging of mines could be heard. "Drum-fire," Schneider said. "That means we'll be thrown into the line again. It's all up with your furlough."

"Yes."

They went on listening. Schneider was right. What they heard did not sound like a local attack. Heavy artillery preparation was going on along the whole unstable front. Early tomorrow, very likely, the general storm would break. Since nightfall the weather had become foggy, and it was growing steadily more impenetrable. The Russians would advance behind the fog as they had done two weeks before, when the company had lost forty-two men.

His furlough was done for. Graeber had never really believed in it anyway. He had not even written his parents about it. He had only been home twice since he had been a soldier and the last time seemed so long ago that it was already unreal. Nearly two years. Twenty years. It was all the same. He did not even feel disappointed. Just empty.

"Which direction do you want to take?" he asked Schneider.

"I don't care. To the right?"

"Good. Then I'll go around to the left."

The fog was settling in and became rapidly denser. It was like wading about in dark milk soup. It already reached to the neck and was billowing and seething coldly. Schneider's head swam away on its surface. Graeber walked to the left in a wide circle around the village. Now and again he was submerged. Then he came up again and saw at the edge of the milky surface the colored lights of the front. The firing was getting steadily heavier.

He did not know how long he had been walking when he heard a couple of single shots. Schneider, he thought. Probably getting nervous. Then he heard renewed shooting and now shouts too. He bent forward, sank into the protection of the fog, and waited, his rifle ready. The shouts came nearer. Someone called his name. He answered.

"Where are you?"

"Here."

He raised his head out of the fog for an instant and at the same time leaped sidewise as a precaution. No one fired. He heard the voice now very close; but in the fog and the night it was hard to estimate distance. Then he saw Steinbrenner.

"The swine! They got Schneider through the head!"

It had been guerrillas. They had crawled up under cover of the fog. Schneider's red beard had apparently been an unmistakable target. No doubt they had expected to find the company asleep and the work of clearing up had spoiled their plan; but they had got Schneider.

"The bastards! We couldn't follow them in this damned soup!" Steinbrenner's face was wet with fog. His eyes sparkled. "We're to patrol in pairs now," he said. "Orders from Rahe. And not too far."

"All right."

They stayed close enough together to recognize each other. Steinbrenner peered sharply into the fog and glided cautiously forward. He was a good soldier. "I just wish we could grab one of them," he whispered. "I'd know what to do with him here in the fog. Jam a rag into his mouth so no one could hear, tie his arms and legs and then to work! You wouldn't believe how far you can pull an eye out before it tears." He made a motion with his hand as if slowly squashing something.

"I believe it," Graeber said.

Schneider, he thought. If he had gone to the left and I to the right they'd have got me. He felt no particular emotion. Similar things had often happened to him before. A soldier lived by accident.

They went on searching until they were relieved, but they found no one. The firing from the front reverberated. The sewing-machine rattle of the machine guns could be heard. The attack was beginning. "Here it comes!" Steinbrenner said. "If I were only up there! In an attack like this lots of replacements are needed. In a couple of days you might be a non-com."

"Or squashed flat by a tank."

"Oh, nonsense! That's what you old goats always think of right away. That's not the way to get ahead. Not everybody gets killed."

"Certainly not. Otherwise there'd be no war."

They crawled into the cellar. Steinbrenner spread out his blanket and arranged himself on his bunk. Graeber looked at him. This twenty-year-old had killed more men than a dozen old soldiers together. Not in battle; behind the front and in concentration camps. He had boasted of it more than once and was proud of having been especially sharp.

Graeber lay down and tried to sleep. He couldn't. He listened to the rumbling on the front. Steinbrenner fell asleep right away.

The day dawned gray and wet. The front was in uproar. Tanks were in battle. Toward the south the line was already pushed back. Airplanes droned. Transports were rolling across the plain. The wounded were coming back. The company was awaiting orders to move into the line.

At ten o'clock Graeber was summoned to report to Rahe. The company commander had changed his quarters. He now lived in another corner of the stone house which was still standing. Next to it was the company office. Rahe's room was at ground level. The furniture consisted of a three-legged chair, a large broken oven on which lay a couple of blankets, a campaign cot and a table. The windows had been mended with cardboard. The room was cold. On the table stood an alcohol burner with coffee.

"Your furlough has come through," Rahe said. He poured the coffee into a brightly colored cup without a handle. "Granted. You're surprised, aren't you?"

"Yes, sir."

"So am I. The form is in the office. Get it right away. And see that you leave immediately. Try to get one of the cars to take you along. I expect all leaves to be canceled any minute. If you're gone you're gone, understand?"

"Yes, sir."

Rahe looked as though he was about to say something more. But then he reconsidered, came around the table and shook hands with Graeber. "All the best. And see that you get away from here. You're long overdue for leave. You've earned it."

He turned away and walked to the window. It was too low for him. He had to bend to look out.

Graeber turned and went around the house to the office. As he passed the window he saw Rahe's decorations. He could not see his face.

The clerk pushed the stamped and signed form toward him. "Damn your luck!" he said ill-temperedly. "And not even married, eh?"

"No. But this is my first furlough in two years."

"Luck," the clerk repeated. "Furlough. When things are as hot as this!"

I didn't pick the time."

Graeber walked across to the cellar. He had stopped expecting the furlough and so he had not packed. There wasn't much to pack. Quickly he threw his things together. There was an enameled Russian icon among them that he intended to give his mother. He had found it somewhere along the way.

When he looked up Hirschland was standing in front of him. He held a piece of paper in his hand.

"What?" Graeber asked, and thought: Leave canceled! They've caught me at the last minute.

Hirschland glanced around. There was no one else in the cellar. "Are you going?" he whispered.

Graeber breathed again. "Yes," he said.

"Could you—here is the address—could you tell them at home that everything's fine with me?"

"Why? Can't you write them that yourself?"

"I do, I do," Hirschland whispered. "Always. But they don't believe me. My mother doesn't believe me. She thinks because—"

He broke off and offered the scrap of paper to Graeber. "Here is the address. If a member of my company comes—then perhaps she'll believe it—do you understand? She thinks I wouldn't dare—"

"Yes," Graeber said. "I understand." He took the paper and laid it in his pay book. Hirschland brought out a package of cigarettes. "Here—for your trip—"

"Why?"

"I don't smoke."

Graeber looked up. That was right. He had never seen Hirschland smoking. "Well, fine," he said, and took the package.

"And don't say anything to them about—" Hirschland motioned toward the front. "Just that we're resting."

"Of course. What else would I say?"

"Good. Thanks."

Hirschland left quickly.

Thanks? Graber thought. Why thanks?

He found a place in an ambulance car. The car full of wounded had slid into a ditch in the snow. The man beside the driver had been pitched out of his seat and had broken his arm. Graeber was being taken along in his place. The car followed the road marked with stakes and wisps of straw, circling the village in a wide curve. Graeber saw the company standing in formation in the town square in front of the church. "They have to move up to the front," the driver said. "They're going into the line. Man, where do the Russians get all that artillery?"

"Yes—"

"And they've got plenty of tanks, too. Where do they all come from?"

"From America. Or Siberia. They're supposed to have a lot of factories there."

The driver made his way around a truck that was stuck. "Russia is too big. Too big, I tell you. One just gets lost in it."

Graeber nodded, and drew a blanket around his boots.

For a minute he seemed to himself like a deserter. The company was standing darkly on the village square; but he was driving back. He alone. The others were staying here and he was driving back. They had to go to the front. I've earned it, he thought. Rahe said so, too. So why do I think about it? Isn't it just that I'm still afraid someone will come after me and take me back?

A couple of kilometers farther they found another car with wounded that had slipped off the road and was stuck in the snow. They stopped and checked over their stretchers. Two men had died. They unloaded them and in their places took on three wounded from the other car. Graeber helped to load them. Two were amputees; the third had a face wound; he could sit up. Those left behind cursed and screamed. They were stretcher cases for whom there was no room. They felt the terror of all wounded men: to be overtaken by war at the last moment.

"What's the trouble?" the driver asked the chauffeur of the car that was stuck.

"Broken axle."

"Broken axle? In the snow?"

"A man once broke his finger picking his nose. Hadn't you heard that, you novice?"

"Sure. At least you're lucky it's no longer winter. Otherwise all of them would freeze to death."

They drove on. The driver leaned back. "It happened to me two months ago. I was having trouble with the transmission. Making very slow time. The fellows on the stretchers froze solid. Couldn't do a thing. Six were still alive when we finally arrived. Hands, feet, and noses frozen, of course. Getting wounded in the winter in Russia is no joke." He got out a piece of tobacco and bit off a chew. "And the ambulatory cases! They were all along the road on foot. At night in the cold. Tried to storm our car. Hung on the doors and running-boards like a swarm of bees. Had to kick them off."

Graeber nodded absently and looked around him. The village had disappeared behind a snow bank. There was nothing left but the sky and the plain through which they were driving westward. It was midday. The sun shone dimly behind the gray. The snow glittered wanly. And suddenly something in him broke, hot and headlong, and for the first time he felt that he had escaped, that he was driving away from death; he felt it and he stared at the track-marked snow disappearing yard after yard under the wheels, and yard after yard it was safety, safety toward the west, toward home, toward the incredible life beyond the rescuing horizon.

The chauffeur jostled him while changing gears. Graeber jumped. He felt in his pockets and brought out a package of cigarettes. They were the ones from Hirschland. "Here—," he said.

"Merci," the driver replied without looking. "I don't smoke. Only chew."

# Chapter Five

THE BRANCH-LINE train came to a stop. A small camouflaged station stood there in the sun. Of the few surrounding houses only ruins remained; in their place barracks had been erected with roofs and walls painted in protective colors. A number of railroad cars stood on the tracks. Russian prisoners were transferring freight. The branch line at this point joined a main line.

The wounded were carried into one of the barracks. Those that could walk sat hunched on rough-hewn benches. A few more men on leave had arrived. They kept together and tried to be as inconspicuous as possible. They were afraid of being noticed and sent back.

It was a weary day. Wilted light played tag over the snow. From a distance came the hum of airplane engines. It did not come from the air; probably there was a concealed airfield nearby. Later a squadron took off over the station and began to climb until it looked like a flight of larks. Graeber dozed. Larks, he thought. Peace.

They were startled into attention by two military policemen. "Papers!"

The M.P.'s were healthy and strong and had the confident bearing of men who are not in danger. Their uniforms were spotless, their weapons polished, and each of them weighed at least twenty pounds more than any of the men on leave.

The soldiers silently brought out their certificates of leave. The M.P.'s examined them methodically before returning them. Then they ordered the pay books to be shown.

"You're to eat in Barracks Three," the older one said finally. "Clean yourselves up. What a sight you are! Do you want to arrive home looking like pigs?"

The group wandered across to the barracks. "These damned spying hounds!" growled a man with a black, stubble-covered face. "Big mouths and a long way from the shooting! Act as if we were criminals."

"At Stalingrad they shot dozens of men who got separated from their regiments," another man said.

"Were you at Stalingrad?"

"If I had been at Stalingrad I wouldn't be sitting here now. No one got out of that stew."

"Listen to me," said one of the older non-coms. "At the front you can talk any way you like. But from now on you'd better shut your trap if you know what's good for you. Understand?"

They lined up with their mess pots. For over an hour they had to wait. No one left his place. They were cold, but they waited. They were used to it. Finally they were given a dipperful of soup with some meat and vegetables and a couple of potatoes floating in it.

The man who had not been at Stalingrad looked around cautiously. "I wonder if those M.P.'s eat this stuff too."

"Man, you have worries!" said the non-com contemptuously.

Graeber swallowed his soup. At least it was warm, he thought.

At home it would be different. His mother would cook. Perhaps even bratwurst with onions and potatoes, and afterwards a raspberry pudding with vanilla sauce.

They had to wait until dark. Twice more they were inspected. More wounded kept arriving all the time. With each new batch the men on leave became jumpier. They were afraid of being left behind. Finally, after midnight, the train was assembled. It had grown colder and the stars hung big in the sky. Everyone hated them; they meant good visibility for the fliers. For a long time now nature had had no significance in itself; it was simply good or bad in relation to the war. As protection or as danger.

The wounded were put on board. Three were taken off again immediately. They had died in the meantime. The stretchers were left standing on the platform—the ones with the dead had no blankets. No light showed anywhere.

Next came the ambulatory wounded. They were carefully checked. We won't get in with them, Graeber thought. There are too many. The train is full. He stared stolidly into the night. His heart pounded. Airplanes hummed above him. He knew they were Germans, but he was afraid. He was much more afraid than at the front.

"Men on leave!" someone shouted finally.

The group hurried forward. Military police were once more standing there. In the afternoon during the last inspection each man had received a slip of paper which he now had to surrender. They climbed into a car. Some of the wounded were already sitting there. The men on leave crowded together, pushing one another. An M.P. shouted commands. They all had to get out again and form up. Then they were led to the next car where there were wounded sitting too. They were allowed to enter. Graeber found a place in the middle. He did not want to sit by the window. He knew what bomb splinters could do.

The train did not start. It was dark in the compartment. They were all waiting. Outside things grew quiet; but the train continued to stand still. They could see two M.P.'s leading a soldier between them. A troop of Russians was moving cases of ammunition. Then came a couple of S.S. men talking together loudly. Still the train did not move. The wounded were the first to begin cursing. They could afford to. For the time being nothing more could happen to them.

Graeber leaned his head back. He tried to go to sleep with the intention of waking up when the train was moving; but he could not do it. He kept listening to every sound. He saw the eyes of the others in the dark. The dim light coming from snow and stars outside made them gleam. It was not bright enough to distinguish faces. Only the eyes. The compartment was full of darkness and restless eyes and between them shimmered the dead white of the bandages.

The train gave a jerk and stopped again immediately. Shouts were heard. After a while there was a banging of doors. Two stretchers were taken out on the platform. Two more dead. Two more places for the living, Graeber thought. If only no new ones come at the last minute so that we will have to get out. They all thought the same.

The train jerked again. The platform began to slide past slowly. Military police, prisoners, S.S. men, piles of crates—and then suddenly the plain was there. Everyone was bending forward. They still did not believe it. The train would stop again. But it moved and moved and by degrees the irregular thrusts were transformed into an even rhythm. They saw tanks and cannons. Troops that stared after the cars. All at once Graeber was very tired. Home, he thought. Going home. Oh God, I don't dare rejoice.

In the morning it was snowing. They stopped at a station to get coffee. The station stood on the edge of a small city of which nothing much remained. Bodies were carried out. The train was being shunted. Graeber ran back to his compartment with his ersatz coffee. He did not dare leave it to get bread.

A group of M.P.'s started through the train, picking out the less seriously wounded; they were to stay in the local hospital. The news ran swiftly through the cars. The men with arm wounds rushed to the toilets to hide themselves. They fought for the place inside. In a fury they pulled each other out at the very minute the door was about to be locked. "They're coming!" someone shouted suddenly from outside.

The crowd dispersed. Two pushed their way into the same toilet and slammed the door. Another who had fallen in the fracas stared at his splinted arm. There was a small red spot growing larger. A third opened the door that faced away from the platform and clambered painfully out into the blizzard. He pressed himself against the outside of the train. The rest kept their seats.

"Shut the door," someone said. "Otherwise they'll know at once what's happened."

Graeber pulled the door shut. For a moment through the eddying snow he saw the white face of the man who was clinging below.

"I want to get home," said the wounded man whose bandage was bleeding. "Twice I've been in one of these damn field hospitals and each time right out to the front again, without any leave at all. I want to get back home. I've earned it."

He stared with hatred at the healthy men on leave. No one answered. It took a long time for the patrol to arrive. Three men were going through the compartments while outside a couple of others watched over the wounded who had been told to stay. One of the examiners was a junior field surgeon. He glanced swiftly at the certificates of the wounded. "Get out," he said indifferently, already examining another slip.

One of the men did not get up. He was small and gray. "Out, grandpa," said the M.P. who accompanied the surgeon. "Didn't you hear?"

The man stayed where he was. He had a shoulder bandage. "Out! Get out!" repeated the M.P. The man did not move. He kept his lips pressed together and stared straight ahead as though he understood nothing. The M.P. stood straddle-legged in front of him. "Do you need a special invitation? Stand up!"

The man went on as though he had not heard. "Stand up!" snorted the M.P. "Can't you see a superior is talking to you? Man, do you want to be courtmartialed?"

"Take it easy!" said the young surgeon. "First take it easy." He had a rosy face without eyelashes. "You're bleeding," he explained to the man who had been fighting at the door of the toilet. "You must have a fresh bandage. Get out."

"I—" the man began. Then he saw that a second M.P. had entered and together with the first had taken hold of the gray soldier by his uninjured arm. They were lifting him. The soldier emitted a thin shriek without moving his face. The second M.P. now seized him around the hips and pushed him out of the compartment like a light package. He did it impersonally, without brutality. The soldier did not go on shrieking either. He disappeared into the herd outside.

"Well?" asked the young surgeon.

"Can I go on with the train when I've been bandaged, Captain?" asked the bleeding man.

"We'll see about that. Possibly. First you must be bandaged."

The man got out with a face full of misery. He had addressed the junior surgeon as captain and even that had not helped. The M.P. tried the door to the toilet. "Of course," he said contemptuously. "Nothing else ever occurs to them. Always the same thing. Open up!" he commanded. "At once!"

The door opened. One of the soldiers came out. "You're a sly one, aren't you?" growled the M.P. "Why did you shut yourself in there? Trying to play hide and seek?"

"I have diarrhea. And I believe that's what a toilet's for."

"So? Just at this moment? Am I supposed to believe that?"

The soldier pushed back his coat. The Iron Cross first class hung there. He looked at the M.P.'s chest, which was empty. "Yes," he replied calmly. "You're supposed to believe that."

The M.P. got red. The doctor intervened. "Get out, please," he said without looking at the soldier.

"You haven't looked to see what's the matter with me."

"I can tell that from your bandage. Get out, please."

The soldier smiled thinly. "All right."

"Well then, we're through here, eh?" the surgeon asked the M.P. nervously.

"Yes, sir." The M.P. glanced at the men on leave. Each of them was holding his papers in his hand. "Yes sir, all through," he announced, and climbed out after the doctor.

The door of the toilet opened silently. A lance-corporal who had been inside slipped out. His face was steaming with sweat. He slid down on a seat. "Has he gone?" he whispered after a while.

"Seems so."

The lance-corporal sat for a long while in silence. Sweat ran down his face. "I'm going to pray for him," he said finally.

Everyone looked up. "What?" one of them asked incredulously. "You're going to pray for that swine of an M.P.?"

"No, not for the swine. For the man who was with me in the toilet. He told me to stay there; he would fix things up. Where is he?"

"Outside. He fixed things up all right. He made the fat pig so mad he didn't look any further."

"I'm going to pray for him."

"Oh, all right, pray if you like."

"Yes, definitely. My name is Luettjens. I'm certainly going to pray for him."

"All right! Now shut up. Pray tomorrow. Or at least wait until the train has started," someone said, bored.

"I'm going to pray. I have to get home. I'll not get any leave to go home if I'm put in the hospital here. I must get to Germany. My wife has cancer. She's thirty-six. Just thirty-six last October. Four months in bed already."

He looked at them one after the other with tormented eyes. No one said anything. It was too common a matter.

An hour later the train went on. The man who had climbed out the door had not shown himself again. Probably they had grabbed him, Graeber thought.

At noon a non-commissioned officer came in. "Does anyone here want a shave?"

"What?"

"A shave. I'm a barber. I have excellent soap. Left over from France."

"A shave while the train is moving?"

"Of course. I've just been working in the officers' car."

"How much does it cost?"

"Fifty pfennigs. Half a Reichsmark. Cheap when you consider I have to cut off your beards first."

"Fine." Someone brought out the money. "But if you cut me you don't get anything."

The barber set down his shaving bowl and produced from his pocket a pair of scissors and a comb. He had a big paper bag into which he threw the hair. Then he began to work up a lather. He was standing beside a window. The foam was as white as though he were using snow for soap. He was adroit. Three men had themselves shaved. The wounded refused. Graeber was the fourth to sit down. He looked at the three who were finished. They looked strange now. Their faces were red and spotted from the weather; underneath shone their white chins. They were half soldiers' faces and half the faces of stay-at-homes. Graeber heard the scraping of the razor. Being shaved made him more cheerful. It was already a bit of home, especially since a superior was serving him. The effect was like being in civilian clothes.

In the afternoon they stopped once more. A field kitchen stood outside. They got out to receive their portions. Luettjens did not go with them. Graeber saw that he was moving his lips rapidly. As he did so he held his uninjured right hand as though folded into the other invisible one. The left was bandaged and hung inside his tunic. They got Swedish turnips. They were lukewarm.

It was evening when they came to the border. The train was emptied. The men on leave were assembled and taken to a delousing station. They turned over their clothes and sat around naked in the barracks to let their body lice die. The room was warm, the water was warm, and there was soap that smelled strongly of carbolic. For the first time in months Graeber was sitting in a really warm room. At the front there had sometimes been ovens, but then it was always just the side you turned to the heat that was warm. The other was icy. Here the whole room was warm. One's bones could finally thaw out. One's bones and one's skull. It was the skull that had been frost-bound longest.

They sat around and looked for lice and cracked them. Graeber had no head lice. Blanket lice and clothing lice did not invade the head, that was an old rule. Lice respected one another's territory. They had no wars.

The warmth made him drowsy. He saw the pale bodies of his comrades, the chilblains on their feet and the red lines of scars. They were suddenly no longer soldiers. Their uniforms were hanging somewhere in the steam; they were naked human beings cracking lice, and their conversation became immediately different. They no longer talked about the war. They talked about food and women.

"She has a child," said a man called Bernhard. He was sitting beside Graeber and was catching the lice in his eyebrows with the aid of a pocket mirror. "I haven't been home for two years and the child is four months old. She claims it's fourteen months old and mine. But my mother has written me that it was fathered by a Russian. Besides, she only began to write about it ten months ago. Never before. What do you think?"

"That sort of thing happens," a bald-headed man replied indifferently. "In the country there are a lot of children fathered by war prisoners."

"I'd kick the woman out," declared a man who was rebandaging his feet. "It's an obscenity."

"Obscenity? What do you mean obscenity?" The baldhead waved contemptuously. "In wartime things like that are not the same. You have to understand that. What is it, a boy or a girl?"

"A boy. She writes he looks like me."

"If it's a boy you can keep it. He'll be useful. On a farm one always needs help."

"But, look, he's half Russian—"

"What difference? The Russians are Aryans. And the fatherland needs soldiers."

Bernhard put away his mirror. "It's not as simple as that. It's easy for you to talk. You're not the one it happened to."

"Would you prefer it if some fat, reconditioned native bull gave your wife a child?"

"Certainly not that."

"All right, then."

"She might have waited for me," Bernhard said softly and embarrassedly.

The baldhead shrugged his shoulders. "Some of them wait and some don't. You can't expect everything if you don't get home for years."

"Are you married too?"

"No, thank God, I'm not."

"Russians are not Aryans," a mouse-like man with a pointed face and a small mouth said suddenly. He had been silent till then.

Everyone looked at him. "You're mistaken," the baldhead replied. "They are Aryans. After all, they were once our allies."

"They're subhumans, Bolshevik subhumans. That's the definition."

"You're mistaken. Poles, Czechs, and French are subhumans. We are freeing the Russians from the Communists. They are Aryans, with the exception of the Communists, of course. Perhaps not master Aryans like us. Simply Aryan workers. But they are not to be exterminated."

The mouse was taken aback. "They were always subhumans," he declared. "I know that for sure. Pure subhumans."

"That was changed long ago. Just like the Japanese. They too are Aryans now, since they're our allies. Yellow Aryans."

"You're both wrong," said the extraordinarily hairy bass. "The Russians were not subhuman while they were still our allies. But they are now. That's the way it stands."

"Then what is he to do with the child?"

"Hand it over to the state," said the mouse with new authority. "Painless mercy-death. What else?"

"And his wife?"

"That's up to the authorities. Branding, head shaving, penitentiary, concentration camp or gallows."

"They haven't done anything to her so far," Bernhard said.

"The authorities probably don't know about it yet."

"They know. My mother reported it."

"Then they are dirty and corrupt. They belong in a concentration camp too."

"Oh, damn it all, leave me in peace!" Bernhard cried, suddenly furious, and turned away.

A bandy-legged, pigeon-chested man who had been wandering restlessly through the room came up to them and stopped. "We are supermen," he said, "and the others are subhuman, that much is clear. But who now are the ordinary men?"

The baldhead reflected. "Swedes," he said presently, "or Swiss."

"Savages," announced the bass. "White savages, of course."

"White savages don't exist any more," said the mouse.

"No?" The bass stared at him hard.

Graeber dozed off. He heard the others starting to talk about women again. He didn't know much about them. The race theories of his country did not correspond very well with what he understood of love. He did not want to get it all mixed up with natural selection, family trees, and the ability to bear children. As a soldier he had scarcely known anything but a few whores in the countries where he had fought. They had been just as matter-of-fact as the members of the German Maidens' Guild; but with them at least it was a profession.

They got their clothes back and dressed. All at once they were privates, lance-corporals, sergeants, and non-coms again. The man with the Russian child turned out to be a non-com. The bass as well. The mouse was a convoy soldier. He shrank into himself when he saw that the others were non-coms. Graeber examined his tunic. It was still warm and smelled of acid. Under the clasp of the braces he found a colony of lice that had taken refuge there. They were dead. Gassed. He scratched them away.

They were conducted into a barracks. A political officer delivered an address. He stood on a podium behind which hung a picture of the Fuehrer and he explained to them that now, since they were going back to the homeland, they had a great responsibility. Nothing must be mentioned about their time at the front. Nothing about positions, locations, troop disposal, or troop movements. Spies were lying in wait everywhere. Therefore silence was of the utmost importance. Whoever talked loosely could count on severe punishment. Idle criticism, too, was treason. The Fuehrer was conducting the war; he knew what he was doing. The situation was brilliant. The Russians were bleeding to death. They had suffered unprecedented losses, and the counterattack was being mounted. Care of the troops was first class and their spirit excellent. Once more: to divulge the names of places or the position of troops was high treason. Alarmism also. The Gestapo was on the alert everywhere. Everywhere.

The officer paused. Then he explained in an altered tone that the Fuehrer, despite his immense task, kept watch over all his soldiers. He had specified that each man on leave was to receive a gift to take back home with him. For this purpose food packages would be issued to them. They were to be handed over to their families at home as evidence that the troops abroad were well cared for and that they could even bring back presents. Anyone who opened his packet on the way and ate it himself would be punished. There would be an inspection at each destination to make sure. *Heil Hitler!*

They stood at attention. Graeber expected *Deutschland, Deutschland ueber alles* and the *Horst Wessel* song; the Third Reich was great on songs. But nothing happened. Instead came the order: "Men with furloughs to the Rhineland, three steps forward!"

A few men stepped in front of the line. "Furloughs to the Rhineland are canceled," announced the officer. He turned to the man standing nearest him. "Where do you want to go instead?"

"To Cologne."

"I have just told you that the Rhineland is restricted. Where do you want to go instead?"

"To Cologne," said the man uncomprehendingly. "I come from Cologne."

"You cannot go to Cologne. Don't you understand? To what other city do you want to go?"

"No other city. My wife and children are in Cologne. I was a locksmith there. My furlough certificate is stamped for Cologne."

"I see that. But you cannot go there. Try to understand! For the time being Cologne is forbidden to men on leave."

"Forbidden?" asked the former locksmith. "Why?"

"Have you gone crazy, man? Whose business is it to ask questions? Yours or the authorities'?"

A captain came up and whispered something to the officer. He nodded. "Men with furloughs to Hamburg and Alsace, step forward," he commanded.

No one stepped forward. "Rhinelanders remain here! The rest

at ease! Left about face! Step up and receive your homecoming packages."


They were standing in the station once more. The Rhinelanders joined them after a while. "What was up?" asked the bass.

"You heard what it was."

"You can't go to Cologne? Where are you going now?"

"To Rothenburg. I have a sister there. What am I to do in Rothenburg? I live in Cologne. What's going on in Cologne? Why can't I go to Cologne?"

"Careful!" someone said and glanced at two S.S. men who were striding by with thudding boots.

"To hell with them! What am I to do in Rothenburg? Where is my family? They were in Cologne. What is happening there?"

"Perhaps your family is in Rothenburg too."

"They're not in Rothenburg. There is no place for them there. My wife and my sister can't stand each other. What is going on in Cologne?"

The locksmith stared at the others. He had tears in his eyes. His thick lips quivered. "Why can you go home and I can't? After all this time! What has happened? What has become of my wife and my children? George is my eldest's name. Eleven years old. What has happened?"

"Listen," said the bass. "You can't do anything about it. Send your wife a telegram. Have her come to Rothenburg. Otherwise you won't see her at all."

"And the trip? Who will pay for that? And where is she to stay?"

"If they won't let you into Cologne they won't let your wife out," said the mouse. "That's certain. That's the way regulations are."

The locksmith opened his mouth but said nothing. Only after a time he asked: "Why not?"

"Think it out for yourself."

The locksmith looked around. He glanced from one to another: "Everything can't have gone to pieces! That's absolutely impossible!"

"Be glad they didn't send you straight back to the front," said the bass. "That could very well have happened, once your district is barred."

Graeber listened in silence. He realized that he was shivering and that the cold did not come from outside. Once more the ghostly and intangible something was there that had haunted him so long and that could never be wholly grasped, that eluded him and came back and stared at him and had a hundred ill-defined faces and no face at all. He looked at the rails. They led toward home, security, warmth and peace, toward the only thing that was left. And now the something from outside seemed to have slipped in with him, it breathed eerily beside him and was not to be frightened away.

"Furlough," said the man from Cologne bitterly. "This is my furlough! What now?"

The others looked at him and said nothing. It was as though a hidden sickness had suddenly shown itself in him. He was innocent but he seemed to be strangely marked, and imperceptibly they edged away. They were glad it had not struck them but they weren't safe yet themselves—and for that reason they edged away. Misfortune was contagious.

The train rolled slowly into the train shed. It was black and it blotted out the last of the light.

# Chapter Six

NEXT DAY the landscape had changed. It rose clearly out of the soft morning mist. Graeber was now sitting by the window, his face pressed against the pane. He saw fallow land and fields still flecked with snow under which the even black furrows of the plow were visible, and the pale green shimmer of the young rye. No shell holes. No destruction. Flat, smooth plains. No trenches. No dugouts. Country.

Then came the first village. A church on which a cross gleamed. A schoolhouse on whose roof a weather vane was slowly turning. A tavern in front of which people were standing. The open doors of houses, maids with brooms, a wagon, the first reflection of the sun in unbroken windows. Roofs that were whole, undamaged houses, trees that had all their branches, streets that were streets, and children on their way to school. Graeber had not seen any children in a long time. He took a deep breath. This was what he had been waiting for. It was there. There after all!

"Looks different already, doesn't it?" said a non-com at the other window.

"Entirely different."

The mist lifted more and more. Woods approached from the horizon. One could see a long way. Telegraph wires accompanied the train. They swooped up and down—lines and staves of an endless inaudible melody. Birds fluttered up from them like songs. The landscape was still. The rumbling of the front had sunk far behind. No more airplanes. It seemed to Graeber as though he had been on his way for weeks. Even the memory of his comrades was suddenly pale.

"What's today?" he asked.

"Thursday."

"So it's Thursday."

"Of course. Yesterday was Wednesday. Do you think there's any chance we'll get coffee somewhere?"

"Of course. Here everything's the way it used to be."

A few of the men got bread out of their knapsacks and began to munch it. Graeber waited; he wanted to have his bread with the coffee. He thought of the breakfast table at home. His mother had a blue and white checkered tablecloth and there had been honey and rolls and coffee with hot milk. The canary had sung and in summer the sun had shone upon the rose geraniums in the window. At that time he had often rubbed the dark green leaves between his hands smelling the strong, foreign perfume and thinking of foreign lands. Since then he had seen plenty of foreign lands but not the way he had dreamed of at that time.

He looked out again. Suddenly he felt comforted. Outside stood field hands looking at the train. Women were there, too, with kerchiefs around their heads. The non-com lowered his window and waved. No one waved back.

"Well then don't, you louts," the non-com said, in disappointment.

A few minutes later came another field with people in it and he waved again. This time he leaned far out of the window. This time, too, no one waved back although the people had straightened up and were looking at the train.

"That's what we're fighting for now," declared the non-com angrily.

"Perhaps they're prisoners who're working there. Or foreign laborers."

"There were enough women among them. They at least could have waved."

"Perhaps they were Russians, too. Or Poles."

"Nonsense. They didn't look like that. And even so, there must have been some Germans, too."

"This is a train with wounded," said the baldhead. "No one waves at them."

"Oxen," declared the non-com, closing the subject. "Village idiots and milkmaids." He put up the window with a jerk.

"In Cologne they're different," said the locksmith.

The train rolled on. Once it stopped in a tunnel for two hours. There was no light in the cars and the tunnel itself was entirely dark. They were accustomed to living underground; nevertheless after a time the tunnel became oppressive.

They smoked. The glowing tips of their cigarettes darted up and down like fireflies. "Probably a mechanical failure," said the non-com.

They listened. They could not hear any airplanes. Nor were there any sounds of explosions. "Were any of you ever in Rothenburg?" asked the man from Cologne.

"It's an ancient city," Graeber said.

"Were you there?"

"No. Haven't you ever been there?"

"No. And what can I possibly do there?"

"You should have gone to Berlin," said the mouse. "You only get leave once. And there's more going on in Berlin."

"I haven't enough money for Berlin. Where would I stay? In a hotel? I want to get to my family."

The train jerked into motion. "Finally," said the bass. "I thought we were going to be buried here."

Light trickled grayly into the gloom. It became more silvery and then the landscape was there again. It seemed more precious than ever. They all crowded to the windows. The afternoon was like wine. Involuntarily they looked for fresh bomb craters. They found none.

A few stations farther on the bass got out. Then the non-com and two others. An hour later Graeber began to recognize the countryside. Twilight was beginning. Blue veils hung in the trees. It was not any definite object that he recognized—no houses or villages or hills—it was the landscape itself that suddenly spoke. It came from all sides, sweet, overwhelming, and full of sudden memories. It was not precise, it had nothing to do with facts, it was hardly more than the presentiment of return, not return itself, but for that very reason it was much stronger. The twilight lanes of dreams were in it and they had no end.

The names of the stations were now familiar. Places remembered from excursions slipped by. In his memory there was suddenly the smell of strawberries and resin and of the heath in the sun. It could only be a few minutes now till the city came. Graeber had strapped up his things. He stood up and waited for the first streets.

The train stopped. People hurried about outside. Graeber peered out. He heard the name of the city. "Well, good luck," said the man from Cologne.

"We're not there yet. The station's in the middle of town."

"Perhaps they have moved it. Better ask."

Graeber opened the door. In the half-darkness he saw people getting in. "Is this Werden?" he asked.

A couple of people glanced up but did not reply. They were in too much of a hurry. He got out. Then he heard the stationmaster shout: "Werden! All out for Werden!"

He seized the straps of his knapsack and forced his way through to the official. "Doesn't this train go to the station?"

The man eyed him wearily. "Do you want to go to Werden?"

"Yes."

"Over there to the right behind the platform. The bus goes the rest of the way."

Graeber walked along the platform. He was unfamiliar with it. It was new and made of green lumber. He found the bus. "Do you go to Werden?" he asked the driver.

"Yes."

"Doesn't the train go through to the city any more?"

"No."

"Why not?"

"Because it only goes this far."

Graeber looked at the driver. He saw it was pointless to go on questioning him. He would get no real answer. He climbed into the bus. There was a vacant seat in one corner. Outside everything was dark now. He could only just make out what seemed to be new rails shimmering in the darkness. They led off at right angles to the direction of the city. The train was already being switched. Graeber squeezed himself into his corner. Perhaps they have just done it as a precaution, he thought without conviction.

The bus drove off. It was an old crate with bad gasoline. The engine coughed. Several Mercedes cars overtook them. In one seat army officers; in two others officers of the S.S. The people in

the bus watched them race by. They said nothing. Hardly anything was said during the drive. Only a child laughed and played
in the aisle. A girl of about two, blonde, with a blue ribbon in
her hair.

Graeber saw the first streets. They were undamaged. He
sighed with relief. The bus rattled on for a few minutes and then
stopped. "All out."

"Where are we?" Graeber asked the man next to him.

"Bramschestrasse."

"Don't we go any farther?"

"No."

The man got out. Graeber followed him. "I'm on furlough,"
he said. "For the first time in two years." He had to tell someone.

The man looked at him. He had a fresh scar on his forehead
and two of his front teeth were missing. "Where do you live?"

"Number Eighteen Hakenstrasse."

"Is that in the old city?"

"On the edge. Corner of Luisenstrasse. You can see the Katharinenkirche from there."

"Yes—" The man stared up into the dark sky. "Well—you
know the way."

"Certainly. That's something you don't forget."

"Certainly not. Good luck."

"Thanks."

Graeber walked along Bramschestrasse. He looked at the
houses. They were whole. He looked at the windows. They were
all dark. Air raid precaution, he thought; of course. It was childish, but nevertheless he had not expected it; he had thought the
city would be lighted. He ought to have remembered from last
time. Quickly he walked along the street. He saw a baker's shop
in which there was no bread. In the window a couple of paper
roses stood in a glass vase. A fancy grocery store came next; the

display window was full of packages; but they were empty containers. Then a saddler's window. Graeber remembered the store. A stuffed brown horse used to stand there. He glanced in. The horse was still standing there and in front of him, his head raised to bark, the old stuffed black and white terrier, too, just as before. He stopped a moment before the window which was unchanged in spite of all that had happened in recent years; then he walked on. Suddenly he felt at home. "Good evening," he said to someone he did not know who was standing in a nearby doorway.

"Evening," the man said after a while, in surprise, behind him.

The pavement resounded under Graeber's boots. Soon he would get rid of this heavy footgear and put on his light civilian shoes. He would take a bath in clear hot water and put on a clean shirt. He walked faster. The street seemed to spring upward beneath his feet as though it were alive or filled with electricity. Then suddenly he smelled the smoke.

He stopped. It was not chimney smoke; nor the smoke of a wood fire; it was the smell of a conflagration. He looked around. The houses stood there undamaged. The roofs were not burned. The sky behind them was dark blue and vast.

He walked on. The street ended in a little square with flower beds. The smell of burning grew stronger. It seemed to hang in the bare treetops. Graeber sniffed; he could not determine where it came from. Now it was everywhere, as though it had fallen from the sky like ashes.

At the next corner he saw the first ruined house. It gave him a start. He had seen nothing but ruins in recent years and never thought anything about it; but he stared at this pile of rubble as though he were seeing a ruined building for the first time in his life.

It's just a single house, he thought. Only a single one. The others are all still standing. He hastened past the pile of rubble, sniffing. The smell of burning was not coming from it. This house had been destroyed quite a long time ago. Perhaps it had been an accident—a forgotten bomb that had been released at random on the flight home.

He looked for the name of the street. Bremerstrasse. It was still a long way to Hakenstrasse. Still at least a half-hour's walk. He went faster. He saw hardly anyone. Under a dark archway some blue electric bulbs were burning. They were shaded and they made the arch look as though it had tuberculosis.

Then came the first ruined corner. This time there were several houses. Only the foundation walls were still standing. They rose into the air jagged and black. Bent girders hung between like dark snakes that had crawled out of the stones. Part of the rubble had been shoveled to one side. These ruins too were old. Graeber went close by them. He clambered over the rubble on the sidewalk and in the darkness saw darker shadows like giant beetles creeping about. "Hello!" he shouted. "Is anyone there?"

Mortar crumbled and stones clattered. The figures slid away. Graeber heard heavy breathing. He listened, then realized that it was he himself who was breathing so loud.

Now he was running. The smell of the fire grew more intense. The destruction increased. Then he came to the old city and stopped and stared and stared. Rows of wooden houses from the Middle Ages had stood there before, with their projecting gables, painted roofs, and bright-colored legends. They were not there any more. In their place he saw the chaotic aftermath of a holocaust, charred beams, foundation walls, heaps of stone, remnants of pavement and over it a billowing whitish mist. The houses had burned like dry chips.

He ran on. Wild fear had suddenly seized him. He had re-

membered that not far from his parents' house there was a small
copper works. That might have been a target. He blundered on
along the street as fast as he could, over smoldering heaps of
damp ruins, he bumped into people, he ran forward, he climbed
over piles of rubble and then he stopped. He no longer knew
where he was.

The city that he had known since childhood was so changed
that he could no longer find his way. He was used to orienting
himself by the house-fronts. They were no longer there. He asked
a woman who was stealing by how he could get to Hakenstrasse.

"What?" she asked, terrified. She was dirty and held her hands
in front of her breast.

"To Hakenstrasse."

The woman motioned. "There—over there—around the corner—"

He went that way. Charred trees stood on one side. Their
twigs and smaller branches had been burned away; the stumps
and a few of the main branches still rose into the air. They looked
like immense black hands stretched up out of the earth toward
the sky.

Graeber tried to get his bearings. From here he should have
been able to see the spire of the Katharinenkirche. He did not see
it. Perhaps the church too had been destroyed. He did not ask
anyone else. Somewhere he saw stretchers standing. People were
digging. Firemen were running about. Water splashed through
dense smoke. A dull glow hung over the copper works. Then he
found Hakenstrasse.

# Chapter Seven

A BENT LAMP POST bore the street sign. It pointed diagonally downward into a bomb crater in which lay the fragments of a wall and an iron bedstead. He walked around the crater and ran on. Further off he saw an undamaged house standing. Eighteen, he whispered. It has to be Number Eighteen. God grant that Eighteen is standing!

He had made a mistake. It was only the front of a house. In the darkness it had looked whole. But as he came up to it he saw that the entire back had fallen in. High up a piano hung jammed between steel girders. The cover had been torn off and the keys gleamed like a gigantic mouth full of teeth, as though a huge prehistoric animal were glaring down in rage. The door of the house-front stood wide open.

Graeber ran across to it. "Look out there!" someone shouted. "Be careful. Where are you trying to go?"

He did not answer. Suddenly he could no longer recall where his parents' house should be. Through all the years he had seen it before his eyes, every window, the front door, the steps—but now on this night everything had become confused. He did not even know on which side of the street he was standing.

"Look out, man!" the voice cried again. "Do you want that wall on your head?"

Graeber stared through the door of the house. He saw the beginning of a staircase. He looked for the house number. An air raid warden came up. "What are you doing here?"

"Is this Number Eighteen? Where is Eighteen?"

"Eighteen?" The air raid warden straightened his helmet. "Where *is* Eighteen? Where *was* Eighteen, you mean, surely."

"Was?"

"Of course. Haven't you eyes?"

"This isn't Eighteen?"

"Wasn't Eighteen! Was! It doesn't exist any more. Was is the word."

Graeber seized the man by the lapels of his coat. "Listen," he said wildly. "I'm not here to listen to wisecracks. Where is Eighteen?"

The air raid warden looked at him. "Let go of me at once or I'll blow this whistle for the police. You have no right to be here. This is a clean-up area. They will arrest you."

"They will not arrest me. I have come from the front."

"How impressive! Do you suppose this isn't a front right here?"

Graeber let the man go. "I live in Eighteen," he said. "Eighteen Hakenstrasse. My parents live here—"

"No one lives in this street any more."

"No one?"

"No one. I ought to know. I used to live here too." The man suddenly showed his teeth. "Used to! Used to!" he shouted. "We have had six air raids here in ten days, you front-line soldier! And you damned scoundrels have been loafing out there! Whole and hearty, as anyone can see! And my wife? There——" He pointed to the house they were standing in front of. "Who is going to dig her out? No one! Dead! No point in doing it now, say the rescue squads. Too much urgent work elsewhere! Too many blasted records and blasted bureaus and blasted agencies that have to be rescued!" He thrust his haggard face close to Graeber. "Do you want to know something, soldier? Nobody has any idea what's happening till it happens to him. And if he knows it then, it's too late. You front-line soldier!" He spat. "You brave front-line soldier with your medals. Eighteen is over there. There where they're digging."

Graeber left the man where he was. There where they're digging, he thought. There where they are digging! It is not true! I'm going to wake up right away and I'll be in the bunker, I'll wake up in the cellar of the nameless Russian village and Immermann will be there cursing, and Muecke and Sauer, this is Russia here, this is not Germany, Germany is whole and safe, it——

He heard shouts and the clattering of shovels, then he saw the men on the bulging ruins. Water was streaming out of a broken main in the street. It glittered in the rays of the shielded lights.

He ran up to a man who was giving orders. "Is this Eighteen?"

"What? Get away from here! What are you looking for?"

"I'm looking for my parents. In Eighteen. Where are they?"

"Man, how should I know that? Am I God?"

"Were they rescued?"

"Ask someone else. That's not our affair. We only dig people out."

"Are there some buried here?"

"Of course. Do you think we're digging for fun?" The man turned back to the crew. "Stop! Quiet! Willmann, knock!"

The workers got up. They were men in sweaters, men in dirty

white collars, men in old mechanics' overalls, men with military trousers and civilian jackets. They were dirty and their faces were wet. One of them knelt down in the rubble with a hammer and knocked against a pipe that was sticking up. "Silence!" shouted the overseer.

There was silence. The man with the hammer pressed his ear against the pipe. The breathing of the men and the trickling noise of mortar were audible. From a distance came the sounds of an ambulance and a fire engine. The man with the hammer knocked again. Then he straightened up. "They're still answering. But they're knocking faster. There can't be much air left."

He knocked a few times very fast in reply. "Get at it!" shouted the overseer. "Farther over there! To the right! We'll have to drive the pipes through so they can get some air."

Graeber was still standing beside him. "Is this an air raid shelter?"

"Of course. What else? Do you think anyone would still be able to knock if he wasn't in a shelter?"

Graeber swallowed. "Are they people from this house? The air raid warden over there said no one lives here any more."

"The air raid warden is off his trolley. People are down there knocking, that's enough for us. Where they live is not our business."

Graeber pulled his knapsack off. "I'm strong. I can help dig them out!" He looked at the men. "I must. My parents—"

"It's all right with me. Willmann! Here's another for relief. Have you an extra ax?"


The man with the crushed legs came first. A beam had shattered them and pinned him down. The man was still alive. He was not unconscious. Graeber stared into his face. He did not know him.

They sawed through the beam and pulled up a stretcher. The man did not scream. He just turned up his eyes and they were suddenly white.

They widened the entrance and found two bodies. Both were crushed flat. The faces were flat; nothing stood out any longer, the noses were gone and the teeth were two rows of flat kernels, somewhat scattered and askew, like almonds baked in a cake. Graeber bent over them. He saw dark hair. His people were blond. They hauled the bodies out and they lay, strange and flat, on the street.

It grew lighter. The moon was rising. The sky became a soft, very cool, almost colorless blue. "When was the raid?" Graeber asked when he was relieved.

"Yesterday night."

Graeber looked at his hands. They were black in the insubstantial light. The blood that ran down from them was black too. He did not know whether it was his own. He did not even know that he had been scratching away rubble and splintered glass with his bare hands. They went on working. Their eyes streamed; the acids in the vapor from the bombs bit into them. They wiped them dry with their sleeves but they quickly filled again.

"Hey, soldier!" someone shouted behind him. He turned around. "Is that your knapsack?" asked a figure that wavered in his tear-blurred vision.

"Where?"

"Over there. Someone's just making off with it."

Graeber was about to turn back. "He's stealing it," the figure said, pointing. "You can still catch him. Quick! I'll take your place here."

Graeber could no longer think. He simply followed the voice and the arm. He ran down the street and saw someone climbing over a pile of rubble. He caught up with him. It was an old man dragging the knapsack. Graeber stepped on the strap. The man let go, turned around, lifted his hands and emitted a thin high squeak. His mouth was big and black in the moonlight and his eyes glittered.

A patrol came up. It consisted of two S.S. men "What's going on here?"

"Nothing," Graeber replied, and slung his knapsack over his shoulder. The squeaking man was silent. He was breathing quick and loud. "What are you doing here?" one of the S.S. men asked. He was a middle-aged troop leader. "Papers."

"I'm helping dig people out. Over there. My parents used to live there. I must—"

"Papers!" said the troop leader more sharply.

Graeber stared at the two. There was no point in questioning whether the S.S. had the right to check on soldiers. There were two of them and both were armed. He fumbled for his furlough certificate. The man got out a flashlight and read it. For a moment the piece of paper was as brightly lighted as though it glowed from inside. Graeber felt his muscles quivering. Finally the light went out and the troop leader returned his certificate. "You live at Eighteen Hakenstrasse?"

"Yes," Graeber said, mad with impatience. "Over there. We are just digging the people out. I'm looking for my family."

"Where?"

"Over there. Where they're digging. Can't you see?"

"That isn't Eighteen," the troop leader said.

"What?"

"That is not Eighteen. That is Twenty-two. Eighteen is here." He pointed to a ruin out of which iron girders rose.

"Is that certain?" Graeber stammered.

"Of course. Everything around here looks the same now. But that is Eighteen. I know that for sure."

Graeber looked at the ruins. They were not smoking. "This part of the street wasn't bombed yesterday," said the troop leader. "I think it was last week. Or perhaps even longer ago."

"Do you know—" Graeber choked and then went on. "Do you know whether the people were saved?"

"I don't know. But some are always saved. Perhaps your parents weren't even in the house. During alarms most people go into the big bomb shelters."

"Where can I find that out? And where can I find out where they are now?"

"Nowhere tonight. The town hall was hit and everything's mixed up. Ask at the district office early tomorrow morning. What were you doing with this man?"

"Nothing. Do you think there are still any people under the ruins?"

"There are bodies everywhere. If we wanted to dig them all out we'd need a hundred times as many men. The damned swine bomb a whole city indiscriminately."

The troop leader turned around to leave. "Is this a forbidden area?" Graeber asked.

"Why?"

"The air raid warden over there said it was."

"That warden is weak in the head. He's been fired from his job. Stay here as long as you like. Perhaps you can get a place to sleep at the Red Cross office. It's where the station used to be. If you're lucky."

Graeber was searching for the door. At one place the rubble had been cleared away, but nowhere was there an opening that led into the cellar. He climbed over the wreckage. In the midst of it rose a section of the staircase. The steps and the landing were intact but they led senselessly into emptiness. The rubble behind them was piled high. A satin-covered chair stood there in a niche, precise and orderly, as though someone had put it there on purpose. The rear wall of the neighboring house had fallen diagonally across the garden and had piled up on the other ruins. Something hurried away in that direction. Graeber thought it was the old man he had just seen, but then he saw that it was a cat. Without thinking he lifted a stone and threw it. He had suddenly had the baseless notion that the animal had been gnawing at corpses. Hurriedly he climbed over to the other side. Now he knew that it was the right house; a small part of the garden had remained undamaged and a wooden arbor still stood there with a bench inside and behind it the stump of a linden tree. Cautiously he ran his hand over the bark and felt the grooves of carved initials that he himself had put there many years before. He turned around. The moon was coming up over the ruined walls and now lighted the scene. It was a landscape of craters, inhuman and strange; something that one dreamed about but that could not be real. Graeber had forgotten that in recent years he had hardly seen anything else.

The back entrances seemed hopelessly buried under rubble. Graeber listened. He knocked on one of the iron girders and stood still, listening again. Suddenly he thought he heard a whimpering. It must be the wind, he thought. It can't be anything but the wind. Then he heard it again. He rushed in the direction of the stairs. The cat leaped away in front of him from the steps on which she had taken refuge. He went on listening. He realized he was shaking. And then all of a sudden he was absolutely certain that his parents lay under the ruins, that they were still alive and shut up in darkness and that they were scratching with desperate, skinless hands and whimpering for him—

He tore at the stones and rubble, then thought better of it and hurried back the way he had come. He fell, gashed his knee, rolled over mortar and stones down to the street and rushed back to the house where he had been working with the others.

"Come! This is not Eighteen. Eighteen is over there! Help me dig them out!"

"What?" asked the overseer, straightening up.

"This is not Eighteen! My parents—over there—"

"Where?"

"There! Quick!"

The other looked over. "That's an old one," he said then, very considerately and gently. "Much too late, soldier. We've got to go on working here."

Graeber threw his knapsack off his shoulder. "They're my parents! Here! I have things, I have food, money—"

The man fastened his red, streaming eyes on him. "That a reason to let the people down here die?"

"No—but—"

"Well then—the ones here are still alive."

"Perhaps you could later—"

"Later! Don't you see these men are dropping with weariness?"

"I have worked with you here the whole night. You might at least—"

"Man," said the overseer, suddenly angry, "be reasonable. There's no longer any point in digging over there. Can't you understand that? You don't even know whether there is anyone underneath. Probably not, otherwise we'd have heard something about it. And now leave us in peace."

He reached for his pick. Graeber stood there. He looked at the backs of the working men. He looked at the stretchers. He looked at the two medical corpsmen who had arrived. The water from the broken main was flooding the street. He felt that all his strength had left his body. He thought of going on shoveling. He could no longer do it. Wearily he dragged himself back to what had been Number Eighteen.

He examined the ruins. Once more he began to push stones aside but soon gave it up. It was impossible. After the debris had been cleared away there were iron girders, concrete and ashlars. The house had been well built and that made the ruin almost impregnable. Perhaps they had really been able to escape, he thought. Perhaps they had been evacuated. Perhaps they're in a village in south Germany. Perhaps they are in Rothenburg. Perhaps they are somewhere asleep in bed. Mother. I'm empty. I no longer have a head or a stomach.

He crouched down beside the stairs. Jacob's ladder, he thought. What had that been? Wasn't it a stair that led to Heaven? And didn't angels climb up and down on it? Where were the angels now? Transformed into airplanes. Where was everything? Where was the earth? Was it only for graves? I have dug graves, he thought, many graves. What am I doing here? Why doesn't anyone help me? I have seen thousands of ruins. But I had never really seen one. Only today. This one is the first. This one is different from all others. Why am I not lying under it? I ought to be lying under it.

It grew quiet. The last stretchers were lugged away. The moon rose higher; the sickle hung pitiless over the city. The cat appeared again. She watched Graeber for a long time. Her eyes shone green in the insubstantial light. She approached cautiously. Silently she glided around him several times. Then she came closer, rubbed against his feet, arched her back and began to purr. Finally she crept beside him and lay down. He did not notice it.

# *Chapter Eight*

THE MORNING dawned radiant. It took Graeber a while to realize where he was; he was so used to sleeping among ruins. But then everything came back to him with a jolt.

He leaned against the stairs and tried to think. The cat was sitting a short distance away under a half-buried bathtub, peacefully washing herself. The devastation made no difference at all to her.

He looked at his watch. It was still too early to go to the district office. Slowly he got up. His joints were stiff and his hands bloody and dirty. In the bathtub he found some clear water, probably left over from the fire fighting or the rain. His face stared back at him from the surface. It looked strange. He got a piece of soap out of his knapsack and began to wash. The water turned black and his hands began to bleed again. He held them in the sun to dry. Then he looked down at himself. His trousers were torn, his coat dirty. He rubbed at it with his moistened handkerchief. That was all he could do.

He had some bread in his knapsack; in his canteen there was still coffee. He drank the coffee and ate the bread with it. Suddenly he was very hungry. His throat was as raw as though he had been shouting all night. The cat approached. He broke off a piece of bread and held it out to her. She took it cautiously, carried it away, and sat down to chew it. At the same time she kept watching him. Her fur was black and she had one white paw. The sun glittered on the splinters of broken glass among the ruins. He picked up his knapsack and climbed down to the street.

Below he stopped and looked around him. He no longer recognized the silhouette of the city. There were holes everywhere like missing teeth in a damaged jaw. The green dome of the cathedral was gone. One spire of the Katharinenkirche had collapsed. On all sides the lines of the roofs were scabby and ravaged as though huge primeval insects had been rooting in an antheap. In Hakenstrasse only a few houses were standing. The city no longer looked like the home he had expected; it looked like Russia.

In the house of which only the façade remained a door opened. The air raid warden of the night before stepped out. There was something ghostly about seeing him emerge, as though everything were in order, from a house that was no longer a house. He looked at Graeber and motioned to him. Graeber hesitated for a moment. He remembered that the troop leader had told him the man was crazy. Then, in spite of it, he went over to him.

The air raid warden bared his teeth in a snarl. "What are you doing here? Pillaging? Don't you know it is forbidden to—"

"Listen!" Graeber said. "Cut out this damn nonsense and tell me whether you know anything about my parents. Paul and Marie Graeber. They used to live over there."

The air raid warden thrust out his haggard stubble-covered face. "Ah, it's you! The front-line warrior! Just don't shout so loud, soldier! Do you think you're the only one who has lost track of his family? What do you think that is over there?" He pointed to the house out of which he had come.

"What?"

"That, over there on the door. Have you no eyes? Do you think that's a collection of jokes?"

Graeber made no reply. He saw that slips of paper were tacked up on the door and he went over to it quickly.

They were addresses and appeals for missing persons. Some were written directly on the door panels with pencil, ink, or charcoal; others were on sheets of paper fastened with thumbtacks or Scotch tape. "Heinrich and Georg, come to Uncle Hermann. Irma dead. Mother," was written on a large lined sheet that had been torn out of a school exercise book and stuck in place with four thumbtacks. Directly under it on the lid of a cardboard shoebox: "For God's sake supply news of Brunhilde Schmidt, Thueringerstr. 4." Next to it on a postcard: "Otto, we are in Iburg, Primary school." And at the very bottom, below the addresses in lead pencil and ink, on a lace-bordered paper napkin in pastel-colored crayon: "Marie, where are you?" without a signature.

Graeber straightened up. "Well?" asked the air raid warden. "Are yours there?"

"No. They didn't know I was coming."

The madman twisted his face as though in silent laughter. "No one knows anything about anyone else, soldier. No one! And the wrong ones always survive. Nothing ever happens to scoundrels. Haven't you found that out yet?"

"I have."

"Then write down your name here! And wait. Wait like all the rest of us. Wait till you turn black!" The warden's face changed. It was suddenly torn as though by helpless anguish.

Graeber searched about in the rubbish for something to write on. All he could find was a colored print of Hitler, hanging in a broken frame. The back of it was white, without any printing. He tore off the upper part, got out a pencil, and paused to think. Suddenly he did not know what to write. "News of Paul and Marie Graeber requested," he finally wrote in block letters. "Ernst here on leave."

"Treason." the air raid warden said softly behind him.

"What?" Graeber whirled around.

"Treason. You have torn a picture of the Fuehrer."

"It was torn already and it was lying in the dirt," Graeber retorted angrily. "And now stop your nonsense and leave me alone."

He could not find anything with which to tack up his notice. Finally he loosened two of the four thumbtacks with which the mother's appeal had been fastened and used them for his own. He did it unwillingly; it was a little like stealing a wreath from a stranger's grave. But he had nothing else and two thumbtacks served for the mother's appeal as well as four.

The warden had been watching over his shoulder. "All right!" he announced, as though giving a command. "And now *Sieg Heil,* soldier. Mourning forbidden! Mourning clothes as well. Weakens the fighting spirit. Be proud that you can make sacrifices. If you swine had done your duty this would never have happened!"

He turned around abruptly and stalked off on long, thin legs.

Graeber forgot him at once. He tore a small piece from the remainder of Hitler's picture and wrote on it an address that he had found on the door panel. It was the address of the Loose family. He knew them and intended to stop there later and ask after his parents. Then he tore the rest of the print out of the frame, wrote on its back the same message he had written on the other half, and went back to Number Eighteen. There he clamped the notice between two stones so that it was easily visible. Thus there were two chances of his appeal being read. That was all he could do at the moment. For a while he continued to stand in front of the heap of stones and rubble, which might or might not be a grave. The satin chair in the niche above gleamed like an emerald in the sun. A chestnut tree on the street beside it was still entirely undamaged. Its delicate foliage shimmered in the sun and chaffinches were twittering in it as they built their nest.

He looked at his watch. It was time to go to the district office.

The counters in the missing persons bureau were made of new boards rudely hammered together. They were unpainted and still smelled of resin and the forest. At one side of the room the ceiling had fallen. Carpenters were hammering, putting beams in place. Everywhere people were standing about waiting with silent patience. A one-armed official and two women sat behind the counter.

"Name?" asked the woman farthest to the right. She had a flat, broad face and wore a red silk ribbon in her hair.

"Graeber. Paul and Marie Graeber. Clerk in the tax department. Eighteen Hakenstrasse."

"What?" The woman raised her hand to her ear.

"Graeber," he repeated more loudly through the noise of the hammering. "Paul and Marie Graeber. Tax department clerk."

The woman official searched the records. "Graeber, Graeber—" Her finger slid down a column and stopped. "Graeber—yes— what was the first name?"

"Paul and Marie."

"What?"

"Paul and Marie!" Graeber was suddenly furious. It seemed to him unendurable, on top of everything else, to have to shout out his misery.

"No. This one is named Ernst Graeber."

"Ernst Graeber is my own name. No one else in our family is called that."

"Well, you certainly can't be this one. We have no other Graebers here." The woman looked up and smiled. "If you like you can inquire again in a few days. Not all the reports have come in yet. Next!"

Graeber stayed where he was. "Where else can I inquire?"

The secretary smoothed the red silk ribbon in her hair. "At the registry office. Next!"

Graeber felt someone poke him in the back. Standing behind him was a little old woman with hands like the claws of a bird. He stepped aside.

For a while he stood undecided beside the counter. He could not grasp the fact that this was all. It had happened so fast. His loss was too disproportionately great. The one-armed official saw him and bent toward him. "Be glad that your relations are not listed here," he said.

"Why?"

"These are the lists of the dead and the seriously injured. As long as they have not been reported to us they are only missing."

"And the missing? Where are the lists for them?"

The official looked at him with the patience of a man who has to deal with strangers' misery eight hours a day without being able to help. "Be reasonable, man," he said then. "The missing are missing. What good are lists in that case? They don't help you to find out what's happened to them. If you knew that, they would no longer be missing. Right?"

Graeber stared at him. The official seemed proud of his logic. But reason and logic are poor companions for loss and pain. And what was one to reply to a man who had lost an arm? "Very likely," Graeber said and turned away.

He asked his way to the registry office. It was in a wing of the town hall and still smelled of acids and fire. After a long wait he came to a nervous woman with a pince-nez. "I know nothing," she chattered instantly. "It's no longer possible to find out anything definite here. The filing system is in complete confusion. Part of it has been burned. The rest was ruined by those blockheads from the Fire Department with their hoses. I'm not responsible!"

"Why didn't you put your records somewhere safe?" asked a non-commissioned officer who was standing beside Graeber.

"Somewhere safe? Where is there safety here? Do you know? I am not the magistrate. Make your complaints to him." The woman glanced helplessly at a disordered heap of wet and torn papers. "Everything destroyed! The whole registry bureau! What will come of it all! Now anyone can call himself whatever he likes!"

"That would be dreadful, wouldn't it?" The non-commissioned officer spat and nudged Graeber. "Come along, comrade. The people here have all gone crazy."

They went out and stood in front of the town hall. The houses around had been burned to the ground. Of Bismarck's statue only the boots remained. A flock of white pigeons was circling around the fallen tower of the Marienkirche. "Hot shit, eh?" said the non-com. "Who are you looking for?"

"My parents."

"I'm looking for my wife. Didn't write her that I was coming. Wanted to surprise her. And you?"

"Same thing. Didn't want to excite my parents unnecessarily. My leave was postponed a couple of times before. Then it came through suddenly. I hadn't time to write."

"A fine mess! What are you going to do now?"

Graeber glanced across the market square. Since 1938 it had been named Hitlerplatz. Before that, in the aftermath of the first war, it had been Ebertplatz; before that Kaiser Wilhelmplatz, and once, sometime or other, Marktplatz. "I don't know," he said. "I still don't understand all this. One can't simply get lost here in the middle of Germany—"

"No?" The non-com glanced at him with a mixture of irony and sympathy. "My dear boy, you will be surprised! I have been looking for my wife for five days. Five days from morning till night, and she's disappeared from the face of the earth as though she'd been bewitched!"

"But how is that possible? She must—"

"Disappeared," repeated the non-com, "and so have a couple of thousand others. Some of them have been transported. To temporary camps and small towns. Just try to find them with the mail not working. Others have fled in swarms to the villages."

"The villages," Graeber said in relief. "Of course! I hadn't thought of that. The villages are safe. That's where they must be—"

"You may well say that's where they must be!" the non-com snorted contemptuously. "That doesn't get you any further! Do you know that this damn city has almost two dozen villages around it? Before you get through with them your leave will be over. Understand?"

Graeber understood and it did not matter to him. All he wanted now was that his parents should be alive. Where they were was of little consequence.

"Listen to me, comrade," said the non-com more calmly. "You've got to get hold of this thing the right way. If you just dash around wildly you'll waste your time and go crazy. You've got to get organized. What do you intend to do first?"

"I don't know yet. I think I'll try to see some acquaintances. I've found the address of some people who were bombed out too. From the same street."

"They won't tell you much. Everyone's afraid to open his mouth. I've found that out. But try it. Now, listen! We can help each other. Wherever you make inquiries ask for my wife too and I'll ask about your parents wherever I go. Agreed?"

"Agreed."

"Fine. My name is Boettcher. My wife's first name is Alma. Write it down."

Graeber wrote it down. Then he wrote his parents' names on a piece of paper and gave it to Boettcher, who read it carefully and put it in his pocket. "Where are you living, Graeber?" he asked.

"I have no idea. I must find some place."

"There are temporary quarters in the barracks for bombed-out men on leave. Report to the commandant's office and you'll get an assignment card. Have you been there already?"

"Not yet."

"Try to get into Room Forty-eight. It's the infirmary. The food's better there than in the other rooms. That's where I am, too."

Boettcher got the butt of a cigarette out of his pocket, looked at it and put it back again. "Today I'm going to make a round of the hospitals. We can meet somewhere this evening. Perhaps by then one of us will know something.

"All right. Where?"

"The best place is here. Nine o'clock?"

"Agreed."

Boettcher nodded and then looked up at the blue sky. "Just look at that," he said bitterly. "Spring. And for five long nights I've been hitting the sack in a room with twelve farts from the

Reserve—instead of with my wife who has an ass like a brewer's horse."

The first two houses in Gartenstrasse had been destroyed. There was no one living in them now. The third was still almost undamaged. Only the roof had been burned; it was the house in which the Ziegler family lived. Ziegler had been a friend of Graeber's father.

He climbed the stairs. On the landings stood pails with sand and water. Directions for use had been pasted on the walls. He rang and was surprised the bell still worked. After a while a careworn old woman opened the door.

"Frau Ziegler," Graeber said, "I am Ernst Graeber."

"Yes—" The woman stared at him. "Yes—" She hesitated and then said: "Come in, Herr Graeber."

She opened the door wider and bolted it again behind him. "Father," she called then to someone behind her. "It's nothing. It's Ernst Graeber. Paul Graeber's son."

The living room smelled of floor wax. The linoleum was as smooth as a mirror. On the windowsill stood pots containing plants whose big, yellow-spotted leaves looked as though butter had been dropped on them. A sampler hung on the wall behind the sofa. *"Hearth and Home are truest Gold"* was cross-stitched on it in red.

Ziegler appeared from the bedroom. He was smiling. Graeber saw that he was nervous. "You never know who's coming," he said. "We certainly didn't expect you. Have you come from the front?"

"Yes. I'm looking for my parents. They were bombed out."

"Put down your knapsack," Frau Ziegler said. "I'll make some coffee. We still have good malt coffee."

Graeber carried his knapsack into the vestiblue. "I'm dirty," he said. "Everything's so clean here. That's something we're not used to any more."

"It doesn't matter. Just sit down. There, on the sofa."

Frau Ziegler disappeared into the kitchen. Ziegler looked at Graeber uncertainly. "Tcha—," he said.

"Have you heard anything of my parents? I can't find them. At the district office they don't know anything. Everything's in confusion there."

Ziegler shook his head. His wife appeared again in the door-way. "We no longer go out at all," she said quickly. "We haven't for a long time. We hear almost nothing, Ernst."

"Then you haven't seen them at all? But you must have seen them some time."

"That was a long while ago. At least five or six months. At that time—" She fell silent.

"What about that time?" Graeber asked. "How were they then?"

"Well. Oh, your parents were well," the woman replied. "Only since then, of course—"

"Yes—," Graeber said. "I've seen. At the front we knew in a way that our cities were being bombed, but not that it would look like this."

The two made no reply. They did not look at him. "The coffee will be ready right away," the woman said. "You will stay and have some, won't you? A cup of hot coffee is always good."

She put cups of a blue flower pattern on the table. Graeber looked at them. In his home there had been some of the same kind. For some reason the name of the design was onion pattern. "Tcha—," Ziegler said again.

"Do you think my parents might have been sent away with a transport?" Graeber asked.

"Perhaps. Mother, are there still some of those cookies Erwin brought home with him? Do get them out for Herr Graeber."

"How are things with Erwin?"

"Erwin?" The old man looked suddenly frightened. "Erwin is all right! All right!"

His wife brought the coffee. She put a big tin box on the table. The labels were in Dutch. There were not many cookies left in it. From Holland, Graeber thought. Just so, at the start, he had brought things back with him from France.

The woman urged them on him. He took one with pink icing. It tasted old. The two elderly people took nothing. Nor did they drink any coffee. Ziegler was drumming absently on the table top.

"Have another," the woman said. "We haven't anything else. But they are good cookies."

"Yes, very good. Thank you. I had something to eat earlier."

Graeber realized he was not going to get anything more out of these two. Perhaps they really knew nothing. He got up. "Could you tell me where I might be able to find out something more?"

"We know nothing. We're sorry, Ernst. That's how it is."

"I believe you. Thanks for the coffee." Graeber went to the door.

"Where are you staying now?" Ziegler asked suddenly.

"I'll find some place. And then there's always the barracks."

"We haven't any room," Frau Ziegler said quickly, looking at her husband. "The army authorities must certainly have made arrangements for men on leave who have been bombed out."

"Yes, certainly," Graeber replied.

"Perhaps he could leave his knapsack here till he finds a place, Mother," Ziegler said. "It's heavy, you know."

Graeber saw the woman's glance. "I'll be all right," he replied. "I'm used to carrying it."

He shut the door and went down the stairs. The air smelled musty. The Zieglers were afraid of something. He did not know what. But since 1933 there had been many possible reasons for fear.

The Loose family was living in the big concert hall of the Harmony Club. The room was crowded with field cots and mattresses. On the walls hung a few flags, swastika decorations with pithy sayings and an oil painting of the Fuehrer in a wide gold frame—leftovers from earlier patriotic celebrations. The room was crawling with women and children. Between the beds stood trunks, pots, stoves, groceries, and odd pieces of salvaged furniture.

Frau Loose was sitting apathetically on a bed in the middle of the hall. She was a gray, heavy person with disorderly hair.

"Your parents?" She gazed at Graeber with lackluster eyes and reflected for a long time. "Dead, Ernst," she murmured finally.

"What?"

"Dead," she repeated. "What else?"

A little boy in uniform ran into Graeber's knees. He pushed him away. "How do you know that?" Suddenly he noticed he had lost his voice. He swallowed hard. "Have you seen them? Where?"

Frau Loose shook her head wearily. "You couldn't see anything, Ernst. It was all fire and the shrieking and then—"

The words became lost in a muttering that presently stopped. The woman stared straight ahead, her arms braced, wholly absent and motionless as though she were alone in the room. Graeber stared at her. "Frau Loose," he said slowly and with difficulty. "Try to remember! When did you see my parents? How do you know that they are dead?"

The woman looked at him blankly. "Lena is dead too," she murmured. "And August. You knew them both—"

Graeber vaguely recalled two children who were always eating honey-covered bread. "Frau Loose," he repeated, forcing himself not to pull her to her feet and shake her. "Please tell me how you know my parents are dead. Try to remember. Did you see them?"

She seemed no longer to hear him. "Lena," she whispered. "I did not see her either. They would not let me near her, Ernst. There wasn't all of her there anymore, you know. And yet she was so small. Why would they do a thing like that? You must know. You're a soldier."

Graeber looked around in desperation. A man made his way toward them between the beds. It was Loose. He had become thin and old. Cautiously he laid his hand on his wife's shoulder. She continued to sit on the bed sunk in despair. He made a sign to Graeber. "Mother still can't grasp it, Ernst," he said.

The woman stirred under his hand. Slowly she looked up. "Can you grasp it?"

"Lena—"

"For if you can grasp it," she said suddenly, clear and loud and distinct, as though she were saying a piece in school, "then you're not much better than the ones who did it."

Loose's eyes slid fearfully over the nearby beds. No one had heard. The youngster in uniform was playing hide-and-seek between the trunks with two other children.

"Not much better," the woman repeated. Then she let her head sink and was once more nothing but a little heap of animal woe.

Loose motioned to Graeber. They moved to one side. "What has happened to my parents?" Graeber asked. "Your wife says they are dead."

Loose shook his head. "She doesn't know at all, Ernst. She thinks that everyone must be dead because our children are. She isn't quite—you noticed—" He swallowed. His Adam's apple went up and down in his thin neck. "She says things—we've been reported already because of them—by people here—"

For a moment Graeber saw Loose very small and far away in the dirty gray light—then he was there again as before and the room stood still. "Then they aren't dead?" he asked.

"I can't tell you, Ernst. You don't know what it has been like here during the last year with everything getting worse and worse. No one could trust anyone else any longer. They were all afraid of one another. Very likely your parents are safe somewhere."

Graeber was breathing more calmly. "Didn't you see them at all?"

"Once on the street. But it must be four or five weeks ago. There was still some snow on the ground then. It was before the raids."

"How did they look? Were they well?"

Loose did not reply at once. "Yes, I guess they were," he said then and swallowed.

Graeber was suddenly ashamed. He realized that it was frivolous in such surroundings to ask whether or not a person had been well four weeks ago; here you asked about the survivors and the dead, and nothing else. "I am sorry," he said in embarrassment.

Loose shook his head tiredly. "Forget it, Ernst. Today each can think only of himself. There is too much unhappiness in the world—"

Graeber stepped out into the street. It had been dismal and dead when he had gone into the Harmony Club—now all at once it appeared brighter, and life had not entirely died out of it. He no longer saw only the ruined houses; he now saw the growing trees too. Two dogs were at play, and the sky was moist and blue. His parents were not dead; they were only missing. An hour earlier when the one-armed clerk had told him this, the news had been desolating and almost unbearable; now it had mysteriously transformed itself into hope. He knew that it was only so because for an instant he had believed his parents were no longer alive—but what needed less nourishment than hope? And from what incomprehensible roots it could draw it!

# Chapter Nine

HE STOPPED in front of the house. It was dark and he could not make out the number. "Where do you want to go?" asked a man who was leaning beside the door.

"Is this Twenty-two Marienstrasse?"

"Yes. Who do you want to see?"

"Health Councilor Kruse."

"Kruse? What do you want from him?"

Graeber peered at the man in the dark. He was wearing boots and an S.A. uniform. A self-important block warden, he thought, just what I need. "I'll explain that to Dr. Kruse myself," he said and went into the house.

He was very weary. It was a weariness that lay deeper than eyes and bones. He had been inquiring and searching all day but he had learned little. His parents had no relatives in the city and not many of their neighbors were still there. Boettcher had been right; it was like witchcraft. People were afraid of the Gestapo and would say nothing. Or, in other cases, they had heard nothing but rumors and handed you on to others who likewise knew nothing.

He climbed the stairs. The hallway was dark. Dr. Kruse lived on the second floor. Graeber barely remembered him, but he knew that his mother had gone to him several times for treatment. Perhaps she had been there recently and he had her new address.

A middle-aged woman with a blurred face opened the door. "Kruse? You want to see Dr. Kruse?"

"Yes."

The woman examined him in silence. She did not move aside to let him in. "Is he home?" Graeber asked impatiently.

The woman made no reply. She seemed to be listening for something downstairs. "Have you come for the consultation hour?" she asked presently.

"No. On a private matter."

"Private?"

"Yes, private. Are you Frau Kruse?"

"God forbid!"

Graeber stared at her. During the day he had run into every variety of caution, hate, and evasion, but this was new. "Listen to me," he said. "I don't know what's going on here and I don't care. I want to talk to Dr. Kruse, that's all. Do you understand?"

"Kruse no longer lives here," the woman announced in a voice suddenly loud and harsh and hostile.

"But there's his name." Graeber pointed to a brass plate beside the door.

"That plate should have been taken down long ago."

"But it's there. Does any member of the family still live here?"

The woman didn't answer. Graeber had had enough. He was on the point of telling her to go to hell when he heard a door being opened behind her in the apartment. A band of light burst from a room diagonally across the dark vestibule. "Is that someone for me?" a voice asked.

"Yes," Graeber said, taking a chance. "I would like to speak to someone who knows Dr. Kruse. It doesn't seem to be easy."

"I am Elisabeth Kruse."

Graeber stared at the woman with the blurred face. She unblocked the door and went back into the apartment. "Too much light!" she snapped in the direction of the open room. "It is forbidden to use so much electricity."

Graeber stayed where he was. A girl of about twenty came toward him through the band of light as though through a river. For a moment he was aware of high-arched brows, dark eyes, and mahogany-colored hair that flowed in a restless wave against her shoulders—then she plunged back into the muddy half-darkness of the corridor and stood before him.

"My father no longer practices," she said.

"I didn't come for treatment. I came for news."

The girl's face changed. She made a quick movement as though to see whether the other woman was still there. Then she opened the door wide. "Come in," she whispered.

He followed her into the room from which the light came. She turned around and looked at him. Her eyes were now no longer dark; they were gray and very transparent.

"But I know you," she said. "Didn't you go to high school here?"

"Yes. My name is Ernst Graeber."

Now Graeber remembered her too. She had been a skinny girl with too big eyes and too much hair. Her mother had died young and she had gone to live with relatives in another city. "My God, Elisabeth," he said. "I didn't recognize you. It must be seven or eight years since we last saw each other. You have changed a lot!"

"You too."

They stood facing each other. "Just what's going on here?" Graeber asked. "You're guarded like a general."

Elisabeth Kruse laughed shortly and bitterly. "Not like a general. Like a prisoner."

"What? Your father—"

Elisabeth Kruse made a swift gesture. "Wait!" she whispered and went past him to a table where a phonograph stood. She turned it on. The *Hohenfriedberger March* rolled out. "So," she said. "Now you can go on."

Graeber looked at her uncomprehendingly. Boettcher seemed to have been right; almost everyone in the city was crazy. "What's that?" he asked. "Turn the thing off! I've had enough marches. Tell me instead what's going on here. Why are you a prisoner?"

Elisabeth came back. "The woman out there is listening. She's an informer. That's why I turned on the phonograph." She stood in front of him and was suddenly breathing hard. "What about my father? What do you know of him?"

"I? Nothing. I only wanted to ask him a question. What in the world has happened to him?"

"You haven't any news of him?"

"No. I wanted to ask him if he knew my mother's address. My parents are missing."

"That's all?"

Graeber stared at Elisabeth. "It's enough for me," he said then. The tension in her face broke. "That's true," she said wearily. "I thought you were bringing news of him."

"What is all this about your father?"

"He's in a concentration camp. It's been four months now. He was denounced. When you spoke of news I thought you knew something about him."

"But I'd have told you that right away."

Elisabeth shook her head. "Not if it had been smuggled news. You would have had to be cautious."

Cautious, Graeber thought. All day long I have heard nothing but that word. The *Hohenfriedberger March* rolled on, brassy and intolerable. "Can we turn that thing off now?" he asked.

"Yes. And it would be better for you to go. I've told you what happened here."

"I'm no informer," Graeber said angrily. "What about the woman out there? Did she denounce your father?"

Elisabeth lifted the phonograph arm. She did not turn off the machine. The disk went on turning silently. In the stillness a siren began to wail. "The alarm!" she whispered. "Again!"

Someone banged on the door. "Lights out! That's what happens! Always too much light."

Graeber opened the door. "What happens?"

The woman was already at the far side of the vestibule. She shouted something else and disappeared. Elisabeth took Graeber's hand off the doorknob and closed the door.

"What kind of intolerable she-devil is that?" he asked. "How does that woman come to be here?"

"An official tenant. Billeted here by the authorities. I can be happy that I'm allowed to keep this room."

From outside new uproar arose. The screams of a woman and the weeping of a child. The howling of the preliminary alarm grew louder. Elisabeth picked up a raincoat and put it on. "We must go to the air raid shelter."

"We've still got plenty of time. Why don't you move away from here? It must be hell for you staying with that spy."

"Lights out!" the woman screamed again from outside. Elisabeth turned around and snapped off the light. Then she glided through the dark room to the window. "Why don't I move? Because I won't run away!"

She opened the window. All at once the noise of the sirens rushed into the room and filled it completely. She stood black against the diffused light from outside and hooked the casement open to prevent the panes from being broken by the force of the explosions. Then she came back. The noise was like a torrent bearing her before it. "I won't run away!" she shouted through the howling. "Can't you understand that?"

Graeber saw her eyes. Now they were dark again as they had been earlier at the door, and full of passionate strength. He suddenly had a feeling that he must protect himself against something, against the eyes, against the face, against the fury of the sirens and against the chaos that was forcing its way in through the window behind them. "No," he said, "I don't understand it. That only drives you mad. A position that can't be held must be given up. That's something you learn as a soldier."

She stared at him. "Then give it up!" she shouted violently. "Give it up and leave me alone!"

She tried to go past him to the door. He took hold of her arm. She tore it away. She was stronger than he had expected. "Wait!" he shouted. "I'm going with you."

The uproar drove them before it. It was everywhere, in the room, in the corridor, in the vestibule, on the stairs—it broke on the walls and threw back echoes against itself as though it came from all sides, and there was no escape from it, it did not stop at the ears or the surface of the skin, it broke through and foamed in the blood, it made the nerves tremble and the bones vibrate, and it extinguished all thought.

"Where is that damned siren?" Graeber shouted on the stairs. "It drives you mad."

The door of the house slammed shut. For an instant the howling was dampened. "It's in the next block," Elisabeth said. "We must go to the cellar in the Karlsplatz. The one in this house is no good."

Shadows were running down the stairs with bags and bundles. A flashlight went on, illuminating Elisabeth's face. "Come along with us if you're alone!" someone shouted.

"I'm not alone."

The man hurried on. The house door flew open again. Everywhere people were tumbling out of houses as though they were tin soldiers being shaken out of boxes. Air raid wardens were shouting orders. A woman in a red silk dressing gown with flying yellow hair galloped by like an Amazon. A few old people were stumbling along beside the walls; they were talking, but in the driving noise none of it could be heard—as though the flabby mouths were silently chewing dead words to a pulp.

They came to the Karlsplatz. At the entrance to the shelter an excited mob was milling. Air raid wardens ran about like sheepdogs trying to create order. Elisabeth stopped. "We can try to get through from the side," Graeber said.

She shook her head. "Let's wait here."

The crowd crept darkly down into the darkness of the stairway and disappeared underground. Graeber looked at Elisabeth. She suddenly stood there as calm as though all this did not matter to her. "You have courage," he said.

She glanced up. "No. Just fear of the cellar."

"Come on! Come on!" shouted the air raid warden. "Down the stairs! Do you have to have a special invitation?"

The shelter was large and low and well constructed, with galleries, side passages, and lights; there were benches there and wardens, and a good many people had brought mattresses, blankets, suitcases, parcels, and folding chairs; life underground was already organized. Graeber glanced around. It was the first time he

had been in an air raid shelter with civilians. The first time with
women and children. And the first time in Germany.

The pale, bluish light took the color out of people's faces as
though they had been drowned. Graeber noticed not far from
him the woman in the red dressing gown. Her gown was now
violet and her hair had a green glow. He glanced at Elisabeth.
Her face looked gray and hollow, too, her eyes lay deep in the
shadows of the sockets and her hair was lusterless and dead.
Drowned people, he thought. Drowned in lies and fear, hunted
under the earth and at war with light and purity and truth!

A woman with two children crouched opposite him. The children were huddled against her knees. Their faces were flat and
expressionless as though frozen. Only their eyes were alive. They
shone with reflected light, they were big and wide open, they
swung toward the entrance when the howling became stronger
and deeper, and then toward the low ceiling and the walls, and
then back once more to the entrance. Their movement was not
rapid and jerky; they followed the noise like the eyes of paralyzed
animals, heavy yet floating, at once swiftly and as though in a
deep trance, they pursued and circled, and the faint light was
reflected in them. They did not see Graeber nor even their own
mother; the power of recognition and of communication had
vanished from them; with anonymous intentness they followed
something they were unable to see: the humming that might be
death. They were no longer young enough not to scent the danger; and not yet old enough to make a useless pretense of courage. They were alert and defenseless and delivered up.

Graeber suddenly saw that it was not only the children; the
eyes of the others moved in the same way. Their faces and bodies
were still; they listened and it was not only their ears that
listened—it was also the bowed shoulders, the thighs, the knees,

the braced arms and hands. They listened motionless, and only their eyes followed the sound as though they were obeying an inaudible command.

Then he smelled fear.


Imperceptibly something changed in the heavy air. The tenseness relaxed. The uproar outside continued; but from somewhere a fresh wind seemed to come. The gallery was all at once no longer full of crouching bodies; it was filled with human beings again and they were no longer submissive and apathetic; they lifted their heads and moved about and looked at one another. They once more had faces and no longer masks.

"They've flown past," said an old man beside Elisabeth.

"They may come back," someone replied. "They do that sometimes. Swing round and come back again when everyone's out of the shelters."

The two children began to move. A man yawned. From somewhere a dachshund appeared and began to sniff about. An infant cried. A few people unpacked their parcels and began to eat. A woman gave a high scream like a Valkyrie. "Arnold! We forgot to turn off the gas! Now dinner will be burned up. Why didn't you remember it?"

"Never mind," said the old man. "When there's an air raid alarm the city turns off the gas everywhere."

"Never mind? If they turn it on again the whole house will be full of gas! That's a whole lot worse."

"The gas is not turned off for an alarm," said a pedantically instructive voice. "Only for an attack."

---

Elisabeth took a comb and mirror out of her hand bag and combed her hair. In the dead light the comb looked as though it were made of dried ink; but under it her hair seemed to spring and crackle. "I wish we could get out," she said. "It's suffocating here."

They had to wait for a half-hour longer; then finally the doors were opened. They walked to the exit. Over the doors hung small shaded lights. From outside moonlight fell squarely on the steps. Elisabeth changed with each step forward as though she were awaking from a trance. The shadows in her eyesockets disappeared; the leaden color flowed away, copper glints showed in her hair; her skin once more became warm and glowing, and life returned again—breathing, full, stronger than before, rewon, not lost, more precious and colorful for the brief period that one felt it thus.

They stood in front of the shelter. Elisabeth was breathing deeply. She moved her shoulders and her head like an animal coming out of a cage. "These mass graves underground!" she said. "How I hate them! You suffocate there!" With a quick gesture she threw back her hair. "Ruins are a relief by contrast. At least they have the sky over them."

Graeber looked at her. There was something wild and impassioned about her as she stood there in front of the huge, bald block of concrete, its steps leading down into a nether world form which they had just escaped. "Are you going back home?" he asked.

"Yes. Where else? I certainly don't want to run around in these unlighted streets. I've had more than enough of that."

They walked across the Karlsplatz. The wind snuffled around them like a great dog. "Can't you move away?" Graeber asked. "Despite everything you say?"

"Where to? Do you know of a room?"

"No."

"Neither do I. Thousands are roofless. So how am I going to move?"

"That's right. It's too late now."

Elisabeth stopped. "I wouldn't go away anyway even if I could. It would be like leaving my father in the lurch. Can't you understand that?"

"Yes."

They walked on. Graeber had had enough of her. She could do what she liked, he thought. He was suddenly very exhausted and jumpy and he had the feeling that his parents, at this very instant, were looking for him in Hakenstrasse. "I've got to go," he said. "I made an appointment and I'm late already. Good night, Elisabeth."

"Good night, Ernst."

He looked after her for a moment. Almost instantly she disappeared in the darkness. I should have taken her home, he thought. But he did not care. He remembered that even as a child he had not liked her much. Quickly he turned around and went to Hakenstrasse. He found nothing there. No one was in sight. Only the moon and the strange paralyzing stillness of fresh ruins, which was like the echo of a silent scream hanging in the air. The old ones were different.

Boettcher was waiting on the steps of the town hall. Above him, dim in the moonlight, shimmered the grotesque mask of a gargoyle. "Have you had any luck?" he asked from a distance.

"No. And you?"

"Not I either. They're not in any of the hospitals, that's pretty sure. I've tried almost all of them. Man, the things you see there!

Whatever anyone says, it's different with women and children than with soldiers! Come along, let's get a beer somewhere."

They walked across the Hitlerplatz. Their boots echoed. "One more day gone," Boettcher said. "What can one do? Soon my whole furlough will be over."

He opened the door of a pub. They sat down at a table inside the window. The curtains were tightly drawn. The nickel taps of the bar gleamed in the half-dark. Boettcher seemed to be at home in the place. The proprietress, without asking, brought two glasses of beer. He glanced after her. She was fat and her hips swayed. She was not wearing a corset.

"Here I am, sitting alone," he said. "And somewhere my wife is sitting. Alone too. Anyway I hope so! Isn't that enough to drive you nuts?"

"I don't know. I'd be happy enough if I only knew for sure that my parents were sitting somewhere. No matter where."

"Well, parents are different. You don't really need them. If they're all right that's fine, and that's all there is to it. But a wife—"

They ordered two more glasses of beer and unpacked their dinner. The proprietress strolled around the table. She looked at the sausage and the fat. "Children, you live high!" she said.

"Yes, we live high," Boettcher replied. "We have a complete homecoming package with meat and sugar and don't know what to do with it."

He took a swallow. "It's easy for you," he said bitterly to Graeber. "You can feed up now and later go out and pick up a whore and forget your misery!"

"You could do that too."

Boettcher shook his head. Graeber glanced at him in surprise. He hadn't expected that much fidelity in an old soldier. "They're too skinny, comrade," Boettcher explained. "The damnable thing is I only warm up to very buxom women. Others give me the willies. It simply doesn't work. I might just as well go to bed with a hat rack. Only very buxom women! Otherwise it's no go on my part."

"Well, there's one!" Graeber pointed to the proprietress.

"You're mistaken!" Boettcher became excited. "There's an enormous difference, comrade. What you see there is flabby, soft fat you sink into. A buxom person, I grant—but a feather bed, not a double inner-spring mattress like my wife. With her everything is of iron. The room used to shake like a smithy when she went off, and the pictures fell off the walls. No, comrade, you can't just go out and find something like that on the street."

He brooded, staring straight ahead. Graeber suddenly smelled violets. He looked around. They were growing in a pot on the windowsill. They smelled infinitely sweet and in one breath they recalled everything: childhood and security and home and expectancy and the forgotten dreams of youth—it was very strong and it came as quickly as a surprise assault and it was over again at once; but it left him confused and exhausted, as though he had been running through deep snow with a full pack.

He stood up. "Where are you going?" Boettcher asked.

"I don't know. Some place or other."

"Have you been to Headquarters?"

"Yes. They gave me a transfer to the barracks."

"Good. Be sure to get into Room Forty-eight."

"Yes."

Boettcher's eyes lazily followed the proprietress. "I'll sit around here for a while. Drink another beer."

Graeber walked slowly along the street that led up to the barracks. The night had grown cold. At a crossing, streetcar rails rose glittering over a bomb crater. In the open doorways the moonlight lay like metal. He heard his steps resounding as though someone were walking with him under the pavement. Everything was empty and clear and cold.

The barracks were on an elevation at the edge of the city. They were undamaged. The parade ground lay in the white light as though covered with snow. Graeber walked through the gate. He felt as if his furlough were already over. His former life had collapsed behind him like his parents' house and he was going to the front again—to a different front this time, without artillery or rifles but with no less danger.

# Chapter Ten

IT WAS THREE days later. At the table in Room Forty-eight, four men were playing skat. They had been playing for two days, stopping only for food and sleep. Three of the players kept changing off; the fourth played uninterruptedly. His name was Rummel and he had arrived on furlough three days before—just in time to bury his wife and daughter. He had identified his wife by a birthmark on her hip; she no longer had a head. After the funeral he had come to the barracks and begun to play skat. He spoke to no one. He sat there impassively and played. He was winning.

Graeber was sitting by the window. Next to him Lance-Corporal Reuter reclined, with a bottle of beer in his hand and his bandaged right foot on the window seat. He was senior there and suffered from gout. Room Forty-eight was not only a haven for luckless men on leave; it was also the non-contagious sick ward. Behind them Engineer Feldmann lay in bed. It was his ambition to make up in three weeks' time the missed sleep of three years of war. He got out of bed only at meal times.

"Where's Boettcher?" Graeber asked. "Not back yet?"

"He's gone to Haste and Iburg. Somebody loaned him a bicycle at noon. Now he can investigate two villages a day. But he still has a dozen ahead of him. And then there are the camps where the evacuees are sent from all over. They're hundreds of kilometers away. How's he going to get to them?"

"I've written to four camps," Graeber said. "For both of us."

"Do you think you're going to get an answer?"

"No. But that doesn't make any difference. You write just the same."

"To whom did you write?"

"To the camp authorities and then, in addition, in each camp directly to Boettcher's wife and to my parents."

Graeber brought a packet of letters out of his pocket and showed them. "I was just going to take these to the post office."

Reuter nodded. "Where were you today?"

"At the public school and the Cathedral school gym. Then I went to an assembly point and tried the registry office again. Nothing."

A card player who had been replaced joined them. "I can't understand why you men on leave sit around here in the barracks," he said to Graeber. "As far away from the Prussians as possible, that would be my motto! I'd rent a room, put on civilian clothes, and be a human being for two weeks."

"Do you get to be a human being just by putting on civilian clothes?" Reuter asked.

"Sure. What more is there to it?"

"You see?" Reuter said to Graeber. "Life is simple when you take it simply. Have you got your civilian things here?"

"No. They're buried under the ruins in Hakenstrasse."

"I can lend you some."

Graeber glanced through the window at the drill field. A few squads were practicing loading and inspection, grenade throwing and saluting. "I don't know," he said. "Out there I thought I'd throw this damn outfit into a corner as soon as I got home and put on decent clothes—and now I don't care one way or the other."

"You're just a perfectly commonplace barracks crapper," the card player declared, consuming a slice of liverwurst. "A dough-foot who doesn't know what he wants. It's a crime the way the wrong people always get furloughs!"

He went back to rejoin the game. He had lost four marks to Rummel and that morning had been declared 1A by the infirmary doctor; that made him bitter.

Graeber got up. "Where are you going?" Reuter asked.

"Into the city. To the post office and then on."

Reuter put down his empty beer bottle. "Don't forget that you're on furlough. And don't forget that it will soon be over."

"That's something I'm not likely to forget," Graeber replied bitterly.

Reuter cautiously lifted his bandaged foot from the window seat and set it down in front of him. "That's not what I mean. Do all you can to find your parents; but just the same don't forget that you're on furlough. It will be a long time before you get another."

"I know that. And before then there'll be lots of chances of getting my ass pinched shut for good. I know that, too."

"Good," Reuter said. "If you know that, everything's in order."

Graeber walked toward the door. At the table where the card players sat Rummel had just drawn a grand with four jacks; plus the whole slate of clubs. It was a hand with drums and trumpets. Impassively he slaughtered his opponents. No quarter was given. "Cleaned out!" the man who had called Graeber a barracks crapper said in despair. "What do you say to a hand like that! And he doesn't even enjoy it!"

"Ernst!"

Graeber turned around. A short, thick-set S.A. commander was standing in front of him. He had to think for a minute; then he recognized the round face with its red cheeks and hazelnut eyes. "Binding," he said. "Alfons Binding!"

"Himself in person."

Binding beamed at him. "Ernst! Man alive! We haven't seen each other in a thousand years! Where have you come from?"

"Russia."

"On leave then! That's something we have to celebrate. Come along to my place. It's not far from here. I have a first-rate cognac! What a surprise! Meeting an old schoolmate who has just come from the front! There's got to be a toast to that."

Graeber looked at him. Binding had been in his class for a couple of years but Graeber had almost forgotten him. It was only by accident that he had heard that Alfons had joined the S.A. Now he stood in front of him in elegant, gleaming boots, happy and unconcerned. "Come on, Ernst. Don't be childish," he urged. "A good schnapps can't hurt us."

Graeber shook his head. "I haven't time."

"But, Ernst! Just one drink between friends! There's always time for that. Between old comrades!"

Old comrades! Graeber examined the uniform with the commander's insignia. Binding had worked his way up in the world. But he might be just the one who could help him find his parents, he thought suddenly. Just because he belonged to the Party! Perhaps he knew ways only open to Party members. "All right, Alfons," he said. "For one schnapps."

"That's right, Ernst. Come along, it's not far."

———

It was farther than Binding had maintained. He lived in the suburbs in a little white villa that lay, peaceful and undamaged, in a garden with tall birch trees. Bird houses hung in the trees and from somewhere came the splashing of water.

Binding preceded Graeber into the house. In the hall hung the antlers of a stag, the head of a wild boar and a stuffed bear's head. Graeber looked at them in amazement. "When did you get to be such a hunter, Alfons?"

Binding grinned. "There's nothing in it. I've never touched a gun. Just decoration. Looks fine, though, doesn't it? Germanic!"

He led Graeber into a room strewn with rugs. On the walls hung paintings in magnificent frames. Huge leather chairs stood about. "What do you think of my den?" he asked proudly. "Cosy, isn't it?"

Graeber nodded. The Party looked after its own. Alfons had been the son of a poor milkman. It had been difficult for his father to send him to the Gymnasium.

"Sit down, Ernst. How do you like my Rubens?"

"What?"

"But, Ernst! The big ham there over the piano!"

It was the painting of a very voluptuous naked woman standing at the edge of a pond. She had golden hair and a tremendous behind highlighted by the sun. That would be something for Boettcher, Graeber thought. "Pretty," he said.

"Pretty?" Binding was greatly disappointed. "Why, man alive, it is simply magnificent. It came from the same art dealer the Reichsmarshal patronizes. A masterpiece! I snapped it up cheap from the man who bought it. Don't you really like it?"

"Of course! It's just that I'm no connoisseur. But I know someone who would go crazy if he saw it."

"Really? A big collector?"

"Not that; but a specialist in Rubens."

Binding beamed. "That delights me, Ernst. It really delights me. I myself would never have thought that I'd be an art collector one day. But now tell me how you are and what you're up to. And whether I can do anything for you. One has certain connections, you know." He laughed slyly.

Against his will Graeber was somewhat touched. This was the first time that anyone had unguardedly offered to help him. "You can do something for me," he said. "My parents are missing. Perhaps they've been evacuated or are somewhere in one of the villages. How can I find out? They don't seem to be here in the city any longer."

Binding sat down in an easy chair beside a hammered copper smoking stand. His gleaming boots stood like stove pipes in front of him. "It's not so easy if they're no longer in the city," he remarked. "I'll see what I can find out. It will take a couple of days. Perhaps even longer. It depends on where they are. Just now everything is in pretty much of a mess—you know that."

"Yes, I've noticed that."

Binding got up and went to a cabinet. He got out a bottle and two glasses. "Let's have a drink first, Ernst. Genuine armagnac. I like it almost better that cognac. *Prost.*"

"*Prost,* Alfons."

Binding refilled the glasses. "Where are you living now? With relatives?"

"We have no relatives in the city. I'm living in the barracks."

Binding put down his glass. "But, Ernst, that's absurd. A furlough in the barracks! That's as good as none at all. You can stay with me! Plenty of room. Bedroom and bath, and you can bring a girl, anything you want."

"Do you live here alone?"

"But of course! Did you think I was married? I'm not as dumb as that. In my position women practically break the doors down to get in!" Alfons winked and pointed to a tremendous leather sofa. "The things that sofa has seen! They come here and plead with me on their knees."

"Really? Why?"

"On their knees, Ernst. There was one here just yesterday! A lady from the highest circles, as a matter of fact, with red hair, superb bosom, a veil, a fur cape, here on this rug. She wept like a fountain and was ready for anything. Wanted me to get her husband out of the concentration camp."

Graeber glanced up. "Can you do a thing like that?"

Binding laughed. "I can get people in. But getting them out isn't so simple. Of course I didn't tell her that. Well, how about it, Ernst? Will you move in?"

"I can't just yet, Alfons. Everywhere I've been I've given the barracks as my address for messages. I must wait and see what comes."

"All right. But remember you always have a home with Alfons. The food is first-class too. I made good advance preparations."

"Thanks, Alfons."

"Nonsense! After all, we're schoolmates. We should help each other. You let me copy your homework often enough. That reminds me, do you remember Burmeister?"

"Our math teacher?"

"He's the one. That ass was responsible for my being fired in upper-middle year. Because of that business with Lucie Edler. Don't you remember?"

"Of course," Graeber said. He did not remember.

"I begged him not to report me. Didn't get anywhere. The fiend was implacable. His moral duty, and a lot more guff. My father almost beat me to death for it. Burmeister!" Alfons savored the name on his tongue. "I've paid him back, Ernst! Got him six months in a concentration camp. You should have seen him when he got out. He stood at attention and almost wet his pants when he saw me. He educated me; so I re-educated him thoroughly. Good joke, eh?"

"Yes."

Alfons laughed. "That sort of thing does one's soul good. That's what's so nice about our movement. Every once in a while you get a chance like that." He noticed that Graeber had stood up. "Are you going so soon?"

"I've got to. I am restless, you understand that."

Binding nodded. His face became solemn. "I understand, Ernst. And I'm dreadfully sorry. You know that, don't you?"

"Yes, Alfons." Graeber knew what was coming next and tried to cut it short. "I'll stop in here then in a couple of days."

"Come tomorrow afternoon. Or toward evening. Around five-thirty."

"Fine. Tomorrow, around five-thirty. Do you think you'll know something by then?"

"Perhaps. We'll see. In any case we can drink a schnapps. By the way, Ernst—have you been to the hospitals yet?"

"Yes."

Binding nodded. "And—just as a precaution of course—to the cemeteries?"

"No."

"Well, go there. Just in case. There are still a lot there who haven't been reported."

"I'll go tomorrow."

"Good, Ernst." Binding was visibly relieved. "And stop in tomorrow for longer. We old schoolmates must stick together. You haven't any idea how lonesome it is in a position like mine. Everyone wants something from you."

"I wanted something too."

"That was different. I mean favors."

Binding took the bottle of armagnac, drove in the cork with the palm of his hand and offered it to Graeber. "Here, Ernst! Take this along. It's good schnapps. I'm sure you'll be able to use it. Wait a minute!" He opened the door. "Frau Kleinert! A piece of paper! Or a bag!"

Graeber held the bottle in his hand. "This isn't necessary, Alfons—"

Binding brushed his words aside stormily. "Take it! I have a whole cellar full of the stuff." He took the paper bag which his housekeeper had brought and put the bottle in it. "Take care of yourself, Ernst! And keep your chin up! Till tomorrow."

Graeber went to Hakenstrasse. He had been a trifle overwhelmed by Alfons. An S.A. commander, he thought. The first human being who wants to help me unreservedly and offers me food and lodging has to be an S.A. commander! He put the bottle in his coat pocket.

It was early evening. The sky was mother-of-pearl and the trees stood out clear against its bright expanse. Twilight hung blue over the ruins.

Graeber stopped in front of the door that served as the Ruins Journal. His notice was missing. He thought at first the wind had torn it off; but in that case the thumbtacks would still have been there. They, too, were gone. Someone had taken the notice down.

He felt the blood rush suddenly to his heart. Eagerly he examined the door for some message. But he found none. Then he ran across to his parents' house. The second notice was still stuck there between the stones. He plucked it out and stared at it. It had not been touched. There was no message on it.

Uncomprehending, he straightened up and looked around. Then far down the street he saw something drifting in the wind like a white feather. He ran after it. It was his notice. He picked it up and looked at it. Someone had torn it off. On the margin was written in a pedantic hand: *Thou shalt not steal.* At first he did not understand what it meant. Then he remembered the two missing thumbtacks and realized that the appeal from "Mother" had all four tacks again. Mother had taken back her property and imparted a lesson. Suffering seemed not always to produce generosity.

He found two flat stones, laid his notice on the ground beside the door, and weighted it down with them. Then he went back to his parents' house.

He stood in front of the ruins and looked up. The green armchair was missing. Someone must have taken it. In the place where it had stood a few newspapers protruded from the ruins. He climbed up and pulled them out. They were old papers filled with victories and famous names, faded, torn, and dirty. He threw them away and went on searching. After a while, between two beams, he saw a little book, yellow and wilted, lying open as though someone had just left it there. He pulled it out and recognized it. It was one of his schoolbooks. He leafed through the pages to the front and saw his name in pale writing on the first page. He must have written it there when he was twelve or thirteen years old.

It was a school catechism, a book containing hundreds of questions and the answers to them. The pages were spotted and on some of them were notes he himself had written. He stared at them absently. For a moment everything seemed to tremble and he did not know what was trembling—the ruined city with the quiet mother-of-pearl sky above it or the little yellow book in his hands that contained the answers to all the questions of mankind.

He put it aside and continued his search. But he found nothing more—no other books nor anything else from his parents' home. It would have been unlikely in any case; they had lived on the third floor and their things must have been buried much deeper under the rubble. Probably in the explosion the catechism had been blown high in the air and then, because it was light, had slowly fluttered down. Like a dove, he thought, a lonely white dove of assurance and peace, with all its questions and answers, in a night full of fire and smoke and suffocation and screams and death.

He sat a while longer on the ruins. The evening wind sprang up and turned the pages of the book. God is merciful, he read, all-bountiful, all-mighty, all-wise, all-knowing; He is infinitely kind and just—

Graeber felt for the bottle Binding had given him. He opened it and took a swallow. Then he climbed down to the street. He did not take the catechism with him.

It had grown dark. There was no light anywhere. Graeber was walking across the Karlsplatz. At the corner by the air raid shelter he almost ran into someone. It was a young officer who was walking very fast in the opposite direction. "Watch where you're going!" he growled angrily.

Graeber looked at him. "All right, Ludwig," he said. "Next time I'll watch."

The Lieutenant stared at him. Then his face broke into a broad grin. "You, Ernst!"

It was Ludwig Wellmann. "What are you up to? Furlough?" he asked.

"Yes. And you?"

"All over. I'm just going back. That's why I'm in such a rush."

"How was it?"

"So-so. You know. Next time I'm going to arrange things differently. I'll not tell anyone and I'll go somewhere else. Not home!"

"Why?"

Wellmann made a face. "My family, Ernst! My parents! It just doesn't work. They ruin your whole leave for you. How long have you been here?"

"Four days."

"Just wait. You'll soon see how it is!"

Wellmann tried to light a cigarette. The wind blew out his match. Graeber handed him his lighter. The flame illuminated for a moment Wellmann's thin, energetic face. "They think you're still a child," he said, exhaling smoke. "If you want to disappear for so much as an evening, right off there are reproachful looks. You're supposed to spend your time only with them. For my mother I'm still fifteen. She was swimming in tears all through the first half of my leave because I had come home—and all through the second because I had to go away. What can you do?"

"And your father? He was a soldier himself in the first war, wasn't he?"

"He's forgotten that. At least part of it. For my old man I'm the hero. He's proud of my hardware. Wanted to be seen with me. Touching old fellow from the gray dawn of time. They don't understand us any more, Ernst. Take care that yours don't catch you."

"I'll take care, all right," Graeber said.

"They mean well. It's all thoughtfulness and love. But that's just the damnable part of it. You can't do anything about it. You always feel like a heartless criminal."

Wellmann glanced after a girl whose bright stockings glimmered in the windy night. "Your leave goes right down the drain," he said. "All I managed to accomplish was their not coming with me to the station. And I'm not even sure that they won't turn up there after all!" He laughed. "Handle it right from the beginning, Ernst. Clear out at least in the evenings. Invent something. A course, or something like that! Duty! Otherwise it will be the way it was with me and you'll have a leave like a schoolboy's."

"I believe in my case it will be different."

Wellmann shook Graeber's hand. "I hope so! Then you'll have better luck than I. Have you been to our old fleabag of a school yet?"

"No."

"Don't go. I went there. It was a great mistake. Makes you want to vomit. The one decent teacher has been kicked out. Pohlmann, the one we had in religion. You remember him, don't you?"

"Of course. I'm even supposed to go and see him."

"Watch out. He's been blacklisted. Better steer clear of the whole mess! One should never go back anywhere. Well, take care of yourself, Ernst! Our short, glorious life, eh?"

"Yes, Ludwig. With free board, foreign travel, and a state funeral."

"Hot shit! God knows when we'll see each other again." Wellmann laughed and disappeared into the dark.

Graeber walked on. He did not know what to do. The city was dark as a grave. He could not go on searching and he realized he would have to be patient. The long evening terrified him. He did not want to go back to the barracks yet; nor to his few acquaintances. He could not bear their embarrassed sympathy and he knew that anyhow they would be glad when he left.

He stared at the gnawed roofs of the houses. Just what had he expected? An island behind the fronts? Home, security, refuge, comfort? Perhaps. But the islands of hope had long since silently sunk under the monotony of pointless death, the fronts were shattered and the war was everywhere. Everywhere, even in the brain and the heart.

He came to a moving picture theater and went in. It was less dark inside than on the street. At any rate sitting there was better than continuing to wander through the black city or sitting and getting drunk in some tavern.

# Chapter Eleven

THE CEMETERY LAY in the bright sun. Graeber saw that a bomb had hit the gate. A few crosses and granite headstones were strewn over the paths and graves. The weeping willows had been turned upside down; as a result the roots seemed to be branches, and the boughs long, trailing green roots. They looked like some strange growth that had been thrown up, decked with seaweed from a subterranean sea. Most of the bones from the bomb-wrecked graves had been gathered up and heaped in a tidy pile; only small splinters and fragments of decaying coffins hung in the willows. No longer any skulls.

A shed had been put up beside the chapel. An overseer and his two helpers were at work there. The overseer was sweating. When he heard what Graeber wanted he waved him away. "No time, man! Twelve more burials before lunch! Dear God, how should we know whether your parents are here? There are dozens of graves without headstones and without names. This has turned into mass production! How can we know about everybody?"

"Don't you keep lists?"

"Lists!" the overseer replied bitterly, turning to the two assistants. "Lists he wants to see, did you hear that? Lists! Do you know how many corpses are still lying outside? Three hundred. Do you know how many were brought in after the last air raid? Seven hundred. How many after the one before? Five hundred. There were just four days in between. How are we going to catch up with that? We're not equipped to do it! We need steam shovels instead of grave diggers to handle what's still lying out there. And can you tell me when the next attack is coming? Tonight? Tomorrow? And he wants to have lists!"

Graeber made no reply. He took a package of cigarettes out of his pocket and laid it on the table. The overseer and his helpers exchanged glances. Graeber waited for a moment. Then he laid down three cigars as well. He had brought them back from Russia for his father.

"Well, all right," the overseer said. "We'll see what we can do. Write down the name. One of us will ask at the cemetery office. Meanwhile you can take a look at the dead that haven't been recorded yet. Those rows over there by the church wall."

Graeber went over. Some of the dead bore names. Others had coffins, stretchers, blankets, flowers, shrouds, or were covered with white sheets. He read the names, lifted the sheets over those that were unnamed and then walked across to the rows of the unknown who lay side by side under a narrow temporary roof that had been put up against the wall. The eyes of some had been closed, the hands of some had been folded, but most of them lay the way they had been found; only their arms had been pressed close to their bodies and their legs straightened so they would take up less room. A silent procession was moving past. Bent over, they examined the pale, rigid faces, searching for their own dead.

Graeber took his place in line. A few steps ahead of him a woman suddenly sank to the ground beside one of the corpses and began to sob. The rest walked silently around her and proceeded, bent over and with faces so intent they seemed empty, without any expression except anxious expectation. Only as they neared the end of the row a pale gleam of covert, uneasy hope gradually appeared, and one could see them sigh with relief when they were through.

Graeber walked back. "Have you been in the chapel yet?" the overseer asked.

"No."

"The badly mutilated ones are there." The overseer looked at Graeber. "It takes strong nerves. But you're a soldier after all."

Graeber went into the chapel. Then he came back. The overseer was standing outside. "Horrible, isn't it?" He glanced at Graeber searchingly. "Several people have folded up on us looking at them," he went on. "Only yesterday a troop leader from the concentration camp, a giant of a fellow."

Graeber did not answer. He had seen so many dead that he found nothing out of the ordinary here. Not even the fact that here they were civilians, and many of them women and children. He had seen that, too, often enough, and the mutilations of the Russians and Dutch and French had been no less hideous than those he now saw. It even seemed to him that the corpses frozen in the Russian winter in every stage of decomposition and dismemberment and a group of fifty hanged men, with bloated heads, burst, protruding eyes, split lips and thick black tongues, had been more horrible than these fragments of humanity in the chapel.

"There's no record in the cemetery office," the overseer announced. "But there are two more big mortuaries in the city. Have you been there yet?"

"Yes."

"They still have ice," the overseer said almost enviously. "They are better off than we are."

"They're overcrowded."

"Yes, but they're refrigerated. That's something we don't have. And it's getting warmer and warmer. If a couple more attacks come close together and we have more sunny days on top of that, there'll be a catastrophe. It will mean that we'll have to resort to mass graves."

Graeber nodded. He did not consider that a catastrophe. The catastrophe was what caused the mass graves.

"We work as hard as we can," the overseer explained. "We have as many grave diggers as we can hire, but even so they're not nearly enough. The procedure here is out of date in this age. Of course religious requirements are a complication." He rubbed his forehead worriedly. "The only institutions that are really modern in every respect are the concentration camps. They can dispose of hundreds of corpses a day. All the newest methods. But, of course, they use a crematorium and that's out of the question for us—"

For a moment he stared out thoughtfully over the wall. Then he waved to Graeber briefly and strode rapidly back to his shed—a loyal, conscientious officer of death.

Graeber had to wait for a few minutes; two funerals blocked the exit. He looked around once more. Priests were praying over the graves, relatives were kneeling beside the headstones, there was a smell of faded flowers and fresh earth, birds were singing, the procession of searchers continued to move along the wall, grave diggers were swinging their picks in half-dug graves, stonecutters and undertakers were wandering about—the abode of death had become the busiest spot in the city.

Binding's little white house lay in the early twilight of its garden. On the lawn stood a bird bath into which water was splashing. Jonquils and tulips were in bloom in front of the lilac bushes and under the birch trees stood the marble statue of a girl.

The housekeeper opened the door. She was a gray-haired woman, wearing a large white apron. "You are Herr Graeber, are you not?"

"Yes."

"The Commander is not here. He had to attend an important Party meeting. But he left a message for you."

Graeber followed her into the house with its antlers and paintings. The Rubens shone of itself in the twilight. On the copper smoking stand stood a bottle already wrapped. Beside it lay a letter. Alfons wrote that he had not been able to find out much so far; but Graeber's parents had not been reported as dead or wounded anywhere in the city. Probably they had been evacuated or had moved. Graeber could come again tomorrow. The vodka was for him to use tonight to celebrate the fact that he was far from Russia.

He put the bottle and the letter into his pocket. Frau Kleinert had remained in the doorway. "The Commander sends his warmest greetings."

"Give him mine too. Tell him I'll be back tomorrow. And many thanks for the bottle. I can use it."

Frau Kleinert smiled. "He will be pleased. He is such a kind man."

Graeber walked back through the garden. A kind man, he thought. But had Alfons been kind to Burmeister, their mathematics teacher, whom he had sent to the concentration camp? Probably everyone was a kind person for somebody. And, for somebody else, the opposite.

He felt for the note and the bottle. To celebrate, he thought. What? The hope that his parents were not dead? And with whom? With the men in Room Forty-eight at the barracks? He stared into the twilight that had grown bluer and deeper. He might take the bottle to Elisabeth Kruse, he thought. She could use it as well as he could. For himself he still had the armagnac.

The woman with the blurry face opened the door. "I'd like to see Fräulein Kruse," Graeber said determinedly and tried to pass her.

She did not move from the doorway. "Fräulein Kruse is not in," she replied. "You ought to know that."

"What do you mean I ought to know that?"

"Didn't she tell you?"

"I forgot. When will she be back?"

"At seven."

Graeber had not reckoned on Elisabeth's being out. He debated where to leave the vodka; but who knew what this informer would make of it? Perhaps she would even drink it herself. "All right, I'll come back then," he said.

He stood in the street outside and looked at his watch. It was a little before six. The evening once more lay long and dark before him. "Don't forget that you're on furlough," Reuter had said. He had not forgotten; but that by itself did not help much.

He went to the Karlsplatz and sat down on a bench in the square. The air raid shelter crouched there massively like a monstrous toad. Cautious people were slipping into it like shadows. Darkness welled up out of the bushes and drowned the last light.

Graeber sat quietly on the bench. An hour earlier he had not thought of seeing Elisabeth again. If he had found her at home he would probably have given her the vodka and gone away, he thought. But now that he had not found her he was waiting impatiently for seven o'clock.

———

Elisabeth opened the door herself. "I wasn't prepared for you," he said in surprise. "I was expecting the dragon that guards your gate."

"Frau Lieser isn't here. She went to a meeting of the National Socialist Women's Auxiliary."

"The flat-foot brigade. Of course! That's where she belongs." Graeber looked around. "The minute she leaves it looks different here."

"It looks different because now the light is on in the vestibule," Elisabeth replied. "I turn it on wherever she leaves."

"And when she's here?"

"When she's here we're thrifty. That's patriotic. We sit in the dark."

"That checks," Graeber said. "That's where they like us to be." He pulled the bottle out of his pocket. "Here's some vodka I brought you. It comes from the cellar of an S.A. commander. A present from a schoolmate."

Elisabeth looked at him. "Have you that sort of schoolmate?"

"Yes. Just as you have a boarder you didn't choose."

She smiled and took the bottle. "I must see whether there's a corkscrew anywhere."

She walked ahead of him into the kitchen. He saw that she was wearing a black sweater and a tight black skirt. Her hair was tied together at the nape of her neck with a thick, lustrous band of red wool. She had straight, strong shoulders and narrow hips.

"I can't find a corkscrew," she said, closing the drawers. "Apparently Frau Lieser doesn't drink."

"She looks as though she did nothing else. But we don't need a corkscrew."

Graeber took the bottle, knocked the varnish off its neck and struck it twice sharply against his thigh. The cork popped out.

"That's the way we do it in the army," he explained. "Have you glasses? Or shall we drink out of the bottle?"

"I have glasses in my room. Come."

Graeber followed her. He was suddenly glad that he had come. He had been afraid he would have to spend another evening sitting around by himself.


Elisabeth took two thin wine glasses from a break-front with books in it that stood against the wall. Graeber glanced around. The room looked different today. It contained a bed, a couple of armchairs covered in green, the books, and a Biedermeier desk; their effect was old-fashioned and peaceful. In his memory it had been more disorderly and wild. It must have been the noise of the sirens, he thought. Noise confused everything. Elisabeth, too, looked different today from the way she had then. Different, but not old-fashioned and not peaceful.

She turned around. "How long is it really since we saw each other?"

"A hundred years. At that time we were children and there was no war."

"And now?"

"Now we're old without the experience of age. Old and cynical and without faith and sometimes sad. Not often sad."

She looked at him. "Is that true?"

"No. But what is? Do you know?"

Elisabeth shook her head. "Does something always have to be true?"

"Probably not. Why?"

"I don't know. But perhaps we'd have fewer wars if everyone wasn't so eager to convince someone else of his own particular truth."

Graeber smiled. The way she said it sounded odd. "Tolerance," he said. "That's what's lacking, isn't it?"

Elisabeth nodded. He took the glasses and filled them. "We'll drink to that. The commander who gave me this bottle certainly didn't have anything like that in mind. But we'll do it for that very reason."

He emptied his glass. "Will you have another?" he asked.

Elisabeth shook herself briefly. "Yes," she said then.

He poured and placed the bottle on the table. The vodka was sharp and clear and clean. Elisabeth put her glass down. "Come," she said. "I'll show you an example of tolerance."

She led him through the vestibule and pushed open a door. "In her hurry Frau Lieser forgot to lock up. Take a look at her room. It's no betrayal of confidence. She searches mine all the time when I'm out."

Part of the room was furnished in the ordinary way. But on the wall opposite the window, in a massive frame, hung a large colored portrait of Hitler decked with wreaths of evergreen and oak leaves. On a table under it a deluxe edition of *Mein Kampf,* bound in black leather and stamped with a gold swastika, lay on top of a huge swastika flag. On either side stood silver candlesticks with photographs of the Fuehrer beside them—one with his sheep dog in Berchtesgaden and another that showed a little girl in a white dress handing him flowers. Honor-daggers and Party badges completed the exhibit.

Graeber was not especially surprised. He had often seen similar things. The cult of a dictator easily turned into a religion.

"Does she write her denunciations here?" he asked.

"No, she writes them over there, at my father's desk."

Graeber looked at the desk. It was old-fashioned, with a high back and a roll top. "It's always locked," Elisabeth said. "You can't get into it. I've tried several times."

"Did she denounce your father?"

"I don't know for sure. She was already living here with her child at that time. She had only one room. After my father was taken away she got the two that belonged to him as well."

Graeber turned toward her. "Do you mean she might have done it for that reason?"

"Why not? It often takes even less reason than that."

"That's true. But from the altar here it looks as though the woman is one of the crazy fanatics of the flat-foot brigade."

"Ernst," Elisabeth said bitterly, "do you really believe that fanaticism can never go hand in hand with personal advantage?"

"No. As a matter of fact it often does. Strange that one keeps forgetting that! There are platitudes you learn somewhere or other and go on using without thinking about them. The world is not divided into compartments with labels. And human beings even less. Very likely this poisonous reptile loves her child, her husband, flowers, and everything noble in existence. Did she know something against your father or did she invent the whole thing?"

"My father was good-natured and careless and had been under suspicion for a long time. Not everyone can keep quiet when he has to listen to Party speeches all day long in his own home."

"Do you know what he might have said?"

Elisabeth shrugged her shoulders. "He didn't believe that Germany would win the war."

"There are many now who do not believe that."

"You, too?"

"I, too. And now let's get out of here. Otherwise that she-devil will catch you and who knows what she'll do then!"

Elisabeth gave a quick smile. "She won't catch us. I bolted the door to the corridor. She can't get in."

She went to the door and pushed back the bolt. Thank God,

Graeber thought. Even if she is a martyr at least she plays the part cautiously and without many scruples. "It smells like a cemetery here," he said. "It must be those damn wilted oak leaves. Come, let's have something to drink."

He filled the glasses. "Now I know why we feel old," he said. "It's because we've seen too much filth. Filth stirred up by people who are older than we and ought to be wiser."

"I don't feel old," Elisabeth replied.

He looked at her. She looked anything but old. "Be glad of it," he answered.

"I feel imprisoned," she said. "That's worse than feeling old."

Graeber sat down in one of the Biedermeier chairs. "Who can be sure that woman won't denounce you too?" he said. "Perhaps she wants the whole apartment for herself. Why do you wait for that to happen? There's no justice for you, you know that."

"Yes, I know that." Elisabeth suddenly appeared headstrong and helpless. "It's like a superstition," she replied hurriedly and tormentedly like someone who has given herself the same answer a hundred times. "As long as I'm here I believe that my father will come back. If I went away it would be like abandoning him. Don't you understand that?"

"One doesn't have to understand it. One acts on it, and that's the end of it. Even if it's unreasonable."

"Good."

She picked up her glass and emptied it. Outside there was the rattling of a key. "There she is," Graeber said. "That was close. The meeting doesn't seem to have lasted long."

They listened to the steps in the vestibule. Graeber glanced at the gramophone. "Haven't you anything but marches?" he asked.

"Yes. But marches are loud. And sometimes when the silence screams you have to drown it out with the loudest thing you have."

Graeber looked at her. "Nice conversations we have! At school they used to tell us that youth was the romantic time of life."

Elisabeth laughed. In the vestibule something fell to the floor. Frau Lieser swore. Then the door slammed. "I left the light on," Elisabeth whispered. "Come, let's get out of here. Sometimes I just can't stand it. And let's talk about something else."

"Where shall we go?" Graeber asked when they were outside.

"I don't know. Anywhere."

"Isn't there a café in the neighborhood? Or a tavern or a bar?"

"I don't want to go indoors again right away. Let's just walk."

"Good."

The streets were empty and the city was dark and quiet. They walked along Marienstrasse, across Karlsplatz, and then over the river into the old city. After a while it became unreal, as though all life had vanished and they were the last human beings. They walked past houses and apartment buildings but when they peered into the windows in the hope of seeing rooms with chairs, tables, evidences of life, they saw nothing but the reflection of the moonlight in the panes and behind them the black curtains or the paper coverings of blackout screens. It was as though the whole city were in mourning, an endless morgue shrouded in black, with coffined homes, a single wake.

"What's going on?" Graeber asked. "Where is everyone? Tonight it's even quieter than usual."

"Probably they're sitting in their homes. We haven't had a raid for a couple of days. So they don't dare come out now. They're waiting for the next one. It's always that way. It's only directly after a raid that there are more people out in the streets."

"There's already a routine even about that, eh?"

"Yes. Isn't it the same with you at the front?"

"Yes."

They walked through a street that lay in ruins. Shreds of cloud drifted across the sky making the light tremulous. In the ruins shadows darted out and withdrew like moon-shy sea monsters. Then they heard the tinkle of china. "Thank God!" Graeber said. "There's someone eating. Or drinking coffee. Anyway alive."

"Probably they're drinking coffee. They distributed some today. Good, as a matter of fact. Bomb coffee."

"Bomb coffee?"

"Yes, bomb coffee or ruins coffee. That's what they call it. It's an extra ration that's issued after heavy bombings. Sometimes there's sugar, too, or chocolate, or a package of cigarettes."

"That's the way it is in the field. There you get schnapps or tobacco before an offensive. Rather ridiculous, isn't it? Two hundred grams of coffee for one hour's fear of death."

"One hundred grams."

They walked on. After a while Graeber stopped. "Elisabeth, this is even grimmer than sitting at home. Let's go somewhere and have a drink. I should have brought along the vodka. I need a schnapps. You too. Where's a place around here?"

"I don't want to go to a bar. You feel as shut in there as though you were in a cellar. Everything's blacked out and all the windows are covered."

"Then let's walk up to the barracks. I still have a bottle there. I'll fetch it and we can have a drink in the open."

"Good."

Through the stillness they heard the rattling of a wagon. Almost immediately they saw a horse galloping toward them. Restive, shying at the shadows, its wild eyes and distended nostrils gave it a ghostly look in the pale light. The driver was pulling on the reins. The horse reared. Foam flew from its mouth. They had to climb onto the ruins at the side of the street to let it by. With a swift movement Elisabeth sprang just high enough to let the horse pass without touching her; she bent over and for a moment it looked as though she were about to swing herself onto the snorting animal and gallop away. Then she was once more standing alone against the empty expanse of the disordered sky.

"You looked as though you were going to jump on his back and ride away," Graeber said.

"If one only could! But where to? The war is everywhere."

"That's true! Everywhere. Even in the countries of perpetual peace—in the South Seas, and in the Indies. We couldn't escape it anywhere."

They came to the barracks. "Wait here, Elisabeth. I'll get the schnapps. It won't take long."

Graeber walked across the barracks courtyard and up the echoing steps to Room Forty-eight. The place was shaking with the snores of half its inmates. Above the table a shaded light was burning. The card players were still up. Reuter was sitting beside them reading.

"Where's Boettcher?" Graeber asked.

Reuter closed his book with a bang. "He left word for you that he had found nothing. He ran his bicycle into a wall and broke it. It's the old story—misfortune breeds misfortune. Tomorrow he's got to go off on foot again. And so tonight he's sitting in a tavern consoling himself. What's happened to you? You look a little pale around the gills."

"Nothing. I'm going out again right away. Just wanted to get something."

Graeber felt around in his knapsack. He had brought a bottle of Geneva and a bottle of cognac from Russia. In addition he still had Binding's armagnac. "Take the cognac or the armagnac," Reuter said. "The vodka isn't there any more."

"How come?"

"We drank it. You might have donated it voluntarily. Anyone who comes from Russia had no business acting like a capitalist. He ought to have some consideration for his comrades. It was good vodka."

Graeber got out the two bottles that were still there. He put the armagnac in his pocket and gave the Geneva to Reuter. "You're right. Here, take this as medicine for your gout. And don't act like a capitalist yourself. Give the others some."

"Merci!" Reuter hobbled to his locker and got out a corkscrew. "I assume you're planning the most primitive form of seduction," he said. "Seduction with the aid of intoxicating beverages. In such cases one usually forgets to draw the cork beforehand. With a broken-neck bottle it's awfully easy to slash your mug to ribbons in the excitement. Here, be a man of foresight."

"Go to hell! The bottle's open."

Reuter opened the Geneva. "How did you come to get Holland gin in Russia?"

"I bought it. Any more questions?"

Reuter grinned. "None. Run along with your armagnac, you primitive Casanova. And don't be ashamed. There are mitigating circumstances. Lack of time. Leave is short and war is long."

Feldmann sat up in bed. "Do you need anything, Graeber? There are some things in my wallet. I don't need them. He who sleeps doesn't get syphilis."

"That's not so certain," Reuter remarked. "There's said to be a kind of simon-pure infection. But our Graeber here is a nature boy. An Aryan stud with twelve thoroughbred ancestors. In a case like his prophylactics are a crime against the fatherland."

Graeber opened the armagnac, took a swallow and put it back in his pocket. "You're all damned romantics," he said. "Why don't you worry about your own affairs?"

Reuter dismissed him with a wave of his hand. "Go in peace, my son. Forget the manual of arms and try to be a human being! It's easier to die than to live. Especially for one of you—the heroic youth and flower of the nation!"

Graeber put a package of cigarettes and a tumbler in his pocket. On his way out he saw that Rummel was still winning at the card players' table. A pile of money lay in front of him. His face was expressionless; but now he was sweating in bright drops.

The barracks stairs were deserted; it was after taps. The corridors re-echoed to Graeber's steps. He walked across the wide square. Elisabeth was no longer at the gate. She's gone away, he thought. He had almost expected it. Why should she wait for him anyway?

"The lady's standing over there," the sentry said. "How does a doughfoot like you come to have a girl like that? That is something for officers."

Graeber saw Elisabeth now. She was leaning against the wall. He tapped the sentry on the shoulder. "It's a new regulation, my son. You get that instead of a medal when you've been at the front for four years. All generals' daughters. Better hurry up and report for front-line service right away, you mooncalf. Don't you know you're not allowed to talk on duty?"

He walked across to Elisabeth. "Mooncalf yourself," said the sentry lamely from behind.

They found a bench on a rise behind the barracks. It stood between a pair of chestnut trees and from it one could look out over the whole city. No light showed anywhere. Only the river glinted in the moon.

Graeber opened the bottle and filled the tumbler halfway. The armagnac shimmered in it like liquid amber. He offered it to Elisabeth. "Drink it down," he said.

She took a swallow and gave the glass back. "Drink it down," he said. "This is an evening for it. Drink to anything you want, to this damnable life of ours, or to the fact that we are still alive— but drink it. We need it, after the dead city. Today we seem to need it badly."

"All right. To all of that together."

He refilled the glass and drank himself. He felt the warmth at once. He felt, too, how empty he was. He had not known that. It was an emptiness without pain.

He filled the glass once more halfway and drank about half of it. Then he placed it between himself and Elisabeth. She was sitting on the bench with her legs drawn up and her arms around her knees. The young foliage of the chestnut trees above her shimmered almost white in the moon—as though a swarm of early butterflies had alighted there.

"How black it is," she said, pointing toward the city. "Like a burned-out coal mine."

"Don't look at it. Turn around. It's different there."

The bench stood at the top of the rise and the hill sloped gradually down on the other side—to fields, moonlit roads, poplar-bordered lanes, the steeple of a village church and then to the forest and to the blue mountains on the horizon. "You see? There is all the peace in the world," Graeber said. "Simple, isn't it?"

"Simple if you can do it—just turn around and not think of the other."

"One learns that fast enough."

"Have you learned it?"

"Of course," Graeber said. "Otherwise I wouldn't be alive now."

"I wish I could learn it too."

He laughed. "You know it already. Life takes care of that. It draws its reserves from any source. And in danger it knows neither weakness nor sentimentality." He pushed the glass toward her.

"Is this part of it too?" she asked.

"Yes," he said. "Tonight for sure."

She drank and he watched her. "For a change," he said, "let's not talk about the war any more for a while."

Elisabeth leaned back. "Let's sit quietly and not talk about anything at all."

"All right."

They sat in silence. It was very still and slowly the stillness became animated with the peaceful sounds of the night that did not disturb it but only made it deeper—the soft wind that was like the breathing of the forests, the cry of an owl, the rustling of the grass—and the unending play of cloud and light. The stillness increased in strength, it rose and surrounded them and filtered into them more and more with each breath, and breath itself turned into stillness, it canceled and dissolved and became softer and more prolonged, and was no longer an enemy but a far-off beneficent sleep.

Elisabeth moved. Graeber started up and looked around. "What do you think of that? I went to sleep."

"So did I." She opened her eyes. The dispersed light was caught in them and made them very transparent. "I haven't slept like this in a long time," she said in astonishment. "Always only with the light on and in fear of the darkness and awakening with the shock of terror—"

Graeber sat in silence. He did not question her. Curiosity dies in times of constant happenings. He only marveled vaguely that he himself was sitting there so calmly, hung with translucent sleep like an underwater rock with waving seaweed. He felt relaxed for the first time since his journey out of Russia. A gentle calm had invaded him like a flood that had risen overnight, whose shining surface seemed suddenly to unite parched and arid regions into a single whole again.

They walked down to the city. The streets engulfed them once more, the cold stench of old fires drew about them, and the blank, black windows accompanied them again like a procession of catafalques. Elisabeth shivered. "Once upon a time the houses and streets were full of light. We were so used to it that we thought nothing of it. Today we're beginning to understand what we have lost—"

Graeber looked up. The sky was clear and cloudless. It was a good night for fliers and so for his taste too bright. "They say it's this way almost everywhere in Europe," he said. "Only Switzerland is supposed to be still full of light at night. They keep the lights burning there so that fliers will see it's a neutral country. A man who was in France and Italy with his squadron told me that. He said Switzerland was like an island of light—of light and peace, for one means the other. Beyond it and around it as though covered by endless funeral palls lie the dark countries, Germany, France, Italy, the Balkans, Austria, and the rest that are at war."

"Light was given to us and it made human beings of us," Elisabeth said vehemently. "But we have murdered it and become cave men again."

Did it make human beings of us? Graeber wondered. That seemed to him exaggerated. But maybe Elisabeth was right. Animals had no light. No light and no fire. And no bombs.

They were standing in Marienstrasse. Suddenly Graeber saw that Elisabeth was weeping. "Don't look at me," she said. "I ought not to have anything to drink. I just can't drink. I'm not sad. It's only that all at once everything seems to come loose."

"Let it be as loose as it likes and don't bother about it. I'm feeling that way too. It's all part of it."

"Of what?"

"Of what we were talking about before. Of turning around and looking in the other direction. But tomorrow evening we're not going to run about in the streets. We are going somewhere where there's as much light as this city has to offer. I'll find out about that."

"You can find gayer company for that than mine."

"I don't need gay company."

"What then?"

"No gay company. I couldn't stand it. Nor the other sort either—the compassionate kind. I get enough of that during the day. The false and the true. You must have known that yourself."

Elisabeth was no longer weeping. "Yes," she said, "I've known that myself."

"With us it's different. We don't have to make any pretenses. That's a lot in itself. And tomorrow evening we're going to the brightest spot in town and we're going to dine and drink wine and for one evening forget this whole damnable existence!"

She looked at him. "Is that part of it?"

"Yes, that's part of it. Put on the brightest dress you have."

"All right. Come at eight."

He suddenly felt her hair on his face and then her lips. It was swift as a breeze and she had disappeared into the house before he fully knew what it was.

He felt for the bottle in his pocket. It was empty. He put it down in front of the house next door. One more day gone, he thought. It's a good thing Reuter and Feldmann can't see me now! What wouldn't they say!

# Chapter Twelve

"ALL RIGHT, all right, comrades, I admit it," Boettcher said. "I slept with the proprietress. What else could I do? I had to do something! What's the use otherwise of having a furlough? After all, I don't want to go back to the front like a calf."

He was sitting beside Feldmann's bed, in one hand his mess-kit cover full of coffee, his feet in a pail of cold water. He had raised blisters on them after wrecking the bicycle. "And you?" he asked Graeber. "What did you do today? Were you out this morning?"

"No."

"No?"

"He was in the sack," Feldmann said. "Till noon. No row could raise him. It's the first time he's shown some sense."

Boettcher withdrew his feet from the water and examined the soles. They were covered with large white blisters. "Just look at that! I'm a big, powerful fellow—but I have feet as sensitive as an infant's. It's been that way all my life. They won't harden up. I've tried everything. And I've got to start off again on these."

"Why? You can take it easy now," Feldmann said. "You've got the proprietress."

"Oh, the proprietress, man! That hasn't anything to do with it. Besides, it was a big disappointment."

"The first time is always a disappointment after you come back from the front. Everyone knows that."

"That's not what I mean. It went off all right; but she was not the right one."

"You can't expect everything all at once. The woman has to adjust herself."

"You still don't understand me. She was very good, but our souls didn't meet. Just listen. There we are in bed, the affair is in progress and all at once I forget myself in the heat of the engagement and call her Alma. But her name is Luise. Alma is my wife's name, you see—"

"I see."

"It was a catastrophe, comrade."

"It serves you right," one of the card players at the table said suddenly and sharply to Boettcher. "That's the proper punishment for adultery, you pig. I hope she threw you right out with drums and trumpets!"

"Adultery?" Boettcher let go of his feet. "Who's talking about adultery?"

"You! The whole time! Or are you an idiot as well?"

The card player was a little egg-headed man. He stared at Boettcher with hatred. Boettcher was highly indignant. "Did anyone ever hear such drivel?" he asked, looking around. "The only one who has said anything about adultery is you! It would be adultery, you fool, if my wife had been here and then I had slept with somebody else. But she isn't here. That's exactly the whole trouble! How can it be adultery? After all, if she were here I wouldn't sleep with the proprietress!"

"Don't pay any attention to Egghead," Feldmann said. "He's just envious. What did she do then, after you called her Luise?"

"Luise? Not Luise! Luise is her right name. I called her Alma."

"All right, Alma. And then?"

"And then? You wouldn't think it possible, comrade. Instead of laughing or raising a row she began to howl. Tears like a crocodile, imagine that! Big women oughtn't to cry—"

Reuter coughed, closed his book and looked at Boettcher with interest. "Why not?"

"It isn't becoming to them. Doesn't go well with their bulk. Big women ought to laugh!"

"Would your Alma have laughed if you had called her Luise?" the egg-headed card player asked poisonously.

"If my Alma had been there," Boettcher announced calmly and with immense authority, "first of all I'd have got the nearest beer bottle in my mug. After that everything that wasn't bolted down. And finally when I came to again she would have taken care of me so that only my shoes were left. That's the way it would have been with my Alma, you camel!"

Egghead was silent for a while. The picture seemed to have overwhelmed him. "And you betrayed a woman like that?" he finally asked hoarsely.

"But man, I didn't betray her at all! If she were here I wouldn't so much as look at the proprietress. Something like that isn't betrayal! It's simple self-preservation."

Reuter turned to Graeber. "And you? What did you achieve last night with your bottle of armagnac?"

"Nothing."

"Nothing?" Feldmann asked. "And that's why you slept till noon like a dead man?"

"Yes. The devil only knows why I'm suddenly so tired. I could go right to sleep again. It's as if I hadn't shut my eyes for a week."

"Then lie down and go to sleep again."

"Wise advice," Reuter said. "The advice of the master sleeper Feldmann."

"Feldmann is a donkey," the egghead declared. "He's sleeping away his whole leave. Then it will be exactly as though he hadn't had one at all. He could just as well have gone to sleep at the front and only dreamed his leave."

"That's what you think, brother. Just the opposite is true. I sleep here, and when I am dreaming I dream that I'm at the front."

"And where are you actually?" Reuter asked.

"What? Here, of course."

"Are you sure?"

The egghead bleated. "That's what I mean," he said. "It makes no difference where he is if he's always in the sack. The ox just doesn't know that."

"It does make a difference if I wake up, you wiseacre," Feldmann declared, suddenly irritated, and lay back.

Reuter turned back to Graeber. "And you, what do you intend to do for your immortal soul today?"

"Tell me where to go if you want a good dinner."

"Alone?"

"No."

"Then go to the Germania. It's the only place. The only trouble is that they may not let you in. Not in your front-line outfit. It's a hotel for officers. The restaurant too. However, the waiter may respect your hardware."

Graeber looked down at himself. His uniform was patched and very shabby. "Couldn't you lend me your tunic?"

"Glad to. You're only thirty pounds lighter than I am. They wouldn't let you get past the door. But I can borrow a corporal's dress uniform in your size, trousers too. If you put your coat on over it no one here in the barracks will notice. By the way, why are you still a doughfoot? You should have been a lieutenant long ago."

"I was a corporal once. Then I beat up a lieutenant and was broken for it. Luckily they didn't send me to a disciplinary company. But after that it was all up with promotion."

"Good. Then you even have a moral right to the corporal's uniform. If you take your lady to the Germania the wine to order is Johannisberger Kochsberg 1937, from the cellars of G. H. von Mumm. It's a wine that can raise the dead."

"Good. That's what I need."

It had grown foggy. Graeber was standing on the bridge over the river. The water was full of refuse, and crawled black and sluggish among the rafters and kitchenware. Opposite, the silhouette of the school rose darkly out of the white mist. He stared over at it for a while; then he went on across the bridge and along a little alley that led to the schoolyard. The big iron gate, dripping with moisture, stood wide open. He went in. The schoolyard was empty. There was no one there; it was too late for classes. He walked across the yard to the edge of the river. The trunks of the chestnut trees stood in the fog as dark as though made of coal. Under them were the damp benches. Graeber remembered sitting there often. None of the things he had dreamed of at that time had come true. He had gone from school to the war.

For a time he stared at the river. A broken bedstead had been swept ashore. On it the white pillows lay like fat sponges. He shivered. Then he went back and stopped in front of the school building. He tried the front door. It was unlocked. He opened it and went in hesitantly. In the entrance hall he stopped and looked around. There was an oppressive school smell and he saw the half-darkened stairway and the dark painted doors that led to the assembly hall and the classrooms. He felt nothing. Not even contempt or irony. He thought of Wellmann. "One must not go back," he had said. He had been right. Graeber felt nothing but emptiness. All the experience he had gained since his school years contradicted what he had learned here. Nothing had remained. It was bankruptcy.

He turned around and went out. At either side of the entrance he saw memorial plaques for the dead. He remembered the one on the right; it was for those who had fallen in the First World War. It had always been decorated with spruce greens and oak leaves for Party celebrations, and Schimmel, the principal, had made glowing orations in front of it about revenge, Greater Germany, and the retribution to come. Schimmel had had a fat, soft belly and always sweated a great deal. The plaque on the left was new. Graeber had never seen it. It was for those fallen in the present war. He read the names. There were many of them; but the plaque was large, and next to it there was space for another one.

Outside in the schoolyard he met the beadle. "Are you looking for something?" the old man asked.

"No. I'm not looking for anything."

Graeber walked on. Then an idea occurred to him. He went back. "Do you know where Pohlmann lives?" he asked. "Herr Pohlmann who used to teach here."

"Herr Pohlmann is no longer employed here."

"I know that. Where does he live?"

The beadle glanced around. "There's no one around to overhear us," Graeber said. "Where does he live?"

"He used to live at Jahnplatz Six. I don't know whether he still lives there. Were you a pupil here?"

"Yes. Is Schimmel still here, the principal?"

"Of course," the beadle replied in astonishment. "Of course, he's still here. Why shouldn't he still be here?"

"Yes," Graeber said. "Why not?"

He walked on. After a quarter of an hour he realized that he no longer knew where he was. The fog had grown heavier and he had lost his way among the ruins. They all looked alike and the streets could no longer be told apart. It was a strange feeling: as though he had lost his way inside himself.

It took him a while to find Hakenstrasse. A wind had suddenly sprung up and the fog began to heave and roll like a noiseless, ghostly sea.

He went to his parents' house. He found no message there and was about to go on when he heard a curious resonant note. It was like the sound of a harp. He looked around. The street was empty as far as he could see. The sound came again, higher now, plaintive and diminishing, as though an invisible buoy were ringing out its warning in the sea of fog. It was repeated, deeper, then higher, irregularly and yet at almost uniform intervals, and it seemed to come out of the air as though someone on the roof were playing a harp.

Graeber listened. Then he tried to follow the notes but he could not determine their direction. They seemed to be everywhere and to come from everywhere, strong and challenging, now singly and now like an arpeggio, an unresolved chord of inconsolable grief.

The air raid warden, he thought. The mad man—who else? He went to the house where only the façade was standing and jerked open the door. A figure inside sprang up out of an easy chair. Graeber saw it was the green chair that had been standing in the ruins of his parents' house. "What's the matter?" the air raid warden asked sharply in alarm.

Graeber saw he had nothing in his hands. The notes went on resounding. "What's that?" he asked. "Where does it come from?"

The warden brought his damp face close to Graeber's. "Ah, the soldier! The defender of the fatherland! What is that? Don't you hear it? That is the requiem for those who are buried. The cry for help. Dig them out! Dig them out! Cease this murdering!"

"Nonsense!" Graeber stared upward through the rising fog. He saw something like a dark cable swinging in the wind and every time it swung back he heard the mysterious gong-like note. All at once he remembered the piano with the top missing that he had seen hanging high among the ruins. The cable was striking against the exposed wires. "It's the piano," he said.

"It's the piano! It's the piano!" the warden mimicked him. "What do you understand about it, you unconscionable murderer! It's the funeral bell and the wind rings it. It is Heaven calling for mercy, for mercy, you rifle-shooting automaton, for that mercy which no longer exists on earth! What do you know about death, you vandal! And what could you know? Those who cause it never know anything about it!" He stooped over. "The dead are everywhere," he whispered. "They lie under the ruins with their trodden faces and outstretched arms, they lie there but they will arise and they will hunt all of you down—"

Graeber stepped back into the street. "Hunt you down," whispered the warden behind him. "They will accuse you and judgment will be exacted for every single one of them—"

Graeber could no longer see him. He only heard the hoarse voice issuing from the eddying wisps of fog. "For whatever ye have done unto the least of these my brethren that have ye done unto me, saith the Lord—"

He walked on. "Go to hell," he muttered. "Go to hell and bury yourself under those ruins you perch on like a bird of death." Death, he thought bitterly. Death, death! I've had enough of death! Why did I come back? Wasn't it to feel that somewhere in this wilderness there is life too?

He rang. The door opened at once as though someone had been standing right behind it. "Oh, it's you—" said Frau Lieser, taken aback.

"Yes, me," Graeber replied. He had expected Elisabeth.

Just then she came out of her room. This time Frau Lieser withdrew without a word. "Come in, Ernst," Elisabeth said. "I'll be ready right away."

He followed her. "Is that your brightest dress?" he asked, looking at the black sweater and dark skirt she was wearing. "Have you forgotten we're going out tonight?"

"Did you really mean it?"

"Of course. Just look at me! This is a dress uniform belonging to a corporal. A friend of mine borrowed it for me. I've become an impostor so that I can take you to the Hotel Germania—and it's still a question whether anyone lower than a lieutenant can get in. That depends on you. Haven't you another dress?"

"Yes. But—"

Graeber saw Binding's vodka on the table. "I know what you're thinking," he said. "Forget it! And forget Frau Lieser and the neighbors. You're not hurting anyone; that's the one thing that counts. And you have to get out of here sometime; otherwise you'll go crazy. Here, have a drink of vodka."

He filled a glass and handed it to her. She emptied it. "All right," she said. "I won't take long. I was already half prepared, but I didn't know whether you'd remember. Only you've got to get out of the room while I change. I don't want to be denounced by Frau Lieser for prostitution."

"She wouldn't get away with it in this case. With soldiers that counts as patriotism. But I'll wait for you outside. On the street, not in the vestibule."

He walked up and down on the street. The fog had grown thinner but it still eddied between the walls of the houses like steam in a laundry. Suddenly a window clattered open above him. Elisabeth leaned out, bare-shouldered in a frame of light, holding two dresses in her hands. One was golden and the other nondescript and darker. They fluttered like flags in the wind. "Which?" she asked.

He pointed to the golden one. She nodded and closed the window. Graeber looked around. The street was still empty and dark. No one noticed the violation of the blackout. He walked up and down again. But the night suddenly seemed to have become vaster and fuller. The weariness of the day, the strange mood of the evening and his determination to turn away from the past had slowly transformed themselves into a mild excitement that now all at once turned into impatient expectation.

Elisabeth came through the door. She came quickly and she was slender and supple and seemed taller than before in the long, golden dress which glittered in the faint light. Her face, too, had changed. It was thinner and her head seemed smaller, and it took Graeber a moment to realize that this was because she was wearing a low-necked dress. "Did Frau Lieser see you?" he asked.

"Yes. She was speechless. She is convinced that I ought constantly to do penance in sackcloth and ashes. For a minute I had a bad conscience."

"It's always the wrong people who have a bad conscience."

"It's not just a bad conscience. It's fear as well. Do you think—"

"No," Graeber replied. "I don't think anything. And tonight we're not going to do any more thinking either. We've thought enough for a while and it's made us edgy enough, too. Now we're going to see for once whether we can't just have a good time—"

The Hotel Germania stood between two wrecked houses like a rich woman between needy relatives. The rubble had been neatly piled up on either side, and as a result the two ruins no longer seemed wild and haunted by death; they had already been made orderly and almost respectable.

The doorman examined Graeber's uniform with an appraising glance. "Where is the wine room?" Graeber asked sharply before he could say anything.

"To the rear at the right of the hall, sir. Please ask for Fritz, the headwaiter."

They walked along the corridor. A major and two captains passed them. Graeber saluted. "They say it's crawling with generals here," he said. "A couple of military commissions have their offices on the second floor."

Elisabeth stopped. "Then aren't you being very reckless? Suppose someone noticed your uniform?"

"What would they notice? It's not hard to behave like a corporal. I used to be one myself."

A lieutenant colonel accompanied by a small thin woman strode by, spurs ringing. He looked straight over Graeber's head. "What will happen to you if they find out?" Elisabeth asked.

"Nothing serious."

"Could they shoot you?"

Graeber laughed. "I don't believe they would do that, Elisabeth. They need us too much at the front."

"What else might happen to you?"

"Nothing much. At most a couple of weeks' arrest. That would be a couple of weeks of rest. Almost like a furlough. When you have to be back at the front in about two weeks there's not much that can scare you."

Headwaiter Fritz emerged from the passage at the right. Graeber slipped a bill into his hand. Fritz allowed it to disappear and made no difficulties. "The wine room, for dinner, of course," he said and solemnly led the way.

He seated them at a table hidden behind a pillar and departed with dignity. Graeber glanced around. "Just what I wanted. I need some time to accustom myself to this. And you?" He looked at Elisabeth. "You certainly don't," he said in surprise. "You look as though you came here every day."

A little old waiter who looked like a marabou appeared. He brought them the menu. Graeber took it, placed a bill inside and handed it back to the marabou. "We'd like to have something that's not on the menu. What have you?"

The marabou looked at him expressionlessly. "We have nothing except what is on the menu."

"All right. Then for the time being bring us a bottle of Johannisberger Kochsberg 1937, G. H. von Mumm, not too cold."

The marabou's eyes lit up. "Very good, sir," he said with sudden respect. Then he bent over. "We happen to have some Ostend sole on hand. Absolutely fresh. With it perhaps a Belgian salad and a few parsley potatoes?"

"Good. And what have you for hors d'oeuvres? No caviar, of course, with the wine."

The marabou became even more animated. "Of course not. But we still have a little Strasbourg goose liver, truffled—"

Graeber nodded.

"And afterwards I recommend a piece of Dutch cheese. It will bring out the bloom of the wine completely."

"Excellent."

The marabou disappeared in excitement. He might at first have taken Graeber for a soldier who had wandered in by chance; now he saw in him a connoisseur who was by chance a soldier.

Elisabeth had listened in amazement. "Ernst," she said, "where did you find out all that?"

"From my friend Reuter. This morning I didn't know any of it. He's such a great connoisseur that he has the gout. That, however, has rescued him from the front. Thus, as always, sin pays."

"But the trick with the tip and the menu?"

"All from Reuter. He knows his way around here. How to behave like a man of the world—he taught me that, too."

Elisabeth laughed suddenly. It was a warm, free and tender laugh. "God knows this isn't how I remember you," she said.

"Nor I you, the way you are now." He looked at her. He had never seen her like this before. She changed completely when she laughed. It was as though all the windows in a dark house had suddenly opened. "That's a very beautiful dress," he said, a little embarrassed.

"It's one of my mother's. I made it over last night."

"Do you mean you can sew? You don't look as if you could."

"I couldn't, either, until some time ago, but I have learned. Now I sew Army overcoats eight hours a day."

"Really? Were you snapped up by the labor service?"

"Yes. I had to join. And I wanted to, too. I thought perhaps it would help my father."

Graeber looked at her and shook his head. "It doesn't suit you. Not any more than your first name. How did you happen to get that?"

"My mother picked it out. She came from southern Austria and looked Italian, and she hoped I would be a blonde with blue eyes—and I was to be called Elisabeth. Then she called me that anyway in spite of her disappointment."

The marabou came with the wine. He held the bottle as though it were a jewel and he poured carefully. "I have brought you very thin, plain crystal glasses," he said. "It's the best way to see the color. Or would you prefer goblets?"

"No. Thin, clear glasses."

The marabou nodded and uncovered a silver platter. The rosy slices of black-truffled goose liver lay surrounded by a circle of quivering aspic. "Fresh from Alsace," he announced proudly.

Elisabeth laughed. "What luxury!"

"Luxury!" Graeber raised his glass. "Luxury," he repeated. "That's it! We'll drink to that, Elisabeth. For two long years I've eaten out of a tin mess kit and was never quite sure whether I could finish my meal—so this is not simply luxury. It is much more. It is peace and security and joy and festivity—it is everything that is lacking out there."

He drank and felt the wine and looked at Elisabeth and she was part of it. It was always the unexpected, he suddenly realized, the thing that transcended need, the unnecessary, apparently useless that produced lightness and elation, and this was so because these qualities belonged to the other side of existence, to the brighter side, to play and superfluity and dreams. After his years close to death the wine was now not just wine, the silver not just silver, and the music that stole into the room from somewhere not just music—they were all symbols of that other life, the life without death and destruction, the life for life's sake that had already become almost a myth and a hopeless dream.

"Sometimes one completely forgets that one's alive," he said. "I found that out today."

Elisabeth laughed. "I've known that all the time. But I could never put it to any use."

The marabou approached. "How is the wine, sir?"

"It must be good. Otherwise I wouldn't suddenly be thinking of things I haven't thought of in a long time."

"That's the sun, sir. The sun that ripened it in the autumn. It shines out of it again. In the Rhineland they call a wine like this a monstrance."

"A monstrance?"

"Yes. It is full-bodied and like gold and it shines in all directions."

"So it does."

"You feel it with the first glass, don't you? Filtered sunshine!"

"Even at the first sip! It doesn't go into the stomach. It goes straight behind the eyes and changes the world."

"You understand about wine, sir." The marabou bent toward him confidentially. "Over there at that table to the right they have the same wine. There where the two troop leaders are sitting. Those persons pour it down as though it were water. They ought to be drinking Liebfraumilch!"

"This seems to be a good day for impostors, Elisabeth," Graeber said. "How's the wine for you? A monstrance too?"

She leaned back and stretched her shoulders. "I feel like someone who has escaped from prison. And like someone who will soon be locked up again for swindling."

He laughed. "That's how we are! Afraid of our feelings. And when we become aware of them we immediately think we are swindlers."

The marabou brought the sole and the salad. Graeber watched him as he served. He felt completely relaxed and seemed to himself like someone who has ventured out on thin ice and to his amazement finds that it holds. He knew it was thin and perhaps would not hold for long, but it was holding now and that was enough.

"There's one good thing about having lain in the dirt so long," he said. "Everything is as new and exciting as though you were seeing it for the first time. Everything—even a glass and a white tablecloth."

The marabou held up the bottle. He was now like a mother. "In general, Moselle is served with fish," he explained. "But sole is different. It has an almost nutty flavor. With it a wine from the Rhinegau is a revelation, don't you think?"

"Absolutely."

The marabou nodded and disappeared.

"Ernst," Elisabeth said, "can we pay for all this, too? It's sure to be frightfully expensive."

"We can pay for it. I have two years' combat pay with me. And it doesn't need to last long." Graeber laughed. "Only for a short life, Elisabeth. Two weeks. It will do all right for that."

They were standing in front of the door to the house. The wind had dropped and it had grown foggy again. "When do you have to go back?" Elisabeth asked. "In two weeks?"

"Just about."

"That's soon."

"It's soon and at the same time it's a long way off. That changes from moment to moment. Time in war is different from time in peace. I'm sure you know that too. It's just as much the front here as out there."

"It isn't the same."

"Yes, it is. And this evening was my first real day of leave. God bless the marabou and Reuter and your golden dress and the wine."

"And us," Elisabeth said. "We could use it."

She stood in front of him. The mist hung in her hair and the pale light glittered on it. It glittered on her dress and the mist

made her face damp as a fruit. It seemed suddenly hard for Graeber to leave all this, the web of tenderness, relaxation, quietude,
and excitement that had woven itself so unexpectedly over the
evening, and go back to the stink and the jokes of the barracks,
into the desolation of waiting and brooding over the future.

A sharp voice cut through the stillness. "Have you no eyes in
your head, corporal?"

A little fat major with a bushy white mustache was standing in
front of them. He must have come up on rubber soles. Graeber saw
at once that he was a superannuated war horse from the reserves
who had been got out of mothballs and was now pulling his rank.
He would have liked to pick the old man up and give him a thorough shaking but he could not risk it. He acted as an experienced
soldier should; he said nothing and stood at attention.

The old man let his flashlight wander over him. For some reason Graeber found this especially insulting: "Dress uniform!"
barked the old man. "You must have an armchair job to be able to
afford something like that! A home-front warrior in a dress uniform! That certainly is something! Why aren't you at the front?"

Graeber made no reply. He had forgotten to take his service
ribbons from his old tunic and put them on the borrowed one.

"Necking and petting, that's all you're good for, eh?" barked
the major.

Elisabeth moved suddenly. The circle of the flashlight hit her
face. She looked at the old man and stepped out of the beam
toward him. The major cleared his throat, threw an oblique
glance at her and went off.

"I'd had just about enough of him," she said.

Graeber shrugged his shoulders. "You can't do anything about
these old goats. They wander around the streets so that people
will have to salute them. That's their life. To think that nature

has labored for a couple of million years to produce something like that in the end."

Elisabeth laughed. "Why *aren't* you at the front?"

Graeber grinned. "That's what I get for cheating with this dress uniform. Tomorrow I'll put on civilian clothes. I know where I can borrow some. I've had enough of saluting. Then we can sit in peace tomorrow in the Germania."

"Do you want to go there again?"

"Yes, Elisabeth. Those are the things you remember later out there. Not the commonplace. I'll come and get you at eight o'clock. And now I'm going. Otherwise that old fool will come by again and ask to see my paybook. Good night."

He drew her to him and she yielded. He felt her in his arms and suddenly everything dissolved; he wanted her and he wanted nothing but her, and he held her close and kissed her and did not want to let her go and let her go.

He went once more to Hakenstrasse. In front of his parents' house he stopped. The moon broke through the mist. He bent down. Then with a sudden jerk he pulled the notice out from between the stones. Something had been written in thick lead pencil on one corner. He reached for his flashlight. "Inquire at Main Post Office. Window Fifteen," he read.

Involuntarily he glanced at his watch. It was much too late; the post office was not open at night and he would not be able to find out anything until eight next morning; but then at last he would know. He folded the notice and put it in his pocket so that he could show it at the post office. Then he walked through the dead-still city to the barracks and it seemed to him that he had no weight and was walking in a vacuum from which he dared not emerge.

# Chapter Thirteen

PART OF THE post office was still standing. The rest had collapsed and burned. There were crowds everywhere. Graeber had to wait for a while. Then he got to Window Fifteen and showed the slip of paper with the message that had been written on it.

The clerk handed the slip back to him. "Have you means of identification?"

Graeber pushed his paybook and his furlough certificate through the grating. The clerk studied them. "What is it?" Graeber asked. "A message?"

The clerk made no reply. He got up and disappeared in the background. Graeber waited, staring at his papers lying open on the counter.

The clerk came back with a small battered package in his hand. Once more he compared the address with the one on Graeber's furlough certificate. Then he pushed the package through the window. "Sign here."

Graeber saw his mother's handwriting on the package. She had sent it to him at the front and it had been forwarded from there. He looked for the sender's address. It was still Hakenstrasse. He took the package and signed the receipt. "Is that all there was?" he asked.

The clerk glanced up. "Do you think we are withholding something?"

"Not that. I thought perhaps you might have gotten my parents' new address."

"We're not responsible for that here. Ask on the second floor in the delivery section."

Graeber went up. The second floor was only half roofed over. Over the remainder one could see the sky with clouds and sun. "We've no new address here," said the woman who sat behind the window. "Otherwise we would not have sent the package to Hakenstrasse. But you can always ask the letter carrier from your district."

"Where is he?"

The woman looked at her watch. "He's on his rounds now. If you come back this afternoon about four he'll be here. That's when the mail is distributed."

"Could he possibly know the address when you don't know it here?"

"Of course not. He only gets the addresses from us. But there are people who like to ask him just the same. It reassures them. That's the way people are. Or aren't they?"

"Yes, probably."

Graeber took his package and went down the stairs. He looked at the date. It had been sent three weeks before and had taken a long time to reach the front but from there it had got back quickly. He stood in a corner and opened the brown paper. A dry cake lay inside, a pair of woolen socks, a package of cigarettes, and a letter from his mother. He read the letter. There was nothing in it about a change of address or about air raids. He put it in his pocket and waited until he was calm again. Then he went out into the street. He told himself that now surely he would soon get a letter with a new address; nevertheless he felt more miserable than he had expected.

He decided to go and see Binding. Perhaps he would have some news.


"Come in, Ernst!" Alfons called. "We're busy emptying a bottle. You can help us."

Binding was not alone. An S.S. man was half lying on the big sofa under the Rubens, as though he had fallen there and could not immediately get up again. He was a thin fellow with a sallow face and hair so extremely blond that he looked as though he had neither eyelashes nor brows. "That is Heini," Alfons said with a certain measure of respect. "Heini, the snake charmer! And this is my friend Ernst, on furlough from Russia."

Heini was fairly drunk. He had very pale eyes and a small mouth. "Russia!" he muttered. "I was there too. Fine times! Better than here!"

Graeber looked at Binding questioningly. "Heini is already one bottle ahead," Alfons explained. "He has trouble. His parents' home was bombed. Nothing happened to the family; they were all in the cellar. But the house is wrecked."

"Four rooms," Heini growled. "All new furniture. The piano, too. Wonderful piano! Beautiful tone. Those swine!"

"Heini will get even for that piano," Alfons said. "Come, Ernst, what will you have to drink? Heini's drinking cognac. There's vodka and kuemmel here too, or anything else you want."

"Nothing at all. I just stopped in for a moment to ask whether you've found out anything."

"Nothing new yet, Ernst. Your parents are no longer in this district. At least they have not been reported anywhere. Nor in the villages. Either they have moved away and haven't reported yet or they've been sent on with the other evacuees. You know how it is nowadays. The whole country is being bombed by those swine. And so it takes a while for communications to be restored. Come along, have something to drink. You can risk one glass, can't you?"

"All right, some vodka."

"Vodka," Heini muttered. "We swilled it in rivers! And then poured it down the beasts' throats and lit it. Made flame-throwers out of them. Children, how they hopped around! You'd die laughing! Fine times then in Russia—"

"What?" Graeber asked.

Heini did not reply. He was staring glassily straight ahead. "Flame-throwers," he muttered. "Magnificent idea."

"What's he talking about?" Graeber asked Binding.

Alfons shrugged his shoulders. "Heini had a hand in all sorts of things. He was with the S.D."

"With the S.D. in Russia?"

"Yes. Have another drink, Ernst."

Graeber picked up the bottle from the copper smoking stand and looked at it. The clear liquor swished back and forth. "What proof is vodka?"

Alfons laughed. "It's pretty strong. Sure to be a hundred and twenty proof. The Ivans can take it strong."

They can take it strong, Graeber thought. And if it's as strong as that then it will burn if someone pours it down your throat and lights it. He looked at Heini. He had heard enough stories about the Security Service of the S.S. to know that what Heini was saying in his drunkenness was no exaggeration. The S.D., under pretext of providing *Lebensraum* for the German people, carried on liquidations in the grand style and by the thousands. They liquidated everything they considered undesirable and to keep the mass killings from becoming monotonous, the S.S. invented humorous variations. Graeber knew about some of them; others had been told him by Steinbrenner. Living flame-throwers were new.

"Why are you staring at the bottle?" Alfons asked. "It won't bite you. Fill your glass."

Graeber put the bottle back. He wanted to get up and go away but he remained seated. He forced himself to remain seated. He had gone away often enough and refused to know. He and a hundred thousand others. And they had thought in that way they could quiet their consciences. He no longer wanted that. He no longer wanted to evade. He had not come back on furlough for that purpose.

"Won't you change your mind and have one more?" Alfons asked.

Graeber looked at Heini who was half asleep. "Is he still with the S.D.?"

"No longer. He's here now."

"Where?"

"He's a commander in the concentration camp."

"The concentration camp?"

"Yes. Have another swallow, Ernst! We'll not be as young when we meet again! And stay a while longer. Don't always run off right away!"

"No," Graeber said, continuing to stare at Heini. "I'll not run off any more."

"At last you're talking sense. What will you have to drink? Another vodka?"

"No, give me kuemmel or cognac. No vodka."

Heini roused himself. "Of course no vodka," he mumbled.

"Much too wasteful. We lapped up the vodka ourselves. It was gasoline. Gasoline burns better—"

Heini was vomiting in the bathroom. Alfons was standing with Graeber in front of the door. The sky was filled with fleecy white clouds. In the birch trees a blackbird was singing, a little black ball with a yellow beak in whose voice was all of spring. "Mad fellow, that Heini, eh?" Alfons said.

He said it like a boy talking about a bloodthirsty Indian chief—with a mixture of horror and admiration.

"He's a mad fellow with people who can't defend themselves," Graeber replied.

"He has a stiff arm, Ernst. That's why he can't be in the regular army. Got it in a beer hall brawl with the Communists in 1932. It's what makes him so wild, too. Man, that was quite a story about the pyre of wood, wasn't it?" Alfons puffed at a dead cigar he had lighted while Heini was recounting his further Russian exploits. In his excitement he had let it go out. "First a layer of wood and then a layer of people, and each layer having to haul its own wood and then lie down on it and be shot in the back of the head—that's something, eh?"

"Yes, that's something."

"And the women! Can you imagine what went on with them!"

"Yes, well enough. Would you like to have been there?"

"With the women?"

"No, with the others. At the burning pyre and the Christmas trees covered with hanged men and the mass machine-gunnings."

Binding reflected for a moment. Then he shook his head. "I don't think so. Perhaps once, just to have seen it. Otherwise I'm not the type for it. Too romantic, Ernst."

Heini appeared in the doorway. He was very pale. "Duty!" he growled. "Late already! Time to get going! I'll twist the swines' snouts for this."

He stamped down the garden path. At the gate he straightened his cap, threw back his shoulders and strode on like a stork.

"I wouldn't like to be the next prisoner to fall into his hands," Alfons said.

Graeber glanced up. He had been thinking the same thing. "Do you think that's right, Alfons?" he asked.

Binding shrugged his shoulders. "They're all traitors to the nation, Ernst. They're not there for nothing."

"Was Burmeister a traitor to the nation?"

Alfons laughed. "That was a private matter. Besides, nothing much happened to him."

"And if something had happened to him?"

"Then that would have been his bad luck, Ernst. Lots of people have had bad luck these days. From bombs, for example. Five thousand in this city alone. Better people than those in the concentration camp. So what does it matter to me what happens there? It's not my responsibility. Nor yours."

A couple of sparrows flew twittering to the bird bath in the middle of the lawn. One of them waded in and began to beat his wings, and all at once they were all in the bath splashing about. Alfons was watching them intently. He seemed to have forgotten Heini already. Graeber looked at the satisfied, harmless face and, with sudden shock, he realized the eternal hopelessness to which justice and sympathy are condemned: always to suffer shipwreck on egoism and indifference and fear—he realized it and he realized, too, that he himself was not exempt, that he too was caught in it in an anonymous, indirect, and sinister fashion, as though he and Binding somehow belonged together, however much he might struggle against it.

"This business of responsibility isn't as simple as all that, Alfons," he said somberly.

"But, Ernst! Don't be funny! You can only be held responsible for what you yourself do. And then only when you're not acting on orders."

"When we shoot hostages we say exactly the opposite—that they are responsible for what others have done."

"Have you shot hostages?" Binding asked, turning around with interest.

Graeber made no reply.

"Hostages are something else again, Ernst. They are exceptions! Necessary exceptions."

"Everything's a necessary exception," Graeber declared bitterly. "Everything that one does oneself, I mean. Of course not what the others do. When we bomb a city that's a strategic necessity; when the others do it it's a hideous crime."

"That's what it is! At last you're thinking sensibly!" Alfons looked at Graeber and grinned slyly from the side. "That's what's called modern politics. The right is what is useful to the German people, as our Minister of Justice has said. And after all, he must know! We only do our duty. We are not responsible." He bent forward. "There—there's the blackbird. Do you see him? The first time he's taken a bath. How the sparrows clear out!"

Graeber suddenly saw Heini in front of him. The street was empty, between the garden hedges lay dull sunlight, a yellow butterfly floated low over the strips of sand that bordered the cement sidewalk, and about a hundred yards ahead Heini swung around the corner.

Graeber walked on the sand. It was very quiet and his footsteps were inaudible. He looked around. If anyone wanted to get rid of Heini this was the right time. There was no one in sight. The street seemed asleep. You could approach almost noiselessly on the strip of sand. Heini would not notice anything. You could strike him down and strangle him or stab him. A shot would make too much noise and attract people too quickly. Heini was not very powerful; you could strangle him.

Graeber noticed that he was walking faster. Alfons would not suspect him, he thought. He would believe that someone had taken revenge on Heini. There were certainly plenty of grounds for that. It was a splendid opportunity for someone to take revenge. And it was an opportunity, too, to rid the world of a murderer who in an hour's time would in all likelihood be torturing to death some terrified, defenseless human being.

Graeber felt his hands sweating. Suddenly he was very hot. He came to the corner and saw that he had gained about thirty yards on Heini. There was still no one in sight. If he ran quickly along the strip of sand everything could be over in less than a minute. He could stab Heini and run on instantly.

All at once his heart was beating like a hammer. It seemed to beat so loud that for a moment he feared Heini might hear it. What's the matter with me? he thought. What concern is this of mine? How have I got involved in it? The idea that a moment before had been fortuitous had now suddenly transformed itself into a dark compulsion. It seemed to fill up all his mind. It was as though he had to do it, as though everything depended on his doing it; as though it were a justification for many things in the past, for his own life, for things in it that he wanted to forget and for things he had done and things he had left undone. Vengeance, he thought in confusion, but it was someone he hardly knew, someone who had done nothing to him! Nor did he have any cause for vengeance! Not yet, he thought, but was it not possible that Elisabeth's father was al-

ready among Heini's victims, or might he not belong to their
number today, or tomorrow, and whom had the hostages
harmed or the countless innocents, and where was the guilt for
that and where the atonement?

He stared at Heini's back. His mouth was dry. A dog barked
from a garden gate. He started and looked around. I've had too
much to drink, he thought, I must stop, all this has nothing to
do with me, it's crazy—but he went on faster, silently, driven by
something incomprehensible, something that seemed a compen-
sation and a justification for all the death that lay behind him.

He had approached within twenty yards without knowing
what he was going to do. Then at the end of the street he saw a
woman coming out of an opening in the hedge. She was wearing
an orange blouse and carrying a basket and she was coming
toward him. He went slack. Everything in him relaxed. He almost stopped and then went on very slowly. The woman swung
her basket and walked at an easy pace past Heini and toward
Graeber. She advanced with quiet strides; she had strong, broad
breasts, a broad, tanned face and smooth, dark hair parted in the
middle. The sky behind her head was pale, flickering, and un-
clear, she alone was clear, everything else swam together, she
alone was real, she was life, she bore it on her broad shoulders,
she brought it with her and it was great and good, and behind
her were wilderness and murder.

She looked at him as she passed. "Good day," she said in a
friendly tone.

Graeber nodded. He could not speak. He heard her steps behind him and the wilderness was there again, flickering, and
amid the flickering he saw Heini's dark figure move around the
next corner, and the street was free.

He looked around. The woman was walking on, calm and unconcerned. Why don't I run? he thought. I still have time to do

it. But he already knew he would not do it. Something had broken. I can't do it now, he thought, the woman saw me, she would recognize me again. But would he have done it if the woman had not come? Would he not have found some other excuse? He did not know.

He came to the crossing where Heini had turned. Heini was not in sight. He saw him again at the next corner. He was standing in the middle of the street. An S.S. man was talking to him and then walked on with him. A mail man was coming out of a gateway. A little farther on two men with bicycles stood talking together. It was past. Graeber felt as if he had suddenly awakened. He looked around. What had that been? he thought. Damn it, I was close to doing it! How did it happen? What's the matter with me? What was it that suddenly burst out of me? He walked on. I must keep watch on myself, he thought. I believed I was calm. I am not calm. I am more confused than I realize. I must keep watch on myself or I'll commit some damn foolishness!

At a newsstand he bought a paper and stood there reading the war news. He had not done this until now. He had not wanted to be reminded of it. Now he read and he saw that the retreat had continued. On the small inset map he found the approximate place where his regiment must be. He could not determine it exactly. The war news only reported army groups; but he could estimate that they had retreated about a hundred kilometers farther.

He stood very still for a while. For the whole time that he had been on leave he had not once thought of his comrades. Memory had fallen from him like a stone. Now it came back.

It seemed to him as though a gray loneliness rose from the ground. It was noiseless. The war news had reported heavy fighting in Graeber's section; but the gray loneliness was noiseless and colorless as though the light and even the protest of battle had long since died in it. Shadows arose, bloodless and empty, they moved and looked at him and through him and when they fell they were like the gray, uptorn ground and the ground was like them, as though it were moving and growing into them. The high gleaming sky above him seemed for a moment to lose its color before the gray smoke of this endless dying, which seemed to rise up out of the earth and throw an overcast across the sun. Betrayed, he thought bitterly; they have been betrayed, betrayed and befouled, their fighting and their dying have been coupled with murder and injustice and lies and might; they have been defrauded, defrauded of everything, even of their miserable, courageous, pitiful, and useless deaths.

A woman carrying a bag in front of her collided with him. "Can't you use your eyes?" she snapped irritably.

"I can," Graeber said without moving.

"Then why don't you get out of my way?"

Graeber did not answer. He suddenly knew why he had followed Heini. It was the darkness that he had so often felt in the field, the question he had never dared to answer, the pressing despair he had evaded again and again; it had finally caught up with him and brought him to bay, and he knew now what it was and he no longer wanted to evade it. He wanted clarity. He was ready for it. Pohlmann, he thought. Fresenburg wanted me to go and see him. I had forgotten. I will go and talk to him. I have to talk to someone I can trust.

"Blockhead!" said the heavily laden woman and dragged herself on.


Half of the Jahnplatz had been destroyed; the other half stood undamaged. Only a few of the windows were broken. The daily round went on there, with women cleaning and cooking, while, opposite, the house fronts had collapsed, revealing only fragmentary rooms where torn carpets hung down like slashed flags after a lost battle.

The house where Pohlmann had lived was on the ruined side. The upper floors had fallen in, burying the entrance. It looked as though no one could still be living there. Graeber was on the point of giving up when he discovered beside the house a narrow, trodden path through the rubble. He followed it and found a passage shoveled out to the undamaged back door. He knocked. No one answered. He knocked again. After a while he heard sounds. A chain rattled and the door was cautiously opened.

"Herr Pohlmann," Graeber said.

An old man peered out. "Yes. What do you want?"

"I am Ernst Graeber. A former pupil of yours."

"Ah, yes. And what would you like?"

"To call on you. I am here on furlough."

"I no longer hold a teaching post," Pohlmann said shortly.

"I know that."

"All right. Then you know too that I was dismissed for disciplinary reasons. I no longer receive students and, in point of fact, do not have the right to do so."

"I am no longer a student; I am a soldier and I have come from Russia and I bring you greetings from Fresenburg. He told me to come and see you."

The old man regarded Graeber more attentively. "Fresenburg? Is he still alive?"

"Ten days ago he was still alive."

Pohlmann continued to regard Graeber for a moment. "All right, come in," he said then, stepping back.

Graeber followed him. They went along a corridor that led to a kind of kitchen and from there through a second short passage. Pohlmann suddenly walked faster, opened a door and said much louder than before: "Come in here. I thought at first you were from the police."

Graeber looked at him in surprise. Then he understood. He did not look around. Probably Pohlmann had spoken so loud in order to reassure someone.

The room was lighted by a small oil lamp with a green shade. The windows were broken and outside the rubble was piled so high one could not see out. Pohlmann paused in the middle of the room. "Now I recognize you," he said. "Outside the light was too strong. I don't go out much and I am no longer used to it. Here I have no daylight; only the oil and there's not much of that; as a result I often sit for a long time in the dark. The electric light connections have been broken."

Graeber looked at him. He would not have recognized him, he had grown so old. Then he glanced around, and it seemed to him as though he had come into another world. It was not only the stillness and the unexpected lamplit room that was like a catacomb after the harsh noonday sun; it was something else besides—it was the rows of brown and gold books on the walls, it was the reading desk, it was the steel engravings of Weimar, and it was the old man with the white hair and furrowed face which seemed in its waxen pallor like that of a man who had been imprisoned for years.

Pohlmann noticed Graeber's glance. "I have been fortunate," he said. "I have been able to save almost all my books."

Graeber turned around. "I haven't seen any in a long time. And in the last few years I have read very little."

"Probably you couldn't. Books are too heavy to cart around with you in a knapsack."

"They were also too heavy to cart around with you in your head. They did not go very well with what was happening. And the ones that did go well with it were the ones you didn't want to read."

Pohlmann gazed into the soft green light of the lamp. "Why did you come to see me, Graeber?"

"Fresenburg told me I ought to."

"Do you know him well?"

"He was the only human being out there I trusted completely. He said I should come here and talk to you. You would tell me the truth."

Graeber looked at the old man. It seemed infinitely long ago that he had been in his class; nevertheless, for the span of a heartbeat, he suddenly had the feeling that he was once again a student facing an examination about his life—and as if in this little half-buried room with all the books and the discredited teacher of his youth his fate was now to be decided. Here was embodied the past that had once been—kindness, tolerance, and knowledge—and the rubble outside the windows was what the present had made out of it. "I would like to know how far I am involved in the crimes of the last ten years," he said. "And I would like to know what I ought to do."

Pohlmann stared at him. Then he got up and walked across the room. He took a book from the shelves, opened it, put it back without looking at it. Finally he turned around. "Do you know what you are asking?"

"Yes."

"People are beheaded for less than that nowadays."

"At the front people are killed for nothing," Graeber said.

Pohlmann came back and sat down again. "By crime do you mean the war?"

"I mean everything that led up to it. The lies, the oppression, the injustice, the use of force. And I mean the war. The war and the way we wage it—with slave camps, concentration camps, and the mass murder of civilians."

Pohlmann was silent. "I have seen certain things," Graeber said. "And I have heard a good deal. I know too that the war is lost. And I know that we are only continuing to fight so that the government, the Party, and the people who caused it all can stay in power for a while longer and create still more misery."

Pohlmann stared at Graeber again. "You know all that?" he asked.

"I know it now. I've not always known it."

"And you have to go out again?"

"Yes."

"That's dreadful."

"It's even more dreadful to have to go out again knowing this and thereby perhaps to become an accomplice. Will I be that?"

Pohlmann was silent. "How do you mean?" he asked after a while almost in a whisper.

"You know what I mean. You instructed us in religion. How far shall I be an accomplice if I know not only that the war is lost but also that we have to lose it so that slavery, murder, concentration camps, S.S. and S.D., mass exterminations and inhumanity shall cease—if I know that and in two weeks I have to go out and fight for it again?"

Pohlmann's face was suddenly gray and extinguished. Only his eyes still had color, a strange clear blue. They reminded Graeber of eyes he had seen somewhere before but he did not remember where. "Must you go out again?" Pohlmann asked finally.

"I could refuse. Then I would be hanged or shot. Or I could desert. Then I would pretty certainly be caught in a short time—you can depend for that on the organization and the informers. And where could I hide? Anyone who gave me shelter would be risking death himself. Besides that they would take revenge on my parents. The least would be a concentration camp for them. They would die there. What else can I do? Go back to the front and do nothing to defend myself? That would be suicide."

A clock began to strike. Graeber had not seen it before. It was an old grandfather's clock in a corner behind the door. Its deep note was suddenly a ghostly indication of time in the quiet, buried room.

"And there is nothing besides?" Pohlmann asked.

"There's self-mutilation. It's almost always discovered. The punishment is the same as for desertion."

"Couldn't you be transferred? Back home?"

"No, I am very healthy and strong. And I think, too, it would not do much to answer my question. It would be an escape but hardly a solution. One can be an accomplice in an office too, don't you think?"

"Yes." Pohlmann pressed his hands together. "Guilt," he then said softly. "No one knows where it begins and where it ends. If you like, it begins everywhere and ends nowhere. But perhaps it is just the other way about. And complicity! Who knows about that? Only God."

Graeber made an impatient gesture. "God should indeed know about it," he replied. "Otherwise there would be no original sin. That is complicity extending over thousands of generations. But where does personal responsibility begin? We cannot simply take refuge behind the fact that we were acting on orders. Or can we?"

"It is compulsion. Not just orders."

Graeber waited. "The martyrs in Christian times did not submit to compulsion," Pohlmann said hesitantly.

"We are no martyrs. But where does complicity begin?" Graeber asked. "When does what is ordinarily called heroism become murder? When you no longer believe in the reasons for it, or in its aim? Where is the dividing line?"

Pohlmann looked at Graeber tormentedly. "How can I tell you that? It is too great a responsibility. I cannot decide that for you."

"Must each one decide for himself?"

"I believe so. What else?"

Graeber was silent. Why do I go on questioning? he thought. I am suddenly sitting here like a judge instead of one accused. Why do I torment this old man and call him to account for the things he once taught me and for the things I have learned later without him? Do I still need an answer? Haven't I already answered myself? He looked at Pohlmann. He could picture how day after day he crouched in this room, in the darkness or beside the lamp, as though in a catacomb of ancient Rome, dismissed from his position, in hourly expectation of arrest, laboriously seeking comfort in his books. "You're right," he said. "To ask someone else always means an attempt to evade a decision. Besides I didn't really expect an answer from you. I was really only questioning myself. Sometimes you can't do that except by putting the question to someone else."

Pohlmann shook his head. "You have the right to ask. Complicity!" he said with sudden vehemence. "What do you know of that? You were young and they poisoned you with lies before you had learned to judge. But we—we saw it and let it happen! What caused it? Hardness of heart? Indifference? Poverty? Egoism? Despair? And how could it become such a plague? Do you suppose that I don't think about it every day?"

Graeber suddenly knew what Pohlmann's eyes reminded him of. It was the eyes of the Russian at whom he had shot. He got up. "I must go," he said. "Thanks for letting me in and talking to me."

He took his cap. Pohlmann roused himself. "What do you intend to do, Graeber?"

"I don't know. I still have two weeks' time to think it over. That's a lot when you're used to living from minute to minute."

"Come again. Come once more before you leave. Promise me to."

"I promise."

"Not many come," Pohlmann murmured.

Graeber saw a small photograph standing between the books near the rubble-blocked windows. It was of a man of his own age in uniform. He remembered that Pohlmann had had a son. But in these times it was better not to ask questions about such matters.

"Send my regards to Fresenburg if you write to him," Pohlmann said.

"Yes. Did you talk to him the way you have just been talking to me?"

"Yes."

"I wish you had talked to me that way before."

"Do you think it made things easier for Fresenburg?"

"No," Graeber said. "Harder."

Pohlmann nodded. "I couldn't tell you anything. But I didn't want to give you any of the many answers that are nothing but excuses. There are plenty of them. All smooth and persuasive, and all evasions."

"Those of the Church, too?"

Pohlmann hesitated an instant. "Those of the Church, too," he said then. "But the Church is lucky. Over against Love Thy Neighbor and Thou Shalt Not Kill there conveniently stands that other saying, 'Render unto Caesar the things that are Caesar's, and unto God the things that are God's.' Given that, a good pulpit acrobat can perform all sorts of feats."

Graeber smiled. He recognized something of the sarcasm that Pohlmann had formerly had. Pohlmann saw him. "You're smiling," he said. "And you are so calm. Why aren't you screaming?"

"I am screaming," Graeber replied. "You just don't hear it."

He was standing in front of the door. Bright spears of sunlight assailed his eyes. The white mortar flickered. Slowly he walked across the square. He had the feeling of someone who, after a long, uncertain trial, has finally received judgment and to whom it is almost a matter of indifference whether it is acquittal or not. It was over; he had wanted it; it was the thing he had planned to think about during his vacation, and now he knew what it was. It was despair, and he no longer drew back from it.

For a while he sat on a bench that had remained standing close to the edge of a bomb crater. He was completely relaxed and empty and could not have said whether he was disconsolate or not. He just did not want to think any more. There was nothing more to think about. He leaned his head back and closed his eyes and felt the sun warm on his face. He felt nothing else. He sat still there, breathing quietly, and felt the impersonal, comforting warmth which knew neither justice nor injustice.

After a while he opened his eyes. The square lay before him very clear and distinct. He saw a large linden tree that stood in front of a demolished house. It was unharmed and thrust its trunk and branches up out of the earth like a giant, wide-open hand, touched with green, straining upward toward the light and the bright clouds. The sky behind the clouds was very blue. Everything gleamed and shimmered as though after a rain, it had depth and power, it was life—strong, open life, self-evident, without questions, without sorrow, without despair. Graeber felt it as though he were emerging from a nightmare, it burst full upon him, and everything melted into it, it was a wordless answer beyond all questions, beyond all thought, an answer that he knew from the nights and days when death had brushed him and when, out of spasm, rigidity, and finality, life had suddenly rushed back into him, a hot and rescuing drive that blotted out the brain in its surge.

He got up and went past the linden tree, between the ruins and the houses. He felt suddenly that he was waiting. Everything in him was waiting. He was waiting for the evening as though for an armistice.

# Chapter Fourteen

"TODAY WE HAVE an excellent Wiener Schnitzel," the marabou said.

"Good," Graeber replied. "We'll take it. And everything with it that you recommend. We put ourselves entirely in your hands."

"The same wine?"

"The same, or a different one if you wish. We leave that to you, too."

The waiter stalked off, gratified. Graeber leaned back and looked at Elisabeth. He felt as though he had been transported from a shell-torn sector of the front into a place of peace. The afternoon was far away. There remained only an afterglow of that moment when life had suddenly been very close to him, when, up through the paving stones and ruins, it had seemed to burst forth in the trees stretching out their green hands to grasp the light. Two weeks, he thought. Two weeks more of life. I must grasp it the way the linden tree grasped the light.

The marabou came back. "How would a young wine do today?" he asked. "We have a Johannisberger Kahlenberg—champagne's common soda water by comparison—"

"The Johannisberger Kahlenberg," Graeber said.

"Very good, sir. You are a connoisseur. The wine will go admirably with the Schnitzel. I will give you a tossed green salad as well. It will bring out the sparkling bouquet."

The condemned man's last meal, Graeber thought. Two weeks of last meals! He thought it without bitterness. Until now he had not looked beyond his furlough. It had seemed endless. Too much had happened and too much seemed still to lie before him. Now, after reading the war news and being with Pohlmann, he suddenly knew how short it was and how soon he would have to go back.

Elisabeth followed the marabou with her eyes. "Blessings on your friend Reuter," she said. "He has turned us into connoisseurs."

"We're no connoisseurs, Elisabeth. We're more than that. We are knights-errant. Knights-errant of peace. The war has turned everything upside down. What used to be the symbol of security and stale bourgeois respectability has today become a great adventure."

Elisabeth laughed. "We make it that."

"Not we. It is the times. But there's certainly one thing we can't complain of—boredom and monotony."

Graeber looked at Elisabeth. She was sitting on the banquette opposite him and was wearing a close-fitting dress. Her hair was hidden under a little cap. She looked almost like a boy. "Monotony," she said. "Weren't you going to wear civilian clothes this evening?"

"I couldn't. Hadn't any place to change."

He had intended to change at Alfons's; but after the afternoon's conversation he had not gone back. "You can do it at my place," Elisabeth said.

"At your place? And Frau Lieser?"

"To hell with Frau Lieser. I've been thinking about it."

"To hell with a lot of things," Graeber said. "I've been think-ing too."

The waiter brought the wine and opened it; but he did not pour. He held his head cocked to one side listening. "There it goes again," he said. "I'm sorry, sir!"

He had no need to explain what he meant. The next moment the howling of the sirens had risen above the chatter in the room.

Elisabeth's glass rang. "Where's the nearest cellar?" Graeber asked the marabou.

"We have one here in the hotel."

"Isn't that reserved for guests?"

"You are a guest, sir. The cellar is very good. Better than a good many elsewhere. We have important officers here."

"All right. What will become of the Wiener Schnitzels?"

"They're not on the fire yet. I'll save them. I can't serve them down there though. You understand why."

"Of course." Graeber took the bottle out of the marabou's hand and filled two glasses. He handed one to Elisabeth. "Drink this. And drink it all."

She shook her head. "Don't we have to go?"

"We have plenty of time. That was just the first alarm. Per-haps nothing at all will happen, like last time. Drink it up, Elis-abeth. It helps you over the first fright."

"I believe the gentleman is right," said the marabou. "It is a shame to toss off so noble a wine—but this is a special case."

He was pale and smiled with an effort. "Sir," he said to Grae-ber, "formerly we used to look up to heaven to pray. Now we do it to curse. That's what we've come to."

Graeber looked at Elisabeth. "Drink it down! We still have lots of time. We could empty a whole bottle."

She lifted her glass and drained it slowly. She did it with a determined gesture that had in it, at the same time, a kind of reckless prodigality. Then she put down her glass and smiled. "To hell with panic too!" she said. "I must get used to this. Look how I'm trembling."

"You're not trembling. It's life in you that's trembling. That has nothing to do with courage. One has courage when one can do something to defend himself. All the rest is vanity. The life in us is smarter than we are, Elisabeth."

"Good. Give me some more to drink."

"My wife," said the marabou. "Our youngster is sick. Tuberculosis. He's eleven. Our cellar is not good. It is hard for her to get the youngster down there. She is delicate; a hundred and six pounds. Twenty-nine Suedstrasse. I cannot help her. I have to stay here."

Graeber picked up a glass from the next table, filled it and offered it to the waiter. "Here! Drink this with us. There's an old soldier's rule: When there's nothing you can do, don't get excited. Does that help you?"

"It's easy to say!"

"Right. We are not all born statues. Empty the glass."

"It is not permitted, on duty—"

"This is a special case. You just said so yourself."

"Very good." The waiter looked around and accepted the glass. "May I take the liberty of drinking to your promotion?"

"To what?"

"To your promotion to corporal."

"Thanks. You have sharp eyes."

The waiter put down his glass. "I can't empty it at one gulp, sir. Not a noble wine like this. Not even in this special case."

"That does you honor. Take the glass with you."

"Thank you, sir."

Graeber refilled Elisabeth's glass and his own. "I'm not doing

this to show how cool-headed we are," he said. "I'm doing it simply because it's better during an air raid to drink whatever you
have. You never know whether you'll find it again."

Elisabeth looked at his uniform. "Won't you be caught if the
cellar is full of officers?"

"No, Elisabeth."

"Why not?"

"Because I don't care."

"Aren't people caught if they don't care?"

"Less often. Fear attracts attention. And now come—we have
got over the first fright."

A part of the wine cellar had been reinforced with steel and concrete and had been fitted up as an air raid shelter. Chairs, tables,
and sofas stood around, a few worn carpets lay on the floor, and
the walls had been newly whitewashed. There was a radio and on
a sideboard stood glasses and bottles. It was a shelter de luxe.

They found a place at one side where the real wine cellar was
shut off by a lattice-work door. A swarm of guests were pushing
their way in. Among them was a very beautiful woman in a
white evening gown. Her back was bare and her left arm flashed
with bracelets. A noisy blonde with a face like a carp followed
her, then came a number of men, an older woman, and a group of
officers. A waiter and a busboy appeared. They began to open
bottles.

"We could have brought our wine with us," Graeber said.

Elisabeth shook her head.

"You're right. It's damned play-acting."

"One oughtn't to do that," she said. "It's bad luck."

She's right, Graeber thought, and looked angrily at the waiter
who was going around with his tray. It's not courage; it's frivol-

ity. Danger is too serious a thing for that. How serious and how profound, one only knew after much death.

"The second warning," said someone behind him. "They're coming!"

Graeber pushed his chair close to Elisabeth. "I'm afraid," she said, "in spite of the Johannisberger Kahlenberg and all my resolutions."

"So am I." He put his arm around her shoulders and felt how tense she was. A wave of tenderness suddenly came over him. She was like an animal that smells danger and draws itself together, she had no pose and wanted none, her courage was her defense; life contracted in her at the changed tone of the sirens, which now meant death, and she did not try to hide it.

He saw that the blonde's escort was staring at him. He was a thin first lieutenant with a pointed chin. The blonde laughed and was being admired from the next table.

A mild tremor ran through the cellar. Then came the muffled rumble of an explosion. The conversation halted and then began again, louder and more self-conscious. Three more explosions followed, quick and nearer.

Graeber held Elisabeth tight. He saw that the blonde had stopped laughing. A heavier blow unexpectedly shook the cellar. The busboy put down his tray and clung to the spiral columns of the buffet. "Don't get excited," someone shouted. "It's a long way off."

Suddenly the walls rippled and cracked. The light flickered as in a bad film. There was a sound of crashing. Darkness and light alternated wildly and, in the jumpy flashes, the groups at the tables seemed like frames of an extremely slow-motion picture. The woman with the bare back was still sitting in the first flash; in the next she was standing, in the third she was running into the next darkness, and then people were there holding her and she was screaming and the light went out completely and in a roar that was re-echoed a hundred times all the earth's gravity seemed neutralized and the cellar hung suspended.

"It's only the light, Elisabeth!" Graeber shouted. "It has gone out. It was just the shock of the explosion. Nothing more. The wiring has been broken somewhere. The hotel has not been hit."

She pressed against him. "Candles! Matches!" someone shouted. "There must be candles somewhere. Hell and damnation, where are the candles? Or flashlights!"

A few matches flared. They seemed like small marsh lights in the great resounding space and they lighted faces and hands as though the bodies had already been destroyed by the roar and only the bare hands and faces were left floating there.

"Damn it, hasn't the management any emergency lights? Where's that waiter?"

The circles of light wavered to and fro and up and down on the walls. For an instant the woman's bare back was there, the glitter of jewelry and a dark open mouth—they seemed to flutter in a black wind, and the voices were like the weak screeches of field mice above the deep rumble of opening abysses. Then a howl arose, increasing until it became maddening and unbearable, as though a huge steel planet were plunging straight at the cellar. Everything shook. The circles of light shuddered and went out. The cellar was no longer suspended; the monstrous roar seemed to break up everything and cast it into the air. Graeber felt as though his head were flying up to the ceiling. He clasped Elisabeth with both hands—it was as though she were being torn away from him. He threw himself against her, over her and pulled her to the floor, tilted a chair over her head and waited for the ceiling to fall.

There was a splintering and clattering, a tearing and roaring and cracking as though a giant paw had struck the cellar and thrown it into a vacuum so that lungs and stomachs were torn out of bodies and the blood forced out of veins. It seemed as if all that could come now was the last thundering darkness and suffocation.

It did not come. Instead there was suddenly light, a quick twisting light as though a pillar of fire had burst up out of the floor, a white torch was there, a woman screaming: "I'm burning! I'm burning! Help! Help!"

She sprang up and beat about her with her arms, sparks cascading under her blows; jewels glittered, her horrified face was starkly lit—then voices and parts of uniforms descended on her, someone pulled her to the floor, she twisted and screamed, a scream that soared above the sirens and the flak and the destruction, high, inhuman, and then muffled, deadened, under coats and tablecloths and cushions in the dark cellar, as though from a grave.

Graeber held Elisabeth's head between his hands, under him, he pressed it against himself and his arm against her ear until the blaze and the screaming had ceased and the whimpering had turned into darkness and the smell of burned clothes and flesh and hair.

"A doctor, get a doctor! Is there a doctor here?"

"What?"

"We must get her to a hospital! Damn it, you can't see a thing. We've got to get her out of here."

"Now?" someone asked. "Where to?"

Everyone fell silent. They were listening. Outside the antiaircraft guns were firing madly. But the explosions had stopped. Only the guns were in action.

"They're gone! It's over!"

"Stay where you are," Graeber said in Elisabeth's ear. "Don't move. It's over. But stay on the floor. No one will step on you here. Don't move."

"We must wait for a while. There may be another wave," a slow, schoolmaster's voice announced. "It's not yet safe outside. The shell fragments of the flak!"

A round beam of light fell through the door. It came from a flashlight. The woman on the floor began to scream again. "No! No! Beat it out! Beat out the fire!"

"It's not a fire, it's a flashlight."

The spot of light wavered feebly through the darkness. It was a very small flashlight. "This way! Come over here! Who is it? Who are you with that light?"

The beam swung rapidly around, glided over the ceiling and back again and lighted a starched shirt front, part of a dinner jacket, a black tie and an embarrassed face. "I'm the headwaiter, Fritz. The dining room is destroyed. We cannot go on serving. If the gentlemen will perhaps pay——"

"What?"

Fritz continued to hold the light on himself. "The attack is over. I have brought this flashlight and the checks——"

"What? That's unbelievable!"

"Sir," Fritz replied helplessly into the darkness, "the headwaiter is personally responsible to the restaurant."

"Unbelievable," snorted a man in the dark. "Are we swindlers? Don't keep lighting up your miserable face! Come here! As quick as you can. Someone is hurt!"

Fritz disappeared again in the darkness. The circle of light wandered over the walls, over a lock of Elisabeth's hair, along the floor to a bundle of uniforms and stopped there. "My God!" said a man, now palely visible in his shirtsleeves.

He leaned back. Now only his hands were lighted. The beam wavered over them. The headwaiter was shaking visibly. Army coats were thrust aside.

"My God!" the man said once more.

"Don't look," Graeber said. "That sort of thing happens. It can happen anywhere. It has nothing to do with the air raid. But you mustn't stay in the city. I'll take you to a village that won't be bombed. I know one. I know people there. They'll take you in. We can live there and you will be safe."

"A stretcher!" said the kneeling man. "Have you a stretcher in the hotel?"

"I think so. Yes, Herr—Herr—" Headwaiter Fritz could not distinguish the man's rank. The blouse of his uniform lay with the others on the floor beside the woman. He was now just a man in braces with a sword around his waist and a commanding voice. "I beg your pardon about the checks," Fritz said. "I did not know that someone was injured."

"Hurry up! Get the stretcher. Or no, wait. I'll go with you. How is it outside? Can we get through?"

"Yes."

The man got up, put on his blouse and was suddenly a major. The light disappeared, and it was as though a ray of hope had disappeared with it. The woman's whimpering became audible. "Wanda," said a frantic male voice. "Wanda, what are we to do? Wanda!"

"We can leave now," someone announced.

"The all clear hasn't sounded yet," replied the schoolmaster's voice.

"To hell with the all clear! Where is the light? Light!"

"No, no—no light!" screamed the woman. "No light—"

"We need a doctor—morphine—"

"Wanda," said the frantic voice. "What can we possibly tell Eberhardt? What—"

The light came back. This time it was an oil lamp carried by the major. Two waiters in evening clothes came behind him carrying a stretcher. "No telephone," said the major. "The wires are down. This way with the stretcher."

He placed the lamp on the floor. "Wanda!" the man said again. "Wanda!"

"Get back!" said the major. "Later." He kneeled beside the woman and then straightened up. "So. That's taken care of. She'll soon be asleep. I had one hypodermic left, for emergencies. Careful! Be careful how you lift her. We'll have to wait outside till we find an ambulance. If we find one—"

"Yes, Herr Major," headwaiter Fritz said obediently.

The stretcher swayed out. The black, burned, hairless head rolled back and forth on it. The body was covered by a tablecloth.

"Is she dead?" Elisabeth asked.

"No," Graeber said, "she'll pull through. Her hair will grow again."

"And her face?"

"She could still see. Her eyes weren't injured. It will all heal. I've seen lots of burned people. This wasn't especially bad."

"How did it happen?"

"Her dress caught fire. She got too close to the matches. Nothing more has happened. This cellar is good. It has withstood a heavy direct hit."

Graeber picked up the chair that he had tilted over Elisabeth. In doing so he stepped on fragments of a broken bottle and saw that the latticed door to the wine cellar had fallen from its hinges. A number of racks hung awry, bottles were broken and strewn everywhere, and wine was flowing over the floor like dark oil.

"Just a minute," he said to Elisabeth, and picked up his coat. I'll be right back." He went into the cellar and returned at once. "All right, now we can go."

Outside stood the stretcher with the woman on it. Two waiters were whistling through their fingers for a car. "What in the world will Eberhardt say?" her escort with the frantic voice asked again. "My God, what damnable bad luck! How can we possibly explain it to him—"

Eberhardt must be the husband, Graeber thought, and tapped one of the whistling waiters on the shoulder. "Where's the waiter from the wine room?"

"Which? Otto or Karl?"

"A little old fellow who looks like a stork."

"Otto." The waiter looked at Graeber. "Otto is dead. The wine room caved in. He was hit by the chandelier. Otto is dead, sir."

Graeber was silent for a moment. "I owe him money," he said then. "For a bottle of wine."

The waiter wiped his forehead. "You can give it to me, sir. What was it?"

"A bottle of Johannisberger Kahlenberg."

The waiter produced a list from his pocket and snapped on his flashlight. "Four marks, if you please. Together with tip, four-forty."

Graeber gave him the money. The waiter put it in his pocket. Graeber knew he would not hand it in. "Come," he said to Elisabeth.

They picked their way through the ruins. Toward the south the city was in flames. The sky was gray and red, and the wind was driving swathes of smoke before it. "We must go and see whether your apartment still exists, Elisabeth."

She shook her head. "There's always time for that. Let's stay somewhere in the open."

They came to the square with the air raid shelter to which

they had gone on the first evening. The entrance gaped in the gloomy dusk like an entrance to the underworld. They sat down on a bench in the park.

"Are you hungry?" Graeber asked. "You didn't get anything to eat."

"That doesn't matter. I couldn't eat now."

He unfolded his overcoat. There was a tinkling sound and he pulled two bottles out of the pockets. "I don't know just what I've got hold of. This one looks like cognac."

Elisabeth stared at him. "Where did you get them?"

"Out of the wine cellar. The door was open. Dozens of bottles were smashed. Let's assume that these would have been broken too."

"You simply took them?"

"Of course. A soldier who neglects an open wine cellar is sick. I was raised to think and act practically. The Ten Commandments don't hold for the military."

"They certainly don't." Elisabeth looked at him. "There's a good deal more that doesn't either." She laughed suddenly. "What does one really know about any of you?"

"You already know rather too much."

"What does one really know about you?" she repeated. "What is here is not really you. You are what you come from. But who knows anything about that?"

Out of the other side of his coat Graeber drew two more bottles. "Here's one I can open without a corkscrew. It's champagne." He twisted the wire off. "I hope you have no moral scruples against drinking it!"

"No. Not any more."

"We'll not celebrate anything with it. So it won't be bad luck. We'll drink it because we're thirsty and haven't anything else. And also because we're still alive."

Elisabeth smiled. "You don't have to explain that to me again. I've learned it already. But explain something else. Why did you pay for the one bottle when you were taking four more away with you?"

"There's a big difference. The other would have been welching on a debt."

It grew still. The red dusk extended more and more. Everything became unreal in the strange light. "Just look at that tree over there," Elisabeth said suddenly. "It's blooming."

Graeber looked at it. The tree had been almost torn out of the ground by a bomb. Some of its roots hung free in the air, the trunk was broken and several of the branches had been torn off; but it was actually full of white blossoms tinged by the reddish glow.

"The house beside it has burned down. Perhaps the heat has forced it," he said. "It's farther out than any of the other trees around here, and yet it's the most damaged."

Elisabeth got up and went over to it. The bench stood in the shadow and she stepped out of it into the wavering glow of the conflagration like a dancer stepping onto a lighted stage. It embraced her like a red wind and blazed behind her like a gigantic medieval comet announcing the end of a world, or the birth of a savior.

"It's blooming." she said. "For it this is spring and nothing else. Nothing else matters to it."

"Yes," Graeber replied. "They teach us lessons. They teach us lessons all the time. At noon today it was a linden tree that was teaching me, and now it's this. They grow and put out leaves and even when they're torn out of the ground the part that still has a bit of root in the earth goes on growing. They teach us lessons unceasingly and they don't complain or feel sorry for themselves."

Elisabeth slowly came back. Her skin shimmered in the strange, shadowless light, and her face seemed enchanted and aroused by a secret that was connected with the bursting buds and the destruction and the imperturbable deliberateness of growth. Then she stepped out of the glow, as though out of a spotlight, and was once more warm and darkly breathing and alive in the shadow beside him. He drew her down to him and the tree was suddenly there, very big, the tree that reached for the red sky and its blossoms seemed very close, and it was the linden tree and then the earth, and it arched and became field and sky and Elisabeth, and he felt himself in her, and she did not resist him.

# Chapter Fifteen

ROOM FORTY-EIGHT was in commotion. The egghead and two other skat players stood arrayed for active service. They had been classified 1A and were going out with a transport to the front.

The egghead was pale. He was staring at Reuter. "You with your miserable foot! You shirker! You're staying here and I, the father of a family, have to go!"

Reuter made no reply. Feldmann straightened up in bed. "Shut your trap, egghead!" he said. "You do not have to go because he is staying here. You have to go because you're 1A. If he were 1A and had to go then you'd have to go just the same. So don't talk nonsense!"

"I'll say what I like," screamed the egghead furiously. "I have to go and I'll say what I like! You're staying here! You're sitting around here, eating and sleeping and we have to go! I, the father of a family, and that fat lead-swinger there swills schnapps so that his damned foot won't heal!"

"Wouldn't you do the same thing if you could?" Reuter asked.

"I? Not I! I've never shirked in my life!"

"Well, then everything's in order. Why are you still complaining?"

"What?" asked the egghead, taken aback.

"You're proud of never having shirked. All right, go on being proud and don't complain any more."

"What? What kind of damn twist is that? That's all you know, isn't it—you pig? Twist the words in a man's mouth. They'll catch you yet. They'll catch you even if I have to report you myself."

"Do not commit a sin," said one of the two skat players who were also 1A. "Come, we've got to go down. Move out."

"I'm not committing a sin. Those are the sinners there. It's an outrage that I, the father of a family, have to go to the front in place of this drunken hog. I only want justice—"

"Oh, man, justice! Where can you find that in the army? Come, we've got to get going. He won't report anyone, comrades. That's just the way he talks. Farewell! Take care of yourselves! Hold the position!"

The two skat players dragged the frantic egghead off with them. White and sweating, he jerked around once more in the doorway and was about to shout something when they pushed him out.

"That babbling fool," Feldmann said to Reuter. "Puts on a show like an actor! Do you still remember the row he made because I was sleeping away my leave?"

"He was losing," Rummel said suddenly. Up to now he had been sitting at the table without taking part. "He was way behind the game! Twenty-three marks! That's no small matter! I should have given it back to him."

"You can still do it. The transport hasn't left."

"What?"

"He's still outside. Go down and give it back to him if your conscience is bothering you."

Rummel got up and went out. "He's gone crazy too," Feldmann said. "What's the egghead going to do with those shekels at the front?"

"He can gamble them away again."

Graeber went to the window and looked out. The contingent was gathering below. "Children and old men," Reuter said. "Since Stalingrad they take everyone."

"Yes."

The contingent formed up. "What's happened to Rummel?" Feldmann asked in sudden astonishment. "Why, he's talking now!"

"He began while you were asleep."

Feldmann came to the window in his undershirt. "There stands the egghead," he said. "Now he has a chance to find out for himself whether it's better to sleep and dream of the front or to be at the front and dream of home."

"We'll all be able to find that out before long," Reuter announced. "Next time my staff surgeon is going to put me down as 1A too. He's a man of spirit and has explained to me that true Germans don't need legs for running. They can fight just as well sitting down."

From outside came the sound of commands. The contingent marched off. Graeber saw it as though through the wrong end of a telescope. The receding soldiers were like live dolls with toy guns.

"Poor egghead," Reuter said. "He wasn't mad at me. He was mad at his wife. He thinks she's going to be unfaithful to him when he's gone. And he's furious because she gets his marriage allowance. He suspects she's going to use it to carry on with her lover."

"Marriage allowance? Is there such a thing?" Graeber asked.

"But man, where have you been?" Feldmann shook his head.

"Two hundred marks a month is what a woman gets. That's real money. Lots of people have married for that. Why should one make a present of it to the State?"

Reuter turned away from the window. "Your friend Binding was here asking for you," he said to Graeber.

"What did he want? Did he leave a message?"

"He's having a little celebration at his house. He wants you to come."

"Was that all?"

"That was all."

Rummel came in. "Did you catch the egghead?" Feldmann asked.

Rummel nodded. His face was working. "At least he still has a wife," he burst out with sudden emotion. "But to have to go out again having nothing any more—"

He turned away abruptly and threw himself on his bed. They all pretended they had not heard. "If the egghead had only been here to see that!" Feldmann whispered. "He made a big bet that Rummel would break down today."

"Leave him alone," Reuter said angrily. "Who knows when you're going to break down yourself? No one's safe. Not even a sleepwalker." He turned to Graeber. "How long do you still have?"

"Eleven days."

"Eleven days! That's a pretty long time."

"Yesterday it was still a long time," Graeber said. "Today it's damn short."

"No one is here," Elisabeth said. "Neither Frau Lieser nor her child. The place is ours."

"Thank God! I believe I'd have killed her if she had said so much as a word tonight. Did you have another fight with her yesterday?"

Elisabeth laughed. "She considers me a prostitute."

"Why? After all, we were only here for an hour yesterday evening."

"It was the day before! You were here the whole evening then."

"But we covered the keyhole and played the phonograph the whole time. How does she get such ideas?"

"Yes, how?" Elisabeth said, brushing him with a quick glance.

Graeber looked at her. A sudden warmth rose to his forehead. Where were my eyes that first evening? he thought. "What's become of the she-devil?" he asked.

"She's gone out to the villages with her child. Collecting contributions for some winter or summer benefit. She's not coming back till tomorrow night. We have tonight and the whole day tomorrow all for ourselves."

"The whole day tomorrow? Don't you have to go to your factory?"

Elisabeth laughed. "Not tomorrow. Tomorrow is Sunday. For the time being we still have Sundays off."

"Sunday!" Graeber said. "What luck! I had no idea of it! So I'll finally be able to see you in the daytime. Up to now it has always been evening or night."

"Has it?"

"Yes. We went out for the first time Monday. With a bottle of armagnac."

"That's true," Elisabeth said in surprise. "I haven't seen you in the daytime either." She was silent for a moment looking at him and then she glanced away. "We lead a rather hectic life, don't we?"

"There's nothing else for us to do."

"That's true too. How will it be when we face each other tomorrow in the harsh light of noon?"

"We'll leave that to divine providence. But what shall we do tonight? Shall we go to the same restaurant as yesterday? It was no damn good. What we need is the Germania. Too bad it's closed."

"We can stay here. There's still enough to drink. I could try to cook something."

"Can you stand it here? Wouldn't you rather go out?"

"Whenever Frau Lieser isn't here it's like a vacation."

"Then let's stay here. Let's have an evening without music. It will be marvelous. And I won't have to go back to the barracks. But what about food? Can you really cook? You don't look as if you could."

"I can try. Besides, there's not much here. Only what you can get for coupons."

"That can't be much."

They went into the kitchen. Graeber looked at Elisabeth's provisions. There was hardly anything there—a little bread, some artificial honey, margarine, two eggs, and a few withered apples. "I still have ration coupons," she said. "We can go out and get something. I know a store that's open in the evenings."

Graeber shut the drawer. "Keep your coupons. You'll need them for yourself. Today we'll have to use other methods of procurement. We'll have to organize."

"We can't steal anything here, Ernst," Elisabeth said in alarm. "Frau Lieser knows every crust that belongs to her."

"I can well imagine. Besides, I'm not going to steal today. I'm going out to requisition like a soldier in enemy country. A certain Alfons Binding invited me to a little party. I'll go there and get what I would have eaten if I'd taken part in the celebration and I'll bring it here. He has a house with enormous supplies. I'll be back in half an hour."

Alfons received him red-faced and open-armed. "There you are, Ernst! Come in! Today is my birthday! I have a few friends here."

The hunting room was full of smoke and people. "Listen to me, Alfons," Graeber said quickly in the corridor. "I can't stay. I only dropped in for a minute and I have to go right back."

"Go back? But, Ernst! That's entirely out of the question!"

"I have to. I had made an appointment before I heard you had asked for me."

"That doesn't matter! Tell the people you have to go to an unexpected official meeting. Or to a hearing!" Alfons laughed boisterously. "There are two Gestapo officers sitting inside! I'll introduce you to them at once. Tell your friends you had to go to the Gestapo. Then you won't even be lying. Or bring them over if they're nice."

"That's impossible."

"Why? Why is it impossible? Everything goes with us!"

Graeber saw that the simplest thing was to tell the truth. "You should be able to imagine, Alfons," he said. "I didn't know you were celebrating your birthday. I came by to get something to eat and drink from you. I'm going to meet someone I can't possibly bring here. I'd be a fine fool if I did. Now do you understand?"

Binding grinned. "I've got it," he announced. "The eternal feminine! At last! I was beginning to give up hope for you. I understand, Ernst. You're excused. However, we have a couple of fancy dames here. Won't you at least take a look at them? Irma is a damned enterprising woman—the blonde over there with the high heels, a hot number, a warden in the women's concentration

camp—and with Gudrun you can unquestionably go to bed tonight. She's always available for front-line soldiers. The smell of
the trenches excites her."

"It doesn't excite me."

Alfons laughed. "Nor the concentration camp smell around
Irma, eh? It gives Steegemann wings. That fat fellow on the sofa.
Not my taste. I'm normal and all for coziness. You see that little
trick in the corner? How do you like her?"

"First class."

"You want her? I'll give her up to you if you'll stay, Ernst."

Graeber shook his head. "It can't be done."

"I understand. It must be someone really high class you've
picked up. You don't need to be embarrassed, Ernst. Alfons is a
cavalier himself. Let's go into the kitchen and find something for
you and later you'll drink a glass to my birthday. Agreed?"

"Agreed."

Frau Kleinert was standing in the kitchen in a white apron.
"We're having a cold buffet, Ernst," Binding said. "Your good
luck! Pick out whatever you like! Or better yet, Frau Kleinert,
make up a nice package. We two will go on down to the cellar."

The cellar was well stocked. "Now you just let Alfons attend
to this," Binding said. "You won't be sorry. Here, to begin with,
is a genuine turtle soup in cans. Just heat it up and eat it. Comes
from France. Take two."

Graeber took the cans. Alfons went on searching. "Asparagus,
Dutch, two cans. You can eat it cold or warm it up. No extensive
cooking. And here's a Polish ham in a can too. That's Czechoslo-
vakia's contribution." He climbed up on a little ladder. "A piece
of Danish cheese and a can of butter—it all keeps, that's the advantage of canned goods. Here are some brandied peaches, too.
Or does the lady prefer strawberries?"

Graeber looked at the short legs standing in front of him in the highly polished boots. Behind them shimmered the rows of bottles and tins. He thought of Elisabeth's pathetic supplies. "There'd be more nourishment in both," he said.

Alfons laughed. "You're right. At last you're the same old boy again. No point in being sad, Ernst. Things are bad enough without that. Grab what you can and let the priests worry about the rest. That's my watchword."

He got off the ladder and went to the other side of the cellar where the bottles lay. "Here we have a respectable selection of booty. Our enemies are great in their liquors. What will you have? Vodka? Armagnac? Here's slivowitz, too, from Poland."

Graeber had not really intended to ask for liquor. The supply from the Germania still sufficed. But Binding was right—booty was booty, and one ought to take it wherever one found it. "There's champagne here too," Alfons said. "I don't like the stuff myself. But it's said to be marvelous for romance. I hope it helps you out tonight!" He laughed loudly. "Do you know what my favorite schnapps is? Kuemmel, believe it or not. Old honest kuemmel. Take a bottle along and think of Alfons when you drink it."

He put the bottles under his arm and went into the kitchen. "Make up two packages, Frau Kleinert. One with the food and one with the bottles. Paper between the bottles so they won't break. And put in a quarter pound of the good bean coffee, too. Will that do you, Ernst?"

"I just hope I can carry it all."

Binding beamed. "Alfons doesn't do things by halves. Not on his birthday! And certainly not for an old schoolmate!" He was standing in front of Graeber. His eyes gleamed and his red face glowed. He looked like a boy who has found a bird's nest. Graeber was moved by his kindliness, but then he reflected that Alfons had looked exactly the same way when he was listening to Heini's stories of Russia.

Binding winked at Graeber. "The coffee is for tomorrow morning. I hope you realize that's Sunday and don't go back to sleep in the barracks! And now come! I'll just introduce you to a couple of friends. Schmidt and Hoffmann of the Gestapo. You can never tell when that sort of acquaintance will be useful. Just for a minute or two. Drink a glass to my health. May everything stay just as it is here and now! The house and everything that goes with it!" Binding's eyes were moist. "We can't help it, we Germans are just helpless romantics."

"We can't leave that in the kitchen," Elisabeth said, overwhelmed. "I must try to hide it. If Frau Lieser saw it she'd immediately report me as a black marketeer."

"Damn it! I hadn't thought of that! Can't she be bribed? With some of the stuff we don't like ourselves?"

"Is there anything we don't like?"

Graeber laughed. "Nothing but your artificial honey. Or the margarine. And we'll be able to use those too in a couple of days."

"She is incorruptible," Elisabeth said. "She takes pride in living exclusively on her ration coupons."

Graeber reflected. "We can eat up part of the stuff by tomorrow evening," he explained then. "But we won't be able to manage it all. What can we do with the rest?"

"We'll hide it in my room. Behind the clothes and books. I still have a trunk too that I can lock."

"And if she comes snuffling around?"

"I lock my room every morning when I go out."

"And if she has another key?"

Elisabeth looked up. "I hadn't thought of that. It's possible."

Graeber opened a bottle. "We'll decide about it tomorrow afternoon. Just now we'll eat as much as we can. Let's unpack the whole lot! We'll crowd the table with it as though it were a birthday spread. All together and all at once!"

"The tins too?"

"The tins too. For decoration! We don't need to open them yet. First let's eat whatever won't keep. And let's put the bottles there as well. All our riches which we have honorably won by theft and corruption."

"The ones from the Germania, too?"

"Those, too. We earned them honestly by fear of death."

They pushed the table into the middle of the room. Then they opened all the packages and uncorked the slivowitz, the cognac, and the kuemmel. They did not open the champagne. It had to be drunk once it was uncorked; the liqueurs could be corked again.

"It looks magnificent," Elisabeth said. "What are we celebrating?"

Graeber handed her a glass. "We're celebrating everything at once. We haven't time any more for a lot of separate celebrations. Nor any time for distinctions. We're simply celebrating everything at once no matter what it is and principally that we are here and that we have two days to ourselves!"

He walked around the table and took Elisabeth in his arms. He felt her and it was as if a second life opened in him, warmer, more colorful and easier than his own, without boundaries and without past, wholly present and without any shadow of guilt. She leaned against him. The laden table gleamed like a feast in front of them. "Wasn't that a bit much for a single toast?" she asked.

He shook his head. "It was only long-winded. At bottom it

always comes down to the same thing—to be happy that we're still here."

Elisabeth emptied her glass. "Sometimes I believe we would know quite well what to do with life if they'd only let us."

"At the moment, we're not doing too badly," Graeber said.

The windows were open. A house diagonally across the street had been hit by a bomb the night before and the panes in Elisabeth's room had been broken. She had covered the frames with black air raid paper and hung thin, bright-colored curtains in front of them. They waved in the breezes. So the room looked less like a vault.

They had no lights on; thus they could leave the windows open. From time to time they heard people going by in the street. A radio was playing somewhere. House doors slammed. Someone coughed. Shutters were closed. "The city is going to sleep." Elisabeth said. "And I'm fairly drunk."

They were lying side by side on the bed. On the table stood the remnants of dinner and the bottles, except for the vodka and the cognac and one bottle of champagne. They had not cleared anything away; they were waiting till they got hungry again. They had drunk the vodka. The cognac was standing on the floor beside the bed, and from behind the bed came the sound of running water in the wash basin. The champagne was lying there cooling.

Graeber placed his glass on a little table beside the bed. He was lying in the darkness and it seemed to him that he was in a small town before the war. A fountain was splashing, a linden tree was humming with bees, windows were being closed, and somewhere a man was playing a final tune on his fiddle before going to bed.

"The moon will rise soon," Elisabeth said.

The moon will rise soon, he thought. The moon, tenderness, and simple creature happiness. They were there already. They were in the sleepy circling of his blood, in the stilled wishes of his mind and in the slow breath that wafted through him like a weary wind. He thought of the afternoon with Pohlmann. It was infinitely far away. Strange, that hard on the heels of such clear hopelessness there could come so much violent feeling. But perhaps it was not strange at all; perhaps it could not be otherwise. As long as one was full of questions one was incapable of perceiving much else. Only when one no longer expected anything was one open to everything and without dread.

A beam of light swept over the window. It disappeared, flickered back and remained. "Is that the moon already?" Graeber asked.

"It can't be. Moonlight is not so white."

They heard voices. Elisabeth got up and slipped on a pair of bedroom slippers. She went to the window and leaned out. She did not look for a cover or a dressing gown. She was beautiful and sure of it and therefore without shyness. "It's a clean-up detail from the air defense," she said. "They have a searchlight and shovels and pickaxes and they're over by the house across the street. Do you think there are still people buried in the cellar?"

"Were they digging there during the day?"

"I don't know. I wasn't here."

"Perhaps they only want to repair the electric cables."

"Yes, perhaps."

Elisabeth came back. "Sometimes after an attack I have wished that I might return here and find this house burned down. The house, the furniture, the clothes, and the memories. Everything. Do you understand that?"

"Yes."

"I don't mean the memories of my father. I mean the others,

the fear, the despondency, the hatred. If the house were burned that would be finished too, I thought, and I could begin all over again."

Graeber looked at her. The pale beam from outside fell on her shoulders. The dull sound of pickax blows and the scraping of the shovels came through the window. "Just give me the bottle from the basin," he said.

"The one from the Germania?"

"Yes. We'll drink it before it's blown up. And put the others from Binding in. Who knows when the next attack will come? These bottles with carbon dioxide in them explode from negative pressure. They're as dangerous in the house as hand grenades. Have we glasses?"

"Water glasses."

"Water glasses are right for champagne. That's the way we drank it in Paris."

"Were you in Paris?"

"Yes, at the beginning of the war."

Elisabeth brought the glasses and crouched beside him. He opened the bottle carefully. The wine flooded into the glasses and foamed up. "How long were you in Paris?" she asked.

"A couple of weeks."

"Did they hate you very much?"

"I don't know. Perhaps. I didn't see much of it. Of course we didn't want to see it either. We still believed most of what we had been taught. We wanted to get the war over in a hurry and sit in the sun on the streets in front of the cafés drinking the wines of a foreign country. We were very young."

"Young—you say that as though it were many years ago."

"That's the way it seems, too."

"Aren't you young any more now?"

"Yes. But in a different way."

Elisabeth lifted her glass against the carbide light that trembled in the window. She shook it and watched the wine foam up. Graeber saw her shoulders and the wave of her hair and her back and the line of her spine with the long, soft shadows—she did not need to think about beginning all over again, he thought. She had nothing to do with this room or her work or Frau Lieser when she was without clothes. She belonged to the quivering outside the window and to the restless night, to the blind excitement of the blood and to the odd estrangement afterward, to the hoarse cries and voices outside and also even to the dead that were being dug out—but she did not belong to the accidental, to emptiness, and to senseless lostness. Not any longer! She seemed to have thrown off a disguise and to be following all at once and without reflection laws that yesterday she had not known at all.

"I wish I had been in Paris with you," she said. "I wish we could go there now and there wasn't a war. Would they let us in?"

"Perhaps. We didn't destroy anything in Paris."

"But in France?"

"Not so much as in the other countries. It went fast."

"Perhaps you destroyed enough so that they will go on hating us for many years."

"Yes, perhaps. One forgets a lot in a long war. Perhaps they do hate us."

"I wish we could go to some other country. Some country where noting has been destroyed."

"There aren't many undamaged countries left," Graeber said. "Is there still something there to drink?"

"Yes. Enough. Where else have you been?"

"In Africa."

"In Africa too? You have seen a lot."

"Yes," Graeber said. "But not the way I once dreamed of seeing it."

Elisabeth lifted the bottle from the floor and filled the glasses. Graeber looked at her. Everything seemed a bit unreal and it was not just because they had been drinking. Their words drifted back and forth in the twilight, they were without meaning and the thing that had meaning was without words and you couldn't talk about it. It was like the rise and fall of a nameless river and the words were sails that tacked back and forth across it.

"Were you other places too?" Elisabeth asked.

Sails, Graeber thought. Where had he seen sails on rivers? "In Holland," he said. "That was at the very beginning. There were boats there that glided through the canals and the canals were so flat and low that it was as though the boats were traveling over the land. They were soundless and had huge sails and it was strange when they glided in the twilight through the countryside like gigantic white and blue and red butterflies."

"Holland," Elisabeth said. "Perhaps we can go there after the war. We could drink cocoa and eat white bread and all those different Dutch cheeses and in the evening we could watch the boats."

Graeber looked at her. Things to eat, he thought. In wartime one's ideas of happiness were inseparably bound up with eating. "Or can't we go there any more either?" she asked.

"I think not. We overran Holland and destroyed Rotterdam without warning. I have seen the ruins. There was hardly a single house left standing. Thirty thousand dead. I'm afraid they won't admit us there either, Elisabeth."

She was silent for a time. Then she suddenly lifted her glass and threw it to the floor. It tinkled and broke. "We can no longer go anywhere!" she cried. "Why do we fool ourselves with dreams? Nowhere. We are captured and excluded and accursed!"

Graeber straightened up. Her eyes shone like gray transparent glass in the quivering, chalky light from outside. He bent over her and looked at the floor. The edges of the splinters glittered whitely there. "We'll have to turn on the light and pick them up," he said. "Otherwise we'll step on them and cut our feet. Wait, I'll shut the window first."

He climbed over the foot of the bed. Elisabeth turned the switch on and reached for a dressing gown. The electric light made her shy. "Don't look at me," she said. "I don't know why I did it. Usually I'm not this way."

"You are fine that way. And you are right. You don't belong here. So it's all right for you to do a little smashing once in a while."

"I wish I knew where I do belong."

Graeber laughed. "I don't know either. In a circus, perhaps, or in a baroque mansion or surrounded by steel furniture or in a tent. Not here in this white, girl's room. And I thought that first evening you were helpless and in need of protection!"

"I am, too."

"We all are. But we manage to get along anyway without protection or help."

He took a newspaper, laid it on the floor and pushed the splinters into it with another one. In doing so he saw the headlines: FURTHER SHORTENING OF THE LINES. HEAVY FIGHTING AROUND OREL. He wrapped the splinters in the paper and put it in the wastebasket. The warm light of the room suddenly seemed doubly warm. From outside he heard the hammering and drilling of the search party. On the table stood Alfons's gifts. Sometimes you could think of a lot of things all at once, he thought.

"I'll just clear this up," Elisabeth said. "All of a sudden I can't look at it any more."

"Where will you put it?"

"In the kitchen. We'll have time before tomorrow evening to hide what's left."

"By tomorrow evening there won't be very much left. But how will it be if Frau Lieser comes back earlier?"

"Well then she'll just come back earlier."

Graeber looked at her in astonishment. "I'm surprised myself how much I change every day," she said.

"Not every day. Every hour."

"And you?"

"I too."

"Is that good?"

"Yes. And even if it isn't good it doesn't make any difference either."

"Nothing makes any difference, is that it?"

"No."

Elisabeth turned off the light. "Now we can open the vault again," she said.

Graeber opened the window. The wind came in at once. The curtains waved. "There's the moon," Elisabeth said.

The orb was rising, distended and red, over the roofs opposite. It was like a monster with a glowing head eating its way into the street. Graeber took two water glasses and filled them halfway with cognac. He handed one to Elisabeth. "Let's drink this now," he said. "Wine is no good in the dark."

The moon rose higher and became more peaceful and more golden. They lay for a time in silence. Elisabeth turned her head.

"What are we really," she asked, "happy or unhappy?"

Graeber reflected. "We are both. And probably that's how it has to be today. Unmixed happiness in our times belongs only to cows. Or not even to them any more. Perhaps only to stones."

Elisabeth looked at Graeber. "That doesn't matter either, does it?"

"No."

"Does anything matter?"

"Yes." Graeber looked into the cold, golden light that was slowly filling the room. "We are no longer dead," he said. "And we are not yet dead."

# Chapter Sixteen

IT WAS SUNDAY MORNING. Graeber was standing in Haken-strasse. He noticed there had been a change in the appearance of the ruins. The bathtub had disappeared; so had the remnant of the staircase, and a narrow path had been shoveled out leading around the wall into the courtyard and from there obliquely into what was left of the house. It looked as though a clean-up troop had started to work.

He squeezed through the cleared entrance and came into a half buried room which he recognized as the former laundry of the house. From there a low, dark passage led further. He struck a match and let the light fall ahead of him.

"What are you doing there?" someone shouted suddenly from behind him. "Come out at once!"

He turned around. He could not see anyone in the darkness and walked back. A man with crutches under his arms stood outside. He was wearing civilian clothes and a military overcoat. What are you up to here?" he barked.

"I live here. And you?"

"I live here and nobody else, understand? Certainly not you! What are you snuffling around for? Something to steal?"

"Man, don't excite yourself," Graeber said, looking at the crutches and the military overcoat. "My parents used to live here and so did I before I joined the Prussians. Now are you satisfied?"

"Anyone could say that."

Graeber took hold of the cripple by the crutches, cautiously pushed him aside and went past him out of the passage.

Outside he saw a woman approaching with a child. A second man was following her with a pickax. The woman had come out of a shack that had been put up behind the house; the man was approaching from the opposite side. They took up positions confronting Graeber. "What's happened, Otto?" the man with the pick asked the cripple.

"I caught this fellow here. Snuffling around. Says his parents used to live here."

The man with the pick gave an unfriendly laugh. "Any more to the story?"

"No," Graeber said, "just that."

"I guess nothing else occurred to you, eh?" The man hefted the pick in his hand and raised it. "Disappear! I'll count to three. Otherwise there'll be a little case of a fractured skull. One—"

Graeber sprang at him from the side and struck. The man fell and Graeber tore the pick out of his hands. "There, that's better," he said. "And now, shout for the police if you like! But probably you don't want to, eh?"

The man who had had the pick got up slowly. His nose was bleeding. "You'd better not try it again," Graeber said. "I got some training in close fighting from the Prussians. And now, tell me what you are doing here."

The woman pushed in front. "We live here. Is that a crime?"

"No. And I am here because my parents used to live here. Perhaps that's a crime?"

"Is that really true?" asked the cripple.

"What else? What is there to steal here anyway?"

"Enough for someone who doesn't have anything," the woman said.

"Not for me. I'm on furlough, and I'm going out again. Have you seen that notice outside in front of the door? The one asking for news about a father and mother? That's mine."

"Is that who you are?" asked the cripple.

"Yes, that's who I am."

"Well, that's different. You understand, comrade, we're suspicious. We were bombed out and fixed things up for ourselves here. After all, you have to have some place to live."

"Did you shovel all that out by yourselves?"

"Partly. People helped us with it."

"Who?"

"People we know who have tools."

"Did you find any dead?"

"No."

"Are you certain?"

"Yes, certain. We didn't. Perhaps there were some there earlier, but we didn't find any."

"That was all I wanted to know," Graeber said.

"You didn't have to smash another man's face to find that out," the woman said.

"Is he your husband?"

"That's none of your business. He's not my husband. He's my brother. And he's bleeding."

"Only his nose."

"His teeth too."

Graeber lifted the pick. "And this? What was he going to do with this?"

"He would not have attacked you."

"Dear lady," Graeber said, "I have learned not to wait till I'm attacked."

He threw the pick in a wide arc onto the rubble. They all watched it. The child set about climbing up after it. The woman held him back. Graeber looked around. Now he saw the bathtub too. It was standing beside the shack. The staircase had probably been used for firewood. In a heap lay empty cans, flatirons, broken crockery, odds and ends of torn cloth, wooden boxes, and fragments of furniture. The family had moved in, had built the shack and now obviously regarded everything they could scrape together out of the rubble as manna from heaven. There was nothing to be said against it. Life was going on. The child looked healthy. Death had been overcome. The ruins had become a shelter once more. There was nothing to be said against it.

"You worked damn fast," he said.

"You have to work fast," the cripple replied, "when you have no roof over your head."

Graeber turned to go. "Did you find a cat here?" he asked. "A little black and white one?"

"Our Rosa," the child said.

"No," the woman replied defiantly. "We did not find a cat."

Graeber climbed back. No doubt even more people lived in the shack; otherwise they could not have done so much in so short a time. But perhaps, too, a commando crew had helped them. At night prisoners from the concentration camps were often sent into the city to help with the clearing.

He went back. It seemed to him that he had suddenly become poorer; he did not know why.

He entered a street that was entirely undamaged. Not even the big plate-glass windows of the stores had been broken. Walking ahead absent-mindedly, he suddenly stopped short. He had seen someone coming toward him and for a moment he had not realized it was himself striding forward in the diagonal side mirror of a clothing store. It was strange—as though he were looking at a *Doppelgänger* and were no longer himself now but only a memory that would be wiped out as soon as he walked a step farther.

He stayed where he was and stared at the image in the dim, yellowish mirror. It was pale and undulating and gray. He saw only the hollows of his eyes and the shadows beneath them, not the eyes themselves. And it was as though he no longer had any and was already a death's head. A chill, alien fear crept upon him. It was not panic and not revolt, no urgent, hasty cry of existence for flight and defense and alertness—it was a tugging, cold, almost impersonal dread, a dread that admitted no hand-hold because it was invisible and intangible and seemed to come out of a vacuum where monstrous pumps had been installed which were silently draining the blood out of his veins and the life out of his bones. He still saw his image in the mirror, but it seemed to him as though it must soon grow indistinct, wavy, and the outlines must dissolve and be absorbed, sucked up by the noiseless, cosmic pumps, drawn away from the surface and out of the accidental form that for a short time had been called Ernst Graeber, back into something limitless that was not simply death but horribly much more than that, extinction, disintegration, the end of the self, a vortex of meaningless atoms, nothingness.

He stood there for a time. What remained? he thought, deeply shaken. What would remain when he was no longer there? Nothing but a dying memory in the heads of a few people, his parents, if they were still alive, certain friends, Elisabeth perhaps—and for how long? He looked at the mirror. It seemed to him he had already become as light as a piece of paper, thin, wholly shadowy, something a breath of wind could sweep away, drained by the pumps, now only an empty husk. What would remain? And to what could he hold fast, where could he drop anchor, where find purchase, where leave behind something to hold him so that he would not be completely swept away?

"Ernst," said someone behind him.

He whirled around. A one-legged man on crutches was standing there. For an instant Graeber thought it was the cripple from Hakenstrasse; then he recognized Mutzig, a classmate.

"Karl," he said. "You? I didn't know you were here."

"Been here a long time. Almost half a year."

They looked at each other. "You wouldn't have imagined this, would you?" Mutzig said.

"What?"

Mutzig lifted his crutches and set them down again. "That."

"Well at least you're out of all the crap. I have got to go back."

"Depends on how you look at it. If the war goes on for a couple of years, then it's luck; if it's over in six weeks it's a damn bad break."

"Why should it be over in six weeks?"

"I don't know. I only said if—"

"Well, of course."

"Why don't you stop in and see us sometime?" Mutzig said. "Bergmann is here too. Both arms at the elbows."

"Where are you?"

"In the City Hospital. Amputees Section. We have the whole left wing. Stop in sometime."

"Good. I'll do it."

"Really? They all say that and then not a single ass turns up."

"Positively."

"Good. It will amuse you. We're a lively crowd. At least in my room."

They looked at each other again. They had not met in three years; but now they had already said everything there was to say. "Well, take it easy, Ernst."

"You too, Karl."

They shook hands. "Did you know Siebert was dead?" Mutzig asked.

"No."

"Six weeks ago. And Leiner?"

"Leiner? I didn't know about him either."

"Leiner and Lingen. They fell the same morning. Bruening went crazy. Have you heard that Hollmann got it too?"

"No."

"Bergmann heard that. Well, take care of yourself, Ernst! And don't forget to visit us."

Mutzig hobbled away. It seemed to give him a definite satisfaction to talk about the dead, Graeber thought. Perhaps it made his own misfortune less. He glanced after him. The leg had been amputated high up on the thigh. Mutzig had once been the best runner in their class. Graeber did not know whether to pity him or to envy him. Mutzig was right; it depended on what was coming.

When he came in, Elisabeth was perched on the bed in a white bathrobe. She had twisted a towel around her head like a turban and she sat there beautiful and still and entirely self-contained like a great bright bird that had flown in through the window and was now resting in order to fly on again.

"I have used up all the hot water for a week," she said. "It was a great luxury. Frau Lieser will set up a fine howl."

"Let her howl. She won't miss it. True National Socialists don't bathe very often. Cleanliness is a Jewish vice."

He went to the window and looked out. The sky was gray and the street was quiet. Opposite, a hairy man in suspenders was standing in a window yawning. From another window came the notes of a piano and a harsh female voice singing scales. Graeber stared at the excavated entrance to the cellar. He was thinking about the strange, cold terror he had felt in the street in front of the clothing store and he felt chilled again. What would remain? Something or other ought to remain, he thought, an anchor to hold him so that he wouldn't drift away and fail to return. But what? Elisabeth? Did she belong to him? He had known her for only a short time and he was going away again for years. Would any of this remain? How could he keep her and himself through her?

He turned around. "Elisabeth," he said, "we ought to get married."

"Get married!" She laughed. "Why?"

"Because it's senseless. Because we have only known each other a couple of days and because in a few days I have to go off again; because we don't know whether we want to stay together and actually could not possibly know in such a short time. That's why."

She looked at him. "You mean because we are alone and desperate and have nothing else?"

"No."

She was silent. "Not for that reason alone," he said.

"Then why?"

He looked at her. He watched her breathing. She suddenly seemed very alien to him. Her breasts rose and fell, her arms were different from his, her hands were different, her thoughts, her life—she would not understand him, how could she after all, when even he himself did not clearly understand why he all at once wanted it.

"If we were married you would not have to be afraid of Frau Lieser," he said. "As the wife of a soldier you would be protected."

"Would I?"

"Yes." Graeber grew embarrassed under her glance. "At least it would help some."

"That's no reason. I'll take care of Frau Lieser all right. Get married! We haven't even time."

"Why not?"

"You have to have papers, permits, proof of Aryan blood, health certificates and I don't know what else. That takes weeks."

Weeks, Graeber thought. She says that so lightly. Where will I be then?

"With soldiers it's different," he explained. "War marriages go faster. In a couple of days. I've heard about it at the barracks."

"Is that where you got the idea?"

"No. I believe it only occurred to me this morning. But in the barracks they often discuss the subject. Lots of soldiers get married on leave. Why not? When a soldier from the front gets married his wife is entitled to a monthly subsidy, two hundred marks, I think. Why make a present of that to the State? If one has to put his head on the block why shouldn't he at least take what he's entitled to? You could use it, and otherwise the State will keep it. Isn't that right?"

"If that's the way you look at it, perhaps it's right."

"That's what I mean," Graeber said, relieved. "Then there's a loan for the heads of families in addition, a thousand marks, I believe. Perhaps, too, you wouldn't have to go to your coat factory any more if you were married."

"Yes, I would. That has nothing to do with it. And what should I do otherwise all day long? Alone."

For a moment Graeber felt very helpless. Just what are they doing with us? he thought. We are young and ought to be happy and free to stay together. What do our parents' wars have to do with us? "We will both be alone," he said. "But if we are married we will be less so."

Elisabeth shook her head.

"You don't want to?" he asked.

"We would not be less alone," she said. "We'd be more so."

All at once Graeber heard again the voice of the singer in the house opposite. She had stopped practicing scales and was now singing octaves. They sounded like shrieks that were answered by an echo. "After all it is not irrevocable, if that's what you're thinking," he said. "We could always get a divorce later on if we want to."

"Then why should we marry?"

"Why should we make a present of anything to the State?"

Elisabeth got up. "Yesterday you were different," she said.

"Different in what way?"

She smiled briefly. "Let's not talk about it any more. We are together; that's enough."

"You don't want to?"

"No."

He looked at her. Something in her had withdrawn and closed against him. "Damn it," he said. "I meant it so well."

Elisabeth smiled again. "Sometimes that's just the trouble. One oughtn't to mean too well. Have we still something left to drink?"

"We still have sliwovitz."

"Is that the one that comes from Poland?"

"Yes."

"Haven't we anything that isn't booty?"

"We must still have a bottle of kuemmel. That's from Germany."

"Then give me that."

Graeber went into the kitchen to get the bottle. He was angry at himself. He stood for a moment in front of the pots and pans and Binding's presents in the half darkened room which smelled of former meals, and felt empty and burned out. Then he went back.

Elisabeth was leaning against the window frame. "How gray it is," she said. "It's going to rain. Too bad!"

"Why is it too bad?"

"It's our first Sunday. We could have gone out. It's spring outside the city."

"Would you like to go out?"

"No. For me Frau Lieser's absence is enough. But for you it would be a change from sitting around here."

"It doesn't matter to me either. I've lived long enough with nature and have no more need of her for quite a while. My dream of nature is a warm room free from bullet holes and with unbroken furniture. That's what we have here. It's the greatest adventure I can imagine and I can't get enough of it. But perhaps you've had more than enough of it. We can go to a movie if you like."

Elisabeth shook her head.

"Then let's stay here and not stir out. If we leave, the day will break into pieces and will be over quicker than if we stay. This way it will last longer."

Graeber went to Elisabeth and took her in his arms. He felt the rough toweling of her bathrobe. Then he saw that her eyes were full of tears. "Was I talking nonsense," he asked, "just now?"

"No."

"But I must have done something. Otherwise why are you crying?"

He held her tight and looked over her shoulder out into the street. The hairy man with the suspenders had disappeared. A couple of children were playing war in the trench that led to the cellar of the demolished house. "We shouldn't be sad," he said.

The singer across the street gave voice again. She was braying forth a song by Grieg. "I love thee! I love thee!" she screamed in her harsh, unsteady voice. "In spite of time and toil I love thee!"

"No, we shouldn't be sad," Elisabeth said.

In the afternoon it began to rain. It grew dark early and the overcast became heavier and heavier. They were lying on the bed without a light; the window was open and rain was falling outside, slanting and pale, a wavering, fluid wall.

Graeber listened to the monotous downpour. He was reflecting that in Russia the time of mud must have set in, the time when everything sank in endless mire. There would still be mire when he got back there. "Don't I have to leave?" he asked. "Frau Lieser will surely be back soon."

"Let her come," Elisabeth murmured sleepily. "Is it so late already?"

"I don't know. But perhaps she'll be back early because of the rain."

"Perhaps because of the rain she won't come back till later."

"That could be too."

"Perhaps she won't even come back till tomorrow," Elisabeth said, laying her face on his shoulder.

"Perhaps she'll even be run over by a truck. But that would be too much good luck."

"You're not much of a philanthropist," Elisabeth murmured.

Graeber stared into the gray sheet of rain outside the window. "If we were married I wouldn't have to go at all," he said.

Elisabeth did not move. "Why do you want to marry me?" she murmured. "After all you hardly know me."

"I have known you long enough."

"How long? A few days."

"Not a few days. I've known you for over a year. That's long enough."

"Why a year? We can't count the time from our childhood; that was too long ago."

"I'm not counting that either. But I was given about three weeks' furlough for two years in the field. I have been here almost two weeks now. That corresponds to about fifteen months at the front. And so I have known you for what amounts to more than a year: the equivalent of almost two weeks' leave."

Elisabeth opened her eyes. "I have never thought about it that way."

"I haven't either. I thought of that just now."

"When?"

"Earlier while you were asleep. In the rain and the dark you think of a lot of things."

"Does it have to be rainy and dark for that?"

"No. But one thinks differently then."

"Did you think of anything else?"

"Yes. It occurred to me how marvelous it is that a man could use his hands and arms for something besides shooting a gun and throwing grenades."

She looked at him. "Why didn't you tell me that at noon today?"

"At noontime one can't say that."

"It would have been better than talking about monthly allowances and marriage subsidies."

Graeber lifted his head. "It was the same thing, Elisabeth," he said. "Only in different words."

She murmured something. "Words are sometimes very important," she said then. "At least in something like this."

"I'm not used to using them so. But I will find some more of them. All I need is a little time."

"Time," Elisabeth sighed. "We don't have much, do we?"

"No. Yesterday we still had a lot. And tomorrow we will think that today we had a lot."

Graeber lay still. Elisabeth's head rested on his arm, her hair flowed darkly over the white pillow and the shadows of the rain moved across her face. "You want to marry me," she murmured. "But do you even know whether you love me at all?"

"How could we know that? One needs much more time and being together for that."

"Perhaps. But then why do you want to marry me?"

"Because I can no longer think of life without you."

Elisabeth was silent for a time. "Don't you believe that what's happened to us could have happened to you with somebody else?" she asked then.

Graeber looked at the wavering gray tapestry woven by the rain outside the window. "Perhaps it could have happened to me with somebody else," he said. "Who can tell about things like that? Only now that it has happened to us I can't imagine the possibility that it could ever have happened to me with anyone else."

Elisabeth moved her head in his arm. "You're learning. You're not talking now the way you did at noon. But of course it's night. Do you think I'll have to wait all my life for it to be night?"

"No. And for the time being I'll not say anything more about monthly subsidies."

"But just the same we won't scorn them, will we?"

"What?"

"The subsidies."

For a moment Graeber held his breath. "Then you want to?" he asked.

"If we've known each other for a year we really almost have to. And we can always get a divorce. Or can't we?"

"No."

She pressed herself against him and fell asleep again. He lay awake for a long time listening to the rain. He suddenly knew many things he might have said to her.

# Chapter Seventeen

TAKE ANYTHING you want, Ernst," Binding said through the door. "Act as though you were at home."

"All right, Alfons."

Graeber was stretched out in the bathtub. His army gear lay on a chair in the corner, gray, green, and disreputable as old rags; next to it hung a blue suit that Reuter had found for him.

Binding's bathroom was a big affair with green tile walls that shimmered with porcelain and nickel plate—a paradise by contrast with the roar and the stink of disinfectants in the shower room at the barracks. The soap was some that had come from France, bath towels and hand towels were piled high, the water pipes had never been knocked out of order by bombs, and there was as much hot water as you wanted. There even were bath salts: a big bottle full of amethyst crystals.

Graeber lay in the water thoughtless and relaxed, enjoying the benison of warmth. He had learned long since that it was only the simple things that never disappointed one—warmth, water, a roof, bread, quietness, and confidence in one's own body. He had decided to spend the rest of his furlough like this, without thought, relaxed, and as happy as possible. Reuter was right: it would be a long time before he got another furlough. He pushed the chair with his army gear to one side so that he would not have to look at it. Then he took a handful of the bath salts and appreciatively strewed them in the water. It was a handful of luxury—and luxury was peace—just like the white tablecloth in the Germania, the wine and the delicacies of his first evenings with Elisabeth.

He dried himself and slowly began to dress. The civilian clothes were light and thin after the heavy uniform. When he had finished dressing he still felt as though he were in his under-clothes, so unaccustomed was he to being without heavy boots, harness, and weapons. He looked at himself in the mirror and hardly recognized what he saw. An unfinished, half-baked young fellow looked out at him in surprise, someone he would not have taken seriously if he had met him at the front.

"You look like someone making his first communion," Alfons said. "Not like a soldier. What's up? Are you going to get married?"

"Yes," Graeber replied, startled. "How did you know?"

"It's the way you look. Not the same as before. No longer like a dog looking for a bone he has hidden and forgotten where. Are you really going to get married?"

"Yes."

"But, Ernst! What a thing! Have you thought it over carefully?"

"No."

Binding looked at Graeber in bewilderment. "I haven't had time for years to think anything over carefully," Graeber said.

Alfons grinned. Then he lifted his head and sniffed. "What—" He sniffed again. "Is that you, Ernst? Damn it, it must be the bath salts! Did you take some? You smell like a whole bed of violets."

Graeber sniffed at his hand. "I don't smell anything."

"You don't but I do. Let it wear off. It's tricky stuff. Someone brought it to me from Paris. At first you hardly notice it, and later you're like a whole bush in bloom. We'll drown it out with good cognac."

Binding brought a bottle and two glasses. "*Prost,* Ernst! So you're getting married! All my congratulations! I myself of course am and will remain a bachelor. Tell me, do I by any chance know your future wife?"

"No." Graeber drank up the cognac. He was angry with himself for having admitted the marriage; but Alfons had caught him off guard.

"One more, Ernst! You don't get married every day."

"All right."

Binding put down his glass. He was becoming a little sentimental. "If you should need any help you must know that you can always count on Alfons."

"What help? Things like that go quickly and simply."

"With you, yes. You are a soldier, you don't need any other papers."

"Neither of us does. After all, it's a war marriage."

"For your wife I believe you will need the usual papers. But you will find out about that. If it takes too long we can always help along a bit. You know we have good friends in the Gestapo."

"The Gestapo? What's the Gestapo got to do with a war marriage? That's no concern of theirs."

Alfons laughed contentedly. "Ernst, there is nothing that isn't a concern of the Gestapo! As a soldier you don't know about that. Besides you don't need to worry about it. After all, you're not going to marry a Jewess. Or a Communist. Nevertheless they'll probably make inquiries. Routine matter."

Graeber did not reply. He was suddenly deeply alarmed. If any inquiries were started, it was bound to come out that Elisabeth's father was in a concentration camp. He had not considered that. Nor had anyone mentioned it to him.

"Are you sure that's how it is, Alfons?"

Binding refilled the glasses. "I believe so. But don't worry about it. You're not going to adulterate your Aryan blood with subhumans and enemies of the State, eh?" He grinned. "You'll get your ball and chain fast enough, Ernst."

"Yes."

"Well then! *Prost!* After all, you met a couple of fellows from the Gestapo right here a while ago. If things go too slowly they can help us out. Put on some pressure. They're big wheels. Especially Riese, the thin one with the pince-nez."

Graeber stared straight ahead. Elisabeth had gone to the town hall that morning to ask for her papers. He had insisted on it. Damn it, what have I started? he thought. What if their attention is called to her! Till now they have left her alone. But wasn't it an old rule to hide when the weather got thick? If they thought of it the Gestapo might send Elisabeth to a camp just because her father was in one. He felt himself growing hot. What if they started making inquiries about her? If they asked that esteemed Party member, Frau Lieser, for example?

He got up. "What's the matter with you, Ernst?" Binding asked. "You haven't finished your drink. Happiness makes you absentminded, eh?"

He laughed at his joke. Graeber looked at him. Only a few minutes before he had been a somewhat inflated, good-natured acquaintance—but now he was suddenly transformed into the representative of a dangerous, incalculable power.

"*Prost,* Ernst!" Binding said. "Drink up. It's good cognac. Napoleon!"

"*Prost,* Alfons."

Graeber put down his glass. "Alfons," he said, "will you do me a favor? Give me two pounds of sugar from your store room. In two bags. One pound in each."

"Lump sugar?"

"That doesn't matter. Sugar."

"All right. But why do you need sugar? You ought to be sweet enough yourself, now."

"I want to bribe someone with it."

"Bribe? But, Ernst, we don't have to do that! Threats are much simpler. And more effective. I can attend to that for you."

"Not in this case. Besides, it isn't really bribery. The sugar is for someone I want to have do me a favor."

"All right, Ernst. And the wedding celebration will be at my house, eh? Alfons will make a good witness."

Graeber thought this over rapidly. A quarter of an hour earlier he would have taken refuge behind some excuse. Now he no longer dared to. "I don't think we'll have much of a celebration," he said.

"Just let Alfons attend to it! You'll sleep here tonight, won't you? Why should you come back here and change your uniform and then go trotting off to the barracks? Better just stay here. I'll give you a key to the house. You can come in whenever you like."

Graeber hesitated for an instant. "All right, Alfons."

Binding beamed. "That's sensible. Then we can at last sit down together and gossip in comfort. We haven't had a chance to do that yet. Come, I'll show you your room." He picked up Graeber's army gear and glanced at the decorations on the blouse. "You must tell me sometime how you got all these. You really must have done something special!"

Graeber looked up. Binding's face suddenly had the same expression as on the day when the S.S. man Heini had drunkenly boasted about his exploits in the S.D. "There's nothing to tell," he said. "You get those things simply with the passage of time."

Frau Lieser stared at Graeber's suit; then she recognized him. "You? Fräulein Kruse is not at home. You should know that."

"Yes, I did know that, Frau Lieser."

"Well then?"

She looked at him hostilely. On her brown blouse shone a pin with the swastika. Her hair was oily and disordered. In her right hand she held a dust cloth as though it were a weapon.

"I would like to leave a package for Fräulein Kruse. Will you put it in her room?"

Frau Lieser looked at him uncertainly. Then she took the bag of sugar which he held out to her. "I have a second small package here," Graeber said. "Fräulein Kruse has told me in what exemplary fashion you sacrifice your time for the common good. I have a pound of sugar here, and I don't know what to do with it. Since you have a child who can use sugar I wanted to ask you whether you would like to have it."

Frau Lieser's face assumed an official expression. "We have no need for hoarders' goods. We are proud to get along with what the Fuehrer allows us."

"Your child too?"

"My child too!"

"That's the proper attitude," Graeber said, staring at the brown blouse. "If everyone at home behaved like that many a soldier at the front would be in a happier frame of mind. But these are no hoarders' goods. This is sugar from a package the

Fuehrer gives soldiers at the front who are leaving on furlough, so they can take it with them to their families. My family is missing; so you needn't hesitate to take it."

Frau Lieser's face lost some of its severity. "You came from the front?"

"Of course. Where else?"

"From Russia?"

"Yes."

"My husband is stationed in Russia, too."

Graeber pretended an interest he did not feel. "Where is he stationed?"

"With the Central Army Group."

"Thank God it's quiet there for the moment."

"Quiet? It is not quiet there! The Central Army Group is fully engaged. And my husband is in the very front line."

The very front line, Graeber thought. As though there still were such a thing as a front line! For a moment he was tempted to explain to Frau Lieser what it was actually like beyond the wall of phrases about Honor, Fuehrer, and Fatherland; but he gave it up at once. "I hope he'll come back soon on leave," he said.

"He'll come on leave when his turn comes. We don't ask any favors."

"Neither did I," Graeber remarked dryly. "On the contrary. The last time I was here was two years ago."

"Were you out there the whole time?"

"From the beginning. When I wasn't wounded."

Graeber stared at the unshakable Party warrior. Why do I stand here and justify myself in the eyes of this woman? he thought. I ought to shoot her down—just as her husband, who is probably in the S.D., is shooting down Russian kulaks in order to gain that notorious *Lebensraum* for his Fuehrer.

The Liesers' child came out of the room in which the desk

stood. She was a thin girl with lusterless hair, who stared at Graeber and then began to pick her nose.

"Why are you suddenly wearing civilian clothes?" Frau Lieser asked.

"My uniform is being cleaned."

"So that's it! I thought perhaps—"

Graeber did not find out what she had thought. He suddenly saw that she was smiling at him with yellow teeth, and it almost terrified him. "Well, all right," she said. "Thank you. I will use the sugar for my child."

She took the two packages and Graeber noticed that she weighed one against the other in her hands. He knew she would open Elisabeth's as soon as he had gone and that was just what he wanted. She would be amazed to find simply the second pound of sugar and nothing more. "That's right, Frau Lieser. *Auf Wiedersehen.*"

"*Heil Hitler!*"

The woman stared at him. "*Heil Hitler,*" Graeber said.

He went out of the house. Beside the front door he found the house warden leaning against a wall. He was a little man with S.A. trousers, boots, and a round little paunch under his rooster chest. Graeber stopped. Even this scarecrow had suddenly become dangerous. "Nice weather today," he said, getting out a package of cigarettes. He took one and offered the package to the man.

The house warden grunted something and accepted one. "Discharged?" he asked with an oblique glance at Graeber's clothes.

Graeber shook his head. He considered saying a few words about Elisabeth, but decided not to. It was better not to arouse the house warden's curiosity. "In a week I am off again. For the fourth time."

The house warden nodded indifferently. He took the cigarette out of his mouth, looked at it, and spat out a few shreds of tobacco. "Doesn't it taste all right?" Graeber asked.

"Oh sure. But I am really a cigar smoker."

"Cigars are in damn short supply, aren't they?"

"They certainly are."

"I know someone who still has some boxes of good ones. Next time I have the chance I'll take a couple and bring them along. Good cigars."

"Imported?"

"Probably. I don't know much about them. Cigars with bands."

"Bands mean nothing. Any bunch of beech leaves can have a band around it."

"The man is a commander in the S.A. He smokes a good weed."

"A commander in the S.A.?"

"Yes. Alfons Binding. My best friend."

"Binding is your friend?"

"An old school friend, as a matter of fact. I have just come from seeing him. He and S.S. Commander Riese are old comrades of mine. I am going over to Riese's house now."

The house warden looked at Graeber. Graeber understood the glance; the house warden did not understand why Health Councilor Kruse was in a concentration camp if Binding and Riese were such old friends.

"Several mistakes have been cleared up," he said casually. "Very shortly things will be in order again. Some people will be surprised, I expect. One ought never to be too hasty, eh?"

"Never," declared the house warden with conviction.

Graeber looked at his watch. "I must be off. I won't forget the cigars."

He went on. That was a pretty good start in corruption, he thought. But presently uneasiness seized him once more. Perhaps what he had done was just the wrong thing. It seemed suddenly childish. Perhaps he should not have done anything at all. He stopped and stared down at himself. This damn civilian outfit! It seemed to be to blame for everything. He had wanted to escape from army regulations and to feel free; instead he had immediately got into a world of fear and uncertainty.

He debated what more he could do. Elisabeth could not be reached before evening. He cursed the haste with which he had applied for the papers. Protection, he thought bitterly. Yesterday morning I was making a big point about marriage being a protection for her—and now it has become nothing but danger.

"What's the meaning of these carnival jokes?" a rude voice shouted at him.

He glanced up. A little major was standing in front of him. "Have you no conception of the seriousness of the times, you clown?"

Graeber stared at him for a moment, not comprehending. Then he understood. He had saluted the major without remembering that he was wearing civilian clothes. The old man had interpreted this as derision. "Mistake," he said. "Forget it."

"What? You have the gall to make stupid jokes? Why aren't you a soldier?"

Graeber looked at the old man more closely. He was the same one who had given him a dressing down the evening he had been standing with Elisabeth in front of her house.

"A slacker like you ought to sink into the earth for shame instead of cutting capers like this," the major barked.

"Oh, don't excite yourself," Graeber said angrily. "And get back into your moth chest."

The old man's eyes took on an almost insane expression. He choked and turned red as a crab. "I'll have you arrested," he wheezed.

"You can't do that, as you should know yourself. And now leave me alone, I have other things to worry about."

"Why, that's—" The major was about to burst forth afresh when suddenly he came a step closer and began to sniff with wide-open, hairy nostrils. His face contorted. "Ah, now I understand," he announced disgustedly. "That's why you're not in uniform! The third sex! *Pfui Teufel!* A fairy! Wearing perfume! A male whore!"

He spat, wiped his white bristly mustache, threw Graeber one more glance full of abysmal disgust, and walked off. It had been the bath salts. Graeber smelled his hand. He could detect it now, too. A whore, he thought. I'm not far from being one, though. How corrupt a little fear for someone else can make you! Frau Lieser, the block warden—and what else mightn't I be ready to do! I've tumbled damned fast from my heights of virtue!

He stood diagonally across the street from the headquarters of the Gestapo. In the entrance drive a young S.S. man was walking up and down yawning. A couple of S.S. officers came out laughing. Then an elderly man approached, hesitated, looked up at the windows, halted and took a slip of paper out of his pocket. He read it, looked around, glanced toward the sky as though taking leave and then went slowly up to the guard. The S.S. man read the summons and let him in.

Graeber stared up at the windows. He felt fear again, stickier, heavier and clammier than before. He was acquainted with many fears, sharp ones and dark ones, breathless ones and paralyzing ones, and also with the last great one, the animal's fear of death— but this was a different one, it was a creeping, strangling fear, undefined and threatening, a fear that seemed to soil, slimy and destructive, that was not to be seized and that could not be brought to bay, a fear of helplessness and gnawing doubt, the corrupting fear for others, for the guiltless victims, the unjustly persecuted, the fear before the caprice of power and automatic inhumanity, it was the black fear of the times.

He turned away. He felt helpless and miserable. Hirschland, he thought, Hirschland had known it too! Hirschland who had become a soldier to protect his family, who had volunteered for patrols because he hoped that if he got a decoration it would keep his father out of a concentration camp; Hirschland whose parents he had promised to visit.

He stopped. Where had he put the slip of paper with the address? All at once it seemed very important to him to go there immediately—as though it had a connection with Elisabeth and as though everything would be all right with her if he only went there at once. It was childish, but as a soldier one learned to believe in strange happenings. He searched in all his pockets and finally he found the slip in his pay book.

It was a small three-storied house. He climbed to the third floor and rang twice more. Then the door was opened cautiously. A pale woman peered out.

"May I speak to Frau Hirschland?"

"I am Frau Hirschland."

The woman looked straight at him with very bright, staring eyes. "I'm in the same company as your son," Graeber said.

The woman continued to look at him. It was like the glance of a terrified animal that has been brought to bay and is ready to fight. "Your son asked me to come and see you," Graeber said. "I'm here on furlough. That's why I've got civilian clothes on."

"Yes." The woman opened the door wider. "Yes, please. Come in please, Herr—"

"Graeber. Ernst Graeber."

The woman preceded him into a living room. She walked noiselessly and very lightly. In the living room against one wall was a wide chaise longue with high legs; over it was thrown a blue cover which had been pulled down low in front. Graeber was about to sit down on the chaise longue when the woman pushed up a chair. "Here, you will be more comfortable in this. That over there—we only have this one room—that's the bed."

Graeber sat down on the chair. The room was clean and furnished in middle-class fashion. Over the chaise longue hung a few pictures; there were others on the two side walls. "About two weeks ago I was still with your son," Graeber said.

The woman had not seated herself. Her glance had lost none of its glassy fixity; but her hands jerked restlessly this way and that. "Perhaps you will—I could—perhaps you'd take a little something—"

Graeber suddenly realized that he was very thirsty. "Thanks," he said. "A glass of water—if you happen to have a glass of water—"

"Yes, certainly." Frau Hirschland looked around the room. "Yes, I will—in the kitchen—just one moment—I'll go and get it—"

She went. At the door she looked around once more. What's the matter with her? Graeber thought. He was used to people being afraid but this was something more than usual.

He got up and looked at the pictures on the wall. They were reproductions. One was a chestnut tree in bloom, another the profile of a Florentine girl. The picture over the chaise longue was a big etching. He stepped closer to get a better view. In doing so his foot jostled something behind the hanging cover. He bent down and lifted the cover to see whether he had upset anything. He saw two narrow cardboard boxes arranged end to end and extending almost the whole length of the chaise longue. One was at an angle. Graeber pushed it straight. As he did so he saw a girl's hand in the crack between the two boxes. Someone was lying behind the boxes next to the wall, with her arm pressed close to her body. He let the cover fall and went back to his chair.

Frau Hirschland came in. She was carrying a lacquer tray on which there was a small glass of red wine; on a plate next to it were two slices of bread. "Please have something," she said.

Graeber took a sip. The wine was very sweet and sticky. "Things are going well with your son," he said. "When I left we were in reserve position. All of us like your son."

The woman looked at him. He took another sip. He was surprised that she did not ask him where they were located, how the food was, whether it was dangerous, and all the questions mothers ask.

"So, things were going well with him?" she asked finally.

"As well as is possible in the field. Now it's just about the same here as out there. Almost equally dangerous."

He waited a while longer. But Frau Hirschland asked nothing more. Perhaps she is worried about the girl she has hidden, Graeber thought. "That's really all," he finally said lamely and stood up. The woman walked noiselessly with him to the door. "Your son and I are good friends. Do you want me to take him some message? I have to go back in a week."

"No," she replied, barely audibly.

"I can take something to him. A letter or a package. I can come and get it before I leave."

She shook her head.

Graeber looked at her in amazement. Parents weren't usually like this. He thought she did not trust him and got out his pay book. "Here are my papers—I'm just accidentally in civilian clothes—"

She raised her hand as though to push the pay book aside, but she did not touch it. "He is dead," she whispered.

"What?"

She nodded.

"But how is that possible? He was the last one I talked to—"

"Dead," the woman whispered. "The news came four days ago." She shook her head rapidly as Graeber was about to ask something more. "No, please don't, forgive me, many thanks, I can't, letters still keep coming from him, one just today, no, please—"

She shut the door. Graeber went down the stairs. He tried to recall Hirschland. He had known very little about him. Not even his first name. He thought of the cigarettes Hirschland had given him. It was too bad he had not taken more trouble with him. But it was too bad about so many others too. Hirschland had had a miserable life. Now his mother was sitting up there hiding another child. Perhaps the child of a second marriage in which more Jewish blood was involved, making her ripe for a concentration camp. He paused on the half-darkened stairs and was suddenly wholly at a loss. Threatening and hopeless, the darkness closed in around him and it seemed as though there was no escape any more. If someone had to be hidden for that reason, he thought, then what might not happen to Elisabeth!

He was standing in front of the factory long before closing time. It took a while before Elisabeth came. He was already beginning to fear that she had been arrested in the factory when he finally saw her. She was taken aback to see him in civilian clothes and began to laugh. "How young you are!" she said.

"I don't feel young. I feel a hundred years old."

"Why? What has happened? Do you have to go back ahead of time?"

"No, all that is all right."

"Do you feel a hundred years old because you are wearing civilian clothes?"

"I don't know. But it seems to me that I've put on all the cares of the world along with this damn outfit. What have you done about your papers?"

"Everything," Elisabeth replied, beaming. "I used my lunch hour. All the applications have been made."

"Everything," Graeber said. "Then there is nothing more to be done."

"What needs to be done?"

"Nothing. I just suddenly got frightfully anxious. Perhaps what we are doing is a mistake. Perhaps it could hurt you."

"Me? How?"

Graeber hesitated. "I have heard that sometimes an inquiry is made by the Gestapo. That's why we perhaps ought to have left everything alone."

Elisabeth stood still. "Have you heard anything?"

"No. Nothing. It was just that I suddenly got frightened."

"You mean I might be arrested because we want to get married?"

"Not that."

"What then? Do you mean they might find out my father is in the concentration camp?"

"Not that either," Graeber interrupted. "They certainly know that already. I mean that perhaps it would be better not to call anyone's attention to you. The Gestapo is unpredictable and someone there might get some idiotic idea. You know how that sort of thing happens. No trace of justice about it."

Elisabeth was silent for an instant. "Then what shall we do?" she asked.

"I've been thinking about it all day. But I believe there's nothing more we can do. If we withdrew your applications they might become all the more suspicious."

She nodded and looked at him strangely. "Just the same we could try to withdraw them."

"It's too late, Elisabeth. Now we must take the risk and wait."

They walked on. The factory was situated on a small square and was clearly visible. Graeber looked at it carefully. "Have you never been bombed here?"

"Not yet."

"The building stands pretty much in the open. It's easy to spot it as a factory."

"We have big cellars."

"Are they safe?"

"Fairly so, I think."

Graeber glanced up. Elisabeth was walking along beside him, not looking at him. "For God's sake, understand what I mean," he said. "I am not afraid for myself. I am simply afraid for you."

"You don't need to be afraid for me."

"Aren't you?"

"I have already had all the fears there are. I have no place left for new ones."

"But I have. When you love someone there are many new fears you didn't know about at all before."

Elisabeth turned toward him. She smiled suddenly. He looked at her and nodded. "I haven't forgotten the speech I made day before yesterday," he said. "Do you really have to be afraid before you know whether you love someone?"

"I don't know. But I think it helps."

"This damned outfit! I won't wear it again tomorrow. And I thought civilians had an enviable life!"

Elisabeth laughed. "Is it just the clothes?"

"No," he said with relief. "It comes from being alive again. I'm alive again and I want to go on living. And when that's how it is, apparently you become afraid again. It was horrible all day long. It's better now though—since I have seen you. And yet nothing has changed. Strange how little foundation there has to be for fear."

"Or love," Elisabeth said. "Thank God!"

Graeber looked at her. She was walking beside him free and unconcerned. She has changed, he thought. She changes every day. It used to be that she was afraid and I wasn't; now it's reversed.

They walked past the Hitlerplatz. Behind the church hung a splendid sunset. "Where's the fire now?" Elisabeth asked.

"Nowhere. It's just the sunset."

"The sunset! We don't count on that any more, do we?"

"No."

They walked on. The sunset became stronger and deeper. It touched their faces and hands. Graeber glanced at the people who were coming toward them. He suddenly saw them otherwise than before. Each was now a human being with a fate of his own. It was easy to judge and to be brave when one had nothing, he thought. But when one possessed something the world changed. It made things easier and harder and sometimes almost impossible. It was still bravery, but it looked different and it had entirely different names and it really began only there. He took a deep breath. He felt as though he had returned from a long, dangerous patrol in enemy territory—less safe than before—but nevertheless secure for the moment.

"Strange," Elisabeth said. "It must be spring. After all, this is a bombed street and there is no sense in it—nevertheless I believe I already small violets—"

# Chapter Eighteen

BOETTCHER WAS packing his things. The others were standing around him. "So you actually found her?" Graeber asked.

"Yes, but—"

"Where?"

"On the street," Boettcher said. "She was simply standing on the corner of Kellerstrasse and Bierstrasse where the umbrella store used to be. In the first second, I didn't even recognize her."

"Where had she been all this time?"

"In a camp near Erfurt. But listen! So she's standing there by the umbrella store and I don't see her. I walk past and she calls after me, 'Otto! Don't you know me?'" Boettcher paused and looked around the barracks day-room. "But how are you expected to recognize a woman, comrades, when she has taken off eighty pounds!"

"What's the name of the camp where she was?"

"I don't know. Forest Camp II, I think. I can ask her. But just listen now! So I start at her and say: 'Alma, you?' 'I!' she says. 'Otto, I had a sort of presentiment that you were on furlough; that's why I came back.' I go on staring at her. A woman that used to be as husky as a brewer's horse stands there, emaciated, only a hundred and ten pounds instead of almost two hundred, a skeleton, her clothes hanging, a beanpole!"

Boettcher snorted. "How tall is she?" Feldmann asked, interested.

"What?"

"How tall is your wife?"

"About five feet three. Why?"

"Then she's average weight now."

"Average weight? But, man, what kind of nonsense is that?" Boettcher stared at Feldmann. "Not for me. As far as I am concerned she's a wisp. What does your damned average weight matter to me? I want to have my wife back the way she was, buxom, with an ass you could crack nuts on and not with a sorry coffee bean instead. What am I fighting for? For something like that?"

"You're fighting for our beloved Fuehrer and for our dear Fatherland—not for your wife's dead weight." Reuter said. "You ought slowly to have found that out after three years at the front."

"Dead weight? Who's talking about dead weight?" Boettcher looked from one to the other in anger and helplessness. "Live weight is what it was! And you can take all the rest and—"

"Stop!" Reuter lifted his hand in warning. "Think what you like but don't say it. And be happy your wife is alive."

"I am, of course! But can't she be alive and as buxom as she used to be?"

"But, Boettcher!" Feldmann said. "After all you can feed her up again."

"Really? And with what? With the little bit you can get for ration coupons?"

"Try and see what you can get the back way."

"It's easy for you to talk! You and your good advice," Boettcher exclaimed bitterly. "I only have three days' furlough left. How am I to feed up my wife in three days? Even if she bathes in cod liver oil and eats seven meals a day, she can't gain more than a couple of pounds at most, and what does that amount to? Comrades, I am in a dreadful situation!"

"Why? After all, you still have the plump proprietress for fat, if that's what matters."

"That's just it! I thought if my wife came back I wouldn't so much as give a passing thought to the proprietress. I'm a family man and not a chaser. And now the proprietress pleases me more."

"You're just a damned superficial character," Reuter said.

"I am not superficial! With me everything goes too deep, that's my failing. Otherwise I could be perfectly satisfied. That's something you don't understand, you jokers."

Boettcher went to his locker and threw the last of his things into his knapsack. "Do you know where you and your wife will stay?" Graeber asked. "Or do you still have your old apartment?"

"Of course not. Bombed out! But I would rather live in a cellar in the ruins than spend another day here. The calamity is simply that my wife no longer pleases me. Of course I still love her, that's why I married her, but she simply no longer pleases me the way she is. There's just nothing at all I can do about it. What am I supposed to do? She feels it too, of course."

"How much more furlough have you?"

"Three days."

"Couldn't you pretend just for that bit of time?"

"Comrade," Boettcher said calmly, "in bed maybe a woman can pretend. Not a man. Believe me, it would have been better if I had gone off without finding her. As it is we simply torment each other."

He picked up his things and left.

Reuter looked after him. Then he turned to Graeber. "And you? What are your plans?"

"I'm going to the commissary. Just as a precaution I'm going to ask again whether I need any more papers."

Reuter grinned. "Your friend Boettcher's bad luck hasn't scared you off, eh?"

"No. It's an entirely different kind of thing that scares me."

"Heavy weather," said the clerk at the commissary. "There's heavy weather at the front. Do you know what you're supposed to do in heavy weather?"

"Take cover," Graeber replied. "Any child knows that. But what has that to do with me? I'm on furlough."

"You think you're still on furlough," the clerk corrected him. "What's it worth to you if I show you an order that arrived today?"

"That depends."

Graeber took a package of cigarettes out of his pocket and laid it on the table. He felt his stomach contracting. "Heavy weather," the clerk repeated. "Severe losses. Replacements required instantly. Men on furlough who have no urgent reason for staying are to be sent back immediately. Get it?"

"Yes. what are urgent reasons?"

"Death in the family, settling important family business, serious illness—"

The clerk reached for the cigarettes. "So disappear! Make yourself invisible. If they can't find you they can't send you back. Avoid the barracks like the plague. Crawl in some place until your furlough is over. Then report for duty. What can happen to you then? Punishment for failure to report a change of address? You're going back to the front anyway, *basta.*"

"I am getting married," Graeber said. "Is that a reason?"

"You're getting married?"

"Yes, that's why I'm here. I wanted to know whether I needed any papers beside my pay book."

"Marriage! Perhaps that is a reason. Perhaps, I say."

The clerk lit one of the cigarettes. "It could be a reason. But why take a chance? You, as a front-line hog, don't need extra papers. And if you do need some, come to me; I will arrange it for you on the quiet so that no one gets a whiff of it. Have you a decent outfit? After all, you can't get married in those rags."

"Can I make any sort of trade here?"

"Go to the sarge in charge of supplies," the clerk said. "Explain to him that you are getting married. Say I sent you. Have you still a few good cigarettes?"

"No. But perhaps I can get hold of another pack."

"Not for me. For the sarge."

"I'll see. Do you know whether in a war marriage the woman has to have any special papers?"

"No idea. But I think not. Since it has to be done fast." The clerk looked at his watch. "Go right over to the supply department. The sarge is there now."

Graeber went to the wing where the supply department was. It was in the attic. The sergeant major was fat and his eyes were different colors. One was of an unnatural, almost violet blue, the other was light brown.

"Don't stare at me," he snapped. "Haven't you ever seen a glass eye before?"

"Sure. But never one that was so different in color."

"This isn't mine, you idiot." The sergeant major tapped the beaming blue eye. "I borrowed it from a friend. Mine fell out on the floor yesterday. It was brown. These things are too fragile. They ought to be made of celluloid."

"Then they would be a fire hazard."

The sergeant major looked up. He examined Graeber's decorations and then grinned. "That's right. Nevertheless, I have no uniform for you. Sorry. They're all worse than yours."

He glanced at Graeber piercingly with the blue eye. The brown one had grown duller. Graeber laid a package of Binding's cigarettes on the table. The sergeant major swept them with a glance from the brown eye, turned around and came back with a blouse. "This is all I have."

Graeber did not touch the blouse. He took out of his pocket a small bottle of cognac which he had brought with him as a precaution and placed it beside the cigarettes. The sergeant major disappeared and then returned with a better blouse and an almost new pair of trousers. Graeber reached for the trousers first; his own were much mended. He turned them over and noticed that the commissary watch-dog had folded them so that a spot as big as a man's hand had been hidden. Graeber looked at the spot in silence and then at the cognac.

"It's not blood," the sergeant said. "It's the best grade of olive oil. The man who wore them came from Italy. A little benzine and the spot will be gone."

"If it's so easy, why did he trade them and not clean them himself?"

The sergeant showed his teeth. "A good question. But the man wanted to have a uniform that smelled of the front. Something like the one you're wearing. Spent two years sitting in an office in Milan and writing letters from the front to his fiancée. Couldn't go home in new trousers that had only a dish of salad spilled on them. It's my best pair, really."

Graeber did not believe him but he had nothing more with

him to improve the trade. Nevertheless he shook his head. "Well, then," said the sergeant major, "another proposition. You don't need to trade them. Keep your old rags, too. That way you'll have a dress uniform. Agreed?"

"Don't you need the old one to make the count come out?"

The sergeant gave a careless gesture. His blue eye caught a beam of sunlight that shot dustily through the window. "The count hasn't come out for a long time. What does come out any more, after all? Do you know?"

"No."

"Well then," said the sergeant major.

He was passing the City Hospital and stopped. Mutzig popped into his mind. He had promised to visit him. For a moment he hesitated, but then went in. He suddenly had the superstitious feeling again that he could bribe fate by doing a good deed.

The amputees were on the second floor. The ground floor of the hospital was assigned to the serious cases and those recently operated on who were still confined to bed; thus they could be more quickly moved to the cellar during an air raid. The amputees were not considered helpless, and so they had been placed higher up. During an alarm they could come to each other's assistance. A legless man could, if necessary, always put his arms around the necks of two armless amputees and get to the cellar between them, while the personnel were rescuing the serious bed cases.

"You?" Mutzig said to Graeber. "I never thought you would come."

"Neither did I. But you see I'm here."

"That's nice of you, Ernst. Stockmann is here too. Weren't you with him in Africa?"

"Yes."

Stockmann had lost his right arm. He was playing skat with two other cripples. "Man alive, Ernst," he said. "What's happened to you?" His eyes slid inquiringly over Graeber. He was instinctively looking for the wound.

"Nothing," Graeber replied. They all looked at him. They all had the same expression as Stockmann. "Furlough," he said in embarrassment. He felt almost guilty at being whole.

"I thought you got enough in Africa for a permanent pass home."

"They patched me up and then sent me to Russia."

"You were in luck there. I was, too, relatively speaking. The others all became prisoners of war. They couldn't fly any more out." Stockmann waved his stump. "If one can call this luck."

The man in the middle slapped his cards down on the table. "Are we playing or are we jawing?" he asked rudely.

Graeber saw that he had no legs. They had been amputated very high up. Two fingers were missing from his right hand, and he had no eyelashes. The lids were new and red and gleaming and looked as if they had been burned.

"Go on playing," Graeber said. "I have time."

"Just this one hand," Stockmann announced. "We'll be through soon."

Graeber seated himself beside Mutzig at the window. "Don't pay any attention to Arnold," Mutzig whispered. "He's having his bad day."

"Is he the one in the middle?"

"Yes. His wife was here yesterday. After that he always has a couple of bad days."

"What are you gossiping about there?" Arnold shouted.

"We are gossiping about old times. There's no law against that, is there?"

Arnold growled something and went on playing. "Usually it's very pleasant here," Mutzig said eagerly. "We really have a lot of fun. Arnold was a Mason; that's not simple, you know. And his wife is cheating on him; his mother told him that."

Stockmann threw his cards on the table. "Damn the luck! The solo cross was a sure thing. How was anyone to know the three knaves would be sitting in one hand!"

Arnold bleated something and shuffled again. "Sometimes one doesn't know which is better when you want to get married," Mutzig said, "to have lost an arm or a leg. Stockmann says an arm. But how can you hold a woman in bed with one arm? And you do have to hold them, don't you?"

"That's not important. The main thing is that you are alive."

"That's true. But you can't support yourself with that all your life. After the war those things are different. Then you're not a hero any more; you're just a cripple."

"I don't think so. They have wonderful prostheses."

"That's not what I mean," Mutzig said. "I don't mean work."

"We have to win the war, that's what we have to do," Arnold suddenly announced in a loud voice. He had been listening. "Let others risk their bones for a change! We have done our part."

He shot an unfriendly glance at Graeber. "If all the slackers were out there we wouldn't have to keep withdrawing all the time!"

Graeber did not reply. You could not quarrel with amputees; anyone who had lost a limb was always in the right. You could quarrel with someone who had been shot through the lungs or had a shell splinter in his stomach and might be in even worse shape; but it was strange—not with an amputee.

Arnold went on playing. "What's your opinion, Ernst?" Mutzig asked after a while. "I have a girl in Muenster; we still correspond. She thinks I have been shot in the leg. I have not written her about this yet."

"Wait. And be glad you don't have to go back any more."

"I am, Ernst. But you can't keep on being glad indefinitely."

"You make me sick," one of the kibitzers sitting around the card players said suddenly to Mutzig. "Get drunk and be men."

Stockmann laughed. "What are you laughing about?" Arnold asked.

"I just thought how it would be if a heavy bomb slammed down on us tonight—right on top of us so that there was nothing left but jelly—then why would we have tormented ourselves with all these worries?"

Graeber got up. He saw that the kibitzer had lost both feet. A mine or frozen, he thought automatically. "What's become of our anti-aircraft guns?" Arnold growled at him. "Do you need them all out there? There are practically none here any more."

"Nor outside either."

"What?"

Graeber realized he had made a mistake. "Outside we are waiting for the new secret weapons," he said. "They're said to be real wonders."

Arnold stared at him. "Damn it all! What sort of way is that to talk? That sounds as if we had lost the war. That's impossible. Do you think I want to sit on a pushcart and sell matches like the men after the first war? We have rights. The Fuehrer has promised!"

He slammed his cards down on the table in excitement. "Come, turn the radio on," the kibitzer said to Mutzig. "Music."

Mutzig turned the knob. A flood of brassy words poured out of the loud-speaker. He turned the dial. "Leave it on," Arnold demanded angrily.

"Why? It's only another of those speeches."

"Leave it on, I say! That's a Party oration. If everyone would only listen to them regularly, things would be better with us!"

Mutzig sighed and turned the dial back. A *siegheil* orator screamed into the room. Arnold listened with clenched jaws. Stockmann made a sign to Graeber and shrugged his shoulders. Graeber went over to him. "Take care of yourself, Stockmann," he whispered. "I've got to go."

"Something better to do, eh?"

"It's not that. But I have to be off."

He walked out. The glances of the others followed him. It seemed to him that he was naked. He walked slowly through the room; he believed that would be less offensive to the amputees. But he saw how they looked after him. Mutzig hobbled with him to the door. "Come again," he said in the faded light of the gray corridor. "Today you had bad luck. Usually we are much gayer."

Graeber stepped out into the street. It was growing dark now, and all of a sudden his fear for Elisabeth came upon him again. All day he had tried to escape from it. But now in the uncertain light it seemed to creep upon him once more out of every corner.

He went to Pohlmann. The old man opened the door at once. It was as though he had been expecting someone else. "It's you, Graeber," he said.

"Yes. I won't bother you for long. I just wanted to ask you something."

Pohlmann opened the door. "Come in. It is better not to stand outside. No need for people to know—"

They went into the room where the lamp stood. Graeber smelled fresh cigarette smoke. Pohlmann did not have a cigarette in his hand. "What did you want to ask me, Graeber?"

Graeber looked around. "Is this all the room you have?" he asked.

"Why?"

"I might want to hide someone for a few days. Is that possible here?"

Pohlmann was silent. "It's not anyone who is wanted," Graeber said. "I would only do it as a precaution. Very likely it won't be necessary at all. I am anxious about someone. Perhaps it is only imagination."

"Why do you come to me for that?"

"I don't know anyone else."

Graeber did not know himself why he had come. He had simply felt that he had to look for a hideaway in case worst came to worst.

"Who is it?"

"Someone I want to marry. Her father is in the concentration camp. I am afraid that she may be taken, too. She hasn't done anything. Perhaps I'm just imagining all this."

"Nothing is imagination in these times," Pohlmann said. "And precaution is better than regret. You can have this room if you need it."

Graeber felt a wave of warmth and relief. "Thank you," he said. "Thank you very much."

Pohlmann smiled. Suddenly he looked less frail than before. "Thank you," Graeber said once more. "I hope I won't need it."

They were standing in front of the shelves of books. "Take any of them you want," Pohlmann said. "Sometimes they help you get through an evening."

Graeber shook his head. "They don't help me. But there's one thing I'd like to know: how does all this fit together—these books, these poems, these philosophies—with the inhumanity of

the S.A., the concentration camps and the liquidation of innocent people?"

"They don't fit together. They simply exist at the same time.
If the men who wrote these books were alive most of them would
be sitting in a concentration camp too."

"Perhaps."

Pohlmann looked at Graeber. "You intend to get married?"

"Yes."

The old man pulled a volume from a shelf. "I can't give you
anything else. Take this. It's nothing to read; it's pictures, just
pictures. There have been times when I was not able to read and
spent whole evenings just looking at pictures. Pictures and
poems—they always helped as long as I had oil for the lamp.
Later, in the dark, of course there was only prayer left."

"Yes," Graeber said without conviction.

"I've thought a great deal about you. And I've thought about
what you said to me recently. There's no answer." Pohlmann hesitated and then said softly: "Only one. You must believe. What
else remains?"

"Believe in what?"

"In God. And in what's good in men."

"Haven't you ever doubted that?" Graeber asked.

"Of course," the old man replied. "Often. How else could I
believe?"

Graeber went to the factory. It had grown windy, and torn fragments of cloud drifted low over the roofs. A company of soldiers was marching across the square in the half darkness. They
were carrying packages and were on their way to the station
and to the front. I might be one of them, he thought. He saw
the linden tree looming darkly in front of the demolished house

and suddenly he felt in his shoulders and his muscles the same strong surge of life he had experienced the first time he had seen the tree. Strange, he thought, I feel sorry for Pohlmann and he cannot help me—but every time I go to see him I feel life deeper and closer than usual.

# Chapter Nineteen

"YOUR PAPERS? Just a moment."

The clerk took off his eyeglasses and looked at Elisabeth. Then he ceremoniously got up and went behind the wooden partition that separated his counter from the large room beyond.

Graeber looked after him and then glanced around. There were people between him and the exit. "Go to the door," he said softly. "Wait there. If you see me take off my cap, go to Pohlmann at once. Don't worry about anything, go at once. I'll come later."

Elisabeth hesitated. "Go!" he said again, impatiently. "Maybe the old goat has gone to get someone. We can't risk it. Wait outside."

"He might want to ask me more questions."

"We'll find out about that. I'll tell him you felt faint and went out for a breath of air. Go, Elisabeth!"

He stood at the counter and looked after her. She turned around and smiled. Then she disappeared.

"Where is Fräulein Kruse?"

Graeber whirled around. The clerk had returned. "She will be here right away. Is everything in order?"

The clerk nodded. "When do you want to get married?"

"As soon as possible. I haven't much time. My furlough is almost over."

"You can get married at once if you like. The papers are ready. With soldiers it's all simple and quick."

Graeber saw the papers in the man's hand. The clerk smiled. All at once Graeber felt weak. His face flushed. "Is everything attended to?" he asked and took off his cap to wipe away the sweat.

"Everything is attended to," the clerk replied. "Where is Fräulein Kruse?"

Graeber laid his cap on the counter. He turned and looked for Elisabeth. The hall was full of people and he could not see her. Then he noticed his cap on the counter and remembered it was the signal they had agreed on. "Just a moment," he said quickly. "I'll get her at once."

He pushed his way swiftly through the crowd. He hoped he could catch up with her in the street; but when he came to the exit she was standing calmly behind a pillar, waiting. "Thank God you're here! Everything is in order. Everything is in order, Elisabeth."

They went back. The clerk handed Elisabeth her papers. "Are you the daughter of the Health Councilor Kruse?" he asked.

"Yes."

Graeber held his breath. "I know your father," the clerk said.

Elisabeth looked at him. "Have you heard anything of him?" she asked after a while.

"Nothing. Haven't you heard from him at all?"

"No."

The clerk took off his glasses. He had short-sighted, watery blue eyes. "Let's hope for the best." He gave Elisabeth his hand. "Good luck. I took your business under my wing and saw it through myself. You can marry today. I can make the arrangements for you. Right now if you like."

"Right now," Graeber said.

"This afternoon," Elisabeth replied. "Would two o'clock be all right?"

"I'll arrange it for you then. You'll have to go to the gymnasium in the high school. That's the registry office now."

"Thanks."

They stood at the doorway. "Why not right now?" Graeber asked. "Then nothing else can interfere."

Elisabeth smiled. "I must have a little time to get ready, Ernst. You don't understand that, do you?"

"Only half."

"Half is enough. Come and get me at a quarter of two."

Graeber hesitated. "It went so simply," he said then. "What didn't I expect! I don't know why I've become so jumpy. Probably it was pretty ridiculous, wasn't it?"

"No."

"I'm afraid it was."

Elisabeth shook her head. "My father thought the people who warned him were being ridiculous too. He thought in our time nothing like that could happen—and then it did. We have had a stroke of luck, that's all, Ernst."


A few blocks away he found a tailor shop. A man who looked like a kangaroo was sitting there sewing a uniform.

"Can I get these trousers cleaned?" Graeber asked.

The man looked up. "This is a tailoring establishment. Not a cleaner's."

"I see that. I want to have my things pressed, too."

"The ones you have on?"

"Yes."

The tailor got up, grumbling. He examined the spot on the trousers. "It's not blood," Graeber said. "It's olive oil. A little benzine will take it right out."

"Why don't you do it yourself if you know so much about it? Benzine doesn't help at all with spots like this."

"Maybe. You must know more about it than I. Have you anything I can wear in the meantime?" he asked.

The tailor went behind a curtain and came out with a pair of checked trousers and a white jacket. Graeber took them. "How long will it take? I need my uniform for a wedding."

"One hour."

Graeber changed. "I'll come back in an hour, then."

The kangaroo looked at him distrustfully. He had expected him to stay in the shop. "My uniform is good security," Graeber said. "I won't run away."

Surprisingly, the tailor bared his teeth. "Your uniform belongs to the State, young man. But go ahead. And get a haircut. You will need it if you are going to get married."

"That's right."

Graeber went to a barber shop. A bony woman was on duty. "My husband is in the field," she said. "I am taking his place for the time being. Sit down. Shave?"

"Haircut. Do you know how to do that?"

"Dear God! I know it so well I've almost forgotten it again. Shampoo, too? We still have excellent soap."

"Yes, shampoo, too."

The woman was quite strong. She cut Graeber's hair and gave his head a thorough going-over with soap and a rough hand towel. "Do you want brilliantine?" she asked. "We still have some of the French."

Graeber glanced up from a half doze and was startled. His ears seemed to have grown, so close had his hair been clipped at the temples. "Brilliantine?" the woman asked again peremptorily.

"What does it smell like?" Graeber remembered Alfons's bath salts.

"The way brilliantine smells. How else? It is French."

Graeber took the bottle and sniffed. The brilliantine smelled of old, rancid fat. The time of victories was already long past. He looked at his hair; where it hadn't been clipped close it stood up in tufts. "All right, brilliantine," he said. "But only very little."

He paid and went back to the tailor. "You're too early," growled the kangaroo.

Graeber did not contradict him. He sat down and watched the tailor ironing. The warm air made him sleepy. The war suddenly seemed far away. Flies hummed drowsily, the iron hissed, and the little room was full of an unaccustomed and forgotten security.

"That's the best I could do."

The tailor held out the trousers to Graeber. He looked at them. The spot was almost gone. "Excellent," Graeber said. The trousers smelled of benzine, but he said nothing about that. Quickly he put them on.

"Who cut your hair?" the tailor asked.

"A woman whose husband is a soldier."

"It looks as though you did it yourself. Hold still a minute."

The kangaroo snipped off a few of the tufts. "So! It will do now."

"What do I owe you?"

The tailor waved him away. "A thousand marks or nothing at all. So, nothing. A wedding present."

"Thanks. Do you know where there's a flower shop?"

"There's one in Spichernstrasse."

The store was open. Two women were standing in it, bargaining with the saleswoman about a wreath. "Those are genuine fir cones," the saleswoman said. "That's always expensive."

One of the women looked at her indignantly. Her soft, wrinkled cheeks trembled. "That's usury," she said. "Usury! Come, Minna! We'll find cheaper wreaths somewhere else."

"You don't need to take it," the saleswoman announced sharply. "I can get rid of my stock easily enough."

"At those prices?"

"Oh yes, at those prices. I never have enough and I am sold out every evening, ladies."

"Then you're a war profiteer."

The two women stamped out. The saleswoman drew in her breath sharply as though to shout something after them; then she turned to Graeber. She suddenly had two bright spots in her cheeks. "And you? Wreaths or a coffin blanket? You see the stock is not large, but we have some very beautiful fir arrangements."

"I don't need anything for a funeral."

"What then?" the saleswoman asked in surprise.

"I would like to buy some flowers."

"Flowers? I have lilies—"

"No lilies. Something for a wedding."

"Lilies are entirely suitable for a wedding, sir! They are the symbol of innocence and virginity."

"That's right. But haven't you any roses?"

"Roses? At this time of year? Where from? The greenhouses are all being used to grow vegetables. It's hard to get anything at all."

Graeber walked around the stall. Finally, behind a wreath in the form of a swastika, he found a bunch of jonquils. "Give me these."

The saleswoman picked up the bunch and let the water drip off. "Unfortunately, I'll have to wrap the flowers in a newspaper. I haven't anything else."

"That doesn't matter."

Graeber paid for the jonquils and left. He immediately felt uncomfortable with the flowers in his hand. Everyone seemed to be staring at him. At first he held the bouquet with the blossoms downward; then he clamped them under his arm. In doing so he saw the paper in which they were wrapped. Under the yellow blossoms appeared the picture of a man open-mouthed in front of some sort of tribunal. It was a photograph of the presiding officer of a People's Court. He read the text. Four persons had been put to death because they no longer believed in a German victory. Their heads had been hacked off with an ax. In the Third Reich the guillotine had long since been discarded. It was too humane. Graeber crumpled up the paper and threw it away.

The clerk had been right—the registry office was in the gymnasium of the high school. The registrar sat in front of a row of climbing ropes, the lower ends of which had been hooked back against the wall. Between them hung a portrait of Hitler in uniform, beneath it a swastika with the German eagle.

They had to wait. A middle-aged soldier was in front of them. There was a woman with him, wearing on her breast a gold brooch in the form of a sailing ship. The man was very excited, the woman calm. She smiled at Elisabeth as though they were fellow conspirators.

"Marriage witnesses," said the registrar. "Where are your witnesses?"

The soldier stammered. He had none. "I thought with war marriages you didn't need any," he finally said.

"That would be nice, wouldn't it? With us, order prevails."

The soldier turned to Graeber. "Could you perhaps help us, comrade? You and the young lady? Just your signatures."

"Of course. Then you can sign for us, too. I didn't think I needed any, either."

"Who thinks of anything like that?"

"Everyone who knows his duty as a citizen," the registrar announced cuttingly. He obviously took the omission as a personal insult. "Do you by any chance go into battle without a gun?"

The soldier stared at him. "That's something entirely different. After all, a witness is not a gun!"

"I didn't say he was. It was simply a comparison. Well, what about it now? Have you your witnesses?"

"My comrade here and the lady."

The registrar looked at Graeber peevishly. It obviously did not please him to have the matter settled so simply. "Have you identification papers?" he asked Graeber hopefully.

"Yes, here. We want to get married ourselves." The official growled and picked up the papers. He entered Elisabeth's and Graeber's names in the register. "Sign here."

All four signed. "I congratulate you in the name of the Fuehrer," the registrar said frostily afterwards to the soldier and his wife. Then he turned to Graeber. "Your witnesses?"

"Here." Graeber pointed to the two.

The registrar shook his head. "I can only accept one of them," he announced.

"Why? You took both of us, after all."

"You were still single. But these two are now a married couple. You have to have two independent persons as witnesses. A wife does not qualify."

Graeber did not know whether the official was right or simply trying to make difficulties. "Isn't there someone here who can do it?" he asked. "Perhaps another clerk?"

"It's not my place to take care of such matters," the registrar announced in cold triumph. "If you have no witnesses you can't get married."

Graeber looked around. "What do you need?" asked a middle-aged man who had come up and was listening. "A marriage witness? Take me."

He stood beside Elisabeth. The official examined him coldly. "Have you your papers?"

"Of course." The man casually drew out a passport and tossed it on the table. The registrar read it, rose to his feet, and yelped: "*Heil Hitler,* Herr Group Leader!"

"*Heil Hitler,*" the group leader replied carelessly. "And let's not have any more play-acting, understand? What's the matter with you, behaving toward soldiers this way?"

"Very good, Herr Group Leader! Will you please be so kind as to sign here."

Graeber saw that S.S. Group Leader Hildebrandt was his second witness. The first was Engineer Klotz. Hildebrandt shook hands with Elisabeth and Graeber and then with Klotz and his wife as well. The registrar got two copies of Hitler's *Mein Kampf* from behind the climbing ropes, which looked as though they had been arranged for a hanging. "A gift from the State," he announced sourly, staring after Hildebrandt. "Civilian clothes," he said. "How's anyone to know!"

They went past the leather exercise horse and the parallel bars to the exit. "When do you have to go back?" Graeber asked the engineer.

"Tomorrow." Klotz winked. "We've been intending to do it all along. Why make a present of anything to the State? If I get killed at least Marie will be taken care of. Or don't you think so?"

"Yes, I do."

Klotz unbuckled his knapsack. "You helped me out, comrade. I have a good Brunswick sausage here. Take it and enjoy it! Don't say a word. I am a farmer, I have enough. I really intended to give it to the registrar. Just imagine, that bastard!"

"Not to him, whatever happens!" Graeber took the sausage. "Here, accept this book in exchange. I have nothing else to give you as a wedding present."

"But, comrade, I just got one myself."

"That doesn't matter. You will be twice as well off now. You can give one to your wife."

Klotz looked at the copy of *Mein Kampf*. "It's a nice binding," he said. "Don't you really want to keep it yourself?"

"I don't need it. In the house where we live there's one bound in leather with silver clasps."

"Of course that's something else again. Well then, take care of yourself."

"You, too."

Graeber caught up with Elisabeth. "I didn't say anything to Alfons Binding about today because I didn't want him as a witness," he said. "I didn't want an S.A. commander's name beside ours. Now we've got an S.S. group leader instead. That's what happens to good resolutions."

Elisabeth laughed. "In return you've been able to trade the bible of the movement for a Brunswick sausage. It evens out."

They walked across the Marktplatz. The monument that showed only Bismarck's feet had been straightened. Pigeons circled above the Marienkirche. Graeber looked at Elisabeth. I really ought to be very happy, he thought; but he did not feel it quite as much as he had expected.

They were lying in a clearing in the woods outside the city. Violet haze hung between the tree trunks. Along the edges of the clearing primroses and violets were in blossom. A light breeze began to blow. Elisabeth suddenly sat up. "What's that over there? It looks like an enchanted forest. Or am I dreaming? The trees are all hung with silver. Do you see it, too?"

Graeber nodded. "It looks like angel's hair."

"What is it?"

"Tinfoil. Or very thin aluminum that has been cut up into narrow strips. Something like the silver paper that comes around chocolate."

"The whole forest is covered with it. Where does it come from?"

"They toss it out of airplanes in bundles. It interferes with radio communication. I believe it makes it impossible to determine where the planes are. Something like that. When the narrow strips of foil flutter down through the air they interrupt or distort the radio waves."

"Too bad," Elisabeth said. "It looks like a Christmas forest. And now it's nothing but the war again. I thought we had finally got away from that for once."

They looked across. The trees around the clearing were covered with strips that fluttered from their twigs, twisting and sparkling in the breeze. The sun broke through the mountainous clouds and transformed the woods into a glittering fairyland. What once had fluttered down in the midst of ravening death and the shrill howl of destruction now hung silent and shiny on the trees and had become silver and a shimmering and the memory of childhood stories and the great festival of peace.

Elisabeth leaned against Graeber. "Let's take the forest for what it seems—and not for what it means."

"Good." Graeber drew Pohlmann's book out of his coat pocket. "We can't take a wedding trip, Elisabeth, but Pohlmann gave me this book—it's a picture book of Switzerland. Sometime after the war we'll go there and make up for everything."

"Switzerland. The place where there still are lights at night?"

Graeber opened the book. "For a long time now there haven't been any lights even in Switzerland. I heard that at the barracks. Our government demanded it. We sent them an ultimatum insisting that their lights must be blacked out, and Switzerland had to comply."

"Why?"

"We had no objection as long as we were the only ones flying over Switzerland. But now the others fly over too. With bombs for Germany. Wherever there are lighted cities the flyers can check their position more easily. That's the reason."

"So that, too, is finished."

"Yes. But we know one thing at least—when we get to Switzerland sometime after the war, everything will be exactly as it is in this book. If we had a picture book of Italy or France or England that wouldn't be so."

"Nor with a picture book of Germany."

"Nor with a picture book of Germany."

They leafed through the book. "Mountains," Elisabeth said. "Isn't there anything in Switzerland but mountains? Aren't there any warm southern places?"

"Of course! Here's Italian Switzerland."

"Locarno. Wasn't there once a great peace conference there? Where they decided war would never be necessary again?"

"I think so."

"That didn't last long."

"No. Here is Locarno. Just look at it. Palms, old churches, and there is the Lago Maggiore. And here are islands and azaleas and mimosa and sun and peace."

"Yes. What's the name of that place?"

"Porto Ronco."

"Good," Elisabeth said sleepily, laying the book down. "We'll make a note of that. We'll go there later on. Just now I don't want to take any more trips."

Graeber clapped the book shut. He looked at the glistening silver in the trees and then he took Elisabeth in his arms. He felt her come toward him and with her the floor of the forest, grass and roots and a reddish flower with delicate narrow leaves that grew larger and larger until it blotted out the horizon, and his eyes closed.

The wind died. It grew dark rapidly. From the distance came a low rumbling. Artillery, Graeber thought, half asleep. But where? Where am I? Where is the front? And then, relieved as he felt Elisabeth beside him: where are the gun emplacements around here? It must be target practice.

Elisabeth moved. "Where are they?" she murmured. "Will they bomb us or fly on?"

"It isn't airplanes."

The rumbling came again. Graeber straightened up and listened. "It's not bombs and not artillery and not airplanes, Elisabeth," he said. "It is a thunderstorm."

"Isn't it still too early for that?"

"There are no rules for thunderstorms."

Now they saw the first lightning. It seemed pale and artificial after the man-made tempests they knew, and even the thunder was hardly to be compared with the roar of massed planes—let alone a heavy bombing.

The rain began. They ran across the clearing and into the fir trees. Shadows seemed to race with them. The rustling of the rain in the treetops above them was like the applause of a distant crowd, and in the pale light Graeber saw that Elisabeth's hair was covered with silver strands that had been brushed from the branches. They were like a net in which the lightning flashes were caught.

They came out of the forest and found a covered streetcar platform where a number of people were huddled. A couple of S.S. men stood with them. They were young and they stared at Elisabeth.

After half an hour the rain stopped. "I no longer know where we are," Graeber said. "Which way do we go?"

"To the right."

They crossed the street and turned off into a twilit avenue. Ahead of them at one side of the street a long row of men were busy laying pipes in the half-darkness. They were wearing striped suits.

Elisabeth was suddenly alert; she turned off the street in the direction of the workmen. She walked along slowly, very close to them, studying them as though searching for someone. Now Graeber saw that the men had numbers on their clothes. They were prisoners from the concentration camp who worked quickly and silently without glancing up. Their heads were like skulls and their clothes hung limp on their emaciated bodies. Two had collapsed and lay in front of a boarded-up soft-drink stand.

"Hey there!" an S.S. man shouted. "Stay away! You're not allowed to go there!"

Elisabeth pretended she had not heard him. She just walked faster and kept peering into the dead faces of the prisoners.

"Come back! You there, lady! At once! Damn it, can't you hear me?"

The S.S. man came up cursing. "What's the matter?" Graeber asked.

"What's the matter? Have you mud in your ears? Or is something else the matter with you?"

Graeber saw a second S.S. man approaching. He was a senior troop leader. Graeber did not dare call to Elisabeth; he knew that she would not turn back. "We are looking for something," he said to the S.S. man.

"What? Come on, speak up!"

"We lost something here. A brooch. It's a sailing ship made of diamonds. We came through here late yesterday and we must have dropped it. Have you seen it by any chance?"

"What?"

Graeber repeated his lie. He saw that Elisabeth had gone past half the row. "Nothing has been found here," the senior troop leader declared.

"That's just a driveling excuse," the S.S. man said. "Have you your papers?"

Graeber looked at him for a while in silence. He would have liked to knock him down. The S.S. man was not more than twenty years old. Steinbrenner, he thought. Heini. The same type. "I not only have papers but I have very good papers," he said then. "Besides that, S.S. Group Leader Hildebrandt is a close friend of mine, in case you're interested."

The S.S. man laughed derisively. "Anything else? The Fuehrer too, no doubt?"

"Not the Fuehrer." Elisabeth had almost reached the end of the line. Graeber drew his marriage certificate out of his pocket with deliberation. "Come over here with me under the lamp post. Can you read that? The signature of my marriage witness? And the date? Today, as you see. Any more questions?"

The S.S. man stared at the paper. The senior troop leader looked over his shoulder. "That's Hildebrandt's signature," he agreed. "I know it. Nevertheless you are not allowed to walk here. It's forbidden. We can't do anything about it. I am sorry about your brooch."

Elisabeth had finished. "So am I," Graeber replied. "Naturally we won't go on looking if it's forbidden. Orders are orders."

He walked on quickly to reach Elisabeth. But the senior troop leader stayed beside him. "Perhaps we'll still find the brooch," he said. "Where shall we send it?"

"To Hildebrandt. That's the simplest thing."

"Good," the senior troop leader said respectfully. "Have you found anything?" he asked Elisabeth.

She stared at him as though she had just been awakened. "I have explained to the officer here about the brooch we lost yesterday," Graeber said quickly. "If it turns up he'll send it to Hildebrandt."

"Thank you," Elisabeth replied in amazement.

The senior troop leader looked her in the face and nodded. "You can depend on it. We in the S.S. are cavaliers."

Elisabeth threw a glance toward the prisoners. The senior troop leader observed it. "If one of those swine has hidden it we'll find it all right," he declared gallantly. "We'll inspect them till they drop."

Elisabeth quivered. "I'm not sure I lost it here. It could just as well have been higher up in the woods. I really think it may have been there."

The senior troop leader grinned. She blushed. "It probably was in the woods," she repeated.

The senior troop leader's grin broadened. "Naturally we are not in charge there."

Graeber was standing close to the emaciated skull of one of the bowed prisoners. He put his hand in his pocket, pulled out a package of cigarettes, and in turning let it fall near the prisoner. "Many thanks," he said to the senior troop leader. "We'll look in the woods tomorrow. It could easily have happened there."

"No need for thanks. *Heil Hitler!* And warmest congratulations on your wedding!"

"Thanks."

They walked in silence side by side until the prisoners were out of sight. Like a flight of flamingos, a row of clouds, mother-of-pearl and rose, drifted across the sky which was now clear.

"I should not have gone over there," Elisabeth said. "I know that."

"It doesn't matter. That's the way people are. Barely out of one scrape and we run the risk of another."

She nodded. "You saved us with the brooch. And with Hildebrandt. You're a really good liar."

"That," Graeber said, "is the thing our country has learned to perfection in the last ten years. And now let's go home. I have the absolute, certified right to move into your apartment. I've lost my home in the barracks; this afternoon I moved out of Binding's place; now at last I want to go home. I want to lie luxuriously in bed while you dash off to work early in the morning to earn bread for the family."

"I don't have to go to the factory tomorrow. I have two days' vacation."

"And you haven't told me till now?"

"I wasn't going to tell you until tomorrow morning."

Graeber shook his head. "No surprises, please! We haven't time for them. We need every minute for rejoicing. And we'll begin right away. Have we enough for breakfast? Or shall I make another trip to Alfons?"

"We have enough."

"All right. We'll have a noisy breakfast tomorrow. To the strains of the *Hohenfriedberger March,* if you like. And then when Frau Lieser comes roaring in full of moral indignation we'll push our marriage lines under that informer's disappointed snout. What a face she'll make when she sees the name of our S.S. witness!"

Elisabeth smiled. "Perhaps she may not make so much of a row after all. Day before yesterday, when she gave me that pound of sugar you left for me, she suddenly said you were an upstanding fellow. Heaven knows what produced the sudden change! Do you know?"

"No idea. Corruption, probably. That's the other thing our country has learned to perfection in the last ten years."

# Chapter Twenty

THE AIR RAID came at noon. It was a mild, cloudy day full of growth and dampness. The overcast hung low, and the flames of the explosions were thrown against the clouds as though the earth were hurling them back at an invisible foe, to claw him down with his own weapons into the vortex of fire and destruction.

It was the lunch hour, the most crowded time in the streets. Graeber had been directed to the nearest cellar by an air raid warden. He had thought it would only be an alarm, but when he felt the first explosions he began to force his way through the crowd of people till he was near the entrance. The moment the door opened again to let in new arrivals he leaped through.

"Back!" shouted the warden outside. "No one is allowed on the streets! Only air raid wardens!"

"I'm an air raid warden!"

He ran in the direction of the factory. He did not know whether he could reach Elisabeth, but he knew factories were the prime targets of the raids and he wanted to try at least to get her out.

He came around a corner. In front of him at the end of the street a house slowly rose. In the air it broke into pieces which separated and seemed to fall silently and gently, without making any noise in that uproar. Graeber threw himself into the gutter with his arms pressed over his ears. The shock-wave of a second explosion seized him like a giant hand and hurled him several yards backward. Stones pelted down like rain. They too fell silently in all the din. He got to his feet, reeled, shook his head violently, pulled at his ears and struck himself in the forehead to clear his mind. From one instant to the next the street in front of him had become a sea of flames. He could not get through and so turned back.

People plunged toward him with open mouths, horror in their eyes. They were screaming, but he could not hear them. They raced past him like hunted deaf mutes. After them came a man with a wooden leg carrying a huge cuckoo clock, whose weights dragged after him. A big shepherd dog followed, slinking. In the corner of a house stood a five-year-old girl. She was holding an infant pressed close against her. Graeber stopped. "Run to the nearest cellar!" he shouted. "Where are your parents? Why have they left you here?"

The girl did not look up. She kept her head bent and pressed herself against the wall. Graeber suddenly saw a warden soundlessly screaming at him. Graeber shouted back and did not hear himself. The warden went on screaming soundlessly and making gestures. Graeber waved him away and pointed at the two children. It was like a ghostly pantomime. The warden tried to keep hold of him with one hand; with the other he reached for the children. Graeber pulled free. In the tumult it seemed to him for an instant as though he had no weight and could make gigantic bounds and immediately afterward he felt as if he were made out of soft lead and was being beaten flat by immense hammers.

A wardrobe with open doors sailed over him like a plump, prehistoric bird. A mighty current of air laid hold of him and whirled him about, flames shot out of the ground, a harsh yellow wiped out the sky, burned away to a more intense white and fell to earth like a cloudburst. Graeber inhaled flame. His lungs seemed on fire, he collapsed, pressed his head into his arms, held his breath until his head seemed to be bursting and looked up. Through the tears and the burning in his eyes a picture slowly formed itself and steadied: a torn, bespattered wall thrust backward over a staircase and on the stairs, impaled upon the splintered steps, the body of the five-year-old girl, her short plaid skirt thrown high, her legs sprawled and bare, her arms outstretched as though crucified, her breast pierced by a bar from an iron fence whose knob extended far beyond her back—and to one side, as though provided with many more joints than in life, the air raid warden, headless, slack and now spouting only a little blood, twisted into a knot with his legs over his shoulders, a dead contortionist. The infant was not to be seen. It must have been hurled somewhere in the gale which now returned hot and flaming, driving the fire before it in the backdraft. Graeber heard someone beside him shouting: "Swine! Swine! Damned swine!" and stared at the sky and looked around him and realized that it was himself who was shouting.

He sprang up and ran on. He did not know how he got to the square where the factory was. It seemed undamaged; only on the right there was a fresh crater. The low, gray buildings had not been hit anywhere.

The factory air raid warden stopped him. "My wife is here!" Graeber shouted. "Let me in!"

"Forbidden! The nearest cellar is on the other side. Over there at the edge of the square."

"Damn it, what isn't forbidden in this country! Get away or—"

The warden pointed to the rear courtyard. A little flat block house of reinforced concrete stood there. "Machine guns," he said, "and a guard! Military shits like you. Go in if you like, you clown. Begin a civil war! You're just what we have been waiting for!"

Graeber needed no further explanation; the machine gun commanded the courtyard. "A guard!" he said furiously. "What for? You'll be standing guard over your own crap next. Have they got criminals in there? Or what is there in your damned army overcoat factory to guard?"

"More than you think," the warden answered contemptuously. "We don't just make army overcoats here and we have more here than women workers. In the munitions factory there are a couple of hundred prisoners from the concentration camp. Do you understand now, you front-line calf?"

"Yes. How are the cellars here?"

"What do I care about the cellars? I have to stay outside. And what's happening meanwhile to my wife in the city?"

"Are the cellars safe?"

"Of course. After all, the people are needed for the factory. And now disappear! No one's allowed on the street. The men over there have noticed you already. They are on the lookout for sabotage!"

The heavy explosions had ceased. The anti-aircraft guns went on firing. Graeber ran diagonally back across the square. He did not run to the nearest cellar; he ducked into the fresh bomb crater at the end of the square. The smell in it almost choked him. He crept up to the edge and lay there staring at the factory. It was a different war here, he thought. At the front each one had only to look out for himself. And if you happened to have a brother in the same company that was a lot; but here each one had a family and it was not he alone that was being shot at; all the rest were being shot at as well. It was a double and triple and ten-fold war. He thought of the body of the five-year-old girl and then of the numberless others he had seen and he thought of his parents, and of Elisabeth, and he felt a spasm of hatred against the ones who had caused all this; it was a hatred that did not halt at the borders of his country and that had nothing to do with any understanding or with justice.

It began to rain. The drops fell like a silver shower of gentle tears through the stinking, violated air. They splashed up as they struck and darkened the ground. Then came the next wave of bombers.

It was as though someone were tearing his breast in two. The roar grew to a metallic delirium and then a part of the factory lifted itself into the air, black in front of the fan-shaped, glowing light, and burst apart as if a giant were playing with toys under the earth and tossing them on high.

Graeber stared at the fire which sprang up white and yellow and green. Then he ran back to the factory gate. "What are you after now?" the warden shouted. "Don't you see that we've been hit?"

"Yes. Where? In what section? In the one for overcoats?"

"Overcoats, nonsense! The overcoat section is way at the back."

"Are you sure? My wife—"

"Oh, kiss my ass with your wife! They are all in the cellar. We have a crowd of wounded and dead here! Leave me alone."

"How can you have wounded and dead if everyone's in the cellar?"

"But these are the others, man! The ones from the concentration camp. They aren't in the cellar. Or do you think we build cellars especially for them?"

"No," Graeber said. "I don't think that."

"Well then! At last you're getting some sense. And now leave me in peace! An old soldier oughtn't to be so damned jumpy. Besides that, it's over for the moment. Perhaps even for good."

Graeber glanced up. Only the A.A. guns were barking. "Listen to me, comrade," he said. "I only want one thing. I want to know whether there was a hit in the overcoat section. Let me in or go and ask. Aren't you married?"

"Of course. I told you that once before! Don't you think I'm in enough of a funk about my own wife?"

"Then go and ask. Do it and you can be sure that nothing has happened to your wife."

The air raid warden looked at Graeber and shook his head. "Man, you've got the haunts! Or are you God Almighty?"

He went into his booth and came back. "I have telephoned. Overcoats are in order. Only the concentration camp brothers got a direct hit. And now beat it! How long have you been married?"

"Five days."

The warden suddenly grinned. "Why didn't you say so at once? That's entirely different."

Graeber walked back. I wanted to have something to hold me, he thought. But I didn't realize that makes one doubly vulnerable.

It was over. The city stank of burning and death and was full of fires. There were red and green and yellow and white ones; some were nothing but crawling, serpent-like flickerings over the fallen ruins, and others glared steadily out of roofs up toward the sky; there were fires that wrapped themselves almost tenderly around the still-standing house fronts, embracing them closely, shyly, cautiously; and others that shot violently out of windows. There were conflagrations and fiery walls and fiery towers, there were blazing dead and there were blazing wounded who burst shrieking out of the houses and spun around and tried to climb up the sides of walls and ran raving in circles until they collapsed and crept, mewing hoarsely, and then only jerked and croaked and stank of burned flesh.

"The torches," someone standing beside Graeber said. "You can't rescue them. They burn up alive. The damnable stuff from incendiary bombs gets spattered on them and burns right through everything, skin, flesh, and bones."

"Why can't they put them out?"

"That would take a separate fire extinguisher for each one, and I don't know even then whether it would help. That devilish stuff eats its way through everything. And the shrieking!"

"They ought to be shot quickly if they can't be rescued."

"Just try it and get hanged as a murderer! And just try to hit one while they're racing round like mad! The miserable part of it is that they run like that! That's what turns them into torches. The wind, you understand! They run and that makes the wind and the wind fans the fire and in an instant they're all in flames."

Graeber looked at the man. He had deep eyesockets under his helmet and a mouth in which many teeth were missing. "You think they ought to stand still?"

"It would be better, theoretically. Stand still or try to smother the flames with blankets or something like that. But who has blankets handy? And who thinks of it? And who will stand still when he's on fire?"

"No one. What are you? Air Defense?"

"Nonsense. I belong to the corpse brigade. Wounded, too, of course, when we find any. There comes our wagon. At last."

Graeber saw a wagon drawn by a white horse rolling up between the ruins.

"Wait, Gustav!" shouted the man with whom he had been

talking. "You can't go any farther this way. We'll bring them over. Have you stretchers?"

"Two."

Graeber followed the man. Behind a stone wall he saw the dead. Like a slaughterhouse, he thought. No, not like a slaughterhouse; a slaughterhouse was more orderly; the animals were killed, bled, and drawn according to rules. Here they were mangled, crushed, mutilated, singed, and roasted. Scraps of clothing still hung on them; an arm of a woolen sweater, a dotted dress, one leg of a pair of brown corduroy trousers, a brassière in the wires of which hung bloody breasts. To one side lay a nest of dead children, every which way. They had been caught in a cellar that was not strong enough. Single hands, feet, trampled heads with a little hair, twisted legs; in the midst of this a schoolbag, a basket with a dead cat, a very pale boy, white as an albino, dead without a wound, stretched out as though he had not yet lived and was waiting to be animated, and in front of him a corpse burned black, not very deeply but quite uniformly except for one foot that was only red and covered with blisters. It was no longer possible to tell whether it was a man or a woman; the sex and the breast had been burned away. A gold ring gleamed brightly on a black, shrunken finger.

"The eyes," someone said. "To think the eyes burn too!"

The corpses were loaded on the wagon. "Linda," said a woman who was following one of the stretchers. "Linda! Linda!"

The sun came out. The rain-wet streets shimmered. Those trees that had not been destroyed glistened wet and bright green. The light after the rain was fresh and strong. "That will never be forgiven," someone behind Graeber said.

He turned around. A woman with a coquettish red hat was staring at the children. "Never!" she said. "Never! Not in this world or the next!"

A patrol came by. "Move on! Don't stand here. Get a move on! Forward!"

Graeber walked on. What would never be forgiven? he thought. After this war there would be horribly much to forgive and not to forgive. A single lifetime would not be enough for that. He had seen more dead children than these—he had seen them everywhere, in France, in Holland, in Poland, in Africa, in Russia, and all had had mothers who wept for them, not the Germans alone—if they still could weep and had not already been liquidated by the S.S. But why did he think about that? Had not he himself an hour ago been shouting, "Swine! Swine!" at the sky that held the airplanes?

Elisabeth's house had not been hit, but an incendiary had fallen on the house two doors away, the wind had blown the flames across and now the roofs of all three houses were on fire.

The block warden was standing in the street. "Why doesn't anyone put it out?" Graeber said.

The warden made a sweeping gesture over the city. "Why doesn't anyone put it out?" he asked in turn.

"Isn't there any water?"

"There is still some water, but we haven't any pressure. It just trickles. And we can't get at this fire. The roof may cave in any time."

On the street stood chairs, suitcases, a cat in a canary cage, pictures and bundles of clothes. From the windows of the lower stories people with excited, sweaty faces were throwing things wrapped in blankets and pillowcases out into the street. Others were running up and down the stairs.

"Do you think the house will burn all the way down?" Graeber asked the block warden.

"Probably. If the fire department doesn't come soon. Thank God, there's no wind. We turned on all the faucets on the top floor and carried out everything that was inflammable. There's nothing more we can do. By the way, where are those cigars you promised me? I could use one."

"Tomorrow," Graeber said. "Tomorrow without fail."

He looked up toward Elisabeth's apartment. It was not yet in immediate danger. There were still two stories in between. Through the window of Elisabeth's room he saw Frau Lieser rushing back and forth. She was struggling with a white sphere which probably contained bedclothes. In the half darkness of the room it looked like an inflated ghost.

"I'll go and pack, too," Graeber said. "That can't do any harm."

"Right," the warden replied.

On the stairway a man with a pince-nez knocked against Graeber's shin with a heavy suitcase. "I beg your pardon," he said politely into the air and hurried on.

The door to the apartment was open. The corridor was full of packages. Frau Lieser ran past Graeber, her mouth shut tight and tears in her eyes. He went into Elisabeth's room and closed the door behind him.

He sat down in a chair by the window and looked around. The room suddenly had a strange, secluded peacefulness. Graeber sat there for a while without thinking of anything. Then he looked for suitcases. He found two under the bed and tried to decide what he should pack.

He began with Elisabeth's clothes. He took out of the wardrobe the ones he considered practical. Then he opened the dresser and got out underwear and stockings. He placed a small package of letters between the shoes. Meanwhile he heard cries and noise from outside. He glanced out. It was not the fire department; it was only people carrying their things out. He saw a woman in a mink coat sitting in a red plush armchair in front of the ruined house opposite, clutching a small case. Probably her jewelry, he thought, and began to look in the drawers for Elisabeth's jewelry. He found a few small pieces; a narrow gold bracelet was among them and an old brooch with an amethyst. He took the gold dress too. There was a remote tenderness about touching Elisabeth's things— tenderness, and a little shame at doing something impermissible.

He placed a photograph of Elisabeth's father on top of the things in the second suitcase and closed it. Then he sat down in the chair again and looked around. The strange peace of the room surrounded him once more. After a while it occurred to him that he ought to take the bedding with him. He rolled the blankets and pillows in a sheet and knotted it as he had seen Frau Lieser do. As he laid the bundle on the floor he saw his knapsack behind the bed. He had forgotten it. As he pulled it out the steel helmet clattered across the floor as though someone were knocking hard from underneath. He looked at it for a long time. Then he kicked it over to the door where the other things were and carried them all downstairs.

The houses were slowly burning down. The fire department did not come; these few dwellings were too unimportant. The burning factories had precedence in fire fighting. Besides, a quarter of the city was in flames.

The inhabitants of the houses had rescued as many of their possessions as they could. Now they did not know where to go with them. There was no means of transportation and no place to stay. The street in front of the burning houses had been roped off for a distance. Next to it on either side, household goods were piled high.

Graeber saw overstuffed armchairs, a leather sofa, kitchen chairs, beds, and a child's crib. One family had rescued a kitchen table and four chairs and were sitting around it. Another had formed a nook and were protecting it against everyone that wanted to pass through as though it were their own property. The block warden was lying asleep on a chaise longue covered in a cloth of Turkish pattern. A big portrait of Hitler rested against the wall of a building. It belonged to Frau Lieser. She had her child on her lap and was sitting on her bedding.

Graeber had brought a Biedermeier chair out of Elisabeth's room and was sitting on it with the suitcases, the knapsack, and the other things close beside him. He had tried to find a place to store them in one of the undamaged houses. In two of the apartments there had been no answer when he rang, although he had seen faces peering out of the windows. In some others he was not admitted because they were already overfilled. At the last one, a woman had screamed at him: "That would suit you fine, wouldn't it? And then afterwards you would want to go on living here, eh?" After that he gave up. When he returned to his things he noticed that a package in which he had wrapped up the bread and provisions had been stolen during his absence. He saw later that the family at the table were eating covertly. They popped bits of food into their mouths with averted faces; but it might just as easily be food that belonged to them and that they did not wish to share.

Suddenly he saw Elisabeth. She had broken through the cordon and stood in the free space with the glow of the fire flickering over her.

"Here, Elisabeth!" he shouted, springing up.

She turned around. She did not see him at once. She stood darkly in front of the fire and only her hair was aglow. "Here!" he shouted again and waved.

She ran to him. "There you are! Thank God!"

He held her tight. "I couldn't come to the factory to get you. I had to keep an eye on your things."

"I thought something had happened to you."

"Why in the world should anything happen to me?"

"But something could happen to you, too!"

She was breathing heavily on his breast. "Damn it, I never thought of that," he said in surprise. "I've only been afraid for you."

She looked up. "What's happened here?"

"The roof of the house caught fire."

"And you? I was worried about you."

"And I about you. Sit down here."

She was still breathing heavily. On the curb he saw a pail of water with a cup beside it. He went over, dipped up a cupful and gave it to Elisabeth. "Come, drink this."

"Hey there! You! That's our water," a woman shouted.

"And our cup," added a freckled twelve-year-old youngster.

"Drink it," Graeber said to Elisabeth and turned around. "How about the air? Does that belong to you, too?"

"Give them back their water and their cup," Elisabeth said. "Or pour the pail over their heads. That's even better."

Graeber held the cup to her lips. "No. Drink it. Did you run?"

"Yes. The whole way."

Graeber went back to the pail. The woman who had shouted at him belonged to the family sitting at the kitchen table. He filled the cup again from the pail, emptied it and then put it down beside the pail. No one said anything; but when Graeber had gone back the youngster ran over, picked up the cup and put it on the table. "Swine," the block warden said to the people at the table. He had waked up, yawned, and lain down again. The roof of the first house caved in.

"Here are the things I packed for you," Graeber said. "They're practically all your clothes. Your father's picture is here, too. Also your bedding. I can try to get the furniture out. It still isn't too late."

"Stay here. Let it burn up."

"Why? There's still time."

"Let it burn up. Then the whole thing will be over. Everything up there. And that's as it should be."

"What will be over?"

"The past. There's nothing we can do with it. It simply weighs us down. Even what was good in it. We must begin again. The past is bankrupt. We can't go back."

"You could sell the furniture."

"Here?" Elisabeth looked around. "We can't hold an auction on the street. Just look at that! There's too much furniture and no place to put it. That's the way it will be for a long time."

It began to rain again. Large, warm drops fell. Frau Lieser put up an umbrella. A woman who had rescued a new flowered hat and had put it on for convenience took it off and put it under her dress. The warden woke up again and sneezed. Hitler in Frau Lieser's oil painting looked, in the rain, as though he were weeping. Graeber unwrapped his coat and got the shelter-half out of his knapsack. He put his coat around Elisabeth and spread the canvas over the bedding.

"We must find a place to sleep tonight," he said.

"Perhaps the rain will put out the fire. Where will all the others sleep?"

"I don't know. This street seems to have been forgotten."

"We could sleep here. With the bed and your overcoat and the canvas."

"Could you?"

"I think one can sleep anywhere if one is tired enough."

"Binding has a house with an empty room. You don't want to go there, do you?"

Elisabeth shook her head.

"Then there's still Pohlmann," Graeber said. "He has a place to sleep in his catacombs. I asked him a few days ago. The emergency quarters are sure to be jammed—if they're still standing."

"We can wait a while. Our floor isn't burning yet."

Elisabeth sat in the army overcoat in the rain. She was not depressed. "I wish we had something to drink," she said. "And I don't mean water."

"We have. While I was packing I found a bottle of vodka behind the books. We must have forgotten it."

Graeber unknotted the bedclothes. He had hidden the bottle in the feather mattress; thus it had escaped the thief. He had also wrapped up a glass. "Here it is. We must drink it cautiously so the others won't notice. Otherwise we'll be reported by Frau Lieser for jeering at a national misfortune."

"If you don't want other people to notice, you mustn't act cautiously. That's something I've learned." Elisabeth took the glass and drank. "Marvelous," she said. "Just what I needed. Now it's almost like an open-air café. Have you cigarettes, too?"

"I brought all we had."

"Good. Then we have everything we need."

"Oughtn't I to bring down a few more pieces of furniture?"

"They won't let you up any more. And we couldn't do anything with them anyway. We couldn't even take them with us wherever we're going to sleep tonight."

"One of us can stand guard while the other is looking for shelter."

Elisabeth shook her head and finished her drink. At that moment the roof of her house collapsed. The walls seemed to rock. Then the floor of the top story caved in. The tenants on the street groaned. Sparks poured out of the windows. Flames licked upward at the curtains. "Our floor is still there," Graeber said.

"Not for long," a man behind him replied.

"Why not?"

"Why should you be better off than we are? I have lived up there on that floor for twenty-three years, young man. Now it's burning. Why shouldn't yours?"

Graeber looked at the man. He was thin and bald. "I thought something like this was a matter of chance, not ethics."

"It's a matter of justice. If you know what that means!"

"Not exactly. But it's not my fault." Graeber grinned. "You must have had a hard life if you yourself still believe in it. Shall I give you a glass of vodka? It's better than getting indignant."

"Thanks! Keep your schnapps! You're going to need it when your place caves in."

Graeber put the bottle back. "Want to bet it won't cave in?"

"What?"

"I asked whether you wanted to bet on it."

Elisabeth laughed. The man with the bald head stared at both of them. "You want to bet, you frivolous fool? And you, Fräulein, you laugh with him? Really that's going too far!"

"Why shouldn't she laugh?" Graeber asked. "To laugh is better than to cry. Especially when neither does any good."

"You ought to pray!"

The upper wall fell in. It broke through the floor of the story above Elisabeth's apartment. Frau Lieser began to sob convulsively under her umbrella. The family around the kitchen table were brewing ersatz coffee over an alcohol stove. The woman in the red plush armchair spread newspapers over the arms and back to protect the chair from the rain. The child in the crib began to cry.

"There it goes, our home of two weeks," Graeber said.

"Justice!" the baldhead declared with satisfaction.

"You ought to have bet. You would have won."

"I am not a materialist, young man."

"Then why did you complain about your apartment?"

"That was my home. You probably don't understand that."

"No, I guess I don't understand that. The German Reich turned me into a world traveler too young."

"You ought to be grateful for that." The baldhead ran his hand over his mouth and pointedly cleared his throat. "Anyhow, I'd have nothing against a glass of vodka now."

"You won't get one now. Pray instead."

Flames burst out of the windows of Frau Lieser's room. "There goes the desk," Elisabeth whispered. "The informer's desk with everything in it."

"Let's hope so. I poured a bottle of kerosene over it. What shall we do now?"

"We'll look for lodgings. If we don't find any we'll sleep somewhere on the street."

"On the street or in a park." Graeber glanced at the sky. "There's my shelter-half to protect us against the rain. It's not very good protection but perhaps we'll find some sort of roof. What shall we do with the chair and the books?"

"We'll leave them here. If they're still here tomorrow we'll decide what to do with them then."

Graeber put on his knapsack and swung the bedding over his shoulder. Elisabeth picked up the suitcases. "Give them to me," he said. "I'm used to carrying loads."

The upper floors of the two other houses crashed in. Burning embers flew in all directions. Frau Lieser screeched and sprang up; a glowing coal had flown out across the roped-off street and into her face. Flames were now pouring out of Elisabeth's room. Then the ceiling fell. "We can go," Elisabeth said.

Graeber looked up at the window. "They were good days," he said.

"The best. Let's go."

Elisabeth's face was red in the glow of the fire. They made their way between the chairs. Most of the people sat silent and resigned. One of them had a package of books beside him and was reading. Two elderly people were sitting close together on the pavement. They had drawn a cape over them and looked like a sad bat with two heads.

"Strange how easy it is to part with something that only yesterday you didn't believe you could get along without," Elisabeth said.

Graeber looked around once more. The youngster with the freckles who had taken back the cup was already seated in the Biedermeier chair. "I stole Frau Lieser's handbag while she was jumping around," Graeber said. "It's full of papers. We'll throw them into a fire somewhere. Perhaps that will save someone from a concentration camp."

Elisabeth nodded. She did not look around again.


He knocked for a long time. Then he shook the door. No one opened it. He came back to Elisabeth. "Pohlmann isn't home. Or he won't open for anyone."

"Perhaps he doesn't live here now."

"Where else would he be living? There's no space anywhere. We've seen that during the last three hours. It could only be—" Graeber went to the door again. "No, the Gestapo haven't been here. It would look different if they had. What shall we do? Do you want to go to an air raid shelter?"

"No. Can't we stay somewhere near here?"

Graeber looked around. It was night, and against the dusky

red of the sky the ruins thrust upward black and angular. "Here's
a piece of ceiling," he said. "It's dry under it. I could hang up the
canvas on one side and my coat on the other."

Graeber took his bayonet and tapped at the piece of ceiling. It
held. He looked around in the ruins and found a couple of iron
bars which he rammed into the ground. On them he hung the
canvas. "That's a curtain. My coat on the other side will make it
into a sort of tent. What do you think?"

"Can I help you?"

"No. Just keep an eye on our things, that's enough."

Graeber cleared the ground of debris and stones. Then he carried in the suitcases and unrolled the bedding. He placed his
knapsack at the head. "Now we have a place to stay," he said.
"I've lived in worse before this. You, of course, haven't."

"It's time I got used to it."

Graeber unpacked Elisabeth's raincoat and alcohol stove and a
bottle of alcohol. "They stole the bread, but we still have a couple of cans in my knapsack."

"Have we something to cook in, too? A pot?"

"My mess kit. And there's rain water all around. We have the
rest of the vodka too. I could make you a sort of grog with hot
water. To keep you from catching cold."

"I'd rather have the vodka straight."

Graeber lit the alcohol stove. The pale blue light illuminated the tent. He opened a can of beans. They heated them
and ate them with what was left of the sausage they had received from their marriage witness Klotz. "Shall we go on
waiting for Pohlmann or go to sleep?" Graeber asked.

"Let's go to sleep. I'm tired."

"We'll have to sleep in our clothes. Can you do that?"

"I'm tired enough to."

Elisabeth took off her shoes and placed them in front of the knapsack so they would not be stolen. She rolled up her stockings and put them in her pocket. Graeber pulled the blankets over her. "How's that?" he asked.

"Like a hotel."

He lay down beside her. "Are you sad because of your home?" he asked.

"No. I counted on losing that as soon as the first raids came. I was sad then. Everything since then has been borrowed time."

"That's right. But can one always live as logically as one thinks?"

"I don't know," she murmured on his shoulder. "Perhaps when one is without hope. But it's different now."

She went to sleep, breathing slowly and regularly. Graeber continued to lie awake for a while. He was thinking that sometimes in the field when the men had been talking about impossible wishes this had been one of them—to have a roof, a bed, a woman and a quiet night.

# Chapter Twenty-one

HE WOKE UP. Cautious footsteps crunched over the rubble. He slipped noiselessly from under the covers. Elisabeth stirred and went on sleeping. Graeber peered under the canvas. It might be Pohlmann returning, but it might as easily be thieves or it might even be the Gestapo—they usually came at this hour. If it was the Gestapo he would have to try to intercept Pohlmann and keep him from returning to the house.

He saw two figures in front of him in the dark. As silently as possible he followed them. He was not wearing shoes. However, within a few yards he ran into a piece of wall so loose it toppled over at once. He crouched. One of the figures swung around. "Is someone there?" a voice asked. It was Pohlmann.

Graeber stood up. "It's me, Herr Pohlmann. Ernst Graeber."

"Graeber? What's happened?"

"Nothing. We were just bombed out and didn't know where to go. I thought perhaps you could put us up for a night or two."

"Who?"

"My wife and me. I was married a few days ago."

"Certainly, certainly." Pohlmann approached. His face glimmered very pale in the darkness. "Did you see me coming?"

Graeber hesitated a second. "Yes," he said then. There was no point in taking unnecessary precautions—not for Elisabeth nor for the man who was now lying somewhere in the ruins. "Yes," he repeated, "and you can trust me."

Pohlmann rubbed his forehead. "Certainly, that's sure." He stood undecided. "You saw I was not alone?"

"Yes."

Pohlmann seemed to have made up his mind. "Well—yes—come along. For the night, you said. There isn't too much room, but—first of all come away from here."

They went around the corner. "Everything's all right," Pohlmann said into the shadows.

A man detached himself from the ruins. Pohlmann unlocked the door and admitted Graeber and the man. Then he locked it from inside. "Where's your wife?" he asked.

"She's sleeping outside. We brought bedding along and put up a sort of tent."

Pohlmann stood motionless in the darkness. "I must tell you something, Graeber. It could be dangerous for you to be found here."

"I know that."

Pohlmann cleared his throat. "It's dangerous because of me. I am under suspicion."

"I meant that."

"Did you mean it for your wife too?"

"Yes," Graeber said after a moment.

The other man had been standing completely silent behind Graeber. Now his breathing became audible. Pohlmann went ahead of them and when the door was shut and the curtains drawn he lighted a very small lamp. "There's no need to mention names," he said. "Better not to know them. Then there's nothing you can give away. Ernst and Josef will suffice."

He looked very exhausted. Josef was a man of about forty with a narrow, Jewish face. He seemed completely calm and he smiled at Graeber. Then he began to brush plaster dust off his clothes.

"It's no longer safe here," Pohlmann said, seating himself. "Nevertheless Josef has to stay here tonight. The apartment where he was yesterday no longer exists. Tomorrow during the day we must see what else we can find. It's no longer safe here, Josef. That's the only reason."

"I know," Josef replied. He had a deeper voice than one expected.

"And you, Ernst?" Pohlmann asked. "I am under suspicion, that you know—but do you know what it means to be found at this hour of the night in the house of someone who is under suspicion in company with someone who is wanted?"

"Yes."

"I think nothing will happen tonight. The city is in too much confusion. But one never knows. Do you want to take the risk?"

Graeber was silent. Pohlmann and Josef looked at him. "There's no risk for me," he said. "I have to go back into the field in a couple of days. But with my wife it's different. She has to go on living here. I hadn't thought of that."

"I didn't say it to get rid of you, Ernst."

"I know that."

"Can you manage to sleep outside?" Josef asked.

"Yes, we're protected from the rain."

"Then stay there. That way you'll have nothing to do with us. Early tomorrow bring your things here. That's what you principally wanted, isn't it? However, you can store them just as well in the Katharinenkirche. The sexton there allows it. He is an honorable man. Part of the church has been destroyed, but the underground vaults are still intact. Take your things there. Then you'll be free for the day to look for a place to stay."

"I believe he's right, Ernst," Pohlmann said. "Josef knows about these things better than we do."

Graeber felt a sudden wave of affection for the weary old man who was again calling him by his first name as he had years ago. "I think so too," he replied. "I'm sorry I startled you."

"Come in early tomorrow morning if you need anything. Give two slow knocks, two quick ones. Don't knock loud; I'll hear you."

"Good. Thanks."

Graeber went back. Elisabeth was still sleeping. She only half awoke when he lay down and at once went back to sleep.


She woke up at six o'clock. A wagon was clattering by on the street. She stretched. "I slept marvelously," she said. "Just where are we?"

"On the Jahnplatz."

"Good. And where will we sleep tonight?"

"We'll see about that during the day."

She lay back. A band of cool morning brightness came in between the canvas and the overcoat. Birds were twittering. She pushed the coat to one side. Outside the early morning sky was yellow and luminous. "A gypsy's life," she said. "Full of adventures."

"Yes," Graeber said. "Let's look at it that way. I met Pohlmann last night. We can wake him up if we need anything."

"We don't need a thing. Do we still have coffee? We can cook here, or can't we?"

"I am sure it's forbidden, like everything else that's sensible. But what difference does that make? We are gypsies."

Elisabeth began to comb her hair. "Behind the house there's some clear rain water in a pot," Graeber said. "Just enough to do a little washing."

Elisabeth put on her jacket. "I'll go around. It's like being in the country. Water from the pump. Romantic is what they used to call it in earlier times, isn't it?"

Graeber laughed. "Even now—compared with the mud in Russia. Everything turns out to be comparative." He rolled up the bedding. Then he lighted the alcohol stove and put on the pot of water. Suddenly it occurred to him he had forgotten to look for Elisabeth's ration coupons in her room. She was just coming back from washing. Her face was clear and young. "Have you your coupons with you?" he asked.

"No. They were in the desk by the window. In the little compartment."

"Damn it, I forgot to take them. Why didn't I think of them? I had plenty of time."

"You thought of things that are more important. My golden dress for instance. We'll just put in a request for new coupons. It's nothing unusual for them to be burned."

"That may take forever. The end of the world wouldn't jog a German official out of his routine."

Eisabeth laughed. "I'll take an hour's leave from the factory and get them. The block warden can give me a certificate to prove I was bombed out."

"You intend to go to the factory today?" Graeber asked.

"I have to. Being bombed out is no excuse. It happens every day."

"I could set fire to that damn factory."

'So could I, but then they would only send me some place else where it might be even worse. I don't want to make ammunition."

"Why don't you simply stay away? How is anyone to know what happened to you yesterday? You might have been hurt saving your things."

"That's something I would have to prove. We have factory doctors and factory police. If they find out someone has cheated there are penalties. Extra work, no vacation—and if that doesn't help, an educational course in patriotism in a concentration camp. Those who have been through that never stay away from work again."

Elisabeth took the hot water and poured it over the ersatz coffee powder in the top of the mess kit. "Don't forget I have just had two days' vacation," she said. "I can't make too many demands."

He knew she thought she must not on her father's account. She hoped in that way to be able to help him. That was the noose around everyone's neck. "Those bandits!" he said. "What they have made of us!"

"Here's your coffee. And don't get angry. We have no time for that."

"That's just what makes me angry, Elisabeth."

She nodded. "I know. We have so little time and nevertheless we can spend so little of it together. Your furlough is passing and most of it is squandered waiting. I ought to have more courage and stay away from the factory for as long as you are here."

"You have courage enough. And it's better to wait than to have nothing to wait for."

She kissed him and smiled. "You've been quick at learning to find the right words," she said. "Now I must go. Where shall we meet this evening?"

"Yes, where? There isn't any place now. We must start all over again. I'll come and get you at the factory."

"And if something happens—an attack or a street blockade?"

Graeber reflected. "I'll pack our things up and go to the Katharinenkirche. Let's make that our second meeting place."

"Is it open at night?"

"Why at night? You don't come back at night."

"One never knows. Once we had to sit in the cellar for six hours. The best thing would be if we had someone to leave a message with if worst comes to worst. Meeting places alone aren't enough any more."

"You mean if something happened to one of us?"

"Yes."

Graeber nodded. He had seen how easy it was to lose track of someone. "We can make it Pohlmann for today. No, that's not safe." He considered. "Binding," he said, suddenly relieved. "He's safe. I've shown you his house. Only he doesn't know we're married. But that doesn't matter. I'll go and tell him about it."

"Are you going there to rob him again?"

Graeber laughed. "I really didn't have that in mind. But we do need something to eat. So I'll become corrupt again."

"Shall we sleep here tonight?"

"I hope not. I have the whole day to find some place else."

Her face darkened for an instant. "Yes, you have. I must be off now."

"I'll pack up right away, leave our things with Pohlmann, and take you to the factory."

"There's no time for that now. I have to run. Goodby till this evening. Factory, Katharinenkirche, or at Binding's. What an interesting life!"

"To hell with an interesting life!" Graeber said.

He looked after her. She was walking rapidly across the square. The morning was clear and the sky now a clean, deep blue. Dew glistened like a silver net over the ruins. Elisabeth turned around and waved. Then she walked on quickly. Graeber loved the way she walked. She set her feet almost in front of each other as though she were walking along a wagon track. He had seen native women in Africa walk that way. She waved once more and disappeared between the houses at the end of the square. It's almost like the front, he thought. When you part, you never know whether you will meet again. To hell with this interesting life!

At eight o'clock Pohlmann came out. "I wanted to see whether you had anything to eat. I could let you have some bread—"

"Thanks, we have enough. May I leave the bedding and the bags with you while I go to the Katharinenkirche?"

"Of course."

Graeber carried the things inside. Josef was not to be seen. "It's possible that I won't be here when you come back," Pohlmann said. "Give two slow taps and two quick ones. Josef will hear you."

Graeber opened one of the bags. "It's like a gypsy's life," he said. "That's not what I expected."

Pohlmann smiled wearily. "Josef has been living it for three years. For several months he spent his nights on electric trains. Rode around all the time. During that time he could only sleep sitting up and only for a quarter of an hour at a time. It was before we had the air raids. Now it's no longer possible."

Graeber took a can of meat out of the bag and gave it to Pohlmann. "I can spare this. Give it to Josef."

"Meat? Don't you need it yourself?"

"No. Give it to him. People like him must survive. Otherwise what will happen when all this is over? What will happen anyhow? Is there enough left to start afresh?"

The old man was silent for a time. Then he walked over to the globe that stood in the corner and spun it. "Look here," he said. "This tiny piece of the world is Germany. You can almost cover it with your thumb. It's a very small part of the world."

"That may be. But from this small part we have conquered a large slice of the world."

"A slice yes. And conquered—but not convinced."

"Not yet. But what would have happened if we had been able to hold onto it? Ten years. Or twenty. Or fifty. Victories and successes are horribly effective persuaders. We have seen that in our own country."

"We were not victorious."

"That's no proof."

"It is a proof," Pohlmann said. "A very profound one." His hand with the thick veins continued to turn the globe. "The world," he said. "The world does not stand still. When one despairs for a time of his own country he must believe in the world. An eclipse is possible but not an enduring period of night. Not on this planet. One must not make things easier for oneself by simply giving way to despair."

He pushed the globe back. "You ask whether there's enough left to begin over again. The Church began with a few fishermen, a few of the faithful in the catacombs, and the survivors of the arenas of Rome."

"Yes. And the Nazis with a few jobless fanatics in a beer hall in Munich."

Pohlmann smiled. "You are right. But there has never been a tyranny that lasted. Humanity has not advanced in an even course. It has always been only by thrusts, jerks, relapses, and spasms. We were too arrogant; we thought we had already conquered our bloody past. Now we know that we dare not so much as look around for fear it will get hold of us again." He picked up his hat. "I must go."

"Here's your book about Switzerland," Graeber said. "It's rather the worse for rain. I lost it, but I found it again and rescued it."

"You need not have rescued it. One doesn't have to rescue dreams."

"On the contrary," Graeber said. "What else?"

"Faith. Dreams always reshape themselves."

"One hopes so. Otherwise you might as well hang yourself."

"How young you still are!" Pohlmann said. "But what am I saying? You really are still very young." He put on his overcoat. "Strange—I had always pictured youth differently—"

"So had I," Graeber said.

Josef had been correctly informed. The sexton of the Katharinen-kirche took charge of their things. Graeber left his knapsack there. Then he went to the Housing Authority. It had been forced to move and was now located in the natural history room of a school. A stand with maps and a glass case with exhibits in alcohol were still there. The woman in charge had used some of the jars as paperweights. There were snakes, lizards, and frogs. In addition there was a stuffed squirrel with glass eyes and a nut between its paws. The woman clerk was a friendly, gray-haired person. "I will note down your name for emergency quarters," she said. "Have you an address?"

"No."

"Then you must stop by from time to time and inquire."

"Is there any point in it?"

"Not the slightest. There are six thousand requests ahead of yours. It would be better to see what you can find for yourself."

He walked back to the Jahnplatz and knocked on Pohlmann's door. No one answered. He waited a while. Then he went to Marienstrasse to see what was left there.

Elisabeth's house had burned down to the block warden's story. The fire department had been there. Water was still dripping from everything. Of Elisabeth's apartment nothing was left. The armchair that had been standing outside was gone, too. A pair of wet blue gloves lay in the gutter, that was all.

Graeber saw the block warden behind the curtains of his apartment. He remembered he had promised him cigars. That seemed a long time ago and no longer necessary; but one could never tell. He decided to go and see Alfons. In any case he needed supplies for the evening.

Nothing else had been hit but just that one house. The gardens lay peaceful in the morning light, the birch trees swayed in the wind, the gold of the jonquils glistened, and the early trees were in blossom as though swarms of white and pink butterflies had alighted on them—only Binding's house was a wild heap of wreckage, overhanging a crater in the garden where dirty water stood, reflecting the sky.

Graeber stood for a moment staring at it as though he did not believe it. He did not know why, but he had always assumed nothing could happen to Alfons. Slowly he walked up to it. The bird bath had been broken from its base and splintered. The front door hung in the lilac bushes. Deer's antlers rose from the grass as though the animals were buried under it. A tapestry hung high in the trees like the gleaming banner of a barbarian conqueror. Bold and upright a bottle of Napoleon brandy stood in a flower bed as though it were a dark bottle-gourd that had shot up overnight. Graeber picked it up, examined it, and put it in his pocket. Very likely the cellar has held up, he thought, and Alfons has been shoveled out.

He walked around to the back of the house. The kitchen entrance was still standing. He opened the door. Something inside moved. "Frau Kleinert?" he said.

A loud sobbing answered him. The woman got up and came

out of the half-demolished room into the open. "The poor gentleman! He was so kind!"

"What happened? Is he hurt?"

"He is dead. Dead, Herr Graeber! And he was such a life-
loving gentleman!"

"Dead?"

"Yes. One can't grasp it, can one?"

Graeber nodded. You could never grasp death even when you
were used to seeing it so often. "How did it happen?" he asked.

"He was in the cellar. But the cellar did not hold."

"The cellar was too weak for heavy bombs. Why didn't he go
to the deep bunker on the Seidelplatz? That's only a few minutes
from here."

"He thought nothing would happen. And then—" Frau
Kleinert hesitated. "There was a lady here too."

"What? At noon?"

"She was still here, you see. From the night before. A big
blonde. The Herr Commandant loved big blondes. I had just
served a chicken when the raid came."

"Was the lady killed too?"

"Yes. They hadn't even got properly dressed yet. Herr Binding in pajamas and the lady in a thin silk dressing gown. That's
how they were found. There was nothing I could do about it.
That he should be found that way! Instead of in his uniform!"

"It doesn't matter. And I don't know how he could have found
a better death if he had to die," Graeber said. "Had he already
eaten lunch?"

"Yes. Very heartily. With wine and his favorite dessert. Ap-
felkuchen with whipped cream."

"There, you see, Frau Kleinert. In that case it was a wonderful
death. That's how I'd like to die, myself, when the time comes.
Truly you don't need to weep about that."

"But it was too soon."

"It's always too soon. Even when one is ninety, I believe. When is he to be buried?"

"Day after tomorrow at nine o'clock. He's already in his coffin. Do you want to see him?"

"Where is he?"

"In the storage cellar. It's cool there. The coffin is already closed. This side of the house wasn't so badly damaged. Only the front was entirely destroyed."

They walked through the kitchen into the cellar. A heap of broken glass had been swept into one corner. There was a smell of spilled wine and preserves. On the floor in the middle of the room stood a walnut coffin. All around on shelves, upset and in confusion, were glass bottles with preserved fruit and canned goods. "How were you able to get a coffin so quickly?" Graeber asked.

"The Party took care of that."

"Will he be buried from here?"

"Yes. Day after tomorrow at nine o'clock."

"I'll come."

"That will certainly please our Herr."

Graeber stared at Frau Kleinert. "In the Beyond," she said. "He was always so fond of you."

"Yes. I really don't know why."

"He said you were the only one who never wanted anything from him. And then because you were in the war the whole time."

Graeber stood for a while in front of the coffin. He felt a confused regret but nothing much besides, and he was ashamed in the presence of this weeping woman not to feel more. "What are you going to do now with all these things?" he asked, glancing at the preserves.

Frau Kleinert recovered herself. "Take as many of them as you can use, Herr Graeber. Otherwise they will only pass into the hands of strangers," she said.

"Keep them yourself. After all you put up most of them personally."

"I've already set aside some for myself. I don't need much. Take what you want, Herr Graeber. The Party members who were here seemed to raise their eyebrows. It's better if there isn't so much. Otherwise it would look too much like hoarding."

"That's true."

"Well, for that reason. And when the others come back it will all pass into the hands of strangers. After all you were a real friend to Herr Binding. He would certainly want you to have it more than the others."

"Doesn't he have any family?"

"His father is still alive. But you know how he felt about him. And anyway there will be plenty left. In the second cellar there are still a lot of unbroken bottles too. Take whatever you can use."

The woman hurried along the shelves, pulling out cans, and brought them back. She placed them on the coffin, was about to go for more, then realized what she had done, picked them up from the coffin and carried them into the kitchen.

"Wait, Frau Kleinert," Graeber said. "If I'm going to take some of this with me then we'll pick it out sensibly." He looked at the cans. "This is asparagus. Dutch asparagus. We don't need that. But we can take the sardines in oil and also the bottled pigs' knuckles."

"That's right. I am so confused."

She got together a pile on a chair in the kitchen. "That's too much," Graeber said. "How can I carry all that?"

"Come back two or three times. Why should it fall into the

hands of strangers, Herr Graeber? You are a soldier, you have more right to it than these Nazis with their armchair jobs!"

Maybe that's true, Graeber thought. And Elisabeth and Josef and Pohlmann have just as much right, and I would be an ass not to help myself. It doesn't help and it doesn't hurt Alfons now. Only later when he was already some distance from the ruined house it occurred to him that it had really been only by accident that he had not been living in Binding's house and been buried with him.

Josef opened the door. "Quick work," Graeber said.

"I saw you coming." Josef pointed to a small hole in the door panel. "I bored that earlier. It's useful."

Graeber placed his package on the table. "I was at the Katharinenkirche. The sexton said we could spend the night there. Thanks for your advice."

"Was it the young sexton?"

"No, an old one."

"The old one is all right. He let me live in the church for a week disguised as an assistant sexton. Then suddenly there was an inspection. I hid in the organ. The young sexton had reported me. He is an anti-Semite. A religious anti-Semite. They exist. Because we killed Christ two thousand years ago."

Graeber opened the package. Then he got out of his pockets the cans of sardines and herrings. Josef looked at them. His face did not change. "A treasure," he said.

"We'll divide it."

"Have you so much to spare?"

"As you can see. I inherited it. From a commander in the S.A. Do you mind?"

"On the contrary. It will give it a certain spice. Do you know commanders in the S.A. well enough to get presents like this?"

Graeber looked at Josef. "Yes," he said. "Anyway this one. He was a harmless and good-natured man."

Josef made no reply. "Don't you believe one can be that at the same time?" Graeber asked.

"Do you believe it?"

"It may be possible," Graeber said, "if one is without character or anxious or weak and goes along for that reason."

"Does one become a commander of the S.A. that way?"

"Even that may be possible."

Josef smiled. "It's strange," he said. "One's likely to assume that a murderer must always and everywhere be a murderer and nothing else. In point of fact it's quite enough if he is a murderer only now and again and with a small part of his being—it's enough to cause horrible suffering. Don't you agree?"

"Yes," Graeber replied. "A hyena is always a hyena. A human being is more various."

Josef nodded. "There are concentration camp commandants with a sense of humor. S.S. guards who are good-natured and friendly among themselves. And camp followers who cling only to the good, overlooking what's horrible, or explaining it away as a temporary product of the times and a regrettable necessity. People with elastic consciences."

"And people who are afraid."

"And people who are afraid," Josef said politely.

Graeber was silent. "I wish I could do something for you," he said then.

"There's not much that can be done. I am alone. I'll either be caught or survive." Josef spoke as impersonally as though he were talking about a stranger.

"Haven't you any relations?"

"I had some. A brother, two sisters, a father, a wife and a child. They are dead. Two beaten to death, one dead of natural causes, the others gassed."

Graeber stared at him. "In the camp?"

"In the camp," Josef replied politely and coldly. "They have extraordinary facilities there."

"And you escaped?"

"I escaped."

Graeber looked at Josef. "How you must hate us!" he said.

Josef shrugged his shoulders. "Hate! Who can allow himself such a luxury? Hate makes one forget to be cautious."

Graeber glanced toward the window, close behind which rose the rubble heap of the demolished house. The dim light of the small lamp seemed to have grown fainter. It gleamed on the globe that Pohlmann had pushed into the corner.

"You are going back to the front?" Josef asked courteously.

"Yes. Back to fight so that the criminals who are hunting you can remain in power a while longer. Perhaps just long enough to catch you and hang you."

Josef made a slight gesture of agreement and was silent.

"I am going because otherwise they would shoot me," Graeber said.

Josef did not reply.

"And I am going because if I deserted they would lock up my parents and my wife or send them to a camp or kill them."

Josef was silent.

"I am going and I know that my reasons are no reasons and yet they are the reasons of millions. How you must despise us!"

"Don't be so vain," Josef said softly.

Graeber stared at him. He did not understand.

"Nobody's talking about despising anyone," Josef said. "Only you. Why is that so important to you? Do I despise Pohlmann? Do I despise the people who hide me every night at the risk of their lives? Would I be alive if it weren't for them? How naive you are!"

Suddenly he smiled again. It was a ghostly smile that flitted over his face without touching it. "We're getting away from the subject," he said. "One oughtn't to talk too much. And one oughtn't to reflect. Not yet. It weakens you. So does remembering. It's too early for all that. In time of danger you should think only about how to save yourself." He pointed to the canned goods. "This will help. I'll take it. Thanks."

He took the cans and the preserves and put them behind the books. He did it in a curiously awkward way. Graeber saw that the last joints of his fingers were deformed and without nails. Josef noticed his glance. "A little remembrance of the camp. The Sunday entertainment of a troop leader. He called it lighting the Christmas candles. Sharply pointed matches. I wish he had used my toes instead. Then it wouldn't be so conspicuous. This way I'm easily recognized. On the street I wear gloves."

Graeber got up. "Would it help you if I gave you an old uniform and my pay book? You could alter it where necessary. I can say it was burned."

"No, thanks. I don't need it. For the immediate future I am going to become a Rumanian. Pohlmann thought that up and arranged it. He's very clever at that sort of thing. You wouldn't think it to look at him, would you? I'll become a Rumanian, a member of the Iron Front, a friend of the Party. My appearance is all right for a Rumanian. And my injuries can be more easily explained. Inflicted by the Communists. Are you going to take your bedding and bags along with you?"

Graeber realized that Josef wanted to be rid of him. "Are you going to stay here?" he asked.

"Why?"

Graeber pushed his own supply of canned goods over toward him. "I can get more. I'll go back again and bring another load."

"It's too much as it is. I don't dare carry much baggage. And now I must go. I can't wait any longer."

"Cigarettes. I forgot cigarettes. There are plenty of them there. I can go and get them."

Josef's face changed. All at once it became relaxed and almost soft. "Cigarettes," he said, as though he were talking about a friend. "That's different. They're more important than food. I'll wait for them, of course."

# Chapter Twenty-two

A CROWD WAS already waiting in the cloister of the Katharinenkirche. Almost all of them were sitting on suitcases and baskets or were surrounded by packages and bundles. Most of them were women and children. Graeber took his place among them with his roll of bedding and bags. An old woman with a face like a horse was sitting beside him. "If only they don't ship us out as evacuees!" she said. "You hear such stories about that. Living in barracks with not enough to eat and the farmers being cross and mean."

"I don't care if they do!" a thin girl replied. "I only want to get away. Anything is better than being dead. It's their duty to take care of us. We have lost all our possessions. It's their duty to take care of us."

"A few days ago a train with evacuees from the Rhineland came through here. What a sight! They were on their way to Mecklenburg."

"Mecklenburg? That's where the rich farmers live."

"Rich farmers!" The woman with the horse's face laughed angrily. "With them you have to work till the flesh drops from your bones. In return you get short rations. The Fuehrer ought to be told about it!"

Graeber looked at Horseface and at the thin girl. Behind them through the open Romanesque colonnade the first green shimmered in the cathedral garden. Jonquils were in bloom in front of the statues in the cloister. A thrush perched singing on the figure of Christ being scourged.

"They'll have to billet us gratis," the thin girl declared. "With people who are well off. We're victims of war. Victims of war," she repeated.

The sexton approached. He was a thin man with a pendulous red nose and drooping shoulders. Graeber could not picture him having the courage to hide anyone the Gestapo were looking for.

The sexton let the people in. He gave each a number for his belongings and stuck a slip of paper with the same number on the bundles and bags. "Don't come too late this evening," he said to Graeber. "We haven't enough room in the church."

"Not enough room?" The Katharinenkirche was a large building.

"No. The nave of the church is not used as a shelter. Only the rooms underneath and the side aisles."

"Where do the people sleep who come late?"

"In those cloisters that are still standing. A good many sleep in the cloister gardens too."

"Are the rooms under the nave of the church bombproof?"

The sexton looked at Graeber mildly. "When the church was built no one had thought up anything of that kind. It was during the Dark Ages."

The red-nosed face was entirely expressionless. It did not betray itself by so much as the tiniest twinkle. We have made great advances in dissimulation, Graeber thought. Almost everyone is a little master.

He walked through the garden and out through the cloisters. The church had been severely damaged; one of its towers had caved in, and daylight poured into it mercilessly, cutting broad, bright bands through its dusky twilight. A number of windows were broken as well. Sparrows sat in them, twittering. The seminary had been entirely demolished. Close behind it was the air raid shelter. Graeber went into it. It was a reinforced ancient wine cellar, which had formerly belonged to the church. The stands for the barrels were still there. The air was damp and cool and aromatic. The wine bouquet of the centuries still seemed able to triumph again and again over the smell of fear from the nights of bombs. In the rear of the bunker Graeber saw a number of heavy iron rings fixed in the square-cut stones of the ceiling. He remembered that before being a wine cellar this place had been a torture chamber for witches and heretics. They had been hoisted by their hands, with irons attached to their feet, and they had been pinched with glowing tongs until they confessed. Then they had been put to death, in the name of God and Christian love of one's neighbor. Very little has changed, he thought. The torturers in the concentration camp have excellent models. And the carpenter's son of Nazareth has strange followers.

He was walking along Adlerstrasse. It was six o'clock in the evening. He had been looking all day for a room and had found nothing. Wearily he had decided to give it up for today.

The section was badly devastated. Row after row of ruins. Listlessly he walked on among them. Then suddenly he saw something that at first he could not believe. In the midst of the devastation stood a small two-storied house. It was old and a little crooked, but it was entirely undamaged. A garden lay around it with a few trees and bushes coming into leaf, and everything was untouched. It was an oasis in the wilderness of ruins. Above the garden fence lilac bushes were budding and not a single picket of the fence was broken. Ten paces on either side the lunar wilderness began again; but this tiny old garden and this tiny old house had been spared by one of those miracles that sometimes go with destruction. *Inn and Restaurant Witte* was painted over the front door.

The garden gate was open. He went in. He was no longer surprised to find that not a pane in the windows had been broken. It almost had to be so. The miraculous always lies in wait close by despair. A brown and white hunting dog lay sleeping beside the door. A few flower beds were abloom with jonquils, violets, and tulips. It seemed to him as though he had seen all this once before. He did not know when; it seemed a long time ago. But perhaps he had only dreamed it. He walked through the door.

The taproom was empty. There were only a few glasses standing on the shelves; no bottles at all. The tap was shiny, but the sieve under it was dry. Three tables with chairs around them stood along the wall. A picture hung over the center one. It was a Tyrolean landscape. In it a girl was playing a zither and a huntsman was leaning over her. There was no picture of Hitler; nor had Graeber expected one.

A middle-aged woman came in. She was wearing a faded blue blouse with sleeves shirred at the shoulders. She did not say: *"Heil Hitler."* She said, "Good evening"—and there was actually something of the evening in it. After a day full of good work it was the wish for a good evening. Once there used to be things like this, Graeber thought. He had only intended to get something to drink, the dust of the ruins had made him thirsty, but now it suddenly seemed very important to spend the evening here with Elisabeth. He foresaw it would be a good evening, beyond the dark circle of destruction that lay as far as the horizon on all sides of this enchanted garden. "Can one get supper here?" he asked.

The woman hesitated. "I have coupons," he said quickly. "It would be wonderful to eat here. Perhaps even in the garden. It's one of my last days before I have to go away. For my wife and me. I have coupons for both of us. If you like I can bring canned goods as well to trade."

"We only have lentil soup. We're really not serving any more."

"Lentil soup will be splendid. I haven't had any in a long time."

The woman smiled. It was a quiet smile that seemed to take form of itself. "If that's enough for you, then come. You can sit in the garden too, if you like. Or here if it's too cool."

"In the garden. It will still be light enough. Can we come around eight o'clock?"

"With lentil soup you don't have to be too punctual. Just come when you like."

A letter had been stuck under the doorplate of his parents' house. It was from his mother. They had forwarded it to him from the front. He tore it open. The letter was brief. His mother wrote that his father and she were going to leave the city next morning with a transport. They did not know yet where they were being taken. He was not to worry. It was just a precautionary safety measure.

He looked at the date. The letter had been written a week before his furlough. There was nothing in it about an air raid; but his mother always was cautious. She was afraid of the censors. It was unlikely that the house had been bombed on the following night. It must have happened earlier; otherwise they would not have been selected to go with the transport.

He slowly folded the letter and put it into his pocket. So his parents were alive! He was as sure of it now as one could be! He looked around. Something like a wavy glass wall seemed to be sinking into the ground in front of him. Suddenly Hakenstrasse looked like all the other bombed streets. The dread and torment that had hung over Number Eighteen had been silently blown away. There was nothing more there but debris and ruins, like everywhere else.

He took a deep breath. He felt no joy; only a profound release. A burden that had oppressed him all the time and everywhere had suddenly dropped from his shoulders. He did not reflect that now he would probably not see his parents during his furlough; the long uncertainty had already buried that hope. They were alive; that was enough. They were alive; with that fact something was terminated and he was free.

During the last raid the street had received a few hits. The house of which only the façade had been standing had collapsed. The door with the Ruins Journal was now propped up, a little farther on, between the piles of rubble. Graeber was just wondering what might have become of the mad air raid warden when he saw him coming from across the street. "The soldier," said the warden. "Still here!"

"Yes. You too, it appears."

"Did you find your letter?"

"Yes."

"It came yesterday afternoon. Can we strike you off the door now? We need the space badly. There are five applicants for it."

"Not yet," Graeber said. "In a couple of days."

"It's high time," the warden declared, as sharply and severely as though he were a schoolteacher rebuking a disobedient child. "We have been very patient with you."

"Are you the editor of this Journal?"

"An air raid warden is everything. He maintains order. We have a widow whose three children have been missing since the last raid. We need a place to announce it."

"Then take mine. Apparently I get my mail at the ruin over there anyway."

The warden took down Graeber's notice and handed it to him. Graeber was about to tear it up, when the warden seized his hand. "Are you crazy, soldier? You don't tear something like that. If you did you'd be tearing up your luck. Once saved always saved, as long as you keep that notice. You really still are a beginner!"

"Yes," Graeber said, folding the notice and putting it in his pocket. "And that's the way I'd like to stay as long as I can. Where are you living now?"

"I had to move. I found a snug cellar corner. Live there now as the sub-tenant of a family of mice. Very entertaining."

Graeber looked at the man. His haggard face betrayed nothing. "I intend to found a society," he announced, "for people whose relations are buried under the ruins. We must stand together, otherwise the city will do nothing. At the very least, each place where people are buried must be blessed by a priest so that it will be consecrated ground. Do you understand that?"

"Yes. I understand."

"Good. There are people who think it's foolish. You, of course, haven't any reason now for becoming a member. You've gotten your damn letter!"

The haggard face suddenly fell apart. An expression of bewildered pain and rage seemed to break it into pieces. The man turned around abruptly and stomped back along the street.

Graeber looked after him. Then he went on. He decided not to tell Elisabeth that his parents were still alive.

She came alone across the square in front of the factory. She seemed very lost and small. The twilight made the square bigger than usual and the low buildings beyond it more bare and menacing.

"I'm going to get some time off, she said breathlessly. "Again."

"How long?"

"Three days. The last three days."

She stopped. Her eyes changed. They were suddenly full of tears. "I told them why," she said. "They gave me the three days right away. Perhaps I'll have to make them up later, but that doesn't matter. Afterwards nothing matters. It's really better if I have a lot to do."

Graeber made no reply. The realization that they would have to part had struck in front of him like a dark meteor. He had known it all the time, the way one knows many things—without actually realizing them or completely feeling them. There had always been so much in between. Now all at once it was there by itself, big and full of a chill horror, and it was radiating a pale, penetrating, skeletonizing light—like X-rays that pierce through the charm and magic of life, leaving nothing but the bare residue and the inevitable.

They looked at each other. Both felt the same thing. They stood in the empty square and looked at each other and each knew what the other was suffering. They had the feeling that they were reeling in a storm, but they did not move. Despair, from which they had found escape again and again, had finally caught up with them, and they saw each other now as they would really be—Graeber saw Elisabeth, alone, in the factory, in an air raid shelter, or in some room, waiting without much hope—and she saw him returning to war for a cause in which he no longer believed. Despair shook them, and at the same time like a cloudburst there descended on them a fatal tenderness, to which they dared not yield because they felt they would be torn to pieces once they admitted it. They were helpless. They could do nothing. They had to wait until it passed.

It seemed forever before Graeber could speak. He saw the tears were gone from Elisabeth's eyes. She had not stirred; it was as though they had flowed inward. "Then we will be together for a couple of whole days," he said.

She smiled. "Yes. Beginning tomorrow evening."

"Good. Then it's as though we still had a couple of weeks, if we count it the old way—a couple of weeks with you having only evenings free."

"Yes."

They walked on. In the empty windows in the wall of a house the red of evening hung like a forgotten curtain. "Where shall we go?" Elisabeth asked. "And where are we going to sleep?"

"We'll sleep in the cloisters of the church. Or in the cloister garden if it's warm enough. And now we are going to eat lentil soup."

The Restaurant Witte emerged from between the ruins. For a moment it seemed odd to Graeber that it was still there. It was as improbable as a fata morgana. They went through the garden gate. "What do you say to this?" he asked.

"It looks like a patch of peace the war has overlooked."

"Yes. And that's the way it's to stay for this evening."

The flower beds smelled strongly of earth. Someone had recently watered them. The hunting dog came around the house wagging his tail. He was licking his chops as though he had just eaten. Frau Witte came toward them. She had put on a white apron. "Would you like to sit in the garden?" she asked.

"Yes," Elisabeth said. "And I should like to wash if that's possible."

"Certainly."

Frau Witte led Elisabeth into the house and upstairs. Graeber went past the kitchen into the garden. A table, with a red and white checked cloth, and two chairs had been made ready. Glasses and plates stood on it and a faintly frosted water pitcher. He drank a glass thirstily. The water was cold and tasted better than wine. The garden was larger than one would have thought from outside. It consisted of a patch of lawn, which was already fresh and green, elder and lilac bushes and a few ancient trees in new leaf.

Elisabeth came back. "Just how did you find it?"

"By accident. How else could one find something like this?"

She walked across the grass and fingered the buds on the bushes. "Lilac buds already. They're still green and sharp. Soon they will bloom."

"Yes," Graeber said. "They will bloom. In a couple of weeks."

Elisabeth came to him. She smelled of soap and fresh water and youth. "It's beautiful here. And it's strange—I feel as if I had been here once before."

"I felt that way too when I saw it."

"It's as though all this had been here before. You and I and this garden—and as though there were only a tiny something missing, the last little bit, and I would be able to recall everything exactly as it was then." She laid her head on his shoulder. "It won't ever happen. One is always stopped just short of it. But perhaps we actually did live all this once before and will go on living it over forever."

Frau Witte came out with a soup tureen. "I would like to give you our ration coupons now," Graeber said. "We haven't many. Some of ours got burned. But these will probably be enough."

"I won't need them all," Frau Witte declared. "We had the

lentils from before. I need just a few for the sausage. I'll bring back the rest later. Would you like something to drink? We have a few bottles of beer."

"That's magnificent. Beer is exactly what we'd like."

The sunset was now only a pale glow. A thrush began to sing. Graeber remembered he had heard one at noon. It had been sitting on a station of the cross. Since then a lot had happened. He lifted the cover of the tureen. "Sausage. Good Bologna sausage. And lentils, cooked thick. A superb dish!"

He filled the plates and for a moment it seemed to him as though he possessed a house and a garden and a wife and a table and food and security and as though there were peace. "Elisabeth," he said, "if you were offered a pact that you could live this way for the next ten years—with the ruins and this garden and we two together—would you sign it?"

"Instantly. And for longer."

"So would I."

Frau Witte brought the beer. Graeber opened the bottles and filled their glasses. They drank. The beer was cool and good. They ate the soup. They ate it slowly and calmly, looking at each other.

It grew darker. A searchlight cut across the sky. It poked at the clouds and slid on. The thrush had stopped singing. Night began.

Frau Witte came to refill the tureen. "You haven't eaten enough," she said. "Young people should eat heartily."

"We have eaten all we could. The tureen is almost empty."

"I'll bring you some salad too. And a piece of cheese."

The moon came up. "Now we have everything," Elisabeth said. "The moon, the garden, and we have eaten and still have the whole evening before us. It's so beautiful you can hardly stand it."

"This is the way people used to live all the time. And they didn't consider it anything special."

She nodded and looked around. "You can't see a single ruin from here. This garden is arranged so that you just don't see them. The trees cover them. To think there are whole countries like this!"

"We will go to them after the war. We will see nothing but undestroyed cities and in the evening they will be lighted and no one will go in fear of bombs. We will stroll past shop windows full of lights and it will be so bright we'll actually be able to recognize one another's face on the street at night."

"Will they let us in?"

"For a trip? Why not? The Swiss, for instance."

"We'll have to have Swiss francs. How can we get them?"

"We'll take cameras with us and sell them there. We can live on that for a couple of weeks."

Elisabeth laughed. "Or jewelry or fur coats that we don't have."

Frau Witte came with the salad and cheese. "You like it here?"

"Yes, very much. Can we stay a little longer?"

"As long as you like. I'll bring you coffee, too. Malt coffee, of course."

"Coffee as well. Today we're living like princes," Graeber said.

Elisabeth laughed again. "It was in the beginning that we lived like princes. With pâté de foie gras and caviar and wine from the Rhine. Now we are living like human beings. The way we will live afterwards. Isn't it beautiful to live?"

"Yes, Elisabeth."

Graeber looked at her. She had seemed weary when she came from the factory. Now she was entirely restored. That never took long with her and it didn't require much.

"It will be beautiful to live," she said. "We're so unused to it. Unused to so much. That's why we have so much before us still. Things that are a matter of course to other people will be a great adventure to us. Even air that doesn't smell of burning. Or a dinner without ration coupons. Stores where you can buy what you like. Cities that haven't been bombed. Or to be able to talk without first looking all around. Not to need to be afraid any more! That will take a long time, but the fear will grow less and less and even if it comes back once in a while it will be a joy because we will know at once that we no longer need to feel it. Do you believe that?"

"Yes," Graeber said with an effort. "Yes, Elisabeth. If you look at it that way, there's still a lot of happiness ahead of us."

They stayed as long as they could. Graeber paid for the meal, and Frau Witte went to bed. Thus they were able to remain there alone for a while longer.

The moon rose higher. The night smell of the ground and the young foliage grew stronger and as there was no wind it drove out for the moment the smell of dust and rubbish that hung constantly over the city. There was a rustling in the bushes where a cat was hunting rats. There were many more rats in the town than formerly; they found plenty to eat under the ruins. At eleven o'clock they left. It was like leaving an island.

"You are too late," the sexton said when they arrived. "All the places are taken." It was not the one who had been there that morning. This one was younger, clean-shaven, stiff and dignified. Probably it was he who had denounced Josef, Graeber thought.

"Can we sleep in the cloister garden?"

"There are already people sleeping in all the covered places in the cloister garden. Why don't you go to the emergency relief station?"

At twelve o'clock at night this was an idiotic question. "We trust more in God," Graeber replied.

The sexton looked at him sharply for a moment. "If you want to stay here you must sleep in the open."

"That doesn't matter."

"Are you married?"

"Yes. Why?"

"This is a House of God. People who are not married can't sleep together here. In the cloister we have a section for men and another for women."

"Even when they're married?"

"Even then. The cloister belongs to the Church. There is no lust of the flesh here. You two don't look married."

Graeber pulled out his marriage certificate. The sexton put on his nickel eyeglasses and studied it in the glow of the eternal light. "A very short time," he said then.

"There's no ruling about that in the catechism."

"Did you have a church wedding too?"

"Listen," Graeber said. "We're tired. My wife has been working hard. We are going now to sleep in the cloister garden. If you have any objections try to drive us out. But bring others with you. It won't be easy."

Suddenly a priest was standing beside him. He had come up noiselessly. "What is this?"

The sexton explained the matter. The priest interrupted him after a few sentences. "Boehmer, don't play God Almighty. It's bad enough that these people have to sleep here." He turned to Graeber. "If you have no place to stay tomorrow come to Domhof Number Seven at nine o'clock in the evening. Pastor Biedendieck. My housekeeper will find a place for you somehow."

"Many thanks."

Biedendieck nodded and walked on. "On your way, you noncommissioned officer of God!" Graeber said to the sexton. "A major has just given you an order. You have to obey. The Church is the one dictatorship that has been successful through the centuries. Which way to the cloister garden?"

The sexton led them through the sacristy. The vestments for the Mass shimmered. Then came a door and a passage and the cloister garden. "But don't camp on the graves of the cathedral capitularies," Boehmer growled. "Stay over there on the side next to the cloister. Also you are not allowed to sleep together. Just next to each other. Each bed must be separate. And undressing is forbidden."

"Even shoes?"

"Not shoes."

They walked across. A polyphonic concert of snores rose from the cloisters. Graeber spread out the canvas and the blankets on the grass. He looked at Elizabeth. She laughed. "What are you laughing at?" he asked.

"I am laughing at the sexton. And at you."

"Good." Graeber placed the bags against the wall and made a kind of bolster of his knapsack. Suddenly a woman's scream rose above the rhythmic snoring. "No! No! Oh—h—" It died away in a gasp. "Quiet!" someone growled. The woman shrieked again. "Quiet! Thunderation!" the other voice shouted more loudly. The scream broke off as though smothered.

"That's why we are the Master Race!" Graeber said. "Even in our dreams we obey orders."

They lay down. They were almost alone beside the wall. Only at either corner dark mounds showed where others were sleeping. The moon stood behind the bomb-shattered tower. It threw a band of light on the ancient graves of the cathedral cannons. Some were broken. It had not been bombs that had done this damage; the coffins had moldered and fallen in. In the middle of the garden a great cross rose amid wild rose bushes. About it beside the walk stood the stone stations of the cross. Elisabeth and Graeber lay between the station of the scourging and that of the crowning with thorns. In front of each group was a kneeling bench. Beyond, in a broad rectangle, shimmered the columns and arches of the cloisters which opened toward the garden.

"Come over here to me," Graeber said. "To hell with the regulations of that ascetic sexton!"

# Chapter Twenty-three

SWALLOWS WERE FLYING around the bomb-torn tower. The first of the sun sparkled on the broken edges of the roof tiles. Graeber unpacked his alcohol stove. He did not know whether cooking was allowed, but he decided to follow the old soldier's rule: act before anyone can forbid you. He took his mess kit and went to look for a faucet. He found one behind the station of the crucifixion. A man with mouth open and red stubble on his face was sleeping there. He had only one leg. His unstrapped prosthesis lay beside him. In the early light its nickel supports glittered like a machine. Graeber glanced through the open colonnade into the cloisters. The sexton had been right; the sexes were separate. On the south side there were only women sleeping.

As he was coming back Elisabeth woke up. She looked fresh and rested, not like the sallow faces he had seen in the cloisters. "I know where you can wash," he said. "Go there before the crowd collects. Religious organizations always have inadequate sanitary arrangements. Come, I'll show you the washroom for cathedral canons."

She laughed. "You stay here and keep an eye on the coffee, otherwise it will disappear. I'll be able to find the washroom by myself. Which way do I go?"

He described the way. She walked through the garden. She had slept so peacefully that her dress was hardly wrinkled. He looked after her and loved her very much.

"So you are cooking in the garden of the Lord!" The pious sexton had stolen up on felt soles. "And what's worse, at the station of the sorrowful crown of thorns!"

"Where's the joyous one? I'd just as soon go there."

"This is all holy ground. Can't you see that the cathedral canons are buried over there?"

"I have sat and cooked in many a cemetery before now," Graeber said calmly. "But tell me where we are to go. Is there any sort of canteen or field kitchen here?"

"Canteen?" The sexton mouthed the word like a rotten fruit. "Here?"

"It wouldn't be a bad idea."

"Perhaps for heathen like you! Fortunately there are people who think differently. A restaurant on Christ's ground! What blasphemy!"

"It's not such a blasphemy. Christ fed a couple of thousand people with a few loaves and fishes, as you ought to know. But he was not a pompous raven like you! And now clear out! There's a war on, perhaps that idea's new to you."

"I will inform Herr Pastor Biedendieck of your sacrilege!"

"Do that! He'll throw you out, you tedious creep!"

The sexton went back, dignified and furious, in his felt shoes. Graeber opened a packet of coffee, part of the legacy from Binding, and smelled it. It was bean coffee. He began to prepare it. The aroma spread and produced an immediate effect. From behind the grave of a cathedral canon a man's tousled head rose sniffing. Then he sneezed, got up, and came closer. "How about a cup?"

"Push off," Graeber said. "This is the House of God; they don't give alms here; they just take them."

Elisabeth came back. She moved lithely and limberly as though strolling. "Where did you get the real coffee?" she asked in amazement.

"It's from Binding. We must drink it quickly, otherwise we'll be overrun by the whole cloister."

The sun glided over the statue of the sorrowful crown of thorns. Near the bench at the station of the scourging a patch of ground was purple with violets. Graeber got bread and butter out of his knapsack. He cut the bread with his pocket knife and spread the butter. "Real butter," Elisabeth said. "From Binding too?"

"Everything. Strange—he did me nothing but kindness and I never really liked him."

"Perhaps that's why he did it. Things like that happen."

Elisabeth sat down beside Graeber on the knapsack. "When I was seven years old I wanted to live just like this."

"I wanted to be a baker."

She laughed. "Instead of that you've become a provider. The best. How late is it?"

"I'll pack up and take you to the factory."

"No. Let's stay here in the sun as long as we can. Packing up and putting away our things will take too long and we'd have a long wait before we could get all our things stored downstairs. The cloister is full of people already. You can do it later when I've gone."

"All right. Do you think we're allowed to smoke here?"

"No. But that certainly won't bother you."

"No. Let's enjoy all we can before we're thrown out. It won't be long. Today I'll try to find a place where we won't have to sleep in our clothes. We don't want to go to Pastor Biedendieck in any case, do we?"

"No. I'd rather go back to Pohlmann's."

The sun rose higher. It fell upon the portico and threw the shadows of the columns against the walls. The people there moved back and forth through a lattice of light and shade as though in prison. Children were crying. The one-legged man in the corner of the garden strapped on his artificial leg and pulled his trousers on over it. Graeber packed up the bread, butter, and coffee. "It's ten minutes to eight," he said. "You must go. I'll come and get you at the factory, Elisabeth. If anything happens we have two meeting places: Frau Witte's garden first; if not there, then here."

"Yes." Elisabeth got up. "It's the last time I'll have to go away for the day."

"We'll stay up for a long time tonight. Hours and hours. That will make up for the wasted day."

She kissed him and left quickly. Graeber heard someone laugh. He turned angrily. A young woman stood between the columns, holding on to a little boy who was standing on top of the wall; the child was snatching at her hair and she was laughing with him. She had not seen Graeber and Elisabeth at all.

He packed up his things. Then he went to rinse out his mess kit. The amputee came after him, his leg stamping and creaking. "Hey there, comrade!"

Graeber stopped. "Wasn't it you who had the coffee?" the amputee asked.

"Yes. We drank it all."

"That's clear." The man had very wide blue eyes. "What I mean is the coffee grounds. If you're going to throw them away give them to me instead. They can be cooked up again."

"Yes, of course."

Graeber scraped out the coffee grounds. Then he got his things and took them to the place where they could be left. He expected a battle with the pious sexton. But instead of him the other, red-nosed one was there. He smelled of communion wine and said nothing.

The warden was sitting at the window of his apartment in the burned house. He waved when he saw Graeber. Graeber went in. "Have you any mail for us?"

"Yes. For your wife. The letter is addressed to Fräulein Kruse. That's quite in order, eh?"

"Yes."

Graeber took the letter. It struck him that the block warden was watching him strangely. He glanced at the letter and went numb. It was from the Gestapo. He turned the envelope over. It was sealed as though someone had already opened it. "When did it come?" he asked.

"Yesterday evening."

Graeber looked at the flap. He felt sure the block warden had read the letter and so he pushed up the flap and took it out. It was a summons for Elisabeth to appear at eleven-thirty that morning. He looked at his watch. It was just before ten. "Good," he said. "At last!" I've been waiting for this for a long time."

He put the letter into his pocket. "Anything else?"

"Isn't that enough?" the warden asked with an inquisitive glance.

Graeber laughed. "Don't you know of an apartment for us?"

"No. Do you still need one?"

"Not for me. But my wife does."

"So?" the block warden said without conviction.

"Yes. I would even pay a good premium to get one."

"So?" the block warden said again.

Graeber walked away. He felt the warden watching him through the window. He stopped and acted as though he were examining the skeleton of the roof with interest. Then he wandered on slowly.

Around the next corner he got out the letter at once. It was a printed form from which it was impossible to tell anything. Even the signature was printed. Only Elisabeth's name and the date had been typed in on a machine that made the "a's" too high.

He stared at the paper. It was an oblong piece of cheap, gray, pulp paper in octavo size—but it suddenly seemed to blot out the world. An intangible threat rose from it. It smelled of death.

He was standing in front of the Katharinenkirche and did not know how he had got there. "Ernst," someone behind him whispered.

He whirled around. It was Josef. He was wearing an overcoat of military cut and he walked on into the church without taking further notice of Graeber. Graeber looked around and a minute later followed him in. He found him in an empty pew near the sacristy. Josef gestured cautiously. Graeber went up to the altar, turned back and knelt down beside him.

"Pohlmann has been arrested," Josef whispered.

"What?"

"Pohlmann. The Gestapo came and got him this morning."

For a moment Graeber was not sure whether Pohlmann's arrest might not have had something to do with the letter to Elisabeth. He stared at Josef. "So, Pohlmann too!" he said finally.

Josef looked up quickly. "Who else?"

"My wife has received a summons from the Gestapo."

"For when?"

"For this morning at eleven-thirty."

"Have you the summons with you?"

"Yes. Here."

Graeber gave Josef the letter. "How did it happen with Pohlmann?" he asked.

"I don't know. I wasn't there. When I came back I could tell what had happened from a stone that was lying in a different place. Pohlmann had kicked it to one side as he was being taken away. That was one of our signals. An hour later I saw his books being loaded into a car."

"Was there anything there to incriminate him?"

"I don't think so. Everything that was dangerous had been buried somewhere else. Even the canned goods."

Graeber looked at the paper in Josef's hand. "I was just going to go and see him," he said. "I wanted to ask him what I ought to do."

"That's why I came here to warn you. It's pretty certain there's an agent of the Gestapo waiting in his room." Josef returned the summons to Graeber. "What are you going to do?"

"I don't know. I just got it. What would you do?"

"Flee," Josef replied without hesitation.

Graeber stared into the semi-darkness where the altars gleamed. "I'll go there by myself and ask what they want," he said.

"They won't give you any information if it's your wife they want."

Graeber felt a chill at the back of his neck. But Josef was just being matter of fact. "If they wanted to get hold of my wife they would have arrested her like Pohlmann. It must be something else. That's why I intend to go. Perhaps it's nothing important," he said without conviction. "In that case it would be a mistake to flee."

"Is your wife Jewish?"

"No."

"Then it's different. Jews should always flee. Can't your wife be on a trip somewhere?"

"No. She's in the labor service. That's a matter of record."

Josef reflected. "It's possible they don't intend to arrest her. You are right—they could have done that directly. Have you any idea why she was summoned?"

"Her father is in a concentration camp. And there was a woman she was staying with who might have denounced her. It's possible, too, that she came to their attention because we got married."

Josef reflected once more. "Destroy everything that might have any bearing on her father's arrest. Letters, diaries, all that sort of thing. And then go. By yourself. That was what you intended to do, wasn't it?"

"Yes. I'll explain that the letter only arrived this morning and I couldn't reach my wife in the factory."

"That's best. Try to find out what's going on. Not much can happen to you. You have to go back to the front anyway. They won't keep you from doing that. If you need a hiding place for your wife I can give you an address. But go first. I'll be here this afternoon." Josef hesitated for a moment. "In Pastor Biedendieck's confessional box. There where the sign saying *Absent* is hanging."

Graeber got up and went out. After the cool semi-darkness of the church the light outside burst upon him as though it were trying to shine through him and were already an instrument of the Gestapo. He walked slowly through the streets. It was as if he were walking under a bell-glass. Everything around him was suddenly strange and unreachable. A woman with a child in her arms became a picture of personal safety that inspired bitter envy. A man sitting on a bench reading a newspaper was an example of unattainable serenity; and two laughing people seemed like beings from an earlier world that had suddenly been destroyed. Over him alone hung the dark shadow of fear, separating him from others as though he were plague-stricken.

He entered the Gestapo building and showed the summons. An S.S. man directed him along a corridor into a side wing. The passages smelled of unaired offices and barracks. He had to wait in a room with three other people. One man was standing at a window that opened on the courtyard. His hands were behind his back and with his right hand he was tapping out piano notes on the back of his left hand. The two other men were slumped on chairs staring straight ahead. One was baldheaded and had a harelip which he kept covering with his hand; the other wore a Hitler mustache and had a pale, spongy face. All three glanced over quickly at Graeber as he came in and then immediately looked away again.

An S.S. man with eyeglasses entered. They all got up at once. Graeber was nearest the door. "What are you doing here?" the S.S. man asked in surprise. Soldiers were usually under the authority of the military court.

Graeber showed him the notice. The S.S. man read it. "This isn't for you at all. This is for a Fräulein Kruse."

"She's my wife. We were married a few days ago. She works in one of the State industries. I thought I could attend to this for her."

Graeber got out his marriage certificate which he had brought with him out of foresight. The S.S. man bored into his ear with one finger, reflectively. "Well, it's all right with me. Room Seventy-two, cellar floor."

He returned Graeber's papers. The cellar floor, Graeber thought. The cellar floor was the most infamous place of all in the stories about the Gestapo building.

He went down the stairs. Two people coming toward him stared at him enviously. They thought he was going out a free man while they still had it all to face.

Room Seventy-two was a large hall with filing cases and partitioned offices. A bored official took Graeber's notice. Graeber explained to him why he had come and showed his papers once more.

The official nodded. "Can you sign for your wife?"

"Yes."

The official pushed two sheets of paper across the table. "Sign here. Write under the signature: Husband of Elisabeth Kruse. And add the date and the registry office of your marriage. You may take the second form with you."

Graeber signed slowly. He did not want to show that he was reading the printed matter, but he did not want to sign blindly either. Meanwhile the official was looking about in one of the filing cabinets. "Damn it! Where are those ashes?" he shouted finally. "Holtmann, you've got everything in a mess again. Bring out the Kruse package."

Someone behind the partition grunted. Graeber saw that he had signed a receipt for the ashes of Bernhard Kruse, prisoner in protective custody. In addition he saw on the second form that Bernhard Kruse had died of heart disease.

The official had gone behind the partition. Now he came back with a cigar box that had been wrapped in a too-small piece of brown paper and was tied with a string. On the sides was the word "Claro," and part of the bright cover of the cigar box was visible; it was a coat of arms in red and gold held aloft by a pipe-smoking Indian.

"Here are the ashes," the official said, looking sleepily at Graeber. "Since you are a soldier I hardly need to tell you that the
most complete silence is mandatory. No death notice—either in
the papers or sent as an announcement through the mails. No
funeral service. Silence. Understand?"

"Yes."

Graeber took the cigar box and left.

He decided at once to say nothing to Elisabeth. He would leave
it to chance whether she found out later. It was not likely; the
Gestapo did not repeat its messages. For the present he felt it was
enough to have to leave her in a few days; to tell her in addition
that her father was dead would be an unnecessary cruelty.

He walked back slowly to the Katharinenkirche. The streets
seemed suddenly full of life again. The threat was past. It had
transformed itself into death; but it was the death of a stranger.
He had only known Elisabeth's father in his childhood.

He felt the cigar box under his arm. Very likely it did not
contain Kruse's ashes at all. Holtmann could easily have made a
mistake; and it was hardly to be assumed that people in a concentration camp took much pains with such matters. Besides, it
would not be possible with mass incinerations. Some stoker
would shovel out a few handfuls of ashes and pack them up, that
was all. Graeber could not understand why it was done at all. It
was a mixture of inhumanity and bureaucracy which made the
inhumanity all the more inhuman.

He considered what to do with the ashes. He could bury them
somewhere in the ruins. There were plenty of opportunities for
that. Or he could try to get them into a cemetery; but that would
require a permit and a grave, and Elisabeth would find out.

He walked through the church. In front of Pastor Bieden-dieck's confessional box he stopped. The absent sign was out. He pushed the green curtain aside. Josef was looking at him. He was awake and sitting in such a way that he could have kicked Grae-ber in the stomach and run away instantly. Graeber walked past to the pew near the sacristy. After a while Josef came. Graeber pointed to the cigar box. "It was that. Her father's ashes."

"Nothing more?"

"That's enough. Have you found out anything more about Pohlmann?"

"No."

They both looked at the package. "A cigar box," Josef said. "Usually they use old cardboard boxes or tin cans or paper bags. A cigar box is really almost like a coffin. Where are you going to put it? Here in the church?"

Graeber shook his head. It had suddenly occurred to him what to do. "In the cloister garden," he said. "That's really a kind of cemetery."

Josef nodded. "How about you? Can I do anything for you?" Graeber asked.

"You can go out through the side door over there and see whether anything suspicious is going on in the street. I have to leave; the anti-Semitic sexton is on duty after one o'clock. If you don't come back in five minutes I'll assume the street is clear."

"All right."


Graeber stood in the sun. After a while Josef came out of the door. He walked by close to Graeber. "Good luck!" he murmured.

"Good luck."

Graeber walked back. The cloister garden was empty at this time. Two yellow butterflies with red dots on their wings were playing around a bush covered with tiny white blossoms. The bush stood beside the grave of the cathedral capitulary Aloysius Bluemer. Graeber went up and examined it. Three of the graves were sunken, but Bluemer's in such a way that a hollow seemed to extend under the grassy surface. It was a good place.

He wrote a note saying these were the ashes of a Catholic prisoner from a concentration camp. He did this in case the cigar box should be discovered. He tucked the note under the brown paper. With his bayonet he cut away a piece of grass and cautiously enlarged the crevice under it until the box would fit in. It was easy to do. He pressed back into the hole the earth he had scraped out and arranged the grass over it. Bernhard Kruse, if that's who it was, had thus found a resting place in consecrated ground at the feet of a high dignitary of the Church.

Graeber went back and seated himself on the cloister wall. The stones were warm from the sun. Perhaps I have committed a sacrilege, he thought, or perhaps it was only a gratuitous act of sentimentality. Bernhard Kruse had been a Catholic. Cremation was forbidden to Catholics; but the Church would no doubt have to overlook this because of the unusual circumstances. And if it was not Kruse at all in the box but the ashes of various victims, among them, perhaps, Protestants and orthodox Jews, even then it would probably be all right, he thought. Neither Jehovah nor the God of the Protestants nor the God of the Catholics could very much object to that.

He looked at the grave into which the cigar box had been slipped like a cuckoo's egg into a nest. At the time he had not felt much; but now after it was all over he experienced a deep and boundless bitterness. It was more than just the thought of Kruse. Pohlmann was in it and Josef and all the misery he had seen and the war and even his own fate.

He got up. He had seen in Paris the grave of the Unknown

Soldier, ostentatious under the Arc de Triomphe on which the great battles of France were chiseled—and suddenly it seemed to him as if this sunken plot of grass, with the funeral slab of the cathedral capitulary Bluemer and the cigar box underneath, was something of the same kind, and perhaps even more so—because it was not surrounded by the rainbow of glory and of battles.

"Where are we going to sleep tonight?" Elisabeth asked. "In the church?"

"No. A miracle has happened. I was at Frau Witte's. She has a spare room. Her daughter moved to the country a few days ago. We can stay there and perhaps you can even keep the room after I've gone. I have already taken all our things over. Did your vacation come through?"

"Yes. I don't have to go back. And you don't have to wait for me any more."

"Thank God! We'll celebrate that tonight! We'll stay up all night and sleep until noon tomorrow."

"Yes. We'll sit in the garden till all the stars are out. But first I am going to hurry and buy a hat."

"A hat?" Graeber asked.

"Yes. This is the day to do it."

"What are you going to do with a hat? Do you intend to wear it in the garden tonight?"

Elisabeth laughed. "That, too, perhaps. But that's not the point. The points is to buy it. It's a symbolic action. A hat's like a flag. It can mean anything. You buy one when you are happy or when you are unhappy. You don't understand that, do you?"

"No. But let's buy one if that's the way it is. We'll celebrate your freedom with it. That's more important than dinner! Are there any stores still open? And don't you need clothing coupons?"

"I have them. And I know a store where they have hats."

"Good. We'll buy a hat to go with your golden dress."

"You don't need a hat with that. It's an evening dress. We'll simply buy any sort of hat. It's absolutely essential. Buying it will do away with the factory."

Part of the store window was intact. The rest was boarded up. They peered in. There were two hats there. One was trimmed with artificial flowers, the other with bright feathers. Graeber regarded them doubtfully; he could not picture Elisabeth in either one. Then he saw a white-haired woman locking the door. "Quick!" he said.

The owner led them into a room behind the store where the windows were blacked out. She immediately began a conversation with Elisabeth of which Graeber understood nothing. He seated himself on a fragile gold chair near the door. The owner switched on the light in front of a mirror and began to bring out hats and materials from cardboard boxes. The gray store suddenly became a magic cave. The blue and red and rose and white of the hats flamed out and, shimmering among them, the golden stuff of brocades made them seem like crowns being tried on for a mysterious ceremonial. Elisabeth moved back and forth in the flood of light in front of the mirror as though she had just stepped out of a picture, and the twilight that shrouded the rest of the room closed like a curtain behind her. Graeber sat there very still, observing the scene which seemed unreal to him after all that had happened that day. He saw Elisabeth for the first time fully detached from time, by herself, absorbed in an unconstrained and profound play, bathed in light and tenderness and love, serious and self-possessed as a huntress testing her weapons for battle. He heard the quiet conversation of the two without listening to it and it was like the murmur of a spring, he saw the bright circle that surrounded Elisabeth as though emanating from her, and he loved her and desired her and forgot all else in this silent happiness, behind which stood the unseizable shadow of loss, making it only deeper, more glowing and as costly and fugitive as the glints on the silks and brocades.

"A cap," Elisabeth said. "A simple gold cap that fits close to the head."

# Chapter Twenty-four

STARS FILLED the window. A wild grape vine had grown around the little rectangle and a pair of its tendrils hung down and swung in the breeze like the dark pendulum of a noiseless clock.

"I'm not really crying," Elisabeth said. "And if I do cry, don't worry about it. It's not me, it's just something in me that wants to get out. Sometimes crying is all you have. It isn't sorrow. I am happy—"

She was lying in his arms with her head pressed against his shoulder. The bed was wide and made of old, dark walnut. Both ends were high and curved. A walnut dresser stood in the corner and in front of the window were a table and two chairs. On the wall hung an old glass case, containing a bride's crown of artificial myrtle, and a mirror in which the vine and the pale, wavering light from outside moved, dark and bright.

"I am happy," Elisabeth said. "So much has happened in these weeks that I can't press it all into myself. I have tried. It won't go. Tonight you must be patient with me."

"I wish I could take you out of this city into a village somewhere."

"It doesn't matter where I am, when you're away."

"It does matter. Villages aren't bombed."

"Sooner or later they are certain to stop bombing us here. There's hardly anything of the city left standing. I can't go away as long as I have to work in the factory. I'm happy that I have this enchanted room. And Frau Witte."

She was breathing more quietly. "I'll be through with me right away," she said. "You mustn't think me too hysterical. I am happy. But it's a fluctuating happiness. Not a uniform cow-happiness."

"Cow-happiness," Graeber said. "Who wants that?"

"I don't know. I think I could stand quite a lot of it for quite a long time."

"So could I. I just don't like to admit it because for the present we can't have it."

"Ten years of safe, good, uniform, middle-class cow-happiness —I believe even a whole lifetime of it wouldn't be too much."

Graeber laughed. "That comes from living such a damned interesting existence. Our forebears had other ideas; they longed for adventure and hated the cow-happiness they had."

"Not we. We have become simple human beings again with simple desires." Elisabeth looked at him. "Do you want to sleep now? A whole night of unbroken sleep? Who knows when you'll have the chance again after tomorrow night?"

"I can get enough sleep while I'm on my way. It may take a couple of days to get there."

"Will you ever have a bed?"

"No. The best I can hope for after tomorrow is a field cot or a sack of hay from time to time. You get used to it fast enough. It's not bad. Summer is coming soon. Russia is only horrible in winter."

"Perhaps you'll have to stay there for another winter too."

"If we go on retreating this way we'll be in Poland by winter or even in Germany. Then it won't be so cold. And it's a cold you're used to."

Now she will ask when I'm coming back on furlough, he thought. I wish we had all that behind us. She has to ask and I have to answer and I wish it was over. Already I am no longer wholly here, but what there is of me here feels as though it had no skin, and nevertheless it can't really be injured. It's just more sensitive than an open wound. He glanced at the vine swinging in front of the window and at the shifting silver and gray in the mirror and it seemed to him as though a mystery stood close behind it and must in the next moment reveal itself.

Then they heard the sirens.


"Let's stay here," Elisabeth said. "I don't want to get dressed and rush off to a cellar."

"All right."

Graeber went to the window. He pushed the table aside and looked out. The night was bright and motionless. The garden shone in the moonlight. It was an unreal night and a good night for air raids. He saw Frau Witte come out of the door. Her face was very pale. He opened the window. "I was just coming to wake you," she shouted through the noise.

Graeber nodded. "Cellar—Leibnitzstrasse—" he heard.

He waved. Then he saw her go back into the house. He waited a moment longer. She did not come out again. She, too, was staying at home. He was not surprised. It was almost as if it had to be that way. She did not need to leave her house; garden and house seemed protected through some unknown magic. It was as though they remained noiseless and untouched in the fury that roared over them. The trees stood still behind the pale silver of the lawn. The bushes did not move. Even the vine outside the window had stopped swinging. The little island of peace lay under the moon as though in a glass shelter from which the storm of destruction rebounded.

Graeber turned around. Elisabeth had sat up in bed. Her shoulders shimmered palely and where they rounded there were soft shadows. Her breasts were firm and bold and looked larger than they were. Her mouth was dark and her eyes very transparent and almost colorless. She had braced her arms behind her on the pillows and she sat in bed like someone who had suddenly come in from far away and for an instant she was as alien and quiet and mysterious as the garden outside in the moon confronting the end of the world.

"Frau Witte is staying too," Graeber said.

"Come."

As he walked toward the bed he saw his face in the gray and silver mirror. He did not recognize it. It was the face of someone else. "Come," Elisabeth said once more.

He leaned over her. She put her arms around him. "It doesn't matter what happens," she said.

"Nothing can happen," he replied. "Not tonight." He did not know why he believed that. It had something to do with the garden and the light and the mirror and with Elisabeth's shoulders and a vast, expansive quietude that suddenly filled him to the uttermost. "Nothing can happen," he repeated.

With one hand she took hold of the covers and threw them to the floor. She lay there naked and strong; from her hips sprang long, powerful legs; it was a body that narrowed from shoulders and breasts to a flat depression at the belly; the upper thighs were not thin but seemed to swell and plunge into the dark triangle. It was the body of a young woman and no longer that of a girl.

He felt her in his arms. She slid against him and it seemed to him as though a thousand hands intertwined and held him and bore him up. Nowhere was there any longer any space between, everything was close and tight, it was no longer the tumult of the first days, it was a slow, steady rising that rushed over everything and swept away words, boundaries, the horizon and then the self—

He lifted his head. He was coming back from a great distance. He listened. He did not know how long he had been away. Outside all was silent. He thought he must be mistaken and lay listening. He heard nothing—no explosions and no more antiaircraft firing. He shut his eyes and sank back. Then he awoke again. "They didn't come, Elisabeth," he said.

"They did," she murmured.

They lay side by side. Graeber saw the covers on the floor and the mirror and the open window. He had thought the night would never end but he felt time creeping slowly back again into the stillness. The vines outside the window swung once more in the breeze, their shadowy images moved in the mirror, and distant sounds began again. He looked over at Elisabeth. She had her eyes closed. Her mouth was open and she was breathing deeply and calmly. She was not yet back. He was back. He had already begun to think again. She was always away longer. I wish I could lose myself too, he thought, completely and for a long time. It was something for which he envied her, for which he loved her and which frightened him a little. She was some place where he could not follow her or not for long enough; it was that perhaps which frightened him. He felt himself suddenly alone and in a strange fashion inferior,

Elisabeth opened her eyes. "What became of the airplanes?"

"I don't know."

She pushed back her hair. "I'm hungry."

"So am I. We have lots of things to eat."

Graeber got up and fetched the canned goods he had brought with him from Binding's cellar. "Here's chicken and veal and there's even a potted hare with compote to go with it."

"Let's have the hare and the compote."

Graeber opened the jars. He loved Elisabeth for not helping him but lying there and waiting instead. He could not stand women who, still surrounded by mystery and darkness, hurriedly transformed themselves again into busy housewives.

"Every time I look at these things I feel ashamed," he said. "I acted pretty badly toward Alfons."

"He may have acted badly toward someone else too. That evens out. Were you at his funeral?"

"No. There were too many Party members in uniform there. I didn't go along. I just listened to Group Leader Hildebrandt's oration. He said we should all imitate Alfons and fulfill his last wish. He meant remorseless strife against the foe. But Binding's last wish was something different. Alfons was in pajamas in the cellar with a blonde in a negligee."

Graeber emptied the meat and the compote into two dishes which Frau Witte had given them. Then he cut the bread and opened a bottle of wine. Elisabeth got up. She stood naked in front of the walnut bed. "You really don't look like someone who has been sitting bent over for months sewing army overcoats," Graeber said. "You look like someone who does gymnastics every day."

She laughed. "Gymnastics! You only do gymnastics when you are in despair."

"Really? That would never have occurred to me."

"Only then," Elisabeth said. "Exercise until you can't move

any more, run around until you are dead tired, clean up the room ten times, brush your hair till your head hurts and so on."

"Does that help?"

"Only with the penultimate despair. When you don't want to think any more. In the final despair nothing helps except to let yourself drop."

"And then?"

"Wait until the tide of life somehow flows back again. I mean the life that keeps you breathing. Not the one you live."

Graeber raised his glass. "I believe we know too much about despair for our age. Let's forget it."

"We know too much about forgetting, too," Elisabeth said. "We'll forget that as well."

"All right. Long live Frau Kleinert who put up this hare!"

"And long live Frau Witte who gave us the garden out there and this room!"

They emptied their glasses. The wine was cold and aromatic and young. Graeber refilled the glasses. The moon stood golden in them. "My beloved," Elisabeth said, "it's good to be up at night. It's so much easier to talk then."

"That's true. At night you are a healthy, young child of God and not a seamstress of military overcoats. And I am not a soldier."

"At night one is what he was intended to be; not what he has become."

"Perhaps." Graeber looked at the hare, the compote, and the bread. "That makes us pretty superficial people. We don't do much at night except sleep and eat."

"And make love. That's not superficial."

"And drink."

"And drink," Elisabeth said, holding out her glass.

Graeber laughed. "Theoretically, we should really be sentimental and sad and should be carrying on deep conversations. Instead of that we've eaten half a hare and we find life wonderful and give thanks to God."

"That's better. Don't you think?"

"It's the only thing. If you make no demands, everything is a gift."

"Did you learn that in the field?"

"No, here."

"That's good. It's really all you have to learn, isn't it?"

"Yes. After that all you need is a bit of luck."

"Have we had that, too?"

"Yes. We have had everything there is."

"You're not sad because it's over?"

"It's not over. It's just changing."

She looked at him. "No," he said. "I am sad. I am so sad I think I shall die tomorrow when I leave you. But when I try to think how it would have to be for me not to be sad, then there's just one answer—never to have met you. In that case I wouldn't be sad but would be going away empty and indifferent. And when I think that, then the sadness is not sadness any more. It's black happiness. The reverse side of happiness."

Elisabeth stood up. "Perhaps I haven't put that right," Graeber said. "Do you understand what I mean?"

"I do understand. And you have put it very well. One couldn't put it better. I knew you would say it." She got up and came over to him. He felt her. Suddenly she no longer had a name and had all the names in the world. For an instant something like an unbearable white light flamed through him, he realized that all was one, departure and return, possession and loss, life and death, past and future, and that always and everywhere the unchangeable countenance of eternity was there and nothing could be obliterated—

———

It was the last afternoon. They were sitting in the garden. The cat stole by. She was pregnant and completely occupied with herself, paying no attention to anyone. "I hope I'm going to have a child," Elisabeth said suddenly.

Graeber stared at her. "A child? Why?"

"Why not?"

"A child! In these times! Do you think you're going to have one?"

"I hope so."

He looked at her. "I believe I'm supposed to say or do something now and kiss you and be surprised and tender, Elisabeth. I can't do it. I hadn't thought about a child until now."

"You have no need to either. It doesn't really concern you at all. Besides, I'm not sure yet."

"A child! It would grow up just in time for a new war as we did for this one. Think of all the misery it would be born to!"

The cat came by again. She was creeping along the path to the kitchen. "Children are born every day," Elisabeth said.

Graeber thought of the Hitler Youth and of the children who had denounced their parents. "Why do we talk about it?" he said. "It's only a wish after all. Or isn't it?"

"Don't you ever want to have a child?"

"I don't know. In peacetime perhaps. I haven't thought about it before. There's so much that has been poisoned all around us that the ground will still be contaminated for years. How can one want a child in such circumstances?"

"For that very reason," Elisabeth said.

"Why?"

"To educate it against that. What's to happen if the people who are against everything that is happening now don't want to have children? Are only the barbarians to have them? Then who's to put the world to rights again?"

"Is that why you want to have one?"

"No. I only thought about that just now."

Graeber was silent. There was nothing to be said against her argument. She was right. "You're too quick for me," he said. "I have not got used to being married and now all of a sudden I'm to decide whether or not I want a child."

Elisabeth laughed and stood up. "You haven't noticed the simplest part of it—that it isn't just a child I want but your child. And now I'm going to discuss dinner with Frau Witte. It's to be a canned masterpiece."

Graeber was sitting alone in his chair in the garden. The sky was full of clouds tinged with red. The day was over. It had been a stolen day. He had overstayed his furlough by twenty-four hours. Although he had reported for departure, he had stayed. Now it was evening and in an hour he had to be off.

He had gone to the post office once more; but no further word had come from his parents. He had arranged everything that could be arranged. Frau Witte had already agreed to let Elisabeth go on living in her house. He had examined its cellar; it was not deep enough to be safe but it was well built. He had gone to look at the public cellar in the Leibnitzstrasse as well; it was as good as most of the others in the city. Calmly he leaned back in his chair. He could hear the clattering of pots in the kitchen. It had been a long furlough. Three years, not three weeks. Sometimes they still seemed to him not altogether secure and they had been built hastily on uncertain ground; nevertheless he wanted to believe they were secure enough.

He heard Elisabeth's voice. He thought over what she had said about a child. It was as though suddenly a wall had been broken through. An opening had appeared and behind it, wavering and indistinct, a garden, a bit of the future. Graeber had never thought beyond that wall. When he had arrived he had hoped to find something and seize it and possess it in order to be able to leave it behind when he went away again, something that bore his name and with it bore himself—but the thought of a child had never occurred to him. He looked into the twilight that hung between the lilac bushes. How unending it would be if one continued to pursue it and how strange it was to feel that the life which had always hitherto ceased for him at the wall might go on, and that what he had up to then regarded almost as booty, hastily seized, might sometime become an assured possession to be handed on to an alien, unborn existence in a future that had no end and was full of a tenderness he had never known. What expanses there were and what presentiments and how greatly something in him wanted it and did not want it and yet wanted it, this poor and comforting illusion of immortality!

"The train leaves at six o'clock," he said. "I have taken care of all my things. Now I must leave. Don't come with me to the station. I want to leave from here, taking you with me in my mind the way you exist here. Not in the crowds and the embarrassment of the station. My mother went with me last time. I couldn't do anything to stop her. It was dreadful for her and for me. It took me quite a while to get over it, and later it was always what I remembered— the weeping, tired, perspiring woman on the station platform— not my mother as she really was. Do you understand that?"

"Yes."

"All right. Then let's do it this way. It will be one burden the less. Besides, you oughtn't to see me when I have been reduced again to a mere number, just another uniform loaded down like a donkey. I want to part from you the way we are here. And now take this money: I have it left over. Out there I won't need it."

"I don't need any money, Ernst. I earn enough for myself."

"I can't spend it out there. Take it and buy yourself a dress. A senseless, impractical, beautiful dress to go with your little gold cap."

"I'll use it to send packages to you."

"Don't send me any. We have more to eat out there than you have here. But buy yourself a dress. I learned something when you bought that hat. Promise me that you will buy a dress. Or isn't there enough for that?"

"There's enough. It will even do for a pair of shoes as well."

"That's perfect. Buy yourself a pair of golden shoes."

"All right," Elisabeth said. "Golden shoes with high heels and light as a feather. I'll run to meet you in them when you come back."

Graeber took out of his knapsack the dark painted icon he had brought with him to give to his mother. "Here's something I found in Russia. Keep it."

She did not take it. Her face was suddenly distracted. "No, Ernst. Give it to someone else. Or take it back with you. It's too much goodby. Too final. Take it back."

He looked at the picture. "I found it in a ruined house," he said. "Perhaps there's no luck in it. I hadn't thought of that." He put it back again. It was a Saint Nicholas on a golden ground with many angels.

"If you like I'll take it to the church," Elisabeth said. "The one where we slept. The Katharinenkirche."

The one where we slept, he thought. Yesterday that was still close; now it's already infinitely far away. "They won't take it," he said. "It's a different kind of religion. The trustees of the God of love are not especially tolerant of one another."

He reflected that he might have put the picture with Kruse's ashes in the grave of Bluemer, the cathedral capitulary. But very likely that, too, would have been just one more sacrilege.

He did not look back. He walked neither too slow nor too fast. The knapsack was heavy and the street was very long. When he turned the corner he turned many corners. For a moment the perfume of Elisabeth's hair was still about him; then it was drowned out by the smell of old fires, by the sultriness of the late afternoon and by the rotten-sweet smell of decay that rose out of the ruins in the warm air.

He crossed the embankment. One side of the Lindenallee was burned black; the other was in green leaf. The river was choked and crept sluggishly over concrete, straw, sacking, the broken remnants of docks and beds. Suppose an air raid should come now, he thought. I would have to take cover and would have an excuse for missing the train. What would Elisabeth say if I suddenly stood before her? He thought about it. He did not know. But everything that had been good this time would probably turn into pain. It was the same as at a station when a train was late in leaving and you still had half an hour's time to labor through in embarrassed conversation. Besides it would do him no good; during a raid the train would not leave and he would get there in time just the same.

He came to Bramschestrasse. It was from here that he had first made his way into the city. The bus that had brought him was standing there waiting. He climbed in. After ten minutes they started. The station, meanwhile, had been moved again. Now it was a roof of corrugated tin camouflaged against airplanes. At one side sheets of gray cloth had been stretched. Next to them, as concealment, artificial trees had been set up and there was a stall out of which a wooden cow peered. Two aged horses were grazing in a field.

The train was ready and waiting. A number of cars bore the sign: *For Military Personnel Only.* A guard was inspecting papers. Nothing was said about the fact that Graeber was a day late. He got in and found a seat beside the window. After a while three more men entered: a non-com, a lance corporal with a scar, and an artillery man who immediately began to eat. A field kitchen was rolled along the platform. Two young student nurses appeared, accompanied by an older nurse with an iron swastika worn as a brooch.

"There's coffee," the non-com said. "Just look!"

"Not for us," the lance corporal replied. "That's for a transport of recruits who are going out for the first time. I heard about it earlier. There's to be a speech too. They don't do that sort of thing for us any more."

A crowd of evacuees was led up. They were counted off and stood in two lines, with their cardboard boxes and valises, staring at the coffee urn. A couple of S.S. officers appeared. They were wearing elegant boots and riding breeches and they wandered like storks along the station platform. Three more men returning from leave entered the compartment. One of them opened the window and leaned out. Outside stood a woman with a child. Graeber looked at the child and then looked at the woman. She had a wrinkled neck, thick eyelids, thin, pendulous breasts, and wore a faded summer dress with windmills printed on it. Everything seemed to him clearer than usual—the light and everything he saw. "Well then, Heinrich," the woman said.

"Yes, take care of yourself, Marie. Regards to all."

"Yes." They looked at each other in silence. A few men with musical instruments stationed themselves in the middle of the platform. "How noble!" the lance corporal said. "The young cannon fodder goes off to a musical accompaniment. I thought they'd cut that out long ago."

"They might at least give us some of the coffee," the non-com replied. "After all we're old fighting men and we're going out, too!"

"Wait until evening. Then you'll get it as soup."

There was the sound of marching feet and commands. The recruits came by. Almost all of them were very young. There was only a scattering of husky, older men; they came no doubt from the S.A. or the S.S. "Not many of those fellows need to shave," the lance corporal said. "Just look at the young sprouts! Children! That's what we've got to depend on out there."

The recruits formed up. Non-coms bawled at them. Then there was silence. Someone began a speech.

"Shut the window," the lance corporal said to the man whose wife was outside.

The man made no reply. The orator's voice rattled on as though it came from tin vocal cords. Graeber leaned back and shut his eyes. Heinrich continued to stand at the window. He had not heard what the lance corporal said. Embarrassed, speechless and sad he stared at Marie. Marie stared back in just the same way. It's good that Elisabeth is not here, Graeber thought.

The voice finally ceased. The four musicians played *Deutschland, Deutschland ueber alles* and the *Horst Wessel* song. They played both songs fast and just one stanza of each. No one in the compartment moved. The lance corporal was picking his nose and staring disinterestedly at the result.

The recruits got into their car. The coffee urn followed them. After a while it came back empty. "Those whores," the non-com said. "They let us old military men die of thirst."

The artillery man in the corner stopped eating for a moment. "What?" he asked.

"Whores, I said. What are you eating anyway? Veal?"

The artillery man bit into his sandwich. "Pork," he said shortly.

"Pork—" The non-com looked over the men in the car one after the other. He was searching for sympathy. The artillery man was not interested. Heinrich was still standing at the window. "Regards to Aunt Bertha, too," he said to Marie.

"Yes."

They were silent again. "Why don't we leave?" someone asked. "It's after six already."

"Perhaps we're waiting for a general."

"Generals fly."

They had to wait for a half-hour more. "Now go along, Marie," Heinrich said from time to time.

"I can wait."

"The little one must have his supper."

"He has the whole evening to eat it."

They were silent again for a time. "Regards to Josef, too," Heinrich said finally.

"Yes, all right. I'll tell him."

The artillery man let out an enormous fart, sighed deeply, and went to sleep at once. It was as though the train had only been waiting for that. Slowly it began to move. "Well then, regards to all, Marie."

"To you, too, Heinrich."

The train moved faster. Marie was running beside the car. "Take good care of the little one, Marie."

"Yes, Heinrich. And you take care of yourself."

"Of course, of course."

Graeber saw the woebegone face of the woman running beneath the window. She ran as though it was a matter of life and death to be able to stare at Heinrich for ten seconds longer. And then suddenly he saw Elisabeth. She was standing behind the station shed. She could not have been seen from the train before. He was in doubt for only a second; then he saw her face clearly. It was so completely at a loss that it seemed lifeless. He leaped up and seized Heinrich by the coat collar. "Let me at the window!" he shouted.

Suddenly everything was forgotten. He no longer understood why he had come to the station alone. He no longer understood anything. He had to see her. He had to shout. He had failed to say the most important thing.

He jerked at the back of Heinrich's neck. Heinrich was hanging far out. He had braced his elbows on the outside of the window frame. "Regards to Lisa, too," he shouted above the rattling.

"Let me by! Get away from the window! My wife's out there!"

Graeber threw one arm around Heinrich's shoulders and pulled. Heinrich kicked out backward. He caught Graeber in the shin. "And take good care of everything!" he shouted.

The woman could no longer be heard. Graeber kicked Heinrich in the knee and pulled at his shoulders. Heinrich did not let go. He waved with one hand; with the other hand and elbow he maintained himself in the window. The train swung around a curve. Over Heinrich's head Graeber saw Elisabeth. She was already far away and very small standing alone in front of the shed. Graeber waved over the strawlike bristles of Heinrich's head. Perhaps she could still see the hand; but she could not see who was waving. A cluster of houses came by and the station was no longer there.

Heinrich slowly detached himself from the window. "You damn—" Graeber began furiously and stopped. Heinrich turned around. Big tears were running down his face. Graeber let his hands fall. "Oh, shit!"

"Man, what language!" the lance corporal said.

# Chapter Twenty-five

TWO DAYS LATER he found his regiment and reported at the company office. There was no sign of the sergeant major. Only a clerk was sitting there, idle, at the desk. The village lay a hundred and twenty kilometers west of the last position Graeber had seen. "How are things here?" he asked.

"Shitty. How was your furlough?"

"Half and half. Has much happened?"

"Plenty. You can see for yourself where we are."

"What's become of the men?"

"One platoon is digging trenches. Another is burying the dead. They'll be back at noon."

"Have there been many changes?"

"You'll see. I don't know who was still here when you left. We've had a lot of replacements. Children. They die like flies in winter. Not the slightest idea what war's about. We have a new sarge. The old one is dead. Fat Meinert."

"Do you mean he went up front?"

"No. He got his in the latrine. Flew into the air along with all the muck." The clerk yawned. "You'll see what's up. Why didn't you arrange to get a nice little bomb splinter in your ass while you were home?"

"Yes," Graeber said. "Why not? You just don't get any good ideas until it's too late."

"I'd have arranged to be a couple more days late, too. No one here would have missed you."

"That's something else that doesn't occur to you until you're back."

Graeber walked through the village. It was like the one he had been in last. All these villages were alike. They were all devastated in the same way. The only difference was that now there was hardly any snow. Everything was wet and muddy; your boots sank in deep and the earth held them fast as though it wanted to drag them off. Along the main street boards had been laid end to end so that you could walk on them. They squelched in the water, and when you stepped on one end the other rose up dripping.

The sun was shining and it was fairly warm. It seemed to Graeber much warmer than in Germany. He listened to the front. Heavy artillery fire rolled and swelled and ebbed away. He located the cellar to which the clerk had assigned him and stowed his things in a vacant spot. He was tremendously irritated that he had not stayed on furlough a day or two longer. Actually no one here seemed to need him. He set out again. Trenches had been dug in front of the village; now they were full of water and the walls were beginning to cave in. In a few places small concrete bunkers had been built. They stood like gravestones in the sodden landscape.

Graeber walked back. On the main street he saw Rahe, the company commander. He was balancing on the boards like a stork with horn-rimmed glasses. Graeber reported to him. "You were in luck," Rahe said. "Just after you left all leaves were canceled." He looked at Graeber with his bright eyes. "Was it worth while?"

"Yes," Graeber replied.

"That's good. We're in a pretty dirty spot here. This is only a temporary position. We'll probably fall back on the reserve position that has just been reinforced. Did you see it? You must have come right through there."

"No. I did not see it."

"No?"

"No, sir," Graeber said.

"It's about forty kilometers from here."

"It must have been night when we came through. I slept a good deal."

"That's it, no doubt." Rahe looked searchingly at Graeber again as though he wanted to ask something more. Then he said, "Your platoon leader was killed. Lieutenant Mueller. Now you have Lieutenant Mass."

"Yes, sir."

Rahe poked with his walking stick in the wet clay. "As long as the mud hangs on this way it's hard for the Russians to move up artillery and tanks. That gives us time to regroup. Everything has its good and bad side, eh? Glad you're back, Graeber. We need old hands to train the young recruits." He went on poking in the mud. "How was it back there?"

"Just about the way it is here. Lots of air raids."

"Really? As bad as that?"

"I don't know how bad it was in comparison with the other cities. But every couple of days there was at least one raid."

Rahe looked at him as though he expected him to say more. But Graeber kept quiet.

———

The others came back at noon. "The furlough boy!" Immermann said. "Man alive, what made you come back into this crap? Why didn't you desert?"

"Where to?" Graeber asked.

Immermann scratched his head. "Switzerland," he said then.

"I didn't think of that, wise guy. Despite the fact that special luxury trains for deserters leave daily for Switzerland. They have red crosses painted on the roofs so they won't be bombed. And all along the Swiss border stand triumphal arches with the inscription: Welcome! Know anything else, you joker? And since when have you dared to talk this way?"

"I've always dared. You've just forgotten that back in the whispering homeland. Besides, we're in retreat. We are almost in flight. With every hundred kilometers we retire the tone gets a bit freer."

Immermann began to clean the dirt off his uniform. "Mueller is dead," he said. "Meinecke and Schroeder are in the hospital. Muecke got shot in the stomach. They say he kicked off in Warsaw. Which of the old crowd were still here? That's right, Berning—lost his right leg. Bled to death."

"Hirschland," Graeber said.

"Hirschland? What's the matter with him?"

"He's dead, too."

"Nonsense. He's sitting right over there."

Graeber looked over. It was true. Hirschland was sitting on an old barrel cleaning his mess kit. Damn it, he thought, what does this mean? "His mother got a report that he'd been killed. I've got to ask him."

He walked over to Hirschland. "I went to see your mother," he said.

"Did you really? You didn't forget? I never thought you'd do it."

"Why not?"

"I'm not used to having people do things for me."

Graeber recalled that he had almost forgotten. "How is she? How is she getting along?" Hirschland asked. "Did you tell her that I was fine?"

"Hirschland, your mother thinks you are dead. She got a report from the company."

"What? That's impossible."

"She told me so herself."

Hirschland stared at Graeber. "But I write to her almost every day."

"She thinks they're letters you wrote before. Have you any idea of how it could have happened? After all, there aren't two Hirschlands."

"No. Someone must have done it on purpose."

"No one would do something like that on purpose."

"No? Not even Steinbrenner?"

"Is he still alive?"

"Of course. And he was assigned to the office for two days after the sergeant major was killed. The clerk was sick at the time."

"But that would be a stinking forgery."

"Yes."

"Rahe is supposed to sign those letters."

"My mother doesn't know that. One signature is as good as another to her."

The thing suddenly appeared more probable to Graeber than it had at first. "What a swinish trick!" he growled. "It's hard to believe. Just why would the bastard want to do it?"

"For fun. To educate me. After all, I have Jewish blood. What did my mother say?"

"She was calm. You must write her right away. Tell her what I have said. She will remember that I was there."

"It will be a long time before she gets it."

Graeber saw that Hirschland's lips were trembling. "We'll go to the office," he announced. "We'll have the correction made from there. They'll have to send a telegram. Otherwise we'll go to Rahe."

"We can't do that."

"Why not? We can do even more. We can report Steinbrenner."

"Not I. I can't do that. I can't prove a thing. And even if—No, I can't make a complaint. Not I. Don't you understand that?"

"Yes, Hirschland," Graeber said grimly. "But all that won't last forever."

He met Steinbrenner after supper. Steinbrenner was brown and cheerful. He looked like a sunburned Gothic angel.

"How's morale at home?" he asked.

Graeber put down his mess kit. "When we got to the border," he said, "we were called together by an S.S. captain and told that no one of us was to say a word about the situation at home under penalty of the severest punishment."

Steinbrenner laughed. "I'm in the S.S. myself. You can tell me safely."

"Then I'd be a pretty ass. 'The severest punishment' means being shot as a saboteur of the Army's plans."

Steinbrenner stopped laughing. "You say that as though there were something to tell. As though there had been catastrophes!"

"I say nothing at all. I am simply repeating what the S.S. captain told us."

Steinbrenner regarded Graeber calculatingly. "You got married, eh?"

"How did you know?"

"I know everything."

"You found it out in the office. Don't give yourself airs. You're in the office a good deal, aren't you?"

"I'm there as much as I need to be. When I get my leave I'm going to get married too."

"Really? Do you know to whom?"

"The daughter of the S.S. commandant in my home town."

"Naturally."

Steinbrenner missed the irony. "The combination of blood lines is first rate," he declared, completely absorbed in his subject. "Nordic-Friesian on my side, Rhenish-Saxon on hers. We'll get every parenthood assistance and racial stipend. The children will naturally have special educational advantages—everything that the Party has to give. In five years my wife will be eligible for an important post in the Reich's Women's Auxiliary as a model mother. If, in the meantime, we have twins or triplets the Fuehrer himself will be their godfather, perhaps in just two or three years. For the fifth child he will be in any case. Then my career will be splendidly assured. Picture that!"

"I am picturing it."

"Selective breeding of the race! We've not only got to root out the Jews, we've also got to replace them with pureblooded Germans. A new race of leaders."

"Have you rooted out many Jews?"

Steinbrenner grinned. "If you could see my conduct records you wouldn't have to ask. Those were the times!" He bent over confidentially toward Graeber. "I've put in for a transfer. Back to an S.S. division. There's more going on there. And you've got better chances. Everything's on a bigger scale. No boring court-martials for every lousy Russian. They get rid of them in batches. Not long ago three hundred Polish and Russian traitors in one afternoon. Six men got the Distinguished Service Cross for that. Here all that turns up is a few measly guerrillas—you don't get any decorations for that. We haven't had more than half a dozen since you left. In the clean-up battalions and in the S.S. Security Service they get hundreds and hundreds. A man can get ahead there!"

Graeber stared out into the red Russian evening. A few crows were flapping about like dark rags. Steinbrenner was the perfect product of the Party. He was perfectly healthy, in perfect physical training, perfectly devoid of any thoughts of his own, and perfectly inhuman. He was an automaton, for whom polishing a gun, exercising, and killing were all the same. "You sent the announcement of Hirschland's death to his mother, didn't you?" Graeber asked.

"Who says so?"

"I know it."

"You know nothing at all. How could you know?"

"I found out. That was a fine joke."

Steinbrenner laughed. He had no ear for irony. His pretty face beamed with satisfaction. "You think so too? Just imagine the expression on that old woman's face! And nothing can happen to me. Hirschland will be careful not to say anything. And even if he did, it was simply a mistake! Could happen any time."

Graeber looked at him closely. "You have nerve," he said.

"Nerve? That doesn't take nerve. Just a sense of humor."

"You're wrong. It takes nerve. Anyone who does a thing like that always dies himself soon after. That's well known."

Steinbrenner laughed aloud. "Drivel! That's an old wives' tale!"

"It's not an old wives' tale. Anyone who does that summons his own death. That's an established fact."

"Oh, listen," Steinbrenner said. "You don't mean you believe that yourself?"

"I do believe it. So should you. It's an old Germanic belief. I wouldn't like to be in your boots."

"You're crazy!" Steinbrenner stood up. He was no longer laughing.

"I knew two people who did something similar. Both were killed shortly after. Another was lucky. He only got shot in the balls. Naturally it made him impotent. Perhaps you'll get off as cheaply as that. Then naturally there won't be any twins or triplets. But of course someone else could always take care of that for you. In the Party the only important thing is purity of blood— not the individual."

Steinbrenner stared at Graeber. "Man, what an unfeeling ass you are!" he said. "Have you really always been like that? Besides, that's all drivel, drivel with gravy on it!"

For a minute longer he stood there waiting. Then he walked off. Graeber leaned back. The front was rumbling. The crows flew about. Suddenly it seemed to him as though he had never been away.

He had sentry duty from midnight until two o'clock. His route lay around the village. The ruins stood out black against the fireworks of the front. The sky shook, brightening and darkening with the muzzle flashes of the artillery. His boots groaned in the tough mud like damned souls.

The pain came upon him swiftly and surprisingly and without any warning. He had not been thinking of anything and had been in a stupor as on the days of his journey. Now suddenly and without transition pain cut through him as though he were being torn to ribbons.

He stood still and waited. He made no move. He waited for

the knife to begin to turn, to become torment and realization of torment, to acquire a name and with the name to become localized and accessible to reason and solace or at least to stoic acceptance.

It did not come. Nothing was there but the clear pain of loss. It was a loss forever. Nowhere was there a bridge. He had had it and it was lost. He listened inward. Somewhere there must still be a voice; an echo of hope must still linger somewhere. But he found nothing. There were only emptiness and nameless pain.

It is too early, he thought. It will come back, later, when the pain is past. He tried to conjure it up; he did not want it to tear itself away; he wanted to hold onto it, even if the pain became unbearable. It would come back if he only persevered, he thought. He whispered names and tried to remember. Shrouded by mist Elisabeth's distracted face appeared. It was the way it had been when he had last seen it. All her other faces were blurred; this one alone became clear. He tried to picture Frau Witte's garden and house. He could do it, but it was as though he were striking the keys of a piano that gave no sound. What has happened? he thought. Perhaps she has had an accident. Perhaps she is unconscious. Perhaps at this very moment the house is caving in. Perhaps she is dead.

He tore his boots out of the mud. The damp earth sighed. He realized that he was sweating.

"That's going to tire you out," someone said.

It was Sauer. He was standing in the corner of a ruined stall. "What's more it can be heard for at least a kilometer," he went on. "What are you trying to do, setting-up exercises?"

"Sauer, you're married, aren't you?"

"Of course. When you have a farm you have to be married. Without a woman a farm's no good."

"Have you been married a long time?"

"Fifteen years. Why?"

"What's it like when you've been married for such a long time?"

"The questions you ask, man! What should it be like?"

"Is it like an anchor that holds you? Something you think about all the time and want to get back to?"

"What do you mean, anchor? Of course I think about it. I've been thinking about it all day, if you want to know. It's time for spring sowing and planting! You get silly in the head just thinking about it."

"I don't mean your farm. I mean your wife."

"They go together. I've just explained it to you. Without a woman a farm's no good. But what do you get from it? Nothing but worry. On top of that here's Immermann always trying to tell you that the prisoners of war lie in bed with every woman who's alone." Sauer blew his nose. "It's a big double bed," he added for some mysterious reason.

"Immermann doesn't know what he's talking about."

"He says that once a woman has found out what a man is she can't hold out for long without one. She's sure to find another for herself."

"Oh, crap!" Graeber said, suddenly furious. "That damned Communist thinks everyone's the same. There's no greater nonsense in the world!"

# Chapter Twenty-six

THEY NO LONGER knew one another. They could not even recognize the uniforms. Often it was only by the helmets and the voices and the language that they knew they belonged together. The trenches had long since caved in. An irregular line of shell holes and bunkers was the front. It changed constantly. There was no longer anything there but rain and uproar and night and the light of the explosions and the flying mud. The sky had fallen. Stormoviks had shattered it. Rain poured down and with it the star shells and the bombs and the grenades.

Searchlights harried the torn clouds like white dogs. Antiaircraft fire shattered through the uproar of the quivering horizon. Blazing airplanes came shooting down and the golden hail of tracer bullets flew after them in a sheaf that disappeared into infinity. Parachute flares hung in indeterminate space and disappeared as though in deep water. Then the drum fire began again.

It was the twelfth day. For the first three the line had held. The hedgehog bunkers had withstood the artillery fire without too much damage. Then the outer blockhouses had been lost and the line penetrated by tanks, but a few kilometers further back the tank defenses had contained the breakthrough. The tanks had stood burning in the gray of morning; a few lay overturned, their treads grinding for a while, like giant beetles lying on their backs. Disciplinary companies had been sent out to lay log roads and restore the telephone connections. They had been forced to work almost without cover. In two hours they had lost more than half their men. Clouds of bombers swooped low and unescorted out of the gray sky and attacked the hedgehog bunkers. On the sixth day the bunkers were out of action; they were no longer good for anything except cover. On the seventh night the Russians attacked and were repulsed. Then it began to rain as though the Deluge had come again. The soldiers were no longer recognizable. They crawled about in the sticky clay of the shell holes like insects that all had the same protective coloration. The company's position was now based solely on two ruined blockhouses with machine guns, behind which stood a few grenade throwers. The rest of the men crouched in shell holes and behind fragments of ruined walls. Rahe held one of the blockhouses. Mass the other.

They held them for three days. On the second they were almost without ammunition; the Russians could simply have marched through. But there was no attack. Late in the last twilight, a couple of German airplanes came over and dropped ammunition and food. The men dragged some of it in and ate. During the night reinforcements came. The work battalions had completed a log road. Weapons and machine guns were brought up. An hour later came a surprise attack without artillery preparation. The Russians suddenly bobbed up fifty yards in front of the line. Some of the hand grenades did not explode. The Russians broke through.

In the flickering of the explosions Graeber saw in front of him a helmet with white eyes beneath it, a mouth gaping open, and behind, like the gnarled, living limb of a tree, an arm drawn back to throw—he shot at it, seized a hand grenade out of the fumbling hands of a recruit beside him and threw. It exploded. "Unscrew the caps, idiot!" he shouted at the recruit. "Give it here! Don't try to pull them off!"

The next hand grenade did not explode. Sabotage, shot through Graeber's mind, sabotage by the prisoners, aimed at us now! He threw the next one and bent down and saw a Russian grenade flying toward him; he burrowed into the mud and felt the pressure of the explosion and a blow like a whiplash and a crack and mud that struck him. He reached back and shouted, "Come on! Quick! Give it to me!" and only when his hand remained empty did he turn his head and see that there was no longer any recruit there and that the mud on his hand was flesh. He worked his way down, searching, found a string of grenades, pulled the last two off, saw shadows clambering over the edge of the shell hole springing, running on; he crouched—

Caught, he thought. Caught. Overrun. He crept cautiously to the edge of the shell hole. The mud protected him as long as he lay still. In the light of a parachute flare he saw that the recruit had been splashed all over, a leg, a naked arm, the shredded body. He had caught the grenade full in the stomach; his body had absorbed the explosion and shielded Graeber.

He remained lying with his head no higher than the edge of the shell hole. He saw a machine gun firing from the blockhouse to the right. Then the one on the left fired too. So long as they were in action he was not lost. They had this sector under crossfire. And there were no more Russians coming over. Apparently only a few had broken through. I must get behind the blockhouse, he thought. His head ached, he was half dazed, but in the back of his mind there was a thought, clear, limited, and sharp. This was what made the difference between an experienced soldier and a recruit; in the recruit everything turned to panic and for that reason he was more likely to be killed. Graeber knew he could play dead if the Russians came back. It would be hard to spot him in the mud. But the nearer he could get to the curtain of fire from the blockhouse the better it would be later on.

He slid over the edge into the next hole, slipped down the side and got his mouth full of water. After a while he clambered on. In the next shell hole lay two dead men. He waited. Then he heard a hand grenade and saw an explosion near the left-hand bunker. The Russians had broken through over there and were attacking from two sides. The machine guns flickered. After some time the detonations of the hand grenades ceased, but the blockhouse went on firing. Graeber crept forward. He knew the Russians would come back. They would look for men in the big shell holes; he would be safer in a smaller one. He reached one and lay there. A heavy shower fell. The firing of the machine guns flickered out. Then the artillery began firing. A direct hit was scored on the blockhouse to the right. It seemed to fly into the air. Morning came wet and late.

Graeber succeeded in slipping through before the first light. Behind a disabled tank he came upon Sauer and two recruits. Sauer's nose was bleeding. A grenade had exploded close to him. The belly of one of the recruits was torn open. His intestines lay exposed. Rain was falling on them. No one had anything to bind him up. Besides, it was useless. The sooner he died the better. The second recruit had a broken leg. He had fallen into a shell hole. It was incomprehensible how anyone could break his leg in that soft mud. In the burned-out tank, the middle of which had burst open, the black skeletons of the crew were visible. The torso of one was dangling outside. Only half his face had been burned away; the other half was grossly swollen, red and violet and split open. The teeth were very white like slaked lime.

A liaison officer got through to them from the bunker on the left. "Assemble beside the bunker," he croaked. "Are there others over there in the shell holes?"

"No idea. Are there any medics?"

"All dead or wounded."

The man crawled on.

"We'll get you a medic," Graeber said to the recruit into whose belly the rain was falling. "Or we'll bring you bandages. We'll come back."

The recruit made no reply. He lay pale-lipped, very small in the clay. "We can't drag you on this piece of canvas," Graeber said to the man with the broken leg, "not in this muck. Rest your weight on us and try to hop on your good leg."

They took him between them and stumbled from hole to hole. It took a long time. The recruit groaned when they threw themselves down. His leg twisted. He could go no farther. They left him behind a fragment of wall near the bunker and put a helmet on the wall so the medics could find him. Besides him lay two Russians; one no longer had a head; the other lay on his stomach and the clay under him was red.

They saw still more Russians. Then came their own dead. Rahe was wounded. He had an improvised bandage on his left arm. Three severely wounded men lay under a piece of canvas in the rain. There were no more bandages. An hour later a Junkers plane flew by and dropped a few packages. They fell too far forward, into the hands of the Russians.

Seven more men joined them. Some others collected in the bunker to the right. Lieutenant Mass was dead. Sergeant Major Reinecke took over the command. There was not much ammunition left. The grenade throwers had been knocked out. But two heavy and two light machine guns were still functioning.

Ten men from the disciplinary company got through. They brought up ammunition and canned rations. They had stretchers and they took the wounded away. Two of them were blown into the air within a hundred yards. The artillery fire prevented almost all liaison during the morning.

At noon it stopped raining. The sun came out. It grew hot at once. A crust formed on the mud. "They'll attack with light tanks," Rahe said. "Damn it, where are the anti-tank guns? We've got to have some or we're finished."

The firing continued. During the afternoon came another Junkers supply plane. It was escorted by Messerschmitts. The Stormoviks appeared and attacked. Two were shot down. Then two Messerschmitts came down. The Junkers did not get through. It dropped its bales farther back. The Messerschmitts fought; they were faster than the Russians, but there were three times as many Russian planes in the air. The Germans had to turn back.

Next day the dead began to smell. Graeber was sitting in the bunker. There were still twenty-two men. Reinecke had assembled about the same number on the other side. The rest were dead or wounded. There had been a hundred and twenty.

He ate and he cleaned his weapons. They were covered with mud. He thought about nothing. He was now simply a machine. He no longer knew anything of an earlier time. He simply sat there and waited and slept and woke and was ready to defend himself.

The tanks came on the following morning. Through the night, artillery, grenade throwers and machine guns had kept the line isolated. Telephone connections had been re-established several times but they were always broken again. The promised reinforcements did not come. The German artillery was now very weak. The Russian fire had been deadly. The bunker had been hit twice more; but it still held out. It was really no longer a bunker; it was a chunk of concrete, wallowing in the mud like a ship in a storm. A half-dozen near misses had shaken it loose. The men fell against the walls when it pitched.

Graeber had not been able to bind up the flesh wound in his shoulder. He had found some cognac and poured it on. The bunker went on pitching and reverberating. It was now no longer a ship in a storm; it was a U-boat rolling on the bottom of the ocean with engines dead. Time, too, had ceased to exist. It, too, had been knocked out of action. The men huddled in the darkness and waited. There was no longer a city in Germany where you had been living a couple of weeks before. Nor had there ever been a furlough. There was no longer an Elisabeth. All that had been simply a wild dream between death and death—a half-hour of delirious sleep during which a rocket had soared into the sky and died out. Only the bunker existed now.

The light Russian tanks broke through. Infantry accompanied them and followed them. The company let the tanks pass and caught the infantry in a cross fire. The hot barrels of the machine guns burned their hands. They went on shooting. The Russian artillery could no longer fire on them. Two tanks turned, rolled toward them, and fired. It was easy for them; there was no defense. Their armor was too heavy for the machine guns. The men aimed at the slits; but hitting them was pure chance. The tanks maneuvered out of range and went on shooting. The bunker shook. Concrete screamed and splintered.

"Grenades!" shouted Reinecke. He gathered a string of them together, hung them over his shoulder and crawled to the exit. After the next salvo he crawled out under cover of the bunker.

"Two machine guns fire at the tanks," Rahe ordered.

They tried to give Reinecke cover as he started to crawl in a circle toward the tanks in an effort to blow off their treads with the combined force of all his grenades. It was almost hopeless. Heavy Russian machine-gun fire had set in.

After a while one of the tanks stopped firing. No one had seen an explosion. "We got him!" Immermann roared. He was no longer a Communist shooting at his fellow party members; he was a creature fighting for his life.

The tank was no longer firing. The machine guns concentrated on the second tank, which turned away and disappeared. "Six broke through," Rahe shouted. "They will come back. All machine guns crossfire. We must stop the infantry!"

"Where is Reinecke?" Immermann asked when they were able to think again. No one knew. Reinecke did not come back.


They held throughout the afternoon. The bunkers were being slowly pulverized; but both continued to fire. They fired more slowly. There was very little ammunition left. The men ate canned rations and drank the water out of the shell holes. Hirschland got a bullet through his hand.

The sun blazed. The sky was hung with great gleaming clouds. The bunker smelled of blood and powder. The dead outside swelled up. Whoever could, slept. They no longer knew whether they had already been cut off or still had communications.

In the evening the firing became heavier. Then suddenly it almost ceased. They rushed out in expectation of the attack. It did not come. For more than two hours it did not come. Those two quiet hours devoured more of their energy than a battle.

At three o'clock in the morning the bunker was nothing more than a mass of twisted steel and concrete. They had to leave it.

There were six dead and three wounded. They had to withdraw. They were able to drag the man with the stomach wound for a couple of hundred yards; then he died.

The Russians attacked again. The company now had only two machine guns. From a shell hole they defended themselves with them. Then they fell back again. The Russians thought them stronger than they were and this saved them. During the second halt Sauer fell. He got a bullet in the head and died at once. A little farther on Hirschland fell as he was running crouched over. He twisted over slowly and lay still. Graeber dragged him into a shell hole. He slid into it and writhed on the bottom. Bullets had torn his breast open. Examining him Graeber found his blood-soaked wallet and put it in his pocket. There was now no longer any need to write his mother that he was alive.

They reached the second line. Later, orders came to retire farther. The company was being disengaged. The reserve position became the front.

They assembled a few kilometers farther back. There were only thirty men of the company left. Next day it was restored to one hundred and twenty.

Graeber found Fresenburg in a field hospital. It was a shed that had been inadequately converted to that purpose. Fresenburg's left leg had been shattered. "They want to amputate it," he said. "Some lousy assistant surgeon. Only thing he can think of. I've managed to arrange transportation for tomorrow. Want to have an experienced man take a look at the leg first."

He lay on a field cot with a wire basket over his knee. The cot stood beside an open window. Outside there was a strip of flat land, a meadow abloom with red and yellow and blue wild flowers. The room stank. There were three other beds. "How's Rahe doing?" Fresenburg asked.

"Shot in the arm. Flesh wound."

"Hospital?"

"No, he stayed with the company."

"That's what I'd expect." Fresenburg's face moved. One half of it smiled; the other with the scar stayed rigid. "A good many don't want to go back. Rahe doesn't."

"Why not?"

"He has given up. No more hope. And no belief."

Graeber looked at the parchment-colored face. "And you?"

"I don't know. This has to be attended to first." He pointed to the wire basket.

The warm wind blew in from the meadow. "Strange, isn't it?" Fresenburg said. "In the snow we thought it would never be summer in this land. Then suddenly it's here. And right away too much of it."

"Yes."

"How was it at home?"

"I don't know. I can't make any kind of connection between the two things, my furlough and this. I could do it before. But not now. They're too far apart. I no longer know what's real."

"Who knows that?"

"I thought I knew. Back there everything seemed right. Now I no longer know. It was too short. And too far away from all this. Back there I even thought I wouldn't do any more killing."

"Many have thought that."

"Yes. Are you in much pain?"

Fresenburg shook his head. "This hole has something you would hardly expect: morphine. They gave me a shot that's still working. The pains are there, but it's as though they belonged to somebody else. I still have one or two hours to think."

"Is a hospital train coming?"

"It's an ambulance from here. It will take us to the nearest station."

"Soon none of us will be here any more," Graeber said. "Now you're going too."

"Perhaps they'll patch me up just once more and I'll be back."

They looked at each other. Both knew it was not true. "I'll believe it," Fresenburg said. "At least for this hour or two of morphine. A section of life can sometimes be damned short, can't it? And then comes another one you know absolutely nothing about. This was my second war."

"What will you do afterward? Have you decided?"

"I don't even know yet what the others are going to do to me. I've got to find that out first. I never thought I would end up this way. I always believed it would catch me properly. Now I have to get used to the idea of having been half caught. I don't know if it's any better. The other seemed easier. There was an end of it; the bloody nonsense no longer mattered; you would pay the price and that was all. Now one's in the middle of it again. I had made a sort of pretense: that death canceled everything and so on. That's not how it is. I'm tired, Ernst. I'll try to sleep before I begin to realize that I'm a cripple. Take care of yourself."

He held out his hand to Graeber. "You, too, Ludwig," Graeber said.

"Of course. Since I'm swimming with the current. The primitive impulse of life. Before it was different. But perhaps that was just a deception. Always a last secret hope hidden in it. Means nothing. One always forgets one can make an end of it oneself. We got that gift along with our so-called mind."

Graeber shook his head.

Fresenburg smiled his half-smile. "You're right," he said. "We don't do that sort of thing. Instead, we'll try to see to it that all this can never happen again. To accomplish that, I'd take up a gun again, if I had to."

He laid his head back. Suddenly he looked completely exhausted. When Graeber got to the door his eyes were already closed.

Graeber went back to his village. A pale, evening red colored the sky. It had not rained again. The mud was drying. In the neglected fields flowers and weeds had sprung up. The front was rumbling. Suddenly everything seemed very strange and all connections dissolved. Graeber knew the feeling; he had often had it when he woke up at night not knowing where he was. It was as if he had fallen out of the world and floated in complete loneliness in the dark. It never lasted long. One always found one's way back; but each time a strange small feeling persisted that some day one would not find the way back.

It was not fear that one felt; one simply shrank into oneself, like a tiny child set down in the midst of a gigantic steppe where every road of escape was a hundred times too long. Graeber stuck his hands into his pockets and looked around. There was the old picture: ruins, unplowed fields, a Russian sunset, and, opposite, the pale, beginning heat-lightning of the front. It was there as always and with it the hopeless chill that went straight through the heart.

He felt Elisabeth's letters in his pocket. Warmth was in them, tenderness and the sweet excitement of love. But they were no quiet lamp to light a well-ordered house; they were will-o'-the-wisps above a swamp, and the farther he tried to follow them the more treacherous the swamp seemed to become. He had wanted to put up a light in order to find his way back, but he had put it up before the house was built. He had placed it in a ruin; it did not adorn it, it only made it more desolate. Back there he had not known. He had followed the light without question, wanting to believe that to follow it was enough. It was not enough.

He had fought against this realization as long as he could. It had not been easy to see that what he had hoped would hold him and support him had only isolated him. It could not extend far enough. It touched his heart but it did not hold him. It was swallowed up; it was a small, private happiness that could not support itself in the limitless morass of general misery and despair. He took out Elisabeth's letters and read them, and the red afterglow of sunset lay on the pages. He knew them by heart; he read them once more, and again they made him more lonesome than before. It had been too short and the other was too long. It had been a furlough; but a soldier's life is reckoned by his time at the front and not by furloughs.

He put the letters back in his pocket. He put them with the letters from his parents which he had found waiting for him at the company office. There was no sense in brooding. Fresenburg was right; one step after another was enough. One ought not to try to solve the riddles of existence when one was in danger. Elisabeth, he thought. Why do I think of her as of someone lost? I have her letters here! She is alive!

The village came closer. It lay there dismal and abandoned. All these villages looked as though they would never be rebuilt. An avenue of birch trees led up to the ruins of a white house. A garden had once been there; flowers bloomed, and at the edge of a dirty pond stood a statue. It was a faun, blowing on his pipes; but no one came to his festive noon. Only a couple of recruits were there searching the fruit trees for green cherries.

# Chapter Twenty-seven

"GUERRILLAS." Steinbrenner licked his lips and looked at the Russians. They stood in the village square. There were two men and two women. One of the women was young. She had a round face and high cheekbones. All four had been brought in by a patrol earlier that morning.

"They don't look like guerrillas," Graeber said.

"They are, though. What makes you think they aren't?"

"They don't look it. They look like poor farmers!"

Steinbrenner laughed. "If that were a test there wouldn't be any criminals."

That's true, Graeber thought. You yourself are the best proof. He saw Rahe coming. "What are we to do with them?" asked the company commander.

"They were captured here," the sergeant major said. "We have to lock them up and wait for orders to come through."

"God knows we have enough trouble on our hands. Why don't we send them to the regiment?"

Rahe did not expect an answer. The regiment no longer had a fixed position. At best the staff would sometime send someone to give the Russians a hearing and then direct what was to be done with them. "Outside the village there's what used to be a manor house," Steinbrenner announced. "It has a shed with bars and an iron door and a lock."

Rahe surveyed him critically. He knew what Steinbrenner was thinking. In his charge the Russians would make the usual attempt to escape and that would be the end of them. Outside the village it could be easily arranged.

Rahe looked around. "Graeber," he said, "take charge of these people. Steinbrenner can show you where the shed is. Examine it to see that it's safe. After that report to me and leave a guard there. Take men from your own squad. It's your responsibility. Yours alone," he added.

One of the prisoners limped. The older woman had varicose veins. The younger was barefoot. Outside the village Steinbrenner gave the younger man a shove. "Hey there! You! Run!"

The man turned around. Steinbrenner laughed and gestured. "Run! Run! Hurry up! Free!"

The older man said something in Russian. The other did not run. Steinbrenner kicked him in the ankle with his boot. "Run, you ass!"

"Stop that," Graeber said. "You heard Rahe's orders."

"We can let them run here," Steinbrenner whispered. "The men, I mean. Ten yards and then we shoot. We'll lock the women up. When it's dark we'll get the young one out."

"Leave them alone. And disappear. I'm in command here."

Steinbrenner looked at the young woman's calves. She was wearing a short dress and her legs were brown and muscular. "They'll be shot anyway," he remarked, "either by us or by the Security Service. We can have some fun with the young one. It's all very well for you to talk. You've just been on furlough."

"Shut up and think about your promised bride! The daughter

of the S.S. commandant," Graeber said. "Rahe ordered you to show us the shed, that's all."

They walked along the avenue that led to the white house. "Here," Steinbrenner announced morosely, pointing to a small building that was in a good state of repair. It was built of stone and was strong and the iron-barred door could be secured from the outside with a padlock.

Graeber examined the building. It seemed to have been a kind of stall or shed. The floor was cement. The prisoners could not get out without tools; and they had already been searched to make sure they had none.

He opened the door and let them in. Two recruits who had come along as guards stood with guns ready. The prisoners went in one after the other. Graeber shut the door and tested the lock. It held.

"Like monkeys in a cage." Steinbrenner grinned. "Banana! Banana! Do you want a banana, you apes?"

Graeber turned to the recruits. "You stay here as guards. It's your responsibility to see that nothing happens. You'll be relieved later on. Do any of you speak German?" he asked the Russians.

No one answered. "Later on we'll see if we can find some straw for you. Come," Graeber said to Steinbrenner.

"Do get them a couple of feather beds, too."

"Come along! And you there, keep an eye out!"

He reported to Rahe that the jail was safe. "Pick out a couple of men and take charge of the guard," Rahe said. "In a few days, when the situation has quieted down, we'll get rid of these people, I hope."

"Yes, sir."

"Do you need more than two men?"

"No. The shed is safe. I could almost do it alone if I slept out there at night. No one can get out."

"All right. Let's do it that way. We need the recruits here to teach them a little combat technique as fast as possible. The reports—" Rahe broke off. He looked ill. "You know yourself what's up. Well, go along."

Graeber got his things. There were only a few men he knew left in his platoon. "Have they made a jailer out of you?" Immermann asked.

"Yes. I can get a good sleep out there. It's better than drilling these young sprouts."

"You won't have much time for it. Do you know what's happening at the front?"

"It sounds like a mess."

"It's another rear-guard action. The Russians are breaking through everywhere. A lot of scuttlebutt has been coming in during the last hour. Big offensive. There's only flat ground around here. No place to make a stand. This time we'll have to go a long way back."

"Do you think we'll quit if we have to retreat across the German frontier?"

"Do you think so?"

"No."

"Neither do I. Who on our side could put an end to it? Certainly not the general staff. They'd never take the responsibility." Immermann grinned crookedly. "In the last war they could always put up a new provisional government slapped together for that purpose. The poor fools would hold out their necks, sign the armistice, and a week later be accused of betraying their fatherland. Today there's nothing like that. Total government, total defeat. There is no second party to negotiate with."

"Except yours, of course," Graeber said bitterly. "You've explained it to me often enough. Another totalitarian government. The same methods. I'm going to sleep. All I want in life is to think what I like, say what I like, and do what I like. But since we have messiahs of the right and left that's a much worse crime than murder."

He was angry at himself for getting involved with Immermann; it was as pointless as with Steinbrenner. He took his knapsack and went to the field kitchen. There he got his dipperful of bean soup, his bread, and his ration of sausage for the evening meal; thus he would not have to come back to the village.

It was a strangely quiet afternoon. The recruits had left after getting the straw. The front was rumbling, but nevertheless the day seemed to remain still. In front of the shed extended a lawn that had run wild; it had been trodden down and there were shell holes in it, but nevertheless it had turned green and a few flowering shrubs were growing at the edge of what once had been a walk.

In the garden beyond the avenue of birch trees Graeber found a small, half-preserved pavilion from which he could keep an eye on the shed. He even found a few books. They were bound in leather and bore tarnished gold lettering. Rain and snow had damaged them so much that only one was still legible. It was a volume with romantic etchings of ideal landscapes. The text was French. He leafed slowly through it. Gradually the pictures captivated him. They aroused a painful and hopeless yearning that continued long after he had closed the book.

He walked along the avenue of birch trees to the pond. Amid dirt and water weeds crouched the pipe-playing faun. One of his horns was missing but aside from that he had survived the Revolution, Communism, and the war. He, like the books, came from a legendary time, the time before the first war. It was a time before Graeber was alive. He had been born during the war, grown up during the misery of the inflation and the restlessness of the postwar years, and had awakened during a new war. He wandered around the pond past the pavilion and back to the prisoners. He looked at the iron door. It had not always been part of the shed; it had been added later. Maybe the man to whom the house and the park had once belonged had himself awaited death behind it.

The old woman was asleep. The young one was crouching in a corner. Both men were standing staring out into the afternoon. Then they looked at Graeber. The girl looked straight ahead. The oldest of the Russians watched Graeber. Graeber turned away and lay down on the grass.

Clouds wandered across the sky. Birds twittered in the birch trees. A blue butterfly floated over the shell holes from blossom to blossom. After a while a second joined it. They played together, chasing each other. The rumbling from the front increased in volume. The two butterflies paired and flew united through the hot sunny air. Graeber fell asleep.

In the evening a recruit brought food for the prisoners. It was the midday bean soup thinned with water. The recruit waited until the prisoners had eaten, then he took the pans away with him. He had also brought Graeber his ration of cigarettes. There were more than usual. That was a bad sign. Better food and more cigarettes were issued only when heavy going lay ahead.

"We've been given two hours' extra duty tonight," the recruit said. He looked at Graeber earnestly. "Combat exercises, grenade-throwing, bayonet drill."

"The company commander knows what he's doing. He's not just taking it out on you."

The recruit nodded. He looked at the Russians as though they were animals in a zoo. "Those are human being too," Graeber said.

"Yes, Russians."

"All right, Russians. Take your gun. Hold it ready. We're going to let the women out one after the other."

Graeber said through the bars: "Everyone into that corner. The old woman is to step up here. Later the others will have their chance to come out."

The oldest Russian said something to the others. They obeyed. The recruit held his gun ready. The old woman came forward. Graeber opened the door, let her out and locked it again. She began to cry. She expected to be shot. "Tell her that nothing is going to happen to her. She is just to look after her needs," Graeber said to the old Russian.

He spoke to her. She stopped crying. Graeber and the recruit led her to a corner of the house where two walls were still standing. He waited till she came out again and then let the young woman out. She walked quickly and lithely in front of him. With the men it was simpler. He led them around behind the shed and kept them in sight. The earnest young recruit held his gun ready, his underlip pushed out, all zeal and attention. Graeber led the last man back and locked the door.

"That was exciting," the recruit said.

"Really?" Graeber put his gun aside. "You can go now."

He waited till the recruit had disappeared. Then he got out his cigarettes and gave the old man one for each of them. He lit a match and handed it through the bars. All of them smoked. The cigarettes glowed in the half-darkness and lit up their faces. Graeber looked at the young woman and suddenly he felt an unbearable yearning for Elisabeth. "You—good," said the old Russian, following his glance.

His face was close to the iron bars. "War lost—for Germans—you good man," he said softly.

"Nonsense."

"Why not—let us go—and come with us?" The furrowed face turned for a moment toward the young woman and then back. "Go with us—and Marusa—hide—good place—live. Live—" he repeated urgently.

Graeber shook his head. That's no solution, he thought, not that. But where is another? "Live—not die—only captured—" whispered the Russian. "You too—not dead—good life with us—we innocent—"

It sounded simple. Graeber turned away. It sounded simple in the soft last light of evening. Probably they really were innocent. No arms had been found in their possession and they did not look like guerrillas. The two old ones certainly did not. If I let them out, he thought, then I will have done something, at least something. I will have saved a few innocent human beings. But I can't go with them. Not there. Not into the same sort of thing I want to escape. He wandered about and came to the fountain again. The birches were now black against the sky. He went back. One cigarette was still glowing in the darkness of the shed. The face of the old Russian shimmered palely behind the bars. "Live—" he said. "Good—with us—"

Graeber took the rest of his cigarettes and pushed them into the big hand. Then he got out a few matches and gave them to the man. "Here—smoke these—for the night—"

"Live—you young—war over for you then—you good man—we innocent—live—you—we—" It was a soft deep voice. It spoke the word "live" like a black marketeer saying "butter." Like a whore saying "love." Tenderly, demandingly, enticingly and falsely. As though he could sell it.

Graeber felt the voice tug at him. "Shut up!" he shouted at

the old man. "No more of this or I'll report it. Then you'll be done for!"

He began his rounds again. The uproar at the front was heavier. The first stars appeared. He felt himself suddenly very much alone and wished he were lying again in a dugout amid the stench and snores of his comrades. It seemed to him as though he had been abandoned by all and had a decision to make.

He tried to sleep and arranged himself on his straw in the pavilion. Perhaps they can break out, he thought, without my noticing it. It did not help. He knew they could not. The people who had rebuilt the shed had taken care of that.

The front grew steadily more restless. Airplanes droned through the night. Machine guns chattered. Then came the dull explosion of bombs. Graeber listened. The uproar increased. Suppose they did break out, he thought again. He stood up and walked to the shed. Everything was quiet there. The prisoners seemed asleep. But then he saw indistinctly the pale face of the oldest Russian and turned away.

After midnight he knew that a heavy battle was raging at the front. Big guns were firing far over the lines. The explosions were now not far from the village. Graeber knew how weak the position was. He could follow the separate phases of the engagement. The tanks would soon attack. The earth was quivering now under the drum-fire. Thunder rolled from horizon to horizon. He felt it in all his bones. He felt that it would soon reach him. And yet it seemed in a strange fashion to circle around him in a whirlwind of thunder and lightning, around the narrow white building where the four Russians crouched, as though amid all the destruction and death they had suddenly become the central point and as though everything depended on what happened to them.

He walked up and down. He approached the shed and went

away, he felt the key in his pocket, he writhed on his straw, and it was close to morning when he suddenly fell into a heavy, restless sleep.

It was gray when he started up. At the front all hell had broken loose. The artillery fire already ranged above and beyond the village. He glanced toward the shed. The iron gate was intact. Behind it the Russians were moving. Then he saw Steinbrenner running up.

"We're retreating!" Steinbrenner shouted. "The Russians have broken through. Assemble in the village. Quick! Everything's in confusion. Get your things." He had come up by now. "We'll take care of the fellows in there right away."

Graeber felt his heart beating violently. "Where is the order?" he asked.

"Order! Man, when you see how things are in the village you won't ask for orders. Haven't you heard any of the offensive here?"

"Yes."

"Then you know. Get going! Do you imagine we could haul the whole crowd with us? We'll finish them off through the bars of the door."

Steinbrenner's eyes blazed very blue. The skin was drawn tight over the bridge of his nose. His hand was at his belt.

"No," Graeber said. "The responsibility here is mine. If you have no orders, clear out."

Steinbrenner laughed. "All right. Then you shoot them."

"No," Graeber said.

"One of us has to finish them off. We can't drag them along with us. Move on, you and your delicate nerves. Go ahead, I'll join you in a minute."

"No," Graeber said. "You won't shoot them."

"No?" Steinbrenner glanced up. "No?" he repeated slowly. "Do you happen to know what you're saying?"

"Yes, I know."

"So, you know? Then you know too—"

Steinbrenner's face changed. He reached for his revolver. Graeber raised his gun and fired. Steinbrenner reeled and pitched forward. He gave a sigh like a child. The revolver fell from his hand.

Graeber stared at the body. A shell screamed over the garden. He roused himself, walked to the shed, took the key out of his pocket and opened the door. "Go," he said.

The Russians looked at him. They did not believe him. He threw down his rifle. "Go, go," he said impatiently, showing his empty hands.

Cautiously the younger man pushed his foot outside. Graeber turned away. He walked back to the place where Steinbrenner lay. "Murderer," he said, and did not know whom he meant. He stared at Steinbrenner. He felt nothing. "Murderer," he said once more, and meant Steinbrenner and himself and countless others.

Then suddenly his thoughts began to come tumbling over one another. A stone seemed to have been rolled away. Something was decided forever. He no longer felt any substance. He had no weight. He knew he ought to do something, but it was as though he had to hold fast in order not to fly away. His head swam. He walked cautiously along the avenue. Something of vast importance had to be done, but he could not keep hold of it, not yet. It was still too far away and too new and so clear that it hurt.

He saw the Russians. They were running bent over in a group with the women in front. One of the men looked back and saw him. All at once the Russian had a rifle in his hand. He lifted it and took aim. Graeber saw the black hole of the muzzle, it grew, he wanted to call out, in a loud voice, there was so much to say quickly and loudly—

He did not feel the shot. He only saw grass suddenly in front of him, a plant, close before his eyes, half trodden down, with a cluster of reddish stalks and delicate, narrow leaves that grew larger, and he had seen this before, but he no longer knew when. The plant wavered and then stood alone against the narrowed horizon of his sinking head, silent, self-evident, with the solace of the tidiness of tiny things and with all its peace; it grew larger and larger until it filled the whole sky, and his eyes closed.

## ABOUT THE AUTHOR

ERICH MARIA REMARQUE was born in Germany in 1898, and was drafted into the German army during World War I. Throughout the hazardous years following the war he worked at many occupations—schoolteacher, small-town drama critic, racing driver, and editor of a sports magazine. His first novel, *All Quiet on the Western Front,* vividly describing the experiences of German soldiers during World War I, was published in Germany in 1928. It was a brilliant success, selling over a million copies, and it was the first of many literary triumphs by Erich Remarque.

When the Nazis came to power, Remarque left Germany for Switzerland. He rejected all attempts to persuade him to return, and as a result he lost his German citizenship, his books were burned, and his films were banned. He went to the United States in 1938 and became a citizen in 1947. He later lived in Switzerland with his second wife, the actress Paulette Goddard. He died in Switzerland in September 1970.